THE WOMAN WITH THE MAP

JAN CASEY

An Aria Book

First published in the UK in 2022 by Head of Zeus
This paperback edition first published in 2022 by Head of Zeus Ltd,
part of Bloomsbury Publishing Plc

9 7 5 3 1 2 4 6 8

A catalogue record for this book is available from the British Library.

ISBN (PB): 9781803281322
ISBN (E): 9781838930776

Printed and bound by CPI Group (UK) Ltd, Croydon CR0 4YY

Head of Zeus Ltd
5–8 Hardwick Street
London EC1R 4RG
WWW.HEADOFZEUS.COM

ALSO BY JAN CASEY

Women At War

The Women of Waterloo Bridge

To my husband, Don. With all my love.

ONE

Wednesday 20 February 1974

The envelope Joyce picked up from the mat was stamped Urgent in large, red, angry letters. She stared at it, turned it over in her palm, then threw it on top of the pile of letters on the table by the front door, each of them marked in the same way. It was cold and damp and all she wanted to do was close the door, light the gas fire, put on the kettle, fire up the geyser and spend the evening curled up in her usual position on the settee. Ignoring the eight – or did this letter make it nine – official notices, she shot the bolt across the door, nudged the sausage dog draught excluder along the gap at the bottom of the wood and pulled the orange flower-scattered curtain tight across the lot. Her eye caught the accumulated stack of correspondence, but she rubbed her hands together to warm them, changed her court heels for a pair of cosy slippers and made her evening round of the flat. There was no hurry to open any of the letters as she was well-aware of the information they contained. And as far as she was concerned, none of it was urgent.

Striking a match, she turned on the gas and held the light against the ring on the stove until, with a click and a whoosh, the gas bit the flame and exploded into a blue aurora of glowing heat. She turned to the sink, held the kettle under the running water and peered out at the yard. Despite the inclement weather, snowdrops returned her gaze. Purple and white crocuses poked their heads above the dirt in clay pots and, remembering her reluctance to kneel on the dank, grey paving slabs and plunge her hands into the potting soil last autumn, she was glad now that she had and the modest display of early spring made her smile.

Two spoonfuls of tea in the pot, a cup and saucer, two digestives nestled on the side. While the tea was drawing, Joyce knelt in front of the fire in the sitting room, turned the dial and pushed on the pilot button to the count of eleven. When she heard the comforting muffled hiss that meant the heat was coming through, she put one hand on the coffee table, the other on her thigh and levered herself up.

She stood for a minute and watched, through the gauze of the net curtains, the steady stream of shoe-clad feet walking past her basement flat. If she had been unaware that it was teatime and the end of the working day, the sound of the boots and heels and loafers making their way to families or the pictures or the pub or to visit friends would have told her more certainly than any clock. The steps were somehow lighter and less troubled than the footfall going towards places of work in the morning. There were muddy shoes, shiny shoes, casual and formal shoes. Black, brown, grey, navy blue, red, green, lace-ups, slip-ons, steel-toe-capped boots and of course, the magnificent multi-coloured platform shoes that so many young people were wearing these days. The girls' dresses and skirts were much too short to be in her line of vision but if she could have seen them, they would be psychedelic swirls of paisley and cubes and stars topped by straggly Afghan coats. They were beautiful, she couldn't deny it, but when she was that age all anyone had wanted out of a coat was that it could be buttoned and belted as tightly as possible against the cold. She couldn't fathom any other point to a coat than that.

A couple went past walking in tandem, their bell-bottomed jeans billowing around their huge, clumpy shoes. His in two flashes of brown; hers in shades of green and blue. Joyce caught a murmur followed by a burst of guffaws and for a split second it looked as though the two pairs of shoes might somehow become entangled, but they moved on leaving an echo of laughter trailing behind them.

If she were thirty years younger, would she dare to wear the latest trendy shoes? It was difficult to imagine that she would. Like coats, the shoes she and her contemporaries had worn were practical and if they were lucky enough to have a special pair, they would have been fashioned from good, solid leather in a colour that matched everything, been polished lovingly and saved for high days and holidays.

Joyce remembered that at twenty-one, she had owned a pair of brown brogues that she wore summer and winter. A treat was buying a new pair of laces and that was only after the old ones had been cut and retied countless times and then become frayed beyond repair. And that was it, apart from a lovely pair of black, patent heels that Auntie Cath had given her when the older woman's bunions made it impossible for her to cram her feet into the leather any longer. There must have been other shoes, she thought. She couldn't have gone through the entire war with the same two pairs of shoes. Or perhaps she had. After all, everyone had been entrenched for years in the spirit of make do and mend.

The geyser burst into action with a comforting clunk, clunk, clunk that increased to a grating crescendo much like the noise of the V-1s as they'd glided over London minutes before falling to the ground in a steep dive. Joyce poured the tea into her cup, gathered the latest copy of *Woman's Realm* under her arm and made for the settee where she intended to relax with her feet up. But the unopened stockpile of letters niggled at her and with a sigh, she grabbed them from the table and placed them on the floor where she could reach them when she'd finished her tea and biscuits. Then an article about the advantages and disadvantages of tea bags versus loose leaves caught her attention. Next there was the problem page; horoscopes; a pattern for a loosely crocheted poncho-type garment; the third instalment of a gripping serial about a woman who was trying to choose between the advances of a vicar and a farmer; and a pull-out section dedicated to recipes for under seventy-five pence each. But what was that in old money? She began to scribble in the margin to convert the costs back to shillings and pence, but the photos of food set out in a mouth-watering colour spread made her thoughts drift to the leftover steak and kidney pie in her fridge. She would pop it in the oven, boil a few potatoes with a handful of chopped carrots and green beans and it would be ready in no time; she was looking forward to it and her stomach rumbled in accordance.

Then her toe caught the letters and she stumbled. Blasted things, she thought. Plucking one from the top of the pile, she took her fingernail to the flap and tore it open. It came as no surprise that it was from the London County Council Housing Department and that every page was marked Urgent. Without bothering to read it or open the other envelopes, she gathered up the letters and put them back on the table by the front door. Urgent, she thought. They had no idea about the meaning of the word.

TWO

February 1941

Joyce nodded at Percy, her partner for the night, and he tapped his cap in her direction in response. He was a slim, energetic man with a thick head of hair who was old enough to be her dad – if her dad had still been alive. Darkness fell, the warning sounded, the bombing started and from the minute they emerged from their basement headquarters into the screeching, smoke-filled night they were caught up in the chaos.

They chased the bombs from one hole in the ground to the next, from flattened buildings to demolished roads; running for all they were worth between incendiary fires to trapped civilians and back again. Each time there was a hit, and within minutes she'd lost count of the dozens and dozens, they raced to the scene to do whatever they could to ascertain who might be inside, who could have escaped, who was injured and how they could help. For each incident Joyce wrote as many details as necessary on an ARPM1, flagged down a messenger on a bike and sent him on his way to alert Report and Control to send an ambulance or firefighters or the rescue services. Then she and Percy administered as much help and comfort as they could or made the decision to leave the casualties on their own and turn their attention to another emergency next door or across the road or two streets over.

Ladbroke Grove was ablaze. At number 53, a young mum of perhaps twenty-three or four – not much older than Joyce – stood in what was left of her doorway with a tiny, crying child covered in brick dust and beetroot-red scratches holding tight around his mother's neck. The front part of the house stood but the back was nothing more than flames licking towards the burnished sky. The minute she and Percy arrived on the scene, the young woman thrust the child into Joyce's arms and hurtled herself upstairs screeching, 'My baby!'

Percy pulled her back but not before the ends of her hair caught alight. The woman, oblivious to the odour of her own scorching hair or the flames lapping her face, screamed again for the baby and fought Percy with thrashing arms, but Percy brought her to the ground and rolled her backwards and forwards to put out the fire, then he covered his face and found the little one – pinned under a pile of rubble. When he emerged from the bedroom, empty-handed and coughing into his elbow, he shook his head and without exchanging a word, they knew they could not give that terrible news to the poor mum, sobbing on the floor. She was in no fit state to hear it.

Joyce felt that her heart, if she let it, would shatter and then she would be done for. She braced every muscle in her body, tensed her shoulders and legs and neck and called on every reserve of discipline she could muster to stop herself from cuddling up next to the young woman and draping her arms around her heaving chest. Instead, she nestled the little boy next to his mum where they clung to each other. 'Here, take this,' Joyce shouted above the incessant bombardment. She handed the mother a length of bandage to mop up some of the blood that was beginning to cake on her forehead and wipe at the snot running from her nose, but she chose to spit on the material and dab at the cuts covering her son's pudgy face and hands instead.

Then without warning, something on the roof shifted and gave way with an almighty crash. 'Lift on three,' Joyce yelled as Percy took the arms and she the legs, and together they lifted the mum and little boy to the street where all around them high-explosives and baskets of incendiaries found their targets. Bricks and mortar fell, the low lights of other wardens played chaotically from one raw, cankerous sore of a crater to another, fires lit the sky in oranges and reds to challenge any summer sunset. For a flash, searchlights picked out one horrible scene before flooding another with light for a split second. Above the din of the sirens, they were assaulted by the ceaseless droning of planes, the clang of ambulances and fire trucks, the hammering of feet, the unnerving sound of collapsing masonry. Four wardens pounded past her going one way then three another. A drunk lurched along the jagged pavement, stumbling around pits and mountains of bricks. A sink lay upturned in what was left of a front porch; a ripped gardening gauntlet was poised on top of a mountain of dirt; an unattached hand, washed clean by water from a burst pipe, floated in the gutter; a flattened hat; a shapely stocking; a shredded book. And everywhere they looked there was fire.

A messenger skidded to a halt, took the ARPM1 from Joyce's outstretched hand and pushed down so hard on his bike pedals that the muscles in his calves popped out like round stones. 'Go!' She bellowed as she pushed the seat of the bike to help him on his way, then felt bad because despite the fact that the scouts who took on the job were supposed to be at least fourteen, Joyce guessed he was no more than twelve at the most and she was grateful to him as he pumped towards Report and Control with her message in his pocket.

Percy pointed to an elderly man dragging an armchair, a potted plant balanced on the seat, from the wreck of a house on the opposite side of the road, his shirt unbuttoned and wearing nothing but tattered socks on his feet.

'I'll wait here until the ambulance arrives,' Joyce shouted. Smoke filled her lungs with every breath she took while she waited, so she bent and wrapped her scarf around the young mum and child's faces. 'Thank you,' the woman managed as Joyce took her pulse, afraid she was going into shock. That was overlooked so often, as everyone tried hard to be stoic and uncomplaining, but almost every casualty Joyce dealt with appeared dazed, their skin waxen, pale and covered in a thin film of clammy sweat. And that went for bystanders and those unharmed, too.

In the distance, Joyce heard the clatter of the ambulance and flailed her arms to let the driver know where to stop. It veered towards them at the exact minute a high-explosive tore into the already ravaged plot behind Percy and the older man. Joyce covered her ears and instinctively closed her eyes for a split second. When she opened them, Percy was hobbling towards her cradling his wrist close to his chest, a thin rivulet of blood flowing from his temple. 'Percy!' She called and ran towards him.

But he batted at her outstretched hand and shouted, 'I'm fine. Don't fuss. It's nothing,'

Ignoring that demand, she bundled him into the ambulance, filled out a form, handed it to a passing messenger and ran towards... she couldn't be sure... the direction of the high street, she thought. But before she got her bearings, she stopped at a large house of three flats that were ablaze. Two women were throwing buckets of water at the conflagration which was about as much good as if they had been using thimbles. Twice she hurled a chipped china chamberpot of water at the flames, but before she could fill it a third time, she heard the shrill cry of 'Warden, we need you here!' And she turned to see a woman dragging a man out from under a heap of rubble. Immediately, Joyce could tell the poor unconscious fellow would have to be made of stern stuff to ever walk again. His trousers were in shreds and his exposed right leg was a pulp of mangled red flesh. Joyce threw her coat over him and shivered when the sweat streaming down her back turned to an icy flow. Another ARPM1; another messenger; another ambulance. And so the night went on. And on. And on.

* * *

The smell of bacon frying in lard drifted along the hallway towards Joyce as she let herself into the terraced house. It was early, but Mum had probably left the underground the minute the all-clear was sounded, eager to get breakfast on the go and start on her other chores. 'Hello, Joy love,' Mum called. She appeared in the doorway, her apron tied around her middle and a cloth in her hand. 'Everything alright?'

Joyce knew her mum was anxious for every minute she was on duty. Or shopping, or visiting her cousin, Flo, or on the bus to work. She worried about everything unremittingly. As a consequence, Joyce tried not to give her mother anything more to feel unsettled about than the burdens she already carried.

She smiled as brightly as she could and said, 'Ta, Mum. I'm fine. How was last night?'

Mum shook her head and twisted the cloth in her hands. 'It's so awful down there, love, really horrible,' she said. 'You know I never liked the underground at the best of times. And all I can think about is you wandering the streets with nothing but that bit of tin on your head to protect you.'

Joyce unbuckled her helmet and said, 'I know, Mum. I stuck my head around a couple of times to see if all was well and it certainly wasn't pleasant. But at least you're safe down there and you have company.'

'But it smells,' Mum said.

Joyce had to laugh. 'That,' she said. 'Is the least of our worries. And we've been over this. If we put an Anderson in the garden, you'd be sitting in it worrying all on your own. And that would be worse.'

'I suppose so,' Mum conceded. 'Five minutes to bacon and a real egg.'

'Oh, luxury.' Saliva pooled in Joyce's mouth at the thought of dipping a crust of toast into the yolk and watching the thick, yellow goo trickle onto the bread. She licked her lips and said, 'Won't be long. I'll just sort myself out.'

Mum turned back to the kitchen and Joyce unlaced her shoes and swapped them for an old pair of socks she wore in the house. Then she stepped out of her dusty, dark blue ARP tunic and skirt and into a faded grey dress. When she checked the serge for stains and tears, which she would have to clean and mend before her shift tonight, pebbles of rubble showered to the floor; she pocketed them so Mum wouldn't have to clear up after her. Next, she gave her whistle a quick clean on her sleeve and twirled the gas rattle once – all in working order.

'Joy,' Mum called. 'There's a bowl of warm water here for your wash. And a flannel.'

'Ta, Mum,' Joyce answered. 'Won't be a minute.'

Taking her full flask and uneaten sandwiches from her satchel, Joyce was overwhelmed by a wave of tiredness, and she had to rest her forehead against the wall.

A chill slithered up her spine and was immediately outstripped by a wave of heat and nausea when the image of the poor young mum from Ladbroke Grove flashed through her mind. As much as she was looking forward to breakfast, she would have loved to skip it and crawl between the sheets on her bed instead and sink into sleep. That might give her a bit of respite from the pictures whirling in her mind. But then she would have to face Mum's questions and Mum wouldn't like the answers she would be forced to give.

'The egg's in the pan, Joy,' Mum called, and Joyce stuffed her untouched flask and sandwiches from the night before back into her satchel so Mum wouldn't fret about her going the whole night without food or drink.

Mum filled Joyce in with all the news from the underground the previous night – everyone she'd seen and everything they'd talked about. Nana and Granddad had been there with Auntie Cath, Uncle Terry and Flo but Mum said, as she did every morning, they'd missed and worried about her, her brother Sid who was in the Merchant Navy, his wife Hettie who was living near her own mother and sister in Liverpool, and their two children who had been evacuated to Shropshire.

They were a close family and Joyce knew Mum loved company so she wondered, as she mopped up her egg with a slice of golden toast, why Mum would even entertain the idea of staying home rather than be in the underground, surrounded by the noise and chatter and gossip of the people she loved. But the fetid air, the lack of privacy, the sense of being hemmed in, queues for tea, anxiety about homes and people on duty above them – all of that must have been so hard to bear, family to take your mind off things or not. While Mum divulged her stories, the lines around her mouth concertinaed up and down like the hinged jaws on a puppet. She had every reason to complain, but never did. She didn't nag, either. All she did was worry.

Try as she might, Joyce could not recall her dad. There was one photo of him in the front room and whenever his name was mentioned it was that image of her father that came into her mind; she had no memories of her own to call upon. Besides the fact that everyone commented on it, she could tell from what she discerned from the photo that she favoured her dad as far as looks were concerned. Since she had been a child, friends and family had enthused about her curly, dark auburn hair and eyes of such a pale hazel they appeared to be amber. Her brother, older than her with a house, a job and responsibilities of his own to attend to, was a combination of both their parents. But there was very little of her mother in Joyce, except perhaps her petite stature and she had always felt proud and honoured to take after the father she had not had the chance to know.

A neighbour had once referred to Joyce as her parents' afterthought, but Mum had corrected her by saying, 'Encore, Mrs Owens. Sid was such a lovely bundle, we went for an encore.' Joyce knew that wasn't the reality of her existence and that Mum and Dad had thought their family was over and done with by the time Joyce made her growing presence known. But despite the non-stop chat that went on in the family, she had never discussed that aspect of her life and didn't intend to. She always felt surrounded by love and attention and care and that was good enough for her. The strength of feeling amongst them had made a much younger Joyce ask her mother why everyone in the family had the same middle name.

'The same middle name?' Mum had been perplexed. 'We don't,' she'd said. 'Your middle name is Margaret, love. After me, although I'm known as Maggie. But no one else has that as a middle name.'"

Joyce had thought for a few minutes then insisted, 'But what about the love name, Mummy? There's Joy love and Auntie Cath love and Nana love.'

Mum had laughed until she'd cried and given Joyce a long, hard hug. She'd tried to explain that 'love' was a generic term of affection, but it took a few years for Joyce to understand. That story had been told to everyone they'd visited or who came to see them or who they'd bumped into at the shops or on the bus and it seemed to delight all of them.

Mum topped up Joyce's teacup and asked her if she wanted a slice of toast.

'No, ta,' Joyce said, shaking her head.

'Then Auntie Cath said to me,' Mum didn't skip a beat. "I don't know how we're all managing to function during the day. What with not getting any sleep at all, night after night." Cruel, that's what it is. Out and out cruel. You know what I mean, Joy, don't you, love?'

Yes, Joyce agreed and the thought of having to change, freshen up, get on a bus and be ready for work in the Accounts Department of Bourne and Hollingsworth in a mere few hours caused fatigue to hit hard again. Instead of breakfast revitalising her as she'd hoped, the heavy, fried food dragged down on her eyelids as it followed its path to her stomach.

'Joy,' Mum sounded alarmed. 'You've gone a bit pale.' She

jumped up and stood beside her daughter, one hand on Joyce's forehead, the other on her back. 'Do you need to put your head between your knees?'

'No, Mum,' Joyce managed a giggle. 'I'm full, that's all.'

'Perhaps you should give today a miss and catch up on some sleep.'

But Joyce knew she couldn't do that, money was tight as it was and hers was the only wage coming in. Joyce took her mother's hand from her forehead and held onto it for a minute. 'No need for that sort of mollycoddling,' she said. 'I'll splash my face and hands and be as right as rain.' She smiled with what she could feel were slightly quivering lips.

Squinting around the door, Mum looked at the clock on the mantelpiece and determined that Joyce had time for half an hour or so in bed before she needed to get ready for the working day. 'That,' Joyce said, 'sounds like bliss. But please don't forget to call me in time so I won't be late.'

'I promise,' Mum said. 'Now up those stairs.'

Joyce closed the window and drew the curtains in her bedroom that Mum had opened to let some air blow through, but smoke from the previous night's bombing clung to the sheets, blankets, the moth-eaten rug and woolly dressing gown that hung behind the door. Flopping down on the bed, she brought the sleeve of her cardigan up to her nose and sniffed. Then she gathered the ends of her hair together and curled them around her top lip like a moustache; they smelled singed, too, and another vivid picture of that young mother from Ladbroke Grove with a halo of flames dancing along the lengths of her hair pushed its way into her mind and she screwed her eyes tight against the forceful image. But that only made the impression of what she'd seen more sickeningly defined and detailed and distinct. She let her head fall back on the pillow and wondered how long it would take for the memory to become blurred. Never, was her guess. Not unless a more distressing situation occurred which, she knew, was more than likely.

From under the soft, heavy, comforting blankets Joyce heard the sounds of Auntie Cath letting herself into the house. 'Alright, Maggie love?' she called out.

'Shh,' her mother hissed. And Joyce smiled when she pictured Mum pointing upstairs and beckoning Auntie Cath into the kitchen, her finger on her closed mouth.

* * *

The next thing Joyce was aware of was Mum, rocking her shoulder and telling her it was time to get up. Joyce sat bolt upright and rubbed at her eyes and hair. 'Have I overslept?' she asked. 'I hope I'm not going to be late.'

'No, Joy love,' Mum's voice had an edge of anxiety and excitement to it. 'There's a messenger named Bill at the door. Says he's come to take you to Report and Control and it's urgent. But won't be drawn to say more.'

'Me?' Joy swung her feet to the floor and shook her head. 'But ...but... it's daylight. What could they want with me at this time? Have I missed a whole day, Mum?'

Mum placed her hand under Joyce's elbow to help her up. 'No love, you've only been in bed for twenty minutes or so.'

Staggering to her feet, Joyce felt a rush of blood pulse against the sides of her skull and dots of coloured lights swam in front of her eyes. She had to steady herself on the chair next to the bed.

'Joy,' Mum's voice rose with alarm. 'You're dizzy again. I'm going to tell that boy to come back later.'

But Joyce forced herself to recover and drew herself up to her full height of five feet three inches. 'I can't do that, Mum,' she quipped with a contrived casual tone. 'I'm too intrigued. Aren't you? Come on,' she said. 'Let's go and see what all this is about.'

Mum followed close on her heels, reminding her to pick up her feet so she wouldn't stumble, hold the banister for support, not to take the stairs two at a time and to wait for her.

The lad at the door was hopping from one foot to the other and blowing into his cupped hands in an attempt to keep warm; his bike, like a trusty steed, was leaning against the wall where he could keep it in sight. When Joyce appeared, he smiled at her as if they were great pals although she could not place him amongst the dozens of other messengers who snatched forms out of her hands during the long, raging, crisis-fuelled nights. 'Warden Cooper,' he said, squaring the scrawny shoulders that were having difficulty holding up his Civil Defence armband. 'On the command of Controller Davis, you're to come with me. It's urgent.'

Despite the perplexing situation and how earnestly the boy was taking his duty, Joyce had to stifle a giggle. *Thank goodness the Germans can't see us depending on schoolboys to deliver our communications,* she thought. *They would think their victory was in the bag.*

'What's all this about, Bill,' Joyce said. 'Do I need to put on my uniform again?'

A group of boys walked behind the young messenger, jostling each other and passing a football backwards and forwards between them. One of them stepped down hard on a patch of ice and cracked it with the heel of his hobnail boot. The sudden, loud report distracted Bill and he turned, alert and ready to offer his help. When he saw who had caused the noise, he relaxed his strained stance and lifted his hand to greet them. 'Oi, Bill,' one of the lads shouted. 'Come on, we need a goalie.'

For a beat, Bill looked tempted but shook his head, turned back to Joyce and said, 'No time for uniforms, Warden Cooper, as I said, you're wanted urgently.'

'Alright then, I'll fetch my coat and hat. Won't keep you a minute.'

But Mum beat her to the cupboard, clapped a billow of brick dust from her felt hat so the silver ARP badge pinned to it was revealed and handed it, along with her coat, to Joyce. 'And don't forget this,' she said.

'No, that wouldn't do,' said Joyce, wriggling into the strap of the gas mask that she hung around her neck.

Bill was on his bike and poised to pedal off when Joyce wheeled her own bicycle through the passage to the front path. 'Thank you, Bill, you can stand down now.'

Bill replied through puffs of white, frosty condensation. 'No,' he shook his head.

'I have been given the responsibility of a task and I will see it through. In fact, you can balance on my handlebars and I'll deliver you to Control myself.'

'I think it would be safer for both of us if we used our own bikes,' Joyce said.

'Then I'll lead the way,' Bill said, straddling his saddle and turning left towards the Civil Defence headquarters.

With a sigh, Joyce decided that nothing she said would deter him, so she manoeuvred her bike into position behind his and allowed him to act as her escort. During last night, the damage had appeared eerie and misshapen, lit by fires that burst upwards from direct hits all over London. As the flames had danced, they'd cast flashes of bright light across the devastation that caught the eye for a fleeting moment of time until searchlights played for a split second on the carcass of a building, a family sitting on a pile of bricks, an abandoned teddy bear, a burst and bubbling water main. But now, in the freezing cold, steely grey morning, the damage from the previous night could be viewed from a clear, unhindered standpoint. What she saw chilled her to the bone, but she managed to quell the surge of panic that tumbled in her stomach – giving into that feeling of alarm wouldn't do anyone any good.

Nothing around her was as it had been since as far back as her first childhood memories. There was nothing left of Webb's Greengrocers, but Mr Webb's son was in position where the shop had stood, a sack of potatoes and another of onions by his side, serving a queue of jaded women. The baker's was missing the flat above the shop; the doctor's surgery was flattened but Dr Smith's wife was helping people around the back to somewhere, a shed perhaps, where Joyce presumed they would be seen to; all that was left of the picture house was a wall with a poster glued to it advertising *Freedom Radio*, starring Clive Brook and Diana Wynyard; The Freemasons Arms, where Granddad and Uncle Terry liked to have a pint was completely gone – not a trace of it could be seen. Buildings stood proud while structures on either side of them were razed to the ground and Joyce wondered at how that could be possible. Firefighters remained in attendance at smouldering buildings with their hoses and stirrup pumps; cordons had been set around gaping pits that workmen were beginning to fill, using material from the numerous rubble mountains that littered the streets. Ruptured water mains were being patched and planks of wood were being nailed across any windows left unscathed. It was all so grim, and Joyce remembered Mum saying how atrocious it was that people had to go about their difficult work every day without getting any sleep at all the night before. It was hard to believe that any of them were standing, let alone able to function, but here they were. And there was Bill, casually weaving between icy puddles and bomb debris and, she could hardly believe her ears, whistling something jaunty. Peddling a bit faster, she drew closer to him and could make out the tune of *Laughing it Off* by Tommy Trinder. She smiled, then wet her lips and hummed along with him.

On the corner of Westbourne Grove, there was nothing else for it but to dismount and walk their bikes the rest of the way to Report and Control. Bill lifted his bicycle over a pothole and said, 'Controller Davis will be wondering where we are. He said it was urgent.'

'He'll understand,' Joyce said, lugging her bike above her head to follow Bill's lead. 'He knows what it's like out here and he knows we will have done our best.'

When they found themselves on a somewhat clear length of road where they were able to walk side by side, Joyce asked Bill if he shouldn't be at school. 'Or... I don't know, evacuated or something?' Then she felt terrible and wished she could snatch back her words when she saw the crestfallen look on Bill's face. 'How old do you think I am?' He was astounded.

'I don't know. I'm not very good with...'

'I'm fourteen. And I'm apprenticed to Barker's. You know the butcher in Bayswater?'

Joyce could vaguely recall the shop Bill was talking about. It wasn't her mother's choice of butcher, so she wasn't familiar with the comings and goings there. 'I think so. Is there a model of a pig in the window?'

'That's the one,' said Bill. He looked almost as proud as he had when he'd reported to take her to headquarters. 'I've helped him out since I was ten, with deliveries and orders and such like, and as he doesn't have any sons he's thinking of leaving the shop to me in time.'

'Lucky you, Bill,' she said. 'Well done.'

'Of course, as soon as I can I'll join up so he might have to keep it going for me until we win the victory.' He shrugged. 'But we all have our duty to do, don't we?'

Joyce considered the shop after shop that no longer existed. The haberdasher's gone; the dry goods gone; the shoe emporium devastated; the fishmonger's nothing but a shell. By the time Bill was old enough to become a soldier Barker's might be nothing more than a memory and old Barker, if he had been minding the premises when the fatal bomb fell, nothing more than ash. It could happen at any time – next year, next month, next week, tomorrow. Then Bill's dream of being proprietor of his own butcher shop would be reduced to a distant boyhood hope that he'd once harboured. And Bill was but a solitary figure amongst thousands, including her, for whom the expectations they had for the future might never be fulfilled.

Then again, it might all be over well before Bill was old enough to join the services and the butcher's might pass seamlessly from master to apprentice. But if it were to finish in a flash, they were already at the point where nothing could ever be the same again. But she didn't want to be the cause of putting paid to the messenger's happy-go-lucky, whistling attitude to life so said, 'Yes, Bill, we all have our responsibilities. But do you know, I don't think it will come to you being called up in three years' time. Mark my words, we'll have won well before that.'

'Shall we have a bet on it?' Bill said.

'What have you got to bet with,' Joyce laughed.

'Probably about as much as you. I'll bet you a pork chop with a kidney attached.'

'You're on,' Joyce said, imagining the meat cooked and on a plate in front of her and Mum. 'And I'll bet with my staff discount.'

'From where?' Bill asked.

'Bourne and Hollingsworth.'

'Oh,' Bill's eyes bulged. 'I'd loved to get my mother a present from there. A lovely, soft, white hanky with her initials embroidered on it. SA. In lavender, her favourite colour. So, it's a deal?'

'Deal,' Joyce said.

* * *

The house that had been seconded to the ARP for Group 1 Report and Control was much less lively during the day than it was at night. The hustle and bustle of firefighters, first aiders, messengers and wardens was missing and although the pattern of night bombing seemed to be set in concrete, a sense of urgency lingered as there were no guarantees that Jerry wouldn't suddenly decide to bomb them all day as well as all night. The lightbox on the wall next to the door that declared the building to be an ARP Control Centre must have recently been extinguished because Joyce got a strong whiff of paraffin as she and Bill passed close to it. But the wooden, glass-fronted noticeboard had been shattered and the poster it held shredded and hanging over itself. *Good,* Joyce thought, *hateful thing*. Then she admonished herself right away, as to be pleased about any bomb damage was shocking and tanta-mount to barbarity. But she could not bear it. How dare that handsome young man in a warden's helmet look down on her from his lofty position next to lettering that declared *Air Wardens Wanted – A Responsible Job For Responsible Men*. It was insulting and Joyce took it personally. Half the wardens in her area alone were women and, as far she was aware, doing the job as responsibly as any man.

Bill held the door for her, but as soon as she was in the hallway, he scooted in front so, she presumed, he could announce her arrival to Controller Davis. She allowed him that privilege as he was a boy trying to make his mark on the world and he had pulled off his duty admirably. They trailed past more posters pinned to the walls; cups, saucers, teapot, tea caddy and a tin of biscuits on a rickety table; a wad of ARPM1 forms hanging from a string on a nail. Joyce wondered if the reason the Controller wanted to see her had something to do with the way she filled in her forms. Perhaps she wasn't as good a warden as the men after all and her hand-writing not as neat as theirs. Or maybe she went into too much detail or not enough? The manner in which she wrote up her forms and reports was the only thing she could think of that she might have done wrong. At Bourne and Hollingsworth she was often complimented for the precise, spotless and elegant way in which she kept her ledgers and dealt with her invoices. During her schooldays, too, there had never been a stray inkblot in her copybooks and any misspellings were put to rights with a ruler line through the incorrect word and the proper spelling written neatly in the margin. She'd been so proud of the immaculate presentation of her work and the headmaster must have felt the same because more than once he'd awarded her with a commendation in assembly. No, incorrect or untidy form filling was not what the Controller wanted to see her about.

The stairs, lit by low lights at night, were not much brighter and no easier to negotiate during the day. Bill marched down them on his way to the basement offices, but Joyce, a bit more cautious, ran her hand along the banister and watched her footing. Perhaps Bill's mother wasn't the worrying sort as her mum was, so he didn't have the same warnings in the back of his mind about being careful on each step.

Again Bill opened the door for her, this time with a flourish, saluted Controller Davis and announced, 'Warden Cooper, Sir, delivered as urgently as possible.'

The Controller looked up from the logbook he was scrutinising, and Joyce could tell he was trying very hard not to burst into laughter at Bill's ardent display of zeal. She hoped he could contain himself, as she had earlier, because she knew Bill would be mortified if he realised he was the recipient of ridicule. But the creases between the Controller's eyebrows deepened and he set his mouth in a serious line, snapped his hand up in a salute and told Bill to stand down. 'And I mean it this time, son,' he said, his voice soft and kindly. 'Go home, get some sleep. We're going to need you tonight.'

'Sir,' Bill said. 'All understood.' And he turned sharply towards the stairs to retrieve his bike, Joyce supposed, and pedal home as commanded or to the butcher's shop if he was expected there.

The Controller smiled at Joyce and said, 'Ah, the enthusiasm of youth. Much the same as yourself, Miss Cooper.'

Joyce nodded and waited patiently to find out what could have been so urgent, as there was nothing pressing about Controller Davis's manner. He asked if she minded awfully if he finished his inspection of the logbook in front of him, called for cups of tea for both of them, picked up his pencil, knitted the lines on his brow together again and left her sitting for some minutes. She felt anxious about the fact that the clock was ticking towards the time she was expected at Bourne and Hollingsworth, but didn't like to disrupt Controller Davis from his important work. Besides, if she asked he would write a note to her manager saying she was late because she'd been summoned to the ARP for war work. No one would argue with that.

Dotted around the bright room were several wardens hard at their paperwork, a black telephone on a desk that Joyce knew connected directly to ambulance and fire stations, maps laid out on tables and folded in corners, a woman in a tabard who had been trying to dust around but was now on tea duty and another who was sticking pins and labels onto a huge map of the area mounted on the wall.

Controller Davis ran his finger down a line of writing in the book then closed it with a huff. A grimace twisting his face, he limped towards a pile of filing and placed the logbook precariously on top of it. 'Mrs Bertrand,' he addressed the woman working on the wall map. She didn't reply, so the Controller raised his voice and, enunciating every syllable, called her name again. When she turned at last with a quizzical look on her face, Joyce could see the older woman had a line of pins with coloured tips in her mouth and was holding another ready to stick into the map.

'Mrs Bertrand,' the Controller lowered his voice now that Mrs Bertrand was looking at him. 'Time to go home now.'

Mrs Bertrand took in the room, the wattles under her chin quivering and from the corner of her mouth said something that sounded like, 'I'll just finish these last few.'

'It's fine for today,' Controller Davis said. 'Miss Cooper's here.' He opened his palm towards Joyce who was more confused than ever. Was she to stand in for Mrs Bertrand? What would be expected of her? Would it be for today, two days, a couple of weeks or would it be permanent? Mrs Bertrand spat out the pins into a tin, yawned, put on her coat and hat, said goodbye to all assembled and then the Controller hobbled back to his desk and sat down next to Joyce.

He sighed and looked so grey and weary that Joyce thought he needed to take his own advice and try to get some sleep. 'Miss Cooper,' he said. 'I'm not going to beat about the bush with you. We need a new Map Plotter. Desperately and urgently.'

'Is that what Mrs Bertrand was doing?'

He nodded. 'She takes one ARPM1 form at a time and is supposed to stick a pin into the exact position where a bomb hit. That helps us to ascertain any pattern to the bombing and also to prioritise services to certain areas. But... I mentioned the enthusiasm of young people, but that is much easier to deal with than the enthusiasm of the elderly. Grateful as we are. Look, come with me.'

He led the way to the wall map and they stood side by side poring over the detailed plan. There were all the streets and parks, alleyways and paths she knew so well drawn out with care and precision and blown up to a huge magnification. And pockmarked all over it were the lurid pins that symbolised a bomb or incendiary that had caused that particular spot to be unrecognisable in the cold, grey reality of day.

'Have a look at this,' Controller Davis said, handing her a form from the top of a stack on a nearby table. It wasn't one she'd written, the writing too small and crowded. 'Now,' he continued. 'Please read the report then take a pin. Black is for total destruction. Purple for damage beyond repair. Dark red stands for seriously damaged and doubtful of repair, light red is for seriously damaged but repairable at cost and the orange denotes general damage that isn't structural. Yellow is used for minor blast damage and green is for clearance areas.' He held the tin towards her, but she hesitated as the thought of Mrs Bertrand spitting into it to release the pins from her mouth a few minutes earlier turned her stomach. Then she suppressed the rising nausea and grasped a black one between her thumb and index finger. Every one of them had to make sacrifices, after all. 'Can you place the pin in the bomb's exact location?' Controller Davis asked.

Joyce cross-referenced the details on the form with the map and within seconds confidently stabbed the precise spot where the incendiary had hit the previous night.

The Controller nodded as if he wasn't in the least surprised. 'I thought that wouldn't be a problem for you judging by the meticulous nature of your reports. And do you think you could strip back the whole map? I mean go back into the files and replot it from when the first bomb struck?' He shook his head. 'It's afraid it's a terrible mess.'

Joyce looked back at the map and took in the hundreds of kaleidoscopic pin marks. 'Yes,' she nodded. 'I believe I could. But Sir, I have a job and my mum couldn't...'

'Ah,' he interrupted. 'You wouldn't be able to do both. But this particular post pays two pounds a week. If that helps? I most certainly hope it does.'

Joyce felt her eyebrows shoot up. Two pounds a week was one shilling more than her salary at Bourne and Hollingsworth – oh, what Mum could do with an extra shilling! She would be thrilled.

'And how would you feel about a second chevron?' Controller Davis prodded. 'You'd be a Senior Warden.'

The thought of that filled her with pride. 'Sir,' she said. 'I'd be honoured. When do I start?'

'Wonderful news,' he said, rubbing his hands together. 'Take a day to make arrangements with your place of work and I will see you for duty on Wednesday afternoon at fifteen hundred hours.'

Joyce stood, thanked the Controller, saluted him and walked with what she hoped was decorum back through the office, up the stairs and out of the door. There she clapped her hands together without making a sound, hopped on her bike and pedalled home as fast as she could to tell Mum the news. Halfway there, she couldn't help but start to hum again, but she didn't want to appear disrespectful or insensitive, so kept the lively thrum as low as possible.

THREE

Saturday 23 February 1974

Joyce loved Saturday mornings. She could make a cup of tea, toast a crumpet and take them back to bed where she would read the *Daily Mirror* or *Woman's Realm* or listen to the 'Top 40 Hits' on BBC Radio One. She had been bereft when it was announced that the Light Programme was to be taken off air but much as she missed it, she very much enjoyed some of the popular tunes being played now, too. It had been such a laugh dancing around the living room years ago with Mum and Auntie Cath and Flo to 'I'll Be With You in Apple Blossom Time' by The Andrews Sisters and they'd loved 'I've Got Sixpence' by the Phil Moore Four. Supposing they were all still with her, she wondered if the four of them would fling themselves about to Mud's 'Tiger Feet' – knowing them, they most certainly would.

Laying her head back on the pillow, she hummed along to Andy Williams singing 'Solitaire'; it was lovely. And anything by the fantastic Perry Como was, in her opinion, sublime. Last week at work she'd started to hum 'For the Good Times' and all the girls in the Payroll Department joined in. It had been great fun and they'd laughed about it for the rest of the day. This week, he was at number forty-nine in the charts with that song and Joyce was sure one or other of her colleagues would comment on that fact on Monday morning.

When she felt ready she would get up, potter around the flat for a little while, have a long soak in a bubble bath, then wander down to Portobello Road Market and get a bit of fruit and veg for the week. Her library books were due back, so she would stop off and exchange them for another six. On Saturdays, she gave herself permission to have the entire day off. From Bourne and Hollingsworth, of course, but also from household chores and cooking. So, she would decide later whether to have cold meats with pickle and a tomato for supper or a pork pie or cheese and biscuits. Whatever she chose, for afters she would treat herself to either a custard tart or a vanilla slice from the bakery and tuck into it while she started on one of the books she'd borrowed earlier.

Then as she was turning back the covers and feeling for her slippers, there was a sharp rap on the door. Joyce sat stock still. No one called on Saturday mornings, in fact no one called at all, ever. She'd left money for the milk in an envelope poking out of an empty bottle and she was sure it held the accurate amount. If there was post for her, the postman would push it through the letterbox. It must be a mistake; someone looking for 38A had knocked on her door, 36A, instead. Any minute now they would realise their error and flee, embarrassed, to the correct flat so she would ignore the knock and sit where she was until she heard their feet ascending the concrete steps.

But pinpricks of apprehension pulsed through her arms when there was another loud, urgent strike at the door followed soon after by another. She couldn't go to the door in her nightclothes or dressing gown, so pulled on a skirt and cardigan that she'd left on a chair to be washed and crept down the hall. Convinced the caller was at her door in error, she peered into the living room and through the nets to see the shape of a young man, his knuckles poised to pound the door again. While she watched, he turned to the window and finding the narrowest chink between the curtains, spied her and raised his hand in greeting. 'Miss Cooper,' he called, his mouth as close to the glass as possible. 'I must speak with you. It's really rather urgent.'

Blast that Mr Taylor. *I should have been more surreptitious*, she admonished herself. But there was nothing for it now, she would have to answer the door. Sliding back the bolt, she looked out through the smallest crack possible and was greeted by the all too familiar Mr Taylor, his sideburns bushier than the last time she'd seen him, his hair longer and more wavy, his tie wider with brighter-coloured stripes, his briefcase more swollen and distended with the paperwork he carried around with him. He smiled at her as if they'd known each other for years and asked if he could please come in.

'You have rather caught me on the hop,' she said, looking down at her mismatched clothes and bare legs.

'I can wait here while you prepare yourself,' he said, his smile not faltering for a second. 'But I won't go anywhere as I must speak with you this morning.'

Joyce sighed and resigned herself to getting the meeting over and done with so she could get on with her Saturday routine. She opened the door, pulled back the flowery curtain, nudged the sausage dog aside and beckoned him in. He made a huge show of wiping his shoes on the mat then followed her into the kitchen. 'How are you, Miss Cooper?' he asked.

Much as she disliked the intrusion, Joyce could not find it in herself to be rude. 'Fine, thank you,' she answered. 'And you? Working overtime on a Saturday? Please sit down.'

He sat at the table and shook his head, long tendrils of hair dancing over his forehead. When she was young, women liked their men clean shaven, neatly groomed and dressed in either immaculate uniform or sharp trousers and jackets in muted colours. But although it was a bit garish, she did like his tie. 'Not overtime,' he answered. 'I have to work six days a week until this phase of the job has been completed, then I can take extended leave until the next tranche begins.'

'Oh, I see. So you're in line for a long holiday.'

'Well, three weeks,' he said, his smile spreading further and meeting the hairy sideboards on each side of his face. He looked young and boyish, although the lines around his eyes gave him away for being in his thirties. He exuded the marvellous traits young people have of optimism, freshness and energy. Even during the war people under forty had gone about their business with an air of hopefulness. 'During which,' Mr Taylor continued chatting, 'I'll be married and my new wife and I will be taking a two-week package holiday to Benidorm as a honeymoon.'

She'd heard of that new way of holidaying – the girls at work raved about booking with Clarksons or Thomson Holidays, taking a two-hour flight and laying around for a fortnight in soft sand and guaranteed sun. Some of them returned the colour of walnut wood, looking relaxed and extolling the benefits of sangria and paella.

The pleasantries wound down and Joyce pointed to the teapot. 'Would you like a cup?' she asked.

'If you're having one, I'll join you, please,' he said.

While she busied herself with the kettle, the gas, the cups and saucers, Joyce could hear Mr Taylor opening his briefcase and spreading papers out in front of him. While her back was to him, he said, 'Miss Cooper, why haven't you come into the office as requested in my letters to you? Or replied to them at least. I know you've received them, they're on your hall table, each one of them marked urgent.'

When the gas took, she extinguished the match with a flick of her wrist, threw it in the bin, crossed her arms over her chest and turned to face him. 'Mr Taylor,' she determined to be forthright. 'I didn't think there was a need as I'm sure I made myself plain three weeks ago when I told you that the new, entirely inappropriate flats we traipsed around were not acceptable.'

The smile left Mr Taylor's face. He lifted his hands upwards then let them fall to the table in exasperation. 'Then where will you go, Miss Cooper,' he asked. 'When the bulldozers come in and begin to raze these tenements to the ground?'

'Young man,' she steadied her voice. 'You wouldn't insult me if you knew how many obliterated homes I was forced to deal with before I was anywhere near your age.'

Mr Taylor dug under his collar and rubbed the back of his neck. He apologised, saying it hadn't been his intention to affront her and that he held her in the deepest respect. 'But you cannot stay here,' he added. 'You simply cannot. And it is my job to ensure you have suitable accommodation to move to within the next two weeks. I'm sure you would rather deal with me than a gang of burly policemen dragging you out and the council placing you in a seedy bedsit? Then of course you would have to be housed permanently in whichever flat they assigned you to, and that could be anywhere in London. You wouldn't have a choice at that stage.'

The monologue seemed to have exhausted him and Joyce thought he was probably not used to dealing with non-compliant tenants. She didn't want to give him any trouble or be thought of as rebellious or awkward. But she liked her flat and wanted to stay put and thought she should have some say in the matter.

As Joyce poured both of them a cup of tea, Mr Taylor asked her a number of questions. 'Have you looked for private accommodation, Miss Cooper?'

She shook her head, put the cups on the table and sat down.

'We did discuss the possibility of you finding a flat through the Notting Hill Housing Trust. Or Shelter. Did you make any enquires with them?'

Joyce pictured the houses being done up by the Trust, split into flats and rented on very reasonable terms to homeless families. It had made such a difference to the area and had all been started by the minister Bruce Kenrick from his fund-raising stall on Portobello Market. She'd given him a pound once right at the beginning of his campaign. 'No, I haven't approached them as I'm not homeless, or unemployed, or on the welfare. So it wouldn't be right for me to take up a place that someone else, a struggling family for example, could really use.'

'But Miss Cooper, you could soon be homeless if we don't get this sorted out.' He paused and waited for her to make some kind of panicked comment, but Joyce didn't rise to the challenge so he tried a different tack. 'All the flats in this house have been vacated,' Mr Taylor said. 'And the ones either side of you are empty and boarded up. Are you aware of that?'

Of course she was, so she nodded.

'Well, have you decided on a moving company or asked someone to help you to transport your belongings when the time comes?'

There was no one she could approach for help, so she said no.

'Three weeks from today, this entire area will be unoccupied. Everyone will have relocated. Even if by some strange... oversight you were allowed to stay, you'd have no neighbours or friends or community left.'

Joyce brought the teacup to her lips and swallowed a mouthful of the warming drink. That would not be a new situation for her and, although she hated the thought of going through it again, she knew that if she had to live like that, she could.

'Look,' Mr Taylor jumped up, the smile brandishing his face yet again. He tinkered with the hot water geyser until it started its familiar clunking noise. 'In the new flats you'd have a modern, streamlined boiler and you wouldn't have to put up with this racket anymore.'

'I find it rather comforting,' Joyce said.

'Well, there would be no more lighting the stove with a match. The new pilots are automatic.'

'I've always used a match for the gas,' Joyce shrugged. 'I'm used to it.'

He sat down again and when he looked at her, his eyes were pleading and earnest. 'There's secondary double glazing, so you could get rid of that draught excluder and the curtain over the door. The bath is new and shiny. The oven turns on with a dial, you'd be on ground level or one of the two floors above if you prefer, the walls are painted cream and there's a double lock on the door. You'd have neighbours again. You could make some friends.'

'That,' she said, 'is the least of my concerns.'

'Miss Cooper,' he lowered his voice again. 'I must insist. This is your last opportunity.'

The thought of looking around more box-shaped, soulless flats devoid of cubbyholes and shelves and idiosyncratic thunks and creaks did not fill her with enthusiasm. But then neither did being manhandled out of her home and onto the streets before being allocated the dregs of accommodation.

'Also,' Mr Taylor said. 'It's worth bearing in mind that the new flats are being snapped up, so soon there won't be many left to choose from.'

They sat in silence for a few moments. Joyce could feel a forceful and unrelenting pressure from outside bearing down on the ceiling and pushing in on the walls. It seemed as if the flat were squeezing her out, and the sense of betrayal hurt.

Joyce glanced at Mr Taylor and he looked as if he had come to the end of his persuasive arguments. In a soft, patient voice, he asked if she would meet him tomorrow morning and allow him to show her three perfect, brand new flats on which he would give her first refusal. Although his hope was that she wouldn't refuse all of them.

Joyce looked at the snowdrops bobbing in the yard, the blue, plastic bowl in the kitchen sink, the tin kettle on the hob, the picture of Big Ben on the wall over the cupboard where she kept vegetables and fruit out of the light, the pile of magazines in the corner, the drawer where she kept her personal papers. She could hear the clock ticking on the mantel in the living room and footsteps on the pavement outside. There was a faint smell of the coal tar soap and Sunlight washing powder she'd used for years. She took a deep, steadying breath and nodded in agreement.

FOUR

BILL

February 1941

It was with a huge amount of pride that Joyce related her reason for leaving to the manager of the Accounts Department at Bourne and Hollingsworth, who sat back in his office chair with a mixture of surprise and disappointment on his face. Then he smiled and said, 'Well, if we have to lose someone as promising as you, Miss Cooper, I'm more than glad it's to the war effort and not because you thought you wanted a change of situation.'

'Oh no, Mr Harris,' Joyce was quick to put the record straight. 'I've loved my time here and hope when this war is done and dusted you'll have me back.'

Mr Harris gazed at a photo of a woman and three young adults on his desk, one of the boys in uniform. Then the filing cabinets seemed to capture his attention. Next, he leaned back, peered out of the window and studied the crowds looping around hills of bricks, smashed glass and gaps in the pavements along Oxford Street. Last September, when the insult of nightly bombing was still an extraordinary phenomenon, a huge hole had been ripped into the store's interior and several of the elegant shop floors had been damaged. It was such a shock to see the merchandise – leather belts, china soap dishes, silk hosiery, tie pins that had been lovingly displayed – strewn under shards of glistening glass. Joyce and some other assistants snaffled ruined white sheets from the linen department, drew makeshift Union Jack flags on them and unfurled them to cover the bomb damage to the store front. The gesture made them laugh out loud, almost to the point of hysteria Joyce thought, but also made them strong in their resolve.

The flags had long been removed and directly beneath the manager, out of his line of sight, the building was shoddily shorn up, like so many of the premises along Oxford Street.

When Mr Harris turned to her again his eyes were sad and resigned. 'Of course,' he said, his voice not full of conviction although she didn't think it had anything to do with him re-employing her at some stage in the future. 'Do you know,' he added, his demeanour brightening, 'I do believe that if anyone can get us out of this whole bloody mess it's you. And others of your ilk. Thank you, Miss Cooper and good luck.'

After that official notification of her intention to leave, Joyce set about saying goodbye to the colleagues and friends she'd made at the store and that wasn't easy. She'd started there, first as a salesgirl on the ladies' perfume counter when she was about the same age as Bill, then as a trainee in the Accounts Department followed by a promotion to become a fully-fledged invoice clerk. And Mr Harris had intimated that she could climb higher, with more responsibility and wages to match, if she carried on in her proven manner.

It had all been down to a customer who came across as if

she were a Lady Somebody or Another. Her requirements were complicated – she'd wanted a bottle of Duchesse for herself, Chanel No 5 to be sent to her daughter-in-law who had moved to the country and a bottle of Black Orchid for her sister who lived in Surrey. Joyce chatted with the woman, who was very pleasant, while writing out order forms that included delivery notes and asking for details of where to send the invoices. The woman complimented her on her neat handwriting and when the purchases were complete said, 'Thank you so much, my dear. You have been most efficient.'

'My pleasure,' Joyce replied. 'I hope we see you in Bourne and Hollingsworth again very soon.'

'Oh, you shall indeed. I'm a very regular customer.'

Joyce had watched the woman weave her way through the counters, stopping to admire a display of hats and again to touch a pair of soft, grey kidskin gloves. When the floor manager approached the woman and they conversed for a few minutes in an animated manner, Joyce turned to tidy her counter and thought no more of the transaction. But at the beginning of the following week, she was called to Mr Harris's office, congratulated on being mentioned as outstanding by a valued customer and told she was being recommended for a trainee position in the Accounts Department, if she wanted it. As if she wouldn't. No one in their right mind would turn down such a wonderful opportunity.

Mum had been thrilled with each step up Joyce accomplished and praised her daughter with a profusion of compliments and accolades. They were nothing, though, compared to the bluster and bombast with which she reported her daughter's achievements to friends and family. 'She's done so well yet again,' Mum crowed to Auntie Cath. 'I knew from when she was a baby that she was a brainbox.'

'Mum, please,' Joyce felt her cheeks and the back of her neck redden.

'Guess what our Joy's gone and done now?' Mum gloated to Nana and Granddad. 'She's only gone and got herself a big advancement.' Mum nodded in agreement with her own boast and carried on, 'And she's only twenty-one. The youngest ever in the Accounts Department. Isn't that right, Joy love?'

Joyce had smiled and demurred and hoped the moment would pass without her having to add anything further. But as well as being elated for herself, she was happy and relieved for Mum who she knew felt guilty that Joyce had been forced to leave school at fourteen. All her teachers had said she was more than able to carry on, but Mum needed Joyce to go out to work and bring in a wage, so there had been nothing else for it. Once the promotions started, though, school and the opportunities Joyce had lost by not being able to stay on no longer mattered. And the same applied to her work at Bourne and Hollingsworth now that she was starting her first shift as a Civil Defence Bomb Plotter. Other than the training it had allowed her in precision, exactitude and conscientiousness, that was in the past. Now Mum was full of it again and Joyce was sure that during the last forty-eight hours her mother had managed to tell everyone in the family and most of the neighbours about the position that Joyce was taking up in the ARP.

* * *

The usual round of sandwiches had been cut and wrapped, the flask of steaming tea placed upright in her canvas bag, her uniform scrutinised, cleaned and mended with care, her helmet and whistle polished, the felt hat she was allowed to wear when there was no immediate danger of bombing folded into the pocket of her blue serge greatcoat.

As Joyce gathered her things together, her mother stood and watched her every move. 'I don't suppose you'll need the helmet or the whistle since you'll be in the Control Centre every night instead of out and about.' She reached across and tenderly pushed a stray tendril of hair from Joyce's cheek. 'You'll be much safer there, thank goodness.'

'Yes,' Joyce said. 'I suppose that's right, but I'm going to take everything with me tonight until I'm settled into a routine. Anyway, I should wear the helmet there and back just in case.'

Mum nodded so fast Joyce thought her head might come off her neck. 'You're so wise, Joy love.' Then she put her hands on her daughter's face and said, 'Do you know how very proud I am of you?'

And although Joyce had heard it many times before she said, 'Ta, Mum. You've always been right behind me. Now, listen. I will be sending Bill, or another messenger, to make sure you are in that underground with everyone else.' She widened her eyes and put her hands on her hips. 'Do you understand?'

Mum groaned. 'If I have to.'

'You have to.' Joyce stood to attention, saluted her mother and said, 'Joyce Margaret Cooper, Senior Warden in the Civil Defence, is commanding you to obey orders.'

'Aye, aye, captain,' Mum said.

'Captain?' Joyce echoed.

'Perhaps you prefer lieutenant then, or brigadier?'

'Field Marshal, if you please,' Joyce said and they laughed until they hugged each other close and the door was closed between them.

It wasn't yet dark, but already the evening was crisp and icy. Every breath Joyce took coated her mouth and throat in a layer of fresh, cold air; every breath out produced a camouflage of steam in front of her face. Everyone was hurrying – women on their way home with shopping bags of rations from which to fashion some semblance of a meal to take down to the underground; men with newspapers under their arms rushing to gather their families into Anderson shelters for the night; the few children who remained in London trying hard not to be distracted from their games; people with hands raised for the bus, intent etched on their faces; ARP personnel making their way to their stations to ready themselves for what would probably be a long, arduous night. Joyce wondered how long the Germans would or could keep up this bombing campaign. It had only been about six months, but it was relentless so seemed interminable. Surely the Jerries didn't have the resources or manpower to bombard them for much longer? *But more to the point*, she thought, with a chill that crawled up her back, *how much longer can London take it?* Then she steeled her nerves and told herself they would take it for as long as they had to – there was no doubt about that.

She'd decided to leave her pushbike at home and walk, as manoeuvring a bicycle through the bomb-damaged streets took much longer than striding out on foot. She pulled her shoulders back, lifted her chin, breathed deeply and walked with purpose towards Report and Control, determined to establish a proud and confident exterior despite the seething turmoil in her stomach.

The landscape was a constantly shifting shadowy scene not only after a night of heavy bombing, but also on an hourly basis during the day when temporary maintenance was being carried out so that the once-familiar shapes of pubs, park railings, libraries and post offices were transformed into unknown, looming outlines and silhouettes. Some demolished pockets were so stark in contrast with what they had been that she felt herself shiver when she darted past, unable to confront the unnerving changes.

Then there was the huge inconvenience of facing diversions that hadn't been in place the last time she'd taken the same route. That was very frustrating as it could make the journey to Report and Control twice or three times as long and although she knew Controller Davis would be understanding, it added to the high level of strain that everyone was living under. Two mornings previously, when she'd walked along this road after being offered the job as Bomb Plotter, white and purple crocuses had been nodding their small, fragile heads next to a rickety fence in the cold, frosty air. She remembered them with clarity as they seemed to reflect how buoyant and hopeful she felt, but now when she looked for them they were trampled into a muddy quagmire, a length of the splintered fence pinning them down. The fact that they were ruined caused a deep stab of regret in the place around her heart. Sighing, she chastised herself. Of all the things to grieve she had chosen a handful of crocuses, but when her eye was drawn again to the sorry sight of petals and stems crushed before they'd had a chance to thrive, she knew there was more to it than that.

Tempting as it was to bend and rescue one of the bedraggled blooms from the dirty pit, Joyce refused to allow herself to be sentimental. Picking her way towards her destination once again, she heard a catchy, chummy whistle from somewhere close behind. She smiled and pushed her maudlin thoughts about crushed flowers to a place in her mind where she tried to cordon them off along with images of the young mum and her two small children, Percy with his injured wrist and blood running down his face, the bombed-out greengrocer's and doctor's surgery, Controller Davis's listing limp, Mrs Bertrand's spittle on the pins she would soon have to handle and people making their way to another cramped, stinking, undignified night in the underground.

'Warden Cooper!' The whistling stopped mid-note and Joyce heard Bill's cheerful voice call out to her.

She turned and as he approached on his pushbike she said, 'Senior Warden to you, Messenger Bill.'

'Well, la-di-dah and excuse me,' Bill said, snubbing his nose with his finger. 'I'm surprised and honoured that you're deigning to speak to me.'

Joyce laughed. 'I can't imagine ever being in a position not to talk to you, Bill,' she said. 'Ready for another busy night?'

'Not merely ready, but willing and able,' Bill quipped. 'And you?'

Joyce hesitated, a chill of anxiety passing through her arms and legs. 'Yes,' she said, on a long exhalation. 'But I am admitting to you, and only you, that I'm feeling trepidatious, too.'

Bill looked both confused and embarrassed.

'You know,' Joyce said. 'A bit nervous as it's my first night on the wall map.'

Mum would have referred to the way in which Bill's features lit up as the penny having dropped. 'Oh, I see. Well, I suppose everyone feels a bit, I don't know... unsettled when they start something new? You'll soon get the hang of it. And Controller Davis wouldn't have chosen you if you weren't up to it, would he.'

That statement reassured Joyce more than she would have given the simple sentiment credit for and she wondered how a boy of fourteen could be so insightful. She smiled at Bill and he resumed his jaunty tune.

'Here we are then,' Bill said as they converged on Report and Control with a number of others wearing blue serge uniforms, helmets on their heads, tin whistles and gas masks swinging from their necks. They nodded to several people they recognised and then Joyce remembered her mum and the underground.

'Bill,' Joyce caught hold of the messenger's sleeve and he stopped and looked down at her hand, gripping his jacket. 'Do you have to go into the underground as part of your duties?'

He shook his head. 'No,' he said. 'All I do is convey messages.'

'If you get a chance tonight,' she said, keeping her voice low, 'could you please stick your head into Notting Hill Gate and check on my mum? You remember her, don't you?'

Bill stood straight and said, 'I'm sure I'd recognise her and I'll do my very best to find the time, Senior Warden Cooper. You can count on me.'

Joyce thanked the boy again and felt as if they had forged an unlikely friendship.

When she'd nestled her coat and beret on a hook amongst the blue sea of identical garments, she made her way to the main control room. It was chilly and the cold bit around her ankles and nibbled at her hands; she thought it might heat up later when the bombing started and they were in the thick of their duties, but she wished she'd brought a cardigan with her in case. Or perhaps she'd ask Auntie Cath to knit her a pair of fingerless gloves so she could pick up the pins without trembling. Controller Davis motioned her to an empty chair and she joined a rather large group for their nightly briefing.

'We expect,' Controller Davis said, his face contorting in

pain as he shifted from one leg to the other, 'that tonight will follow the pattern of all those since the seventh of September last in terms of continuous bombing from nightfall until dawn.'

With a sideways glance, Joyce cast a stealthy look around the room to gauge her colleagues' reactions. What she ascertained was remarkable: not one of them looked fed-up – as they had every right to be – or worried or defeated or disbelieving. Tired, certainly, with dark rings around red eyes, sallow skin, a couple of stifled yawns and rather hurried, but imaginative, solutions to unwashed hair. There was a smell, too, of the musty breath that lingered after waking, faces and hands washed with haste and clothes caught in the damp.

Then she was drawn back into the meeting with a start when she heard her name mentioned. 'And Miss Joyce Cooper,' Controller Davis was saying, 'is starting tonight as our Senior Warden Bomb Plotter. Some of you know her already as she's been with us from the beginning.' He gestured towards her and she was glad she wasn't wearing that cardigan after all. She felt blood rush to the surface of her skin as the others began to mumble and nod in her direction, or peer around each other for a closer look. From the back of the room, Bill winked and looked as if he were basking in her spotlight.

'Mrs Bertrand,' Controller Davis continued, 'is now our Chief Tea and Biscuit Warden and she will also have responsibility for minor first aid.' A few people started to titter, but Controller Davis let it be known, by the sincere and austere look on his face, that he would not entertain any form of humiliation to reach the eyes or ears of Joyce's predecessor. As luck would have it, the water in the urn rose to the boil at that very moment followed by the heartening sound of paper being torn off a packet of biscuits. 'I'm sure you're all very grateful, as am I, that such a lovely lady has agreed to take on those most important roles.' Goodness, thought Joyce, the man was so persuasive she was sure any of them would follow him to the ends of the earth if he said it was the right thing to do; he should be Prime Minister. And she, for one, would find a cuppa and a biccy most welcome during the long night ahead.

When Mrs Bertrand appeared from the kitchen with cups and saucers on a tray, Joyce was pleased to see that all the assembled smiled at her and that she, in return, looked happy – not the least bit put out that her place at the map had been taken by a young girl, as Joyce thought she might.

'Now,' Controller Davis said, announcing the impending air raids in a cool, calm manner as if he were talking about something no more dangerous than an evening stroll to the pub. 'If anything, Jerry is consistent and punctual so any minute now the telephone will ring and we shall have to implement the red warning for the first time tonight. If there are no questions,' he rubbed his hands together with vigour, 'let's get into position.'

Joyce hated the urgent, wailing siren that made her inwardly gasp for breath every time it pierced the air. It set every nerve in her body on alert and that, she supposed, was the whole point; the terrible noise refused to allow them to become complacent. She sprang to her feet and faced the wall map, dotted with misplaced pins, and decided that while she waited for the first report of the night to reach her, she would make herself useful and begin to go through the hundreds of previous forms and put to rights the little arrows that had been placed incorrectly. But as she opened the top drawer of the first filing cabinet the telephone rang, which meant the Royal Observer Corps had spotted Luftwaffe aircraft heading towards Britain. A wire broadcast system had sent messages to police stations throughout the country, the police, in turn, had contacted Civil Defence stations and the ARP would initiate powered sirens in towns and cities, whistles or hand-operated alerts in rural areas. It sounded as if it could be a hit and miss system, but in fact it was well thought out and it seemed to work.

For an imperceptible split second everyone froze, then Controller Davis picked up the telephone receiver, listened to the voice of authority on the other end and said, 'Understood.'

Joyce held her breath and along with everyone else present, watched Controller Davis lean towards the siren, which was protected by a wire box, and press the button that activated the warbling high and low-pitched scream that would be heard all over Notting Hill. Although her stomach flipped, she stood rigid and imagined Mum, tea towel in hand, bending over a few sausage rolls or a bit of cheese she was about to cut; Auntie Cath on her way to Nana and Granddad's house to help them to the underground; her cousin Flo coming in from work and beginning to change her shoes for indoor slippers only to have to revert to the outdoor pair again. Each small, simple act of everyday life interrupted night after night. Never before had it occurred to her how precious it had been to go about those tasks in peaceful, calm circumstances. She promised herself that if she were ever to experience blithe moments again in the future, she would not let them pass her by unappreciated.

To a man and woman, the wardens and messengers knew what they had to do and got on with it like tightly wound pieces of machinery. They made for the streets above equipped with their low-level torches, helmets, whistles, ceiling-testing poles and the ARPM1 forms that would soon be filled in and piled up in front of her. She raised her hand to Percy, a scab healing on his forehead, and returned Bill's smart salute.

Controller Davis deactivated that first red alert warning that meant the Jerries had been spotted so those involved in very important war work could carry on but soon, very soon, another siren would be sounded and that would signal, in no uncertain terms, that attack from the air was imminent and enemy aircraft were overhead ready to drop their weapons. The wardens knew they had a limited amount of time to undertake their first job of encouraging and helping people to shelter, whether that was in an Anderson or, like her family, down in the deep pits of the underground.

With everyone gone except Joyce, Mrs Bertrand, Controller Davis and a handful of other wardens who performed administrative tasks, it might have been reasonable to suppose the atmosphere was less charged. But the opposite was true. They understood the implications of what was going to happen next and yet, at the same time, had no comprehension of what would materialise. Both the stark certainty and flagrant uncertainty were enough to fill anyone with dread. Joyce felt a cold, uncomfortable trickle of sweat swim along her hairline. They all watched Controller Davis who, in turn, didn't take his eyes off the telephone.

She decided to use any remaining, unrestricted time to study the map that was now her responsibility and get to know its idiosyncrasies as fully as possible. It was painstakingly detailed, as enormous as the wall it hung on and framed in dark wood which was helpful as the edges wouldn't curl or tear. Joyce had been told that it was drawn up by the Council's Architecture and Surveyors' Department and that they were now involved in the Rescue Services as no one knew the intricacies of the buildings and alleyways, crescents and streets as they did. There was the little terraced house she shared with Mum in Rabbit Row, complete with their patch of a front garden and the passage that led to a tiny shed at the back. The fences that separated them from their neighbours were drawn in as faint pencil lines.

Taking an old form from the filing cabinet, she read through the information, removed the pin and label that pertained to it and moved it to the correct position. It was not complicated, but finding the time to bring the map up to scratch would be difficult, unless she put in a good few hours during daylight. As she stood back to survey her handiwork, Mrs Bertrand appeared at her elbow asking how she liked her tea.

Joyce started as if caught in the act of sabotage and she felt guilty, although she knew she had no reason to. 'Oh, ta, Mrs Bertrand.' She could hear how overly effusive she sounded. 'Milk and one speck of sugar if there's enough to go around, please.'

Mrs Bertrand nodded and then looked her up and down. For a disquieting moment Joyce thought she was about to get taken to task for laying claim to the older woman's property, but all Mrs Bertrand said was, 'And you look like you could use a biscuit to plump you out.' She lowered her voice and smiled as though they shared a secret. 'I'll put two on your saucer, love.'

'That will be a treat. Ta,' Joyce said.

Mrs Bertrand shuffled towards the kitchen and Joyce peered at Controller Davis to see if he'd been observing her making a fool of herself, but his eyes were stuck fast on the telephone. Then, with a jolt that brought her back to reality, the strident ringing of the bell sliced through the heavy atmosphere. Controller Davis answered it with one hand and pushed the alert with the other. This time, Joyce knew, the screeching, grating wail would not stop until the all-clear. Any minute now a messenger would appear with a form, pass it to Controller Davis who would decide what, if any, further action needed to be taken and then the report would find its way to her and the map.

There was just enough time for half a cup of tea and one of the welcome digestives that Mrs Bertrand handed to her before Bill appeared with a form and the accoutrements of that civilised beverage had to be abandoned and forgotten on a side table. Red in the face and puffing from exertion, Bill handed the form to the Controller and without a backward glance, headed for the fray once again. She heard his heavy footfall as he took the stairs two, or perhaps three, at a time.

Controller Davis read through the report and Joyce could see the concentration pull his thick, grey eyebrows together until they met and the lines on each side of his moustache deepened. He reeled off an address to a Senior Warden standing by and told him to phone the Fire and Rescue Service and get a crew sent out as quickly as possible. When he'd fulfilled that duty, he passed the form to Joyce. 'Miss Cooper,' Controller Davis called across the room. 'Do not file the report once you've pinpointed the hit. All details must be recorded in a logbook and if more than one ARPM1 is written up about the same incident, we must transfer the information onto an ARPM2. Then all intelligence needs to be collated and sent to London Regional Report and Control each morning.'

'Yes, Sir,' Joyce replied, and felt rather naïve that she'd thought the job involved sticking pins in a map and nothing else.

Joyce was relieved to find she could read the writing on the form without any trouble. She knew the place, but she had to brace herself when she realised that she would recognise almost every address that was presented to her. It was a bonus, though, that she was familiar with the format of the report so knew how each section was laid out. AIR RAID DAMAGE, the headline on the form read. Then there was a line where the reporting agent had to fill in his or her name and their designation, or the number of their post – theirs was Group 1, but it was plausible and possible to have wardens report from out of area, too. The next section was the address of the occurrence, then the type of bomb involved with three tick boxes to choose from – HE, incendiary or poison gas. The following section was the place to list the approximate number of casualties and to say if any were trapped under wreckage. Then the wardens had to answer yes or no to whether there was fire. There was yet another tick box to inform the authorities if there was damage to mains – either water, coal, gas, overhead electric cables or sewers. And there were places to put the names of blocked roads, and where there were unexploded bombs; the approximate time of the occurrence; whether services were on the spot or on the way; and lastly a few lines to write any further necessary remarks.

When she'd been a warden patrolling the streets and dashing from one emergency to the next, writing out the paperwork had seemed inconsequential. Now when she was on the receiving end, she could appreciate the importance of the documentation more than ever, but also understand that it could be an onerous task; no wonder some wardens made a bit of a hash with their handwriting or the content of their reports.

With studied concentration, Joyce plucked a light red pin

between her thumb and index finger and pierced the map in the exact location of the hit – on a tiny label she wrote out the necessary details: Inc for incendiary; and in the shorthand that had been adopted, one S/I or seriously injured and another L/I – lightly injured. The fire service was on the way and as far as the warden had been able to ascertain, the mains had not taken any damage.

Then there was Bill again and another messenger followed by another who was wearing short trousers. Their faces glowed pink from the sudden heat of the basement after the cold outside; none of them wore gloves, so their hands were red and raw. What had been an almost empty space a few minutes earlier was now crawling with people – a fire chief, a high-up in the ambulance service, two first-aiders, a woman who was in charge of the local WVS – all gathered to be on hand to make decisions with Controller Davis about who should be seconded where and when. Gone was any thought of decorum about picking up the pins one at a time – Joyce lined her lips with the sharp implements and if she had to speak, she did so through clenched teeth. If she swallowed one of the little daggers then no matter, others were being hit with far worse.

Controller Davis clumped towards the map, followed by five or six others and they stood so close behind her that she could feel the heat of their agitation and smell the damp sweat from under their arms. 'Carry on, Miss Cooper,' Controller Davis said. 'You must not stop on our account.'

So she pushed pin after pin into the map, each one a minute spot of oddly-coloured blood that she imagined had seeped from a broken heart. One of the men watching made a comment about the re-allocation of services and the others agreed. Another projected his theory about which row of premises would be targeted next and after some discussion, it was decided to tell messengers to alert wardens so that if any of them were able, they could make their way to that area.

Bill appeared with a form again, a streak of black across his cheek and this time Controller Davis grabbed him by the shoulder and told him he must sit and have a cup of tea. But Bill shook his head and said, 'I wouldn't disobey an order under normal circumstances, Sir, but I'm needed up there.'

'Miss Cooper,' Controller Davis said, tightening his grip on Bill, 'talk some sense into this young man, please.'

Joyce spat her pins into the tin and said in a firm voice, 'Bill, you must have a break. There's so much to worry about, don't let us have to worry about you, too.'

Bill hesitated and the Controller loosened his hold on the boy. Then Bill looked from one to the other and said, 'I'll stop next time.' And he bolted for the stairs without a backwards glance.

Joyce knew there was no hope of stopping him, but tried calling his name in a rather tired, resigned voice as if she were talking to a petulant toddler. She shrugged her shoulders at Controller Davis and placed the pins back in her mouth.

There was no let up. Every once in a while, Joyce glanced at the clock on the wall; 11.28, 12.56, 2.02 – the hours flew past. Her job on the streets as a warden had been intense and so was this, but in a very different way. This work was so much more structured as to be almost robotic. Take a form, read it, pin the position on the map, put it in a pile to be added to an ARPM2 later if necessary, then written up in a logbook and finally consolidated for Regional Control. She knew she was a methodical person, so the work suited her but the tension of not seeing or hearing, first-hand, what was going on above her was enough to make her limbs feel paralysed, if she gave into the apprehension. Her neck ached and she rolled her head from side to side; her shoulders felt like blocks of concrete; her arms were stiff from strain. At 2.27, Mrs Bertrand brought her a cup of tea and she relieved herself of the pins so she could gulp it down. It was amazing how revived she felt after a couple of mouthfuls – but where was Bill? Had he appeared, turned in his forms, been true to his word about stopping long enough for a cuppa and gone on his way again without her noticing?

It wasn't like her to be so unobservant or like him not to say at least a quick hello or bring her news of having seen her mum in the underground, as he'd promised he would try to do.

The boy in the shorts rushed in and thrust a form at Controller Davis and before he could mount the stairs again she tapped him on the shoulder and asked if he'd seen Bill. When he looked perplexed, she said, 'You know – Bill. He whistles all the time. He's going to be a butcher.'

'Oh, Bill,' the lad said. 'No, I ain't seen him in a while. But you can't see much of anything out there.'

Of course, she reasoned to herself and got back to the map. 3.15 came and went, 4.37 ticked past, form after form appeared but somehow she managed to stop the reports from piling up, on which Controller Davis congratulated her. Soon it would be 6.18 when dawn would break and they could hopefully sound the all-clear, the bombing would stop and the work of clearing up in as haphazard a way as possible would begin – with all of them going about the motions like haunted apparitions. And for so many people, represented by one or other of her pins, they would start their day with a beloved member or members of their family injured or worse. It was an achingly cruel way to live.

At 5.26 a bedraggled, slick-faced messenger arrived and placed a form into Controller Davis's hand.

'You look like you need a break, son,' the Controller said.

The boy scout nodded, and Controller Davis called for Mrs Bertrand to take the lad to the small room set aside for the treatment of minor injuries and then he began to read the report. Joyce turned to look at him at the same time as his eyes widened and he sat in his chair with a graceless bump, as if all the stuffing had been knocked out of him. She abandoned her station and strode across the room. He held up his hand and shook his head. 'Go back to your map, Senior Warden Cooper,' he said.

She did as she'd been ordered, but felt entangled in an unsettling mantle of foreboding. Was it Mum? No, Mum was in the underground, she hoped. And the Controller had no idea where Nana and Granddad or Auntie Cath or Flo lived. Was it his home, with news of his wife buried under tons of masonry? Joyce saw him take off his hat and rake through his hair, then his moustache got the same treatment. But when he buried his face in his hands for a moment, alarm pulsed straight from her heart to every other part of her body. Something terrible must have happened for this to be the same man who had commanded them so confidently twelve hours previously. She began to imagine London and its entire population annihilated and them the only ones left to face the city in the morning.

But Controller Davis was much too professional to give in to his emotions entirely and he pulled back his shoulders, replaced his cap, re-arranged his features to neutral and hobbled towards her with the form outstretched. He passed it to her with slow deliberation and said, 'We must be brave and continue to go about our vital work. But,' his voice softened, 'if you need a quiet minute, please take it.'

Joyce nodded without knowing what she was agreeing to. She was transfixed, but knew she must get on with it as other messengers were appearing with more forms and she didn't want to get behind. None of them was Bill, though, and at the very second she brought the form up to her eyes the truth of the matter hit her. Her hand flew to her mouth; her heart hammered so hard it felt as if her ears would explode; she was afraid that if she looked up, the room would spin. All she took in of the report was K for killed and in the box for Further Remarks – *I think the messenger's name was Bill Adams*.

Joyce let her arms fall to her side. She hadn't even known Bill's surname and something about that made her stomach churn with an intense sadness. Then Mrs Bertrand was beside her, putting her hand on Joyce's elbow. 'Come with me, Miss Cooper,' Mrs Bertrand said in a low voice.

'No, I haven't the time,' Joyce said, trying to prise herself away from Mrs Bertrand's hold.

'Yes, you have, my dear. Five minutes. None of us are indispensable, are we? I know that better than anyone.'

So Joyce allowed herself to be taken to the small first aid room where she was seated next to the messenger who looked as if he were shocked. She thought she mirrored his yellowish, glistening, sticky skin. With shaking hands, she took a cup of tea from Mrs Bertrand who stood over her while she sipped it. *Bill*, she said over and over again in her mind. He was a mere seven years younger than her. How could this have happened to him? When she read the report in detail, which she would have to do in a minute, she would find out the answer to that question. But why Bill? That could never be explained. He had been so lively and fun and cheerful and ambitious and...

She stopped as that was about the sum of her knowledge of the boy. But she knew there must have been so many other things about Bill that she hadn't had the time to discover and now never would. The enormity of the war was suddenly reduced to this one casualty – her new friend, Bill – and then her understanding seemed to broaden and the whole picture became clear and terrible.

'Ta, Mrs Bertrand,' Joyce said, testing her legs as she stood. 'I'll get back to the map now.'

Mrs Bertrand nodded. 'Good girl,' she said.

When Joyce strode across the room and plucked the report from the top of the pile with resolve, Controller Davis limped into position next to her and said, 'I appear to have a blessed few minutes of calm. Let's do this one together.'

Blinking to clear her eyes, Joyce nodded and they stood and read through the ghastly details. It became apparent that two incidents had been reported on one ARPM1 – and both involved Bill. Warden John Clayton had written that an incendiary device had exploded on the roof of a house in Pembridge Square. A woman was rescued from the premises but said her sister, who was blind and very frightened, had been pinned under a pile of rubble.

Before I could stop him, a messenger pushed past me and went into the unstable house. When challenged from a safe distance, he said he would stay with the distressed woman until the rescue services turned up. I ordered him to keep out of the building, but he disobeyed my command. After an hour, the woman was pulled from the wreckage and she was most grateful to the messenger who, she said, held her hand while they waited and whistled a number of jolly tunes to keep up her spirits. The lad appeared, apparently unscathed, and said he would return to Report and Control to hand in the ARPM1 of the incident. After completing my duties at that address, I ran towards Kensington Park Road which had taken a hit from an HE and was ablaze. On arrival, I asked the assembled, who were passing buckets of water along a line, if they knew who might be inside. I was told that an elderly couple were probably in their bedroom as they refused to use any kind of shelter. Another witness said that in the moments after the bomb hit, faint cries of help could be heard and that a passing messenger had dashed into the flames.

I believe this was the same lad as had held the blind woman's hand. Someone said they thought his name was Bill Adams. The fire is now under control and the fire service has stated that no one in the house would have survived.

Without exchanging a word, Controller Davis wrote on the appropriate labels and Joyce picked out two pins and fixed them into the map with reverence. All anyone else who peered over her shoulder would see were two insignificant dots among many. But to Joyce, those two pins stood out like no others as she knew the story behind them. And every single one of those rainbow specks, she realised, had a haunting tale to tell.

'We could have stopped him, Sir,' Joyce said, her voice cracking. 'Or should have.'

Controller Davis shook his head. 'There were a lot of people who should have perhaps tried to do that,' he said. 'His mother, me, the wardens on the job. But no one could have stopped a boy like Bill. So please, Miss Cooper, don't dwell on that.'

They stood quietly for a minute then Joyce said, 'What about Bill's mum?'

'I guarantee you she knows already,' Controller Davis

replied. 'But I must, of course, pay her a visit tomorrow.' He turned to Joyce. 'Do you know her?'

'No, Sir,' Joyce shook her head. 'And there's also Mr Barker the Butcher in Bayswater. Bill told me he considered him his son.'

'Do you think you might accompany me?' Controller Davis asked.

Exhaustion flooded every part of Joyce's being and she would have given anything to go home, have a cup of tea and put up her feet. But she knew she wouldn't be able to rest for some time and she would feel terrible about herself if she ran off to hide and cocoon herself in self-pity. 'Of course,' she said. 'But can I see my mum first? She'll have been worried about me during my first night as Bomb Plotter.'

'Yes, let's arrange to meet here again at eleven, visit Mrs Adams and then we will have to complete our paperwork.' With a jarring screech, the telephone rang. Controller Davis lifted the receiver, listened and set the alarm to the all-clear. The night was over, but Joyce did not feel any sense of victory or relief.

* * *

The bomb damage that had materialised overnight hardly registered with Joyce as she dragged herself towards home. The girl with the straight back, business-like demeanour and smart step seemed to have been lost somewhere between dusk and dawn. She walked with her head down, refusing to be drawn in by the sight of any minuscule thing that might bring her a flash of happiness or joy. Avoiding Pembridge Square and Kensington Park Road, she dreaded hearing the playful whistle of a popular tune which she knew would cause tears to flood her eyes. There were burst water mains and gas leaks to avoid; glass reduced to powder and broken roofing tiles to step over; the sickening sight of a toddler's coat hanging by a thread from guttering, an exposed room behind it; a piano stool with a red velvet seat cover sliced neatly in half, laying in the middle of the road. Each of those objects would matter to someone, but they could be fixed. Bill couldn't be and nor could the hundreds of others who'd taken it last night.

There was no bacon that morning, but Joyce could smell porridge and toast as she let herself into the house.

'Is that you, Joy love?' Mum called from the kitchen. 'I've been so worried. How was your first night?' Her mother appeared wearing the same apron and twisting another tea towel in her hands. 'Come in, love and tell us all about it. Flo's here to see you.'

'Oh, lovely,' Joyce squealed, kicking off her shoes and shrugging her arms out of her coat. 'Hello, Flo.'

Flo ducked under her aunt's arm to get to Joyce and they hugged each other hard.

'Anyone would think it was months since you'd seen each other,' Mum said.

Joyce laughed. 'It seems like it.' She sat at the kitchen table and thanked her mother for her breakfast.

'Tell us all about it,' Flo said, pushing back her fine, light brown hair. She usually wore it behind her ears in clips, but they had probably been abandoned in the underground when she'd tried to sleep. Joyce thought her cousin looked drained as if the colour had seeped out of her rosy cheeks and found its way to the whites of her soft grey eyes. She was well aware that she looked at least as jaded.

In between mouthfuls of porridge, Joyce started at the beginning and related the details of her night, but she played down some of the particulars so Mum wouldn't be overwhelmed with worry. When she got to the point where she had to explain about Bill, she put down her spoon and looked into her bowl. She tried to concentrate on the leftover bits she hadn't eaten, cold and grey like tiny pellets of concrete stuck around the rim. When she finished the account, she felt as if she could look up without getting too emotional, but Mum and Flo were staring at her, disbelief on their faces.

'But we saw him. Last night. That was the one, wasn't it, Auntie Maggie?'

'Yes,' Mum nodded slowly. 'Poor Bill.'

'You saw him?' Joyce said, surprised to learn the messenger had made it to the underground.

'He said you'd asked him to check up on us.' Mum wrung her hands in her lap. 'Oh, he was a nice boy. Blast this bloody — blasted war!'

'He had a lovely straight way of standing and walking, I thought,' Flo said, her eyes now redder than they had been. 'Did he finish the cup of tea you gave him?'

'Yes,' Mum said. 'And he said ta ever so politely. His mother would have been proud.'

'For that amongst other things,' Joyce said. Somehow, the image of Bill drinking tea with her family, chatting and sharing a joke with them comforted her and lifted her disposition. 'Flo,' she said while she spread a thimbleful of margarine on her toast. 'What time do you start work?'

'Not until half past ten,' Flo said.

'Oh, Joy,' Mum started to clear away the dishes with trembling hands. 'I do so wish you had a sensible hairdressing job, like Flo. I get so worried about you in that blasted Report and Control Centre.'

'I won't be able to stay at the hairdressers for much longer,

Auntie Maggie. You know that. I'll have to find war work soon or else it will be found for me.'

'Blasted war,' Mum grumbled.

Both girls looked at Joyce's mother, but they'd heard her anxieties so many times before that they didn't make time to address them. Instead, they tried to quell the bubbles of laughter that were forcing their way up into their throats.

'Why?' Flo asked Joyce.

'I have an idea about something I can take to Mrs Adams. Do you want to come to Bourne and Hollingsworth with me?'

'I've never turned down an outing to Bourne and Hollingsworth and I'm not going to start now,' Flo said. 'But let me help Auntie Maggie with the dishes first.'

'You're right,' Joy said. 'Nothing's going to stop us. Not even a war.'

Mum shooed them towards the door. 'You go,' she said. 'I've got all day to tidy up here. Just be careful and mind yourselves. I'll tell your mum where you've gone when I see her, Flo love.'

* * *

Out in the fresh air, the icy breeze brought a glow back to Flo's face and Joyce thought it must be doing the same for her. They trotted arm in arm to the bus stop and Joyce told Flo about the bet she'd had with Bill and how he dearly wanted to give his mother an expensive handkerchief. 'She will be over the moon,' Flo said and squeezed Joyce's hand. 'But have you got enough money?'

Joyce bit her lip. 'I'm hoping Mr Harris will honour my old store discount.'

'Fingers crossed,' Flo said. 'Oh look, there's the bus.' They ran as fast they could, their arms pumping at their sides and their breath leaving their mouths in short, explosive puffs. 'Or should I say,' Flo turned to Joyce. 'The blasted bus.'

For a minute Joyce doubled over, sudden laughter making it impossible for her to run. Then she carried on, feeling light and almost carefree.

Mr Harris was more than generous when he heard Joyce's request and after disappearing to the managers' offices for a few minutes, came back saying the store would like Mrs Adams to have the handkerchief as a gift. Joyce beamed with gratitude, but Mr Harris said it was the least they could do. The gift was wrapped in tasteful paper, fit for a bereavement and a chit for a local seamstress was included so that Mrs Adams, when she was ready, could take it to be embroidered with her initials in lavender.

* * *

Surrounded by sisters and neighbours, Mrs Adams told Joyce and Controller Davis that the house would seem empty as her two younger children had been evacuated to Suffolk. 'Bill should have gone, too,' she said, her tears starting up again. 'But he insisted on staying here.' A look of complete understanding passed between Joyce and Controller Davis; they knew how stubborn and single-minded Bill could be.

When Joyce presented the handkerchief to Mrs Adams, the older woman held it close. 'He was a lovely boy,' she said, tears spilling into the troughs of her eyes.

'He was,' said Controller Davis. 'And a very heroic young man.'

Mrs Adams stopped short as if the thought hadn't occurred to her, although it was one of the first things that had come into Joyce's mind. She stared into the distance, not seeing anything except, Joyce speculated, Bill's face. 'Yes,' she said. 'I suppose he was.'

'He is a hero, not was,' the Controller corrected himself. 'He will live on in our memories. Won't he, Senior Warden Cooper?'

'Always,' she said.

Mr Barker's shop had a closed sign hanging from the door, but Joyce and the Controller rang the bell for the flat upstairs. Mrs Barker answered, dishevelled and distracted. She said Mr Barker had heard the news, taken it badly, closed his shop and had that minute dropped into sleep. She didn't want to disturb him, if that was alright, as she was worried about his health. They asked her to give her husband their condolences.

Controller Davis quietly read a few words at the shared funeral service, others milling around near them doing the same. A line of Boy Scouts stood to attention; Mr and Mrs Barker clung to each other; Mrs Adams balled the hanky to her chest, her knuckles white and her fist tight. *And that,* Joyce thought, *is the best we can do for Bill.* Although it didn't seem anything like good enough in light of the fact that he could not possibly have given more.

Night after night went by in Report and Control, with Joyce becoming more accustomed during each shift to her job as Bomb Plotter. And after a few weeks had passed, she no longer dreaded hearing a chipper whistle, but thought of it as a reminder from Bill to be brave, to be happy and to look forward with hope.

FIVE

Sunday 24 February 1974

Resentment at this change to her Sunday routine overwhelmed Joyce as she was choosing what to wear to view flats with Mr Taylor. When she opened the doors of the old mahogany wardrobe that stood off kilter in the corner of her bedroom, the lilac scent of a wardrobe sachet and a blast of cold air escaped and hit her with full force. She peered into the dark depths and wondered if it would be acceptable to wear the slacks she'd recently purchased and that were, much to her surprise, comfortable and rather smart at the same time. Almost as revolutionary as the wonder of tights, or panty hose as the Americans called them – gone for ever were scratchy, complicated suspender belts and it was goodbye to the draughty gap at the tops of the thighs. She'd had the option of wearing trousers in the Civil Defence during the war, but she hadn't been able to afford those as well as a regulation skirt so had opted for the latter. Often, especially on cold, damp, smoke-choked winter nights she'd regretted that decision, but she would have felt hampered by the serge covering her legs during the summer. Either way, she couldn't win.

Last Christmas, she'd treated herself to a blouse in a lovely shimmery polyester, dotted all over with a ditsy flower design. She thought it would make her feel glamorous if she wore it with a black skirt and jacket to the Bourne and Hollingsworth Christmas party, but in the end she'd decided not to go and now it hung, unworn, in her wardrobe amongst her every day, serviceable clothes. Perhaps she should take this chance outing to give it an airing. Huffing, she dismissed the thought because, if she turned up dressed for a celebration, Mr Taylor might get the incorrect impression and think she'd had a change of heart and welcomed the idea of being thrown out of the flat she loved. So, work clothes it was, and she pulled on a knee-length navy skirt, a pale blue crew neck jumper and over them she would wear her camel mac. She rubbed a dot of unctuous Vitapointe between her hands and spread the residue over her freshly washed hair to tame it. Parting the front strands, she moved closer to the mirror and studied the grey hairs that seemed to have multiplied overnight. Blast, she thought and made up her mind to get a box of dye to use one evening during the week. The neutral lipstick she'd applied earlier had remained in place, so she left well enough alone as far as that was concerned.

A good ten minutes early, Joyce checked the back door and made sure the gas was turned off, put on her mac, checked in her bag for a hanky, then hung the strap over her arm, stepped into her shoes and stood by the front door. Mr Taylor wouldn't be late, she knew that and he wouldn't be early – he would knock on the door at the exact time they had agreed and she wanted to be ready to leave and get the viewings over and done with so she could get back to her routine.

She looked down the narrow dingy hallway. Green and blue flocked paper covered the walls except in the places where it was peeling due to the insidious damp. Patches of fuzzy mould clung to the corners where the walls met the ceilings or skirting boards and try as she might, with scrubbing brush and special cleaners, the obnoxious fur re-appeared with fierce persistence. The landlord had assured her many times that he would get the flocked wallpaper replaced with woodchip and painted a light colour, but he had never lived up to that promise. Now she knew why. Negotiations for the sale of these houses to the council had been going on for some time so he'd probably never had the slightest intention of carrying out maintenance on them – but he had been charging the same rent, nevertheless.

Joyce was used to things not being fair; many years ago nothing had been just, although no one knew it at the time. Most people accepted their circumstances as they hadn't had the time or schooling to realise how hard done by they were – they'd been too busy trying to put a meal of bread and dripping in their children's hands or stave off TB or find the money to pay for the doctor or dodge an incoming incendiary or flying bomb.

Taking a flap of the green and blue tinged wallpaper between her finger and thumb, Joyce pulled upwards. Powder rained on to the carpet and another patch of musty mildew stared back at her.

She checked her watch, half hoping that Mr Taylor would be tardy and give her good reason to cancel their appointment. But he had five minutes so she shifted from one foot to the other and thought about what it would be like to have a new boiler. Lovely, probably, as would an electric cooker that snapped into life without the cloying smell of gas. It would be welcoming to come home from work to light, bright paint on the walls and windows and doors that fitted without the need for draught excluders. Electricity that came from safe, unfrayed wiring; wardrobes that didn't need moth repellent or perfumed pellets to keep them fresh; a step down into the garden that didn't permanently teeter backwards and forwards from bomb damage. But to leave this place that had provided her with a sense of security and sanctuary for so many years? She shook her head, that would be an unfathomable wrench. It would be like turning her back on a structure that had been not merely four walls but a substitute family, a close supportive friend and ally, a confidante, a confessor, a sanctuary, a haven, a refuse – the one solid, immovable, dependable fixture in her life. Until now, when she was being asked to give it up as if it were nothing more than bricks and mortar.

For a moment she trailed her hands along the wall, the raised flocking sticky and damp under her fingers, and thought about how she knew this flat more intimately than any living being. Some might think that pitiful, but it had been enough for her for years.

There was a rat-a-tat-tat on the door. Joyce stood tall, re-arranged her mac, drew back the bolt and turned the key in the lock. 'Good morning, Mr Taylor,' she said. 'Punctual as always.' She took in his open-necked, psychedelic shirt, oranges and yellows swirling over a white background. It was Sunday, so she thought that excused, in his eyes, the lack of a tie. In its place, he sported a chain that sat in the curve of his throat and collars so long and pointed they looked like dangerous weapons. Instead of suit trousers he was wearing bell-bottomed jeans held up with a snazzy leather belt. She felt cheated when she realised she could have got away with the slacks and flowery blouse.

'Of course, Miss Cooper,' the young man said. 'As are you. All ready?' His eagerness was the complete opposite of the apathy she felt.

'Yes,' she replied. 'But not willing and able, I'm afraid.'

'Well, let's see if we can change that attitude,' Mr Taylor said.

Joyce sighed, locked the door behind her and climbed the six stone steps to the street in front of Mr Taylor.

Spring was teasing Notting Hill with a cool, dry, crisp morning. Feathery clouds spread thinly across a blanched blue sky and here and there around spindly trees and in patches of earth, snowdrops like the ones in Joyce's garden hung their heads. In the distance there was a burst of giggles followed by the yap of what sounded like a small dog. On Sundays, people who lived in flats with tiny concrete yards or no access to the outdoors enjoyed walking their dogs and children in Hyde Park. And she liked to join them, smiling at the antics of toddlers for whom grass and leaves and birds and fountains were all new; nodding to other regulars; having an ice cream cornet on a bench in the summer and a cup of hot chocolate in the winter. A feeling of nostalgia washed over her, as if she had missed her Sunday outing for months instead of this once. Perhaps she could hurry the proceedings along and still have time for her usual walk.

Joyce went to turn left, but Mr Taylor beckoned her with an open palm towards the right. 'Oh,' she said. 'Are we going to a different estate? I thought there was only the Shakespeare.'

'There is,' Mr Taylor said. 'But we're not walking. We're travelling in style.' He pointed to a dark green sports car on the opposite side of the street. 'Your carriage awaits.'

Joyce stared at the car, then at Mr Taylor who looked very pleased with himself.

A little boy who'd been given his wish of a Meccano set for Christmas.

'Have you ever been in a sports car, Miss Cooper?' he asked.

Joyce shook her head, too dumbstruck to answer. After a beat she said, 'I've never been in a car before. Full stop.'

Now it was Mr Taylor's turn to stand stupefied, his mouth open in disbelief. 'Well,' he said, coming back to life. 'Let's make the most of it, shall we?'

Joyce wasn't sure she wanted to make the most of it, whatever that meant. But she could not ignore the twist of a thrill she felt in the pit of her stomach at the thought of giving it a go.

They strolled across the street and Joyce could see the make of the car emblazoned in silver relief on the bonnet – Triumph. 'It's a Spitfire Mark 4,' Mr Taylor said.

'Oh, that used to be the name of an RAF plane,' Joyce said. 'During the war.'

'Yes, it says a lot, doesn't it?' Mr Taylor walked around the vehicle admiring the tyres, the windows polished to a sheen, the headlamps that sat flush with the bonnet. 'The dashboard,' he said, 'is moulded from plastic, but you'd think it was wood. And the seats are leather.'

'Well,' Joyce said. 'I've seen cars like this flashing past but

I've never been close to one and I must say, it has a certain beauty.'

Mr Taylor beamed. 'Here,' he said. 'Allow me.' And he unlocked the door and pulled on the recessed handle. 'Are you cold or shall we drive with the top down?'

'I couldn't pass comment,' Joyce said, feeling out of her depth. 'But if we're going to be in the wind, I should perhaps go back for a scarf.'

'There's no need,' Mr Taylor said with desperation, no doubt afraid that if Joyce went back into her flat she might never come out again. He disappeared into the car and bobbed out holding a long piece of fabric in his hands. 'Here, please borrow Jacqueline's.'

Taking the distinctively patterned scarf from him, Joyce let the material stream between her fingers and knew that it was a Liberty. 'Your fiancée's?' she asked. 'Mr Taylor, I couldn't possibly.'

'She would be more than happy to let you borrow it, if she were here.' Mr Taylor's voice had a pleading edge to it. 'She's lovely and generous and...'

Kind, like you. Joyce thought. *And you don't deserve to have to deal with stubborn middle-aged women like me.* 'I'm sure she is,' she said. 'And please thank her for me.'

Mr Taylor handed Joyce into the opulent-smelling interior of the car, the seat softly sculpting itself to her back and legs. She heard cranking behind her and then, as if by magic, the roof glided past her head and she was sitting both inside a car and out in the open. She fashioned the scarf over her head then crossed it around her neck. 'Miss Cooper,' Mr Taylor said, 'there's a definite look of Audrey Hepburn about you.'

Joyce laughed aloud and wondered how she could ever have mourned a walk around Hyde Park.

'Here we go then, for the time of your life,' the young man said. The engine started with a low purr, they pulled out and for a split-second Joyce saw a sight she never imaged she would see – her flat from the seat of a sports car.

SIX

DEREK

March 1941

Joyce shuffled along behind Flo in the queue for tea at the ABC in Queen's Road. It was their regular meeting place when their days off coincided but today the café was busier than she'd ever seen it and the usual prompt, clipped service slow and inexpert. It didn't matter, because apart from a bit of shopping and getting home to washing and mending, neither of them had anything planned.

Looking for what might be a possible vacant table, Joyce was disbelieving at the number of people who were out and about enjoying themselves. There were very few children, but those who sat with parents or grandparents were having a lovely time tucking into cream cakes and gingerbread. One little girl, in a pink party dress that was so tight across her chest and stomach that the buttons were straining, looked from one to the other of the two women with her and when they were engrossed in conversation, stuffed half a fruit scone into her pink, cavernous mouth. The sight made Joyce giggle;

she remembered Mum insisting she could fit into clothes and shoes long after they were functional. But now, what with clothing rations and bombing and fires and flooding, keeping up with children's needs was bound to be more difficult.

A supervisor appeared and checked the till, then beckoned to a waitress and asked her to stop clearing tables and serve at the counter. The line moved forward and Flo let out a sigh. 'What are you having, Joy love?' she asked.

Over time they'd made their way through most of the menu and now had their favourites, so Joyce didn't have to think for long before she replied. 'Unless you fancy a change, shall we stick to what we usually do?'

'Yes,' Flo said, 'I'm happy with that.'

When it was their turn, they ordered two cups of tea, one potted ham and tongue sandwich to share, a rich seed and sultana cake for Joyce and a currant bun for Flo. They each produced fivepence, paid, then stood to the side to wait for their order to be handed to them on a tray.

A heavy, yeasty aroma of bread and buns hung in the air and Joyce thought it must be trapped in the upholstery of chairs, the waitresses' uniforms, the carpets and the cutlery.

A waitress walked past with a plate piled with roasted beef, mashed potatoes, vegetables and steaming gravy. For a minute, the smell of meat drifted after her and both girls followed her with their eyes. The plate ended its journey in front of a rotund man sitting on his own reading a newspaper and they watched as he picked up his knife and fork and tucked in with enthusiasm.

'Perhaps we should save up and treat ourselves,' Joyce said. 'What do you think?'

'No,' Flo said. 'I have an idea for something much better we can do with our money.'

'Oh,' Joyce raised her eyebrows. 'I'm intrigued.' She took their loaded tray and together they wound their way through the tables, past potted palms nestled behind pillars and found a table for two next to a wall on which hung two pictures of birds, one precariously lopsided.

They transferred their lunch from the tray to the table, spread serviettes over their knees, separated the sandwich onto two plates and settled down for a chat.

'So,' Joyce said. 'What do you suppose we should do with our hard-earned wages?'

Flo wiped the corners of her mouth then took a sip of tea through her plump, voluptuous lips, so different from Joyce's tiny mouth which she knew looked as though it could barely open wide enough to slake her thirst. Neither of them looked like their mothers who, as sisters, did look very much like each other, and people often found it hard to believe they were cousins. Flo was well-made and everything about her was soft – her pale brown hair hung to her shoulders in a gentle wave; faint diffused freckles spread across the backs of her hands; the tilt of her nose was almost imperceptible and her eyes were a first light of dawn grey. She sometimes said she envied Joyce her more petite features and striking, distinctive colouring. 'Wishy-washy, that's what I am,' Flo would say.

Joyce didn't think that was the case and there was certainly nothing innocuous and feeble about Flo's ambition to do well and better herself – they did have that in common.

'I think we should take dancing lessons,' Flo said, cutting her currant bun into quarters.

This wasn't the first time Flo had mentioned dancing to her. First, she had wanted Joyce to go with her to a tea dance, then it was a club in the West End, now it was lessons. But Joyce didn't know how she could fit it in with her job at the

Civil Defence. 'It's not practical. Leastways, not at the moment,' Joyce said. 'Besides, our mums taught us to dance.'

Flo laughed, her head back and her mouth wide. 'You can't call that dancing,' she said. 'Not in the real sense.'

'I know.' Joyce started to giggle, too and reminded Flo of the many times they'd messed about with their mums, trying to form some sort of Charleston or Cakewalk that merged into a bit of a waltz or foxtrot. Each time their efforts descended into them throwing themselves around, pulling haughty faces and stepping on each other's toes.

'It would be fun,' Flo said. 'Look, I picked up this flyer today.' She rooted around in her handbag, setting aside a lipstick, a mirror, a comb and a bus pass before she found what she was looking for – a piece of paper with the silhouette of an elegant man and woman on the front, holding each other in a perfect dance pose. Madame Beaupre's School of Dance. Lessons Six Days a Week in a Modern, Airy Studio above Carter's the Fishmonger on Westbourne Grove. And then underneath in smaller letters – No Need to Book.

'Is this a new place?' Joyce asked. 'I don't remember seeing it before.'

'Yes,' Flo answered. 'It opened a week or so ago. It's right across the road from work and you should see the people coming and going. So busy.' She shook her head. 'Men, women, children. It's a wonder there are so many people who can concentrate on learning to dance in the middle of a war.'

'And that's it for me,' Joyce said, putting up her hand to a passing waitress whose white apron crackled with starch. 'I don't know how I'd find the time. Excuse me,' she said to the waitress. 'Would it be possible to have two more small cups of tea, please?'

'Of course, Miss,' the waitress bowed her head slightly and

Joyce noticed a handful of wiry, silver hairs escaping from under her stiff uniform cap. 'Fourpence when I return, if you please.'

'Ta,' Flo said. When the waitress was out of earshot, Flo turned to Joyce and in a low voice said, 'She needs to visit us at the hairdresser's.'

'I shouldn't think she can afford your prices,' Joyce answered. 'I know I couldn't.'

'But you don't need us, do you? Not with that lustrous mane.'

Without thinking, Joyce's fingers went to her hair and she pulled through it, loosening the curls that bounced back into place like graceful lengths of dark coiled ribbon. From across the café, a woman squealed with such a high-pitched laugh that she and Flo were compelled to turn and seek her out. They glimpsed the woman, dressed in a dark mauve jacket with a necklace and earrings that glinted when they caught the light, her hair coiffed in an elaborate style. 'She,' said Flo, 'is in no need of our services either.'

'How *are* things at the salon?' Joyce turned to her cousin again and watched her push the last of her cake crumbs onto her fork. She had gone full-time at the hairdresser's where she'd swept the floor and prepared perm and dye solutions since she was twelve.

Flo shrugged. 'Oh, I'm still enjoying it,' she said. 'But for all her promises Mrs Neville is holding back on signing apprenticeship papers for me.'

The waitress appeared with their tea and Joyce paid the bill. 'Ta very much,' she smiled and the woman hurried towards another raised finger a few tables away.

Stirring a couple of grains of sugar into her cup, Joyce thought about how unfairly Flo was being treated by the owner of the salon. In her heart, she suspected that Mrs Neville was jealous of Flo's appetite for success and the speed at which she picked up everything presented to her. That and how well she got on with everyone. 'Perhaps,' Joyce ventured, 'you can move on now. You know, war work?' She reached out and touched Flo's hand. 'Soon it will be compulsory for women to do their bit and once you make the break, you'll forget all about old lady Neville and find something else you like doing.'

'I'm thinking about it,' Flo sniffed. 'But I don't want the ARP,' she said, digging in her verbal heels.

'I know, I know,' said Joyce. 'You want a more glamorous uniform.'

'That's right, the thought of wearing that blue serge makes me shudder. Now, how about those dancing lessons?'

Flo looked hopeful, her grey eyes bright and shining, her round, smooth mouth poised and waiting for a reason to smile. The loud, brash woman laughed another donkey bray, everyone jumped when a spurt of steam was released from an urn, an older woman walked past reeking of mothballs and lily of the valley. All of a sudden, Joyce felt a fierce urge to do something other than pin labels bearing devastating news to a map or shopping for rations or catching up on sleep.

Flo watched Joyce deliberating and egged her on. 'We could go out dancing together when we learn. Think of the great fun we'd have.'

When Joyce hesitated, Flo continued to cajole. 'We have to carry on the tradition of sticking together, don't we? You know, Colville Infants right up to our last year. Chalking hopscotch on the pavement, swimming lessons in the baths. Birthdays. Christmases. Trying lipsticks. Looking at brassieres without telling our mums.'

Joyce laughed. 'Well before we had anything to put in them.'

'Well,' Flo leaned back as if she were resting on her laurels. 'I wouldn't want to be the one who tore apart our unbroken chain of friendship.'

Joyce shook her head in disbelief. 'I take back what I said about you doing war work,' she said. 'You'd be much better off taking an acting course. You're so dramatic.'

'Please?' Flo batted her eyelashes.

Why not? Joyce thought, it would be a lovely diversion, but she was cautious when she replied to Flo. 'Let's go and have a look and if some of the lessons fit in, then yes, let's,' she said.

Clapping her hands, Flo allowed her smile to spread. She packed her bag, put on her coat, grabbed her cousin's arm, and almost broke into a run before Joyce could change her mind.

* * *

The studio was an impressive oasis away from the constant noise and chaos of bombing throughout the night and rebuilding during the day. The walls were off-white as were the sheer curtains that could be pulled over the blackouts when they were drawn. In the corner stood a tall vase containing silk flowers in vivid reds and greens and blues and behind an imposing desk, a tall, slender woman in a full-skirted ballgown sat with a ramrod straight back. Sparkles seemed to radiate from her. 'Hello, girls,' she said when they walked gingerly towards her. She held out a manicured hand which Joyce and Flo shook in turn. 'Have you come to join us?' Her accent was hard to place, as Joyce was not used to talking to anyone who didn't sound like her, but she thought it had a slight French resonance to it.

The cousins exchanged a look which they both knew meant they were out of their depth. But before they could retrace their steps, they were guided into a studio that was equally spacious and light, with mirrors covering one wall and being shown around as if they were royalty. And the sophisticated woman had such a way about her that Joyce, for one, felt as if she were the centre of the universe.

'I'm Madame Beaupre,' the woman said, 'and my husband, who also teaches dance, is Monsieur of the same name.'

The cousins nodded and Joyce, feeling intimidated, listened in awe.

'My husband and I were competition ballroom dancers,' Madame Beaupre continued. 'And long before this wretched war began, we planned to open a studio.' She shrugged, her smooth, curved shoulders lifting and falling seamlessly. 'So, despite everything ghastly happening in the world we decided to go ahead, to give ourselves and others something refined and erudite to cling to. Do you understand?'

'Yes,' Flo said in a small voice.

Joyce agreed, but was thinking about her little coloured pins and how each of them represented a random act of sabotage. The bombs had no knowledge of whether it was a damp, dirty hovel that would take their hit or a newly kitted out dance studio.

'Now, let me see you, young ladies.' Madame Beaupre stood back, one hand under her chin and appraised what Joyce thought was the sorry sight in front of her. She looked them up and down in turn and Joyce felt both naked and acutely aware of her straight skirt, laced-up brogues, hair in a clip and uniform serge greatcoat. 'I think... yes, you are inter-mediate dancers.'

'No,' both girls said at once.

'Beginners,' Flo said.

'If that,' emphasised Joyce.

Madame Beaupre selected a 78rpm record from a neat pile on a table, put it on a phonograph and when the music started, turned to them with eyes closed as if in a trance. With lights steps she caught Joyce in her arms and waltzed with her around the entire space of the studio. Up close to Madame Beaupre, Joyce was surprised to see that the older woman's face was not as flawless as she had supposed, but that she had artfully disguised the signs of age with face paint. Layers of lacquer held her hair in place and pressed against the dance instructor's torso, Joyce could feel a girdle so rigid she was surprised Madame Beaupre could breathe. She smelled lovely, though, with something that was reminiscent of the perfume counter at Bourne and Hollingsworth.

They swept around a corner of the dance floor and Joyce caught a blurred glimpse of herself in the full-length mirror, stumbling along in Madame Beaupre's firm grip. When the record stopped, they stood back from each other and Madame Beaupre laughed, her hand on her chest. 'Beautiful,' she gasped, out of breath from the effort and forgetting her French accent. Now she sounded more Paddington than Paris. 'You are a beginner, but you have aptitude so will advance in no time. Come my darling,' she signalled to Flo.

Another record was placed on the phonograph and Joyce stood and watched as Madame Beaupre guided Flo around the room. This time, she gave more instruction so the girls could get a taste of what lessons would be like for them. It took all of Joyce's willpower not to laugh at poor Flo, for whom the ordeal must have been worse as she had watched Joyce go through it and knew what was coming. She also wanted to giggle at the absurdity of Madame Beaupre, camouflaging her real age in make-up, hair pomade and undergarments stiff with whale-bones, putting on airs and graces with the charade of an accent that she couldn't keep up, pulling a veil over the reality of the war by dancing on. But as she watched the older woman mentor Flo through the intricate steps, Joyce wondered if perhaps she had the right idea, after all. She seemed to be fulfilled, she was trying to bring people together and make them happy with a few hours respite; she was ambitious and she wanted desperately to hold on to something graceful and beguiling that had existed for her in more peaceful times. All of a sudden, the urge to laugh disappeared and, instead, Joyce felt admiration for Madame Beaupre. When the record finished, she clapped and smiled.

Madame Beaupre explained there was no need to book lessons in advance, they could just turn up and join in. 'During scheduled classes,' she said, flowing into faux French again, 'you will always have someone to partner. Yourselves of course, if you come together, or me or Monsieur Beaupre or another student.'

'Shall we, Joy love?' Flo said, her cheeks pink and her eyes bright from the exhilaration of her free lesson.

'I'll do my best,' Joyce said, conscious of her other commitments. Madame Beaupre took some details in exquisite hand-writing, gave them each a lesson timetable and walked them to the door. She held out her hand and said goodbye in a digni-fied manner.

Back on Westbourne Grove, Joyce blinked and had to steady herself. She caught hold of Flo and said, 'Did that really happen?'

Flo shook her head. 'It was a different world, wasn't it?'

'But one I certainly enjoyed.'

'Despite Madame Beaupre and her funny ways.'

Joyce thought for a moment. 'Because of them, I think,' she said.

* * *

Every night was the same. Joyce made her way to Report and Control, listened to Controller Davis's briefing, put a row of pins in her mouth and one by one drilled the tiny bayonets into the map. Each one of them stabbed her deep inside. She wondered if there would come a time when she was immune to the significance of the pins and labels and what she had to do with them. Somehow she doubted that. The mother with the two small children visited her still in the middle of the night, as did Percy with his head open and bleeding and Bill, whistling his way into a burning building to help complete strangers.

She spent at least part of every day at Report and Control, too, trying to replant the pins that Mrs Bertrand had misjudged. Now, there was another woman she admired; perhaps she hadn't had Madame Beaupre's opportunities, but she was as gracious in her own way.

At first, the old ARPM1 forms that Joyce had to work her way through had seemed endless. No sooner did she come to the end of a pile than there was another from the filing cabinet for her to tackle. And some days she was so tired, she could only manage an hour or two and then she was compelled to devote the rest of the day to sleep. But now she was nearing the end and Controller Davis was pleased with her efforts.

'You're very dedicated to that map, Senior Warden Cooper,' he said.

'Not the map so much as the war work,' Joyce said.

'Of course,' the Controller said. 'But you certainly have an eye for detail.'

Joyce felt herself colour at the compliment and tried to diffuse it by saying, 'Ta, I don't know about that. But it is sending me cross-eyed, I think. What will my duties be during the day when the map is up to scratch?'

Controller Davis put his hand on a teetering stack of paperwork that had been partially hidden from view behind a box of gas masks, torches and gas rattles waiting to be repaired. Joyce had seen it loitering there, but hadn't thought it had anything to do with her. Plucking a form from the top of the pile, she saw that it was a daily report the Controller had filled in and was then supposed to send to Regional Control. Joyce's stomach flipped. The report was dated last November so had it been lying around since then and not on the Regional Commissioner's desk or in his filing cabinet where it belonged? This seemed most irregular.

Controller Davis must have noticed how she blanched, because he took the report from her and came to his own defence. 'Please don't worry, Miss Cooper. These are copies. I can assure you that all paperwork is transported to where it needs to be on time.'

Joyce smiled at him and breathed out a long sigh of relief.

'But these copies haven't been filed as they should be.' Controller Davis looked sheepish. 'I'm afraid that my organisational skills are negligible.'

'My mum says you can't be good at everything,' Joyce said.

'My dear old mother used to say that, too,' Controller Davis chuckled. They both turned their heads towards the sound of the urn bubbling in the kitchen. 'And I'll bet Mrs Bertrand uses that same saying. So,' he pointed to the forms. 'Would you mind awfully...'

'Of course not,' Joyce said. 'I'm glad to do whatever I can.'

Controller Davis limped towards his desk and over his shoulder said, 'There are, in fact, mountains of the damn things everywhere. It will help if I get them all together, won't it?'

All Joyce could do was nod. She didn't mind. Really she didn't. But soon she would start dreaming of reports and memos and forms. But perhaps, she reasoned, that would be better than some of the spectres that visited her during her sleep.

'And,' Controller Davis was stuffing handfuls of dispatches and official letters into a box, 'it will look so much better when we have our visit from Regional Control.'

When the sirens were turned off and they were in the all-clear, the Controller was informal and friendly. He chatted away about his wife and son, who was training to be a doctor and two daughters, both Princess Mary nurses in the RAF. They had a dog, who they'd refused to have put to sleep as the government had instructed two years previously, and on the rare occasions the Controller had time off he regaled his staff with anecdotes about how his vegetables were growing on his allotment. During the nightly Luftwaffe raids, however, when he was at his authoritative best, no one would dare to question him or mention Bonzo or start a discussion about onions or runner beans, but now Joyce felt she could ask for more information about the visit without being told to attend to her duties with the map.

'Ah, yes,' said Controller Davis. 'I'm going to make an announcement to that end at tonight's briefing. But as you're here, I'll tell you that it won't be the Regional Commissioner himself who comes to see us. He'll send one of his senior officers.'

'Oh?' Joyce said, flapping her hands through the dust created by taking up a handful of forms. She began to lay them out on a table in order of type and date. 'Was it a random choice or have we been singled out?'

'No, we're not being shown favouritism. London Regional Control wants to find out what works and what doesn't so they can advise on the best working methods.'

'I see,' Joyce said. 'Is our visit imminent?'

Controller Davis's eyes leaped from one box of paperwork to another. His bottom lip curled downwards under his moustache. 'I've been led to believe that we won't be given any warning.'

'Well, I'll do my best with this lot,' Joyce said, concentrating on the task at hand.

'Thank you, Miss Cooper,' the Controller said. 'But only for an hour or two every day. You must get some rest.'

'And you,' Joyce ventured. 'Please take your own advice.'

Controller Davis stifled a yawn. 'Oh, I do beg your pardon,' he said. 'I'm off home now for a short period of time.' When he'd donned his coat, cap and gloves, Joyce could feel him studying her. She looked up from her close work and smiled at him. 'You are a jolly good egg, Miss Cooper,' the Controller said, and Joyce felt as if she'd been awarded the George Cross.

* * *

A soft hubbub rose from the wardens at the staff briefing when Controller Davis announced the forthcoming visit from the Regional Control Centre. Already privy to the news, Joyce was not caught up in the momentary ado so was able to observe her colleagues' reactions. *How little we have to look forward to,* she thought, *that we should cling to this for a bit of diversion.* She was glad then that she'd signed up for dancing lessons, though she had no idea when she'd be able to go along to a session. The air warning burst their bubble of excitement as quickly as it had formed and they were intent, once again, on their responsibilities. A week went by, then two and if the intended visit did happen to float into her mind, it was soon pushed aside by the relentless spiking of the map with the tiny, ferocious pins and besides, there were often so many men hovering that she presumed the visit had taken place without anyone being the wiser.

The night of 19th of March was as terrible a night as any of them had experienced. Messenger after messenger ran into Report and Control with forms that let them know, in no uncertain terms, that the Luftwaffe was trying its hardest to get rid of every single building and the entire population of London in one night. Telephone call after telephone call took place between the Controller and other bigwigs; report after sooty, crumpled report found its way into Joyce's hands and pin after pin was drilled into the map. Twice the whole Centre rocked with the reverberations of a hit close by and another thin snake of sweat slithered down Joyce's temple when she pictured all of them being buried alive. Thank goodness Mum was in the underground. She bared her teeth and breathed deeply past the parade of pins in her mouth. She and Flo had seen a short film at the cinema last November about the Blitz and now Joyce recited the title to herself over and over again until it became a mantra and was all she could think about –

London Can Take It! London Can Take It! London Can Take It!

Then she was aware of the Controller's voice talking in soft, smooth, assuaging tones. 'And this is Senior Warden Cooper,' he said. 'Our woman with the map.'

In one coherent movement, Joyce looked over her shoulder and plucked another ARPM1 form from the table next to her. In the flash of time that she was looking away from the wall, her eyes focused on a very tall man who was taking in the activity surrounding him with ordered scrutiny. She turned back to her duties, winced inwardly when she read about a hit taken by a row of terraced houses at the other end of the road from Auntie Cath and Uncle Terry. Then she aimed a minute black missile through a black label and pinned them both to the map.

'And over here...' The telephone squawked and the Controller hobbled towards it. 'Excuse me, Sir,' he said.

So this was the Senior Regional Officer. What a night he had taken to visit. Wouldn't he have been of better use undertaking his usual job at the Regional Control Centre? But perhaps he didn't have any say in the matter and had to go where instructed and when. Out of the corner of her eye, Joyce could see him standing with his hands behind his back and looking out of place in the co-ordinated pandemonium around him. She felt sorry for him on that account, but there was nothing she could do to help him tonight.

Busy with another report, she was not aware of his presence close to her until his chest rattled with an almost paralysing cough. When the frenzied fit subsided, his breath came in laboured shudders. It was alarming and Joyce wondered if she should abandon her pins and take him to the first aid room. But apart from his puce face his attitude was nonchalant, so she carried on with the map which must, in her view, come first. Eventually, the Regional Officer's breathing returned to a steady rhythm and Joyce could feel the blood that had been pounding in her own ears quieten down.

Another report, another pin. 'Your map is a beautiful work of art, Senior Warden Cooper,' the Regional Officer wheezed. 'It's a joy to watch your precision.'

As he was standing beside her, Joyce allowed herself a good look at the man who was kicking about for something to do. Her first impression of him had been incorrect, he wasn't merely tall, he towered above her. She thought that no matter where she stood, she would be in his shadow. And she liked the way his uniform jacket rested just below his hips and was pulled a tiny bit too taut across his broad back. She swivelled her head back to the map, embarrassed in case he'd caught her sizing him up. He was young – thirty, if that. She had imagined anyone with the title Senior before his name to be older, although that, she chided herself, was silly as she, at twenty-one, also had that appellation. But she had thought all the younger men would be in the Forces and not stuck here at home in the Civil Defence. That, she supposed, would have been left up to older or disabled men or those who were medically exempt. But except for a crooked smile and a puckered scar next to his left ear, which she longed to reach out and trace with a light touch, there was nothing about this young man to suggest that. He had thick dark hair that was combed back from his face and his sculpted jawline was clean shaven to highlight a fresh-faced complexion. He didn't walk with a limp, or have a withered arm, or pigeon chest and all his fingers were present and correct. There was no cast or squint in either of his eyes which were the colour of coal cinders and in fact, seemed to be focused without any problem on her.

Controller Davis clumped back towards them and conducted the visitor away. She heard him asking the Senior Officer to man the telephone for half an hour or so while he sorted out something else and she chanced another peek at him just in time to see his shoulders drop with relief at having something practical to do. For a minute, she watched his smartly clad back as he strode away from her with a quick, athletic step.

Many hurried, half-drunk cups of tea later, the all-clear sounded to an inaudible sigh of relief followed by a tremble of dread about what they would find when they mounted the stairs and began to make their way home. The Controller shook the Regional Officer's hand and thanked him for visiting and helping on such a night. 'It's been my pleasure,' the young man said. 'I will produce a report soon with my recommendations.'

'Of course,' Controller Davis said. 'I will make sure I action your advice.'

The young officer made for the door, but stopped and put his finger in the air as if a sudden thought had come to him. 'Controller Davis,' he said. 'I might like to return at some stage, perhaps when it's quieter and talk at more length with Senior Warden Cooper. I think she has a lot to offer other Map Plotters.'

'Well,' said Controller Davis. 'She certainly is excellent at her job. Senior Warden Cooper,' he called across to her. 'A minute of your time, please.'

Joyce spat the pins into their tin, swiped under her eyes, patted her hair and walked towards the two men. Controller Davis smiled at her with the smallest hint of sympathy and said, 'It's been a long night, Miss Cooper, hasn't it?'

'London can take it, Sir,' she said, not at all sure she

believed her own words, but it did her good to say them out loud.

'Derek... I beg your pardon,' he half bowed to the younger man, who looked embarrassed at the deference. 'Senior Regional Officer Nicholls would like to discuss your methods in more detail. How would that be?'

Joyce's immediate reaction was one of pride that her work had been mentioned, followed quickly by a feeling of anticipation at spending an hour or two with Officer Nicholls. 'Yes, Sir.' She nodded. 'Of course, if you think it might help.'

Officer Nicholls nodded in return.

'May I suggest a time during the day?' Controller Davis ventured. He turned his palms upwards. 'Nights are too hectic, as you are more than aware.'

Officer Nicholls took a small, leather diary and a jet-black Waterman's Taperite Citation fountain pen from his inside pocket. It took all the self-discipline Joyce had left not to gasp when she saw the beautifully crafted object. She knew how much it must have cost – at Bourne and Hollingsworth they were kept under lock and key. When he uncapped the pen to reveal a solid gold nib, Controller Davis raised one eyebrow imperceptibly. Joyce thought of her and Mum at home, scrabbling around for the stub of a pencil they had to pare with a knife when they wanted to write a note or a list.

Officer Nicholls held the pen as if it was the most natural and ordinary implement in the world to have about his person. It was then that Joyce noticed his fingers. Each one was as hefty as a butcher's sausage and the nails were all the same length and cleaner than any she'd seen since the war started. *This man doesn't dig about in the mud on an allotment*, she thought. Or claw amongst bricks to prop up a damaged

Anderson shelter. 'I won't suggest today,' he said. 'We must all rest after the night we've had.'

The thought made exhaustion crush down on Joyce and grind away at her bones and the sinews of her muscles. 'Yes,' she said. 'I agree.'

'Shall we say Friday the twenty-second? Would that be a good day?' he asked, emphasising the word good and chuckling.

Joyce was bemused, but didn't like to say she hadn't understood the joke.

The officer's face, dark shadowy whiskers now apparent in its contours, reddened. 'Good Friday,' he said. 'It's difficult to remember when every day and night are the same.'

'Of course,' Joyce said. 'I'd forgotten. That day is fine for me.'

They arranged the time of eleven o'clock, shook hands and then Joyce left the Officer and Controller to take their leave of each other.

* * *

Every usual route was blocked by buildings that had collapsed and spilled their guts out onto the pavements. Gas mains were ringed off; water pipes were being patched up; the remnants of families were wandering about between ruins, holding fast to whoever they had left. Joyce's heart beckoned her to stop and try to comfort each and every one of them, but her head told her to get home and prepare for the upcoming night. She hopped over what looked like the shreds of a child's copy book, red corrections peeking through the mud-splattered fragments. Sympathy engulfed her for the poor little boy or girl who might be searching for the notebook so they could have their homework ready to hand in. Then again, the owner of the little book would have, hopefully, been evacuated and if not, they had probably lost much more important things. It was strange to Joyce that seeing simple, everyday objects in a state of ruination had such a profound impact on her. She wondered about the people who had owned them, the stories behind them, how they had been treasured and cared for and then ripped from their owner's possession as if they were nothing. And of course, they were merely things that could be replaced but Joyce thought they said much more than that about the identity of the people who had kept and used and treasured them.

Looking up, Joyce tried to concentrate on the budding trees, the clouds scudding through the sky, Officer Nicholls' solid, capable handshake and the cut of his trousers, but the ubiquitous smoke blurred the scene so there was no respite from the nagging insistence of war anywhere. She passed what had been, the day before, a rather refined block of flats in Moscow Road that had been worth a pretty penny. Three bricks from a wall that had enclosed a driveway were left standing in a vertical chunk and on top of them sat a middle-aged woman, staring straight ahead. All around her was the jumbled ruin of the lovely apartments. Bits of vases, a foot pedal still attached to the base panel of a piano, pots, pans, atomisers, books and journals, a cat's tail, a ration book, the sleeve of a jumper.

Women from the WVS were milling all over what was now a bombsite, but no one was sitting with the woman whose bare feet, barely touching the ground, were turned in towards each other. She had a rough, brown shawl or blanket over her shoulders and a cup of tea in one hand, so perhaps she had been left alone to come to terms with what she had experienced. She could have been Joyce's Nana and there was something so sad about her that Joyce went to sit beside her.

'Hello, my dear,' the woman said without looking at Joyce.

'Hello,' Joyce said. 'Is there anything I can do to help you?'

With a calm demeanour, the woman continued to gaze into the distance and then, with an equally serene voice said, 'My friend. Amelie. She lives on the first floor. Do you think she made it?'

Joyce clasped the woman's hand and stroked the thin, leathery fingers. To be doubly sure, she looked over her shoulder and took in the rubble again. 'No,' she said, her voice echoing the woman's placid tones. 'I'm sure she can't have.'

Taking a handkerchief from the pocket of her dressing-gown, the woman wiped around her eyes once. All she said was, 'Thank you, my dear.' Then she patted Joyce's arm and continued to stare at something a very long way away.

* * *

Breakfast was on the go when Joyce arrived home and Mum's face, turning from the stove, was a comforting sight.

'What a night, Joy love,' Mum said.

'I know,' Joyce said from the understairs cupboard. 'But you know what they say.'

'What do they say?' Mum asked, sounding genuinely perplexed.

'Things have to get worse before they get better.'

Joyce was glad to hear Mum's laugh. 'Oh, do they now?' she said. 'Well, they don't know the half of it, do they?'

They gave a cursory nod to the previous night's events while they ate but kept their chat to more superficial, ordinary things. Mum had seen a woman in the underground wearing mismatched shoes and said that she was probably wondering why she had an identical pair at home.

'I suppose people get muddled when the warning sounds,' Joyce said by way of explanation. 'I'll bet she was trying on an outfit in front of a mirror, one type of shoe on one foot and another on the other and when the air raid siren went off, she didn't stop to think.'

'I know,' Mum said. 'But the sight struck me as funny.'

Joyce told her about the Senior Regional Officer's visit and how he had made an arrangement to come back to talk to her in more detail on Friday. As Joyce watched Mum's eyes widen with pride, she became aware of the extra folds of skin that had recently begun to droop over her eyelids.

'Oh, Joy love,' Mum was giddy with excitement. 'He said that about you? You're to be put up as an example. How wonderful. I always knew you had it in you to...'

Grateful as she was, Joyce felt she could not have this included in her mother's usual round of praise. 'Mum,' she put up her hand. 'This is top secret. You cannot tell anyone or else...'

'What?'

'Or else I will lose my job and not get another,' Joyce said with determined finality.

'Oh,' Mum's animated demeanour faded and Joyce felt a little bit sorry. 'No one at all?'

'No,' Joyce stuck to her guns. 'Not Nana and Granddad, or Auntie Cath, or Hettie, or Sid, or anyone.'

'But *I* know,' Mum said, a small, contented smile on her face. 'And,' she reached out for Joy's hand, 'I know that your dear old dad is watching over you and he's very proud, too.'

Mum had never before mentioned Dad in that context

and the remark took Joyce by surprise. 'Ta, Mum,' she said in a soft voice.

The kettle released a low whistle that rose to a crescendo. Mum took it off the gas and filled the teapot for another cup each. Indoors, the grating sound of rebuilding work was muffled by the walls around them and Joyce felt warm and cushioned and her eyelids began to grow heavy. She thought about the woman she'd sat with outside what remained of the toffee-nosed flats and wondered where she would go to give into the sleep that would eventually overtake her.

'I think I can manage another piece of toast for you, Joy love,' Mum said. 'I know you don't mind the heel.'

'Ta, Mum,' Joyce said. 'But I'm going to get my head down for a couple of hours.'

Joyce took her dishes to the sink and started to wash them, as she always did, but Mum flapped her away and said she had all day to clean and tidy. Joyce was grateful to be able to put down the dishcloth and tea towel and told herself she'd make it up to Mum when she'd had a nap. As she made her way along the hall on legs that were beginning to feel as if they were filling with lead, she could feel her mum's eyes following her, but hoped it was with a sense of pride and not concern.

Mum had opened the blackouts in her bedroom, but the curtains were still drawn over the windows so the room was shadowy and hushed. The bedsheets had been pulled back and when Joyce nestled in between them, they smelled of soap powder, earth and the hedges that bordered their tiny garden. From the kitchen she heard Mum say, 'Oh hello, Nana love, mind that step,' followed by a subdued reply. And for the split second before she succumbed to sleep, Joyce felt an overwhelming sense of peace.

* * *

Senior Regional Officer Nicholls asked Joyce a few questions about her job which she answered in as much detail as possible. Again, he complimented her by saying her map was a 'work of art'. She told him she had an advantage because she knew the area so well, but he insisted he thought there was more to her meticulousness than that.

Sitting across from each other at a table recently cleared of paperwork, one thing led to another and they found themselves chatting about a number of things not in the least related to the war. Joyce liked Officer Nicholls' lopsided smile and the way he shuffled his long legs into contorted shapes to avoid touching hers under the table. They were on the verge of swapping opinions on pictures they had enjoyed when Mrs Bertrand asked them if they'd like yet another cup of tea. 'Ah, no thank you,' Officer Nicholls replied. 'I for one could not manage another mouthful of the stuff.'

'No, ta,' said Joyce, wondering why she felt deflated at the idea of Officer Nicholls bringing the meeting to an end. She looked at the clock and feigned shock. 'Is that the time? Goodness, I must get home so I can get ready for tonight.'

'And I must make my way to the Tube,' Officer Nicholls said, unfolding his legs from beneath him. He replaced his pen and notepad in his inside pocket and buttoned his greatcoat. He watched Mrs Bertrand bustle back to the kitchen, then lowered his voice and said, 'Do you pass the underground on your way home?'

For a moment, Joyce wondered if he was unsure of the way. But Officer Nicholls laughed, not unkindly, when she mentioned that.

'No, I merely thought it would be pleasant to pass the time together.'

Yes, Joyce thought, *it would.* But when they climbed the stairs and opened the door from the fusty Control Centre, the cold air hit them and another spasm of coughing saw Officer Nicholls bent over from the waist, his hands on his chest. It seemed to go on for ever and Joyce was torn between offending his dignity by asking if she could help and ignoring the situation, which was hard to do. People standing at a bus stop on the opposite side of the road stopped staring at the overnight bomb damage and gawped, instead, at the young man who sounded as if he were taking his last breath. When she could stand by no longer, she bent low and looked at his face, engorged veins under the bright red skin, and asked him if there was anything she could do. 'A glass of water?'

He shook his head.

'A sit down on the bench over there?'

Another shake of his head.

'Perhaps I ought to call for a first aider or an ambulance?'

Officer Nicholls put his hand up and waggled it from side to side.

So she stood next to him, feelings of anxiety and helplessness causing her to bob from one foot to another. As last time, the paroxysm abated and the officer began to straighten up, wiping the spittle that had gathered in the corners of his mouth on a handkerchief he fished from his pocket. Much to Joyce's surprise he smiled at her and other than looking exhausted, was not perturbed in the slightest. 'Sir,' she said, aware of worry creasing her forehead. 'Are you quite alright?'

He took off his cap and when he brushed his hair back with his hands, Joyce noticed they were trembling. 'Damn asthma,' he said. 'Excuse my language.'

'Never mind that,' Joyce said. 'I've heard worse from my brother, believe me.'

'Shall we,' was all the young man said. And once more the smart, composed Senior Regional Officer, he gestured towards where they intended to walk with the flat of his hand.

Joyce glanced across at the people waiting at the bus stop, whose mouths were still hanging open as if they were sitting in the front row of the cinema. She felt defensive of Officer Davis and embarrassed for him, but he seemed to take the entire episode in his stride.

Neither of them began a conversation, Officer Nicholls because his rasping breath would not allow him to do so and Joyce because she couldn't bear to put him under the pressure of having to reply to her. Joyce thought that when he could, he would give her some explanation of his condition – asthma, which she knew nothing about. Instead, when he had recovered, the first thing he said was, 'Do you enjoy music, Senior Warden Cooper? I'm rather fond of many genres myself.'

They hesitated at a roadblock and Joyce hoped the diversion would give her a couple of minutes grace to think about why he had moved on with such flippancy from his coughing fit. Surely he couldn't imagine that sort of thing was an everyday event? There were so many questions she wanted to ask him but she had been brought up to be polite, so she answered his question. 'Yes, Sir, I do love music. Especially the Forces Programme. We have a lovely dance around when that's on the wireless. Me, Mum, Auntie Cath, Flo and whoever else is visiting.'

He turned to her and his skewed smile was wide. 'Oh, dancing,' he said. 'Now there's a popular pastime. Do you?'

'My cousin and I have just signed up for lessons,' Joyce answered. 'So no, I don't. But soon I will.'

'That's what I like about you, Miss Cooper,' Officer Nicholls said. 'You seem like the kind of young woman who never thinks she might not achieve whatever she sets her mind to.'

Joyce had to duck under the torn awning of a shoe shop to let an elderly couple pass, but Officer Nicholls must have caught the pink that crawled up from under her coat collar.

'I do beg your pardon, Miss Cooper,' he said. 'Have I spoken out of turn?'

'No, of course not,' she stuttered. 'Oh, it's starting to rain,' she said, as a few fat, grimy drops skimmed her hair and eyelashes.

'In that case, we'd better make a run for it.'

Joyce was petrified that running would start the officer's disturbing cough again. It's alright, she was desperate to tell him, they could walk as sedately as necessary, but he cupped her elbow and took off at a steady trot. The refreshing rain on her face, his warm hand on her arm, the exhilaration of not worrying about the war for a few minutes, the splash of rain-water on her stockings from a puddle they couldn't avoid culminated in a burst of laughter from both of them. A gust of wind took the beret from Officer Nicholls' head and he had to chase it back in the direction they'd come from. That set them off again and they ended up outside Notting Hill Gate grinning and out of breath.

'Ta, Sir,' Joyce said. 'You've given me a good laugh.' She thought she should offer him her hand to shake, but she didn't want to say goodbye.

But he took her hand in his and instead of shaking it, held onto it fast. 'Perhaps,' he said in a timid voice, as if he'd suddenly lost all confidence. 'We could meet for a cup of tea when you next have time off?'

Joyce kicked herself for having made an arrangement with Flo for her next day off. *Blast Madame Beaupre's*, she thought. 'I'm afraid I'm meeting my cousin for our first dance lesson,' she said, hoping he wouldn't leave it at that.

He looked crushed, the corners of his mouth turning down towards his boots. Then he brightened and said, 'How about after the lesson? We could meet up West and go for a drink before the siren?'

Joyce wondered how this could possibly be happening. Him with his handsome face and tall physique, his Taperite pen and perfect nails and music of different genres. But it was and she didn't hesitate before she answered. 'I'd love that,' she said.

They arranged the day, time and place and when they said goodbye, Officer Nicholls walked backwards so he could smile at her until the crowd obscured her from his view.

* * *

Flo had been told about her upcoming meeting with Derek, but Joyce didn't want to let Mum know. If she and the Senior Regional Officer liked each other's company and decided to meet another time and another time after that, then she would tell her mother and perhaps introduce him to her. But not yet. The fluttery anticipation she felt in her stomach every time she thought about meeting Officer Nicholls was lovely, and she wanted to keep it as her secret for now. Besides, when she'd been seeing Michael Flanagan for a few months, Mum became so fond of him that Joyce found it difficult to break it off. Not because she didn't think it was the right thing to do but because she knew Mum would be upset. And then there had been Charlie Simons, a colleague at Bourne and

Hollingsworth. When they'd decided to part company, Mum had taken it badly all over again.

Besides, it was only a first meeting. There was nothing to tell, really. People made dates with no fuss all the time. Flo was forever going to meet this one or that one or the other. So why, she wondered, as she chose what to wear in her chilly bedroom, was she so concerned about her outfit? She'd tried on every combination of the few clothes she possessed and nothing looked quite right. But when she hit on the black skirt with a sparkly paste brooch pinned onto the mauve blouse, she thought she looked presentable. She would wear her old, but passable navy jacket over the top and that would brighten up the ensemble. She didn't have any ear clips, but placed a glittery comb into her pinned back hair. Scooping out the last of her lipstick with her fingernail, she spread it over her lips and smacked them together. A smidgen of rouge and one sweep of mascara from the bit left in the tin and she was done.

Then she looked down at her feet and for the first time she could remember, felt a stab of self-pity. Her stockings had been mended and they would do, but the only shoes she had were the brown brogues in the cupboard under the stairs. She shrugged and told herself it didn't matter. The date would probably not lead to much anyway.

Tiptoeing down the stairs, she hoped to cover up her outfit with her mackintosh and put on her shoes before she said goodbye to Mum. Breathing quietly, she stole across the hall, then Mum's voice rang out. 'That you, Joy love? Auntie Cath's here. All ready for your first dancing lesson?'

'Oh, yes,' Auntie Cath said. 'Flo's told me all about it. She's ever so excited.'

Joyce had her hand on the cupboard door when Mum appeared, as if she knew something was going on. But she looked taken aback when she saw her daughter dressed for more of an occasion than meeting her cousin. 'Joy love,' she said. 'You're looking gorgeous. Even more so than usual.'

'Let's have a look at you,' Auntie Cath said, joining Mum in inspecting Joyce up and down.

'I just fancied a change from that dark, scratchy, serge uniform,' Joyce said. She made a lunge for her mac.

Auntie Cath raised her eyebrows and smiled knowingly. 'I don't think so,' she shook her head. 'You're meeting someone. A young man, I think.'

'Joy,' Mum sounded shocked and a little bit hurt. 'You never said. Who is he?'

'It's nothing,' Joyce said, leaning down to lace her shoes. 'Just a quick drink uptown.'

'Doesn't look like nothing to me,' Mum sniffed.

But Auntie Cath was excited and told Joyce she had something for her. 'Wait five minutes,' she said. 'And promise not to leave this house until I return.'

During that time Mum wiped her hands on her apron, blinked a number of times and swallowed hard. Then she said, 'I don't mind that you didn't tell me, Joy love. Really I don't. But... are you ashamed of me? I wouldn't blame you if you...'

Joyce threw her arms around her mum and held on tight. 'Never, Mum,' she said. 'I love you and I'm proud of you and I will tell you all about it when there's something to tell.'

Auntie Cath re-appeared holding up a pair of black patent court shoes as if they were a trophy. She presented them to Joyce with a triumphant smile. 'They pinch my poor old bunions now,' she said. 'Try them on and see if they fit.'

They did, as if they had been made for her. Joyce hugged her aunt and left the house feeling as if she'd been transformed into a film star.

The dancing lesson was great fun. Joy and Flo partnered each other, then they danced with two middle-aged women who'd arrived together followed by one dance each with Madame and Monsieur Beaupre. They were taught the rudiments of the waltz, the foxtrot and the jive and they both picked the steps up so easily they thought they could soon hold their own at a proper dance. As soon as the lesson finished, Joy said goodbye to Flo and made a dash for the Tube.

Long before Officer Nicholls clocked her, Joyce saw him standing as straight and tall as a sentry outside the Dog and Duck in Bateman Street. She wasn't late, so she slowed down to watch him and liked very much that he towered above everyone else. His gaze didn't linger on other girls either and that impressed her, too. When he spotted her, his face brightened and he gave her his idiosyncratic smile. In three strides he was by her side, threading her arm through his and guiding her into the pub. His shoulders were back and his chin was up, which increased his height further and she thought he looked proud to have her next to him.

She'd never been in the Dog and Duck, but it was beautiful – all mirrors and Victorian fittings. As soon as they found a table, Officer Nicholls said, 'We're off duty now so I'm Derek and may I call you Joyce?'

'Of course,' Joyce said, giggling as she took the hand Derek held out to her as if they had only just been introduced. Derek ordered a pint of bitter for himself and a port and lemon for her. They talked and ordered another. Derek told Joyce about how having asthma had stopped him from joining the Forces. 'I tried, but as soon as they heard the wheeze in my chest they said I was medically exempt.'

'But,' Joyce said, feeling inadequate and uneducated, 'what exactly is asthma?'

Derek explained that the condition made his airways narrow and swollen so that his breathing became difficult and triggered coughing attacks. 'As you were well aware,' he said, smiling as if he were talking about something no more serious than a hangnail.

'But can't the doctor give you something for it?' Joyce asked.

'Oh yes,' he replied. 'I take regular medication and have injections, too. They won't cure me, there is no cure. But they help.'

'But you seem so... I don't know,' Joyce said. 'Unfazed?'

'I am,' he stated with resolution. 'It won't kill me, so I'm not going to let it ruin my life. It's just damned annoying that it's stopped me from joining up.'

Without so much as a moment's hesitation, their conversation moved on to what they had done before the war and Joyce squealed softly when Derek told her he had been an accountant. 'I worked in the Accounts Department at Bourne and Hollingsworth,' she said. 'That's an incredible coincidence.'

'And it answers a lot,' he said. 'About how organised and fastidious you are. One more?' Derek said, pointing to Joyce's empty glass. 'We have time.'

Shaking her head, Joyce explained that she never had more than two drinks as she didn't want to feel woozy during the night when she was on duty. That made Derek throw back his head and cry with laughter.

Feeling a bit offended, Joyce asked him what he found so hilarious.

Derek wiped a tear from his cheek and said, 'I adhere to the same rule, but I'd convinced myself that such a special occasion warranted a one-time regression. I salute you, Senior Officer Cooper,' and he did just that. 'For keeping me on the straight and narrow. Excuse me while I get each of us a lime and soda.'

Joyce couldn't take her eyes off him as he stood at the bar, towering over everyone else. She loved the way he carried his height with such ease, one hand in his trouser pocket the other holding a ten-bob note. When he sat down again, he didn't bother to keep his lengthy legs from touching hers but pressed his ankles, calves, knees and thighs against her in such a confident manner that she felt sure he would feel the heat rising from her toes to the top of her head. He said something funny and she inclined her head towards him until it almost met his shoulder.

They spent the last half an hour together exchanging rather sketchy, basic information about their families. Derek's father had died, too, but his mother was living with his older sister and four nephews in Norfolk, where they had a holiday home. And she told him about her mum and their life together in Rabbit Row.

When they couldn't stretch the time out a minute longer, they left the pub to make their way to their homes to change and then to their separate Report and Control Centres. 'Joyce,' Derek said, sounding very earnest.

'Yes, Derek?'

'I would love to repeat this afternoon, if you would?'

Joyce breathed a sigh of relief. There was no question of what her answer would be. 'I'd like that very much.'

Then he put his arms around her and kissed her on the mouth, there in the street in the middle of Soho. He tasted of hops and foamy beer and smelled like a fresh lemon. Her neck was craned back and his was doubled in half; he stooped down and she had to balance on tiptoes. 'And do you know what I would like even more than that?'

All Joyce could do was shake her head.

'If I could call you my special friend.'

For a moment, Joyce wondered if this was going too fast. She'd never before been hasty or irrational or impetuous. But then she thought about how everything could be taken from her in a bombing raid tonight or tomorrow – her limbs, her ears, her sight. Why not give her heart to this lovely young man before she lost it to an incendiary. 'I'd like that very much too, Derek,' she said.

Fire spread through Joyce as Derek pressed her to him again. Then, smiling, she ran for the Tube. She no longer wanted to keep him a secret, she wanted to shout about him to anyone who would listen. And now that there was definitely something to tell, she would start with Mum.

SEVEN

Sunday 24 February 1974

Joyce hoped the Liberty scarf went some way to ensuring she looked sophisticated and cosmopolitan as it ruffled out behind her in the slipstream of air rushing past the little green Triumph. When they stopped at a red light, the beautiful material spilled onto her arm and pooled across the interior of the door where it served to enhance the sheen of the handle, the window winder and the polished door panels. Then she caught sight of herself in the mirror positioned on the side of the vehicle and, despite living in London for her entire life, her dappy grin gave her away for the parochial, unrefined country bumpkin she was at heart.

She glanced at Mr Taylor and he, too, was grinning broadly, but somehow he managed to give the appearance of being much more accustomed to a well-heeled lifestyle than she could muster. His right elbow sat comfortably in the well of his open window, his hand caressed the steering wheel as he tinkered with the mysterious knobs and buttons on the dashboard and he didn't make eye contact with any of the pedestrians who stared, open-mouthed at the car and its occupants. Young women in particular seemed to take in both the vehicle and driver with one bat of their spider leg eyelashes. How knowing and predatory they seemed – and beautiful, there was no denying that. But Mr Taylor paid them as little attention as he did the portly middle-aged man, eyes round and covetous behind his spectacles, who drew up next to them at the traffic lights. The man leaned forward to peer at Joyce, but finding nothing more than an older has-been in the passenger seat, he reverted to taking in the sports car with greedy eyes until she was convinced he had fallen head over heels for it. *Mind you*, Joyce thought, *there's a lot to fall in love with – I'm rather besotted myself.*

Mr Taylor nudged a lever and a muted rhythmic tick, soft and gentle, bounced around the car. They glided right, in the opposite direction from the Shakespeare Estate and Joyce supposed the detour was part of them making the most of the car, the outing, the day. 'This,' Mr Taylor said, leaning towards her, 'is where Mick Fleetwood first laid eyes on Jenny Boyd.'

Jenny Boyd, Jenny Boyd, Jenny Boyd, Joyce ruminated. She shook her head. 'I'm sorry, Mr Taylor, I don't know who you're talking about.' A group of people on the opposite pavement stopped in their tracks to watch the Spitfire float down the street and a small flock of pigeons started up from where they had been pecking at something objectionable in the middle of the road.

'You know,' he said. 'Mick Fleetwood of Fleetwood Mac and his wife Jenny Boyd? The model?'

'I know Fleetwood Mac,' Joyce said. 'I love some of their tunes.'

'So do we, me and Jacqueline.' Whenever he mentioned

his fiancée's name his voice was thick and sweet, like treacle on the back of a spoon.

'But I'm not aware of Jenny Boyd. Should I be?'

Mr Taylor chuckled. 'No, of course not. It's just that their meeting has become quite a well-known local story.'

The car came to a stop at a zebra crossing and a gaggle of giggling young girls, some in the miniest of skirts, others in flared jeans, sauntered across the road. 'She was a schoolgirl when Fleetwood first clapped eyes on her walking somewhere near here and decided, then and there, to pursue her.'

Joyce shook her head and watched the girls reach the other side of the street. As one, they tossed their hair as they turned their heads to see if the driver of the car was watching them. He wasn't, but she was. 'Well,' Joyce said. 'The girls look so much older than they are these days. And the clothes they're allowed to wear. Even on a school day their skirts barely cover their personal business. And their ties are all unknotted and sloppy. When I was young, children dressed like children, not mini-adults.'

Mr Taylor took his eyes from the road and studied her. Looking beyond the vast amount of hair around his face and shoulders, she could see why the young women they passed were entranced by him – and his car. His carved cheekbones stood out on his slim face, his jawline, under the sideburns, was strong and his eyes sparkled. He pushed on a little button and a shelf fell out of the dashboard. He rooted around behind it and extracted a pair of dark glasses which he flicked open and placed on his nose. On someone else they might have looked affected, but on Mr Taylor they were rather suave.

'The Jenny Boyd story is interesting,' Mr Taylor said, 'because so many bands and models and film stars and artists are gravitating towards this area now. It's becoming gentrified and I'm not sure, Miss Cooper, if you realise just what a des-res this part of London is becoming.'

Joyce felt as if she were being left behind – first Jenny Boyd, now des-res. 'I'm afraid I don't quite...'

'Sorry,' he said. 'Desirable residence.'

Joyce could see herself reflected in Mr Taylor's sunglasses and smoothed down the windswept strands of grey hair that were poking out from under the scarf. 'I've lived in Notting Hill all my life,' Joyce said. 'And I've heard it called many things but never a... a des-res.'

Taking both hands off the steering wheel, Mr Taylor shrugged and looked bemused. 'Well, there you have it.'

The mellow ticking sound filled the car again and this time they turned right. On the left, a demolition site of tall, once-grand houses was cordoned off for the weekend, a digger abandoned precariously in a pit. Joyce caught the messages on some of the signs posted along the fence. 'Hardhats must be worn on site'. 'Do not forget to clock in and out'. 'We are aware of the infestation of rats and are working with the council to bring them under control'. She shivered at the thought of that last one.

At the end of the block, a few raggedy children were playing with a broken baby carriage, a deflated football and an inside out umbrella on a cleared piece of land that had formerly been a bombsite and latterly a slum. It was the next plot to be built on if the sentry line of waiting cranes behind it was anything to go by.

One of the little boys stopped trying to head the ball and followed the progress of the car. Joyce could see a river of blackened snot running from his nose to his lips. As he smeared it across his cheek with his sleeve, Joyce said, 'That's not very gentrified, is it? I wonder what Mr and Mrs Fleet-wood would think about that spectacle.'

'Well,' Mr Taylor chuckled. 'It can't all be perfect. But it's much better than it was, isn't it?'

Joyce looked out at the passing streets, the new high-rise flats and the older houses, some renovated, others in various states of disrepair and the incongruity that accompanied the so-called gentrification of the area. A Wimpy Burger Bar and a tea shop; the launderette and the dry cleaner; pubs and wine shops; the library; second-hand book sellers; comprehensives and private schools; the fishmongers; the greengrocers; a self-service Co-op; the Odeon; the bingo hall and the churches. There were so many people, too, strolling along with nothing more pressing to think about than their dogs, sniffing at lamp posts or their tots, balancing on bikes and skates. Yes, a world where you didn't have to rush home before the blackout, or try to make a meal out of rations, or wash in an inch of scummy, cold water, or mend the same pair of stockings for the umpteenth time was preferable to how they'd had to live during the war.

'Miss Cooper?' Mr Taylor encouraged. 'Surely you agree?'

Joyce looked at the young man, so eager to have his view of the world affirmed. 'Of course, Mr Taylor,' she said. 'But it's come with a price.'

Her companion nodded sagely and said, 'When I think of it, you must have seen some changes, living here as you have all your life.'

'Oh yes, huge changes.'

'Did you never feel like trying somewhere else?'

Joyce shook her head. 'No, not really. I lived in a lot of houses and flats for various amounts of time but...'

'Did you?' Mr Taylor's eyes grew wide and Joyce was

reminded that he really did not know much about her at all. 'Where did you live? And when?'

'It was during the war,' Joyce said, then put up her hand to divert the route the conversation was taking. 'It's not worth talking about,' she said. 'Except to say, all of them were in Notting Hill.'

Mr Taylor took the hint and being a somewhat cultured and well-mannered young man, Joyce knew he would not question her for more information. The car crossed Queensway and both occupants gazed out at Whiteleys.

'Not a patch on your Bourne and Hollingsworth,' Mr Taylor said.

'Not now, at any rate,' said Joyce. 'But when it was built it was on a par with Harrods, believe it or not. When I left school, I was directed to Whiteleys first for a job on the shop floor, but I tried Bourne and Hollingsworth instead and they took me on.'

Mr Taylor let out a low whistle from between pursed lips. 'Let me get this straight,' he said. 'You worked at Bourne and Hollingsworth before the war, then had a break, then resumed employment at B&H when the war finished?'

'That's chronologically correct,' Joyce said. 'But I'd hardly call the war years a break.'

Mr Taylor waggled his head from side to side in a disbelieving attitude. 'I've been away to university, worked for three different councils, lived in two separate digs in London and Jacqueline and I are going to buy a new build in Potters Bar after we're married.'

How quickly she could have been caustic and cutting to Mr Taylor, reminding him that he had it easy because people like her had had it hard. But she couldn't hold him accountable for what hadn't been his fault.

He cleared his throat and fiddled with the chain around his neck. 'I hope you don't mind me asking,' he faltered. 'But what did you do during those war years?'

'I was a bomb plotter.'

'Miss Cooper,' he drawled out her name as if she'd told him she'd been a burlesque dancer. 'Well, I never. So you arranged where and when the RAF would drop bombs on the enemy?'

'Nothing as glamorous as that, I can assure you,' said Joyce. 'I worked for the Civil Defence. You know, the ARP. I plotted on a map where bombs hit in this area. The maps are still kicking around somewhere, as far as I know.'

'And then you just... you just... went back to your old job at Bourne and Hollingsworth? After all that training and the skills you'd acquired?'

Joyce laughed out loud. 'There was no training,' she said. 'One day I was patrolling the streets as a warden, the next I was plotting bombs.'

'But why did you go back to your old job?'

Joyce shrugged. 'They said I could, when the war ended. So I did. It was rather comforting.'

Mr Taylor idled the car behind two others waiting to turn left. He took off his dark glasses, rubbed his eyes with the back of his hand, replaced them on his face and shook his head again. Joyce thought he found her life hard to comprehend and looking back objectively, so did she.

They sailed along the road, Joyce closing her eyes for a few moments and savouring the air on her face, the smell of damp earth and Sunday roasts, children squealing in the distance. When she opened them and saw where they were, she sat up and said, 'Down here, Mr Taylor. This is where our Report and Control Centre was housed.'

Mr Taylor veered around the corner at the last minute. 'Tell me when to stop,' he said. 'Or will I see the monument or plaque?'

Again, Joyce laughed. 'There's no such thing,' she said. 'Stop. There it is.' She pointed to a three-storey house that sat back from the road behind thorny rose bushes and woody hydrangeas waiting for spring.

They parked right outside and looked at the stone steps that led up to the blue front door and at the other set that went down to the basement. Snowy white nets hung gracefully behind draped brown curtains. 'Our headquarters was in the basement. There used to be a noticeboard outside, but that was taken down long ago. And a cupboard type thing that housed a paraffin lamp so people could find us in the blackout.'

'And you spent all of the war down there?' Mr Taylor said.

'Yes, six years on and off.'

'And when it ended, you just took up where you'd left off at the department store. As if nothing had happened.'

'Oh, I knew something had happened,' Joyce said. 'We all did.'

'Your whole life in Notting Hill,' Mr Taylor said, drumming his fingers on the steering wheel. 'And at Bourne and Hollingsworth. Except for the war. You must know London very well.'

'I used to meet friends and my cousin up West from time to time. And occasionally I've taken myself off to one museum or another. But no, I should be ashamed to say, I'm not that familiar with most of it.'

Mr Taylor looked over at her and touched his forehead with his index finger. 'Paul Taylor,' he said. 'Of Taylor's Tours. Stick with me for the time of your life.'

The Spitfire tore away from the kerb and Joyce planted her hand on her head to make sure the scarf stayed in place. 'I don't think I have much choice in the matter, Mr Taylor,' she said, a grin spreading across her face.

As they turned left onto Bayswater Road, Mr Taylor did something with a pedal on the floor and the engine roared. She'd heard the same racket more and more frequently over the last couple of years and it always made her jump and move as far away from the edge of the pavement as possible. But from inside the car, the noise was so sudden and animalistic, that she threw back her head and laughed aloud. If she thought they'd been stared at and scrutinised before, now they were the day's entertainment.

The car turned right into Hyde Park and, Joyce was pleased to observe, Mr Taylor drove sensibly down West Carriage Drive, although twice he was forced to beep his horn to alert pedestrians that he was coming through. They passed over the Serpentine, busy with boats and swans and passed Kensington Palace on their right. Coming out of the park, the car nosed right on Kensington Gore, then made a loop around the Albert Hall. Joyce hung out of the window and found the door that she and Derek had used when they were lucky enough to get tickets for the very first Opening Night of the Proms held at the RAH after the Queen's Hall had been bombed out. It was the twelfth of July 1941 and behind the smell of smoke that lay over the city, there was a trace of lilac in the air. Joyce could still picture the pale grey dress she'd borrowed from Flo which she'd worn with her soft, navy blue jacket over her shoulders – and, of course, the black, patent court shoes. Derek had worn his uniform and on the top of his cheekbone there was the tiniest of nicks from where his razor had caught the skin when he'd been shaving. Joyce remembered the thrill she'd felt when she realised she was the only person in the world who would get close enough to Derek to be aware of that minute cut. The memory was so vivid, that she could almost see Derek and her younger self disappearing into the exquisite interior of the concert hall. 'God Save the King' had opened the programme at 7.00 and the orchestra, conducted by Sir Henry Wood, closed with Wagner's *Der fliegende Holländer* promptly at 9.00 to accommodate the blackout. Never before or since had she experienced anything as heady and evocative.

They then seemed to double back on themselves and drive past Harrods, Harvey Nicks and then around Hyde Park Corner and up Park Lane to Marble Arch. They made their way down Oxford Street, Joyce waving to the empty Bourne and Hollingsworth building. 'Oh, I do wish the girls could see me,' she shouted. 'They won't believe me tomorrow when I tell them how I spent my Sunday.'

'If they'd like to phone me at the office,' Mr Taylor roared back at her. 'I will be happy to verify your whereabouts to them.'

Mr Taylor drove so fast and the air whooshed about their ears at such a speed, that they couldn't talk much while they were moving. All they could do was point and laugh.

Sweeping through Mayfair, they sped down Piccadilly to see the young people hanging out on the steps of Eros. Then, on what felt like two wheels, they took in Leicester Square, Covent Garden and the theatres in Shaftesbury Avenue. Spinning around Trafalgar Square, they passed Horse Guards Parade, Downing Street and the Cenotaph. They cruised down Birdcage Walk to the Palace and Joyce was sure the Queen had never had so much fun in any of her myriad of royal vehicles as she, Joyce Cooper, was having in the little green Spitfire. They drove a circuit of Green Park, then back up to Westminster Abbey, Big Ben, the Houses of Parliament, Somerset House, across Waterloo Bridge to the Royal Festival Hall on the South Bank. Then they were speeding across London Bridge and past the Bank of England. They cruised through the City, empty and eerie on weekends, then somehow Joyce was pointing out the Tower to Mr Taylor as if he'd never set eyes on that landmark before when in reality, he seemed to be familiar with every side street, lane and round-about in London and where each one led.

When they stopped at a red light, Joyce said, 'You could have easily been a cab driver. Are you sure you haven't taken the knowledge test?'

'Jacqueline and I love to explore when we have the chance,' Mr Taylor said. 'And there's always something wonderful to see in London.'

But this, Joyce thought, *doesn't seem like London to me.* Of course, she knew it was, but it was as if she had landed in some romantic and alluring city – Paris or Rome or New York or somewhere she'd read about but didn't have the experience to name.

Then they were off again, laughing their way to the Observatory, back across the river to Spitalfields, out to Ally Pally, back through Hampstead Heath, past the Swiss Cottage pub, around Regents Park, along the length of Lord's Cricket Ground and down the Edgeware Road to Paddington Station. Eventually, the roads and shops became familiar once more. There was the bakery, the second-hand shop and Portobello Road Market – all closed on Sundays – and the flattened site that used to be Rillington Place, where the unsavoury John Christie had lived; the road had been renamed Runton Close before the whole thing had been torn down, just last year.

Joyce wondered if that could be classed as an early example of crude gentrification.

And then before she knew it, or had a chance to protest if she had been ill-mannered enough to dare, Mr Taylor was parking on the road outside Hamlet House on the Shakespeare Estate. The engine was silenced, Joyce took off the Liberty scarf, folded it neatly and handed it to Mr Taylor with her thanks. Then all that remained of their shrieks of laughter was an intangible echo.

EIGHT

MUM

April 1941

What the papers were calling the Blitz, people on the streets were calling utter exhaustion. No one said the word aloud, though, because to do so would be tantamount to admitting a personal defeat and no one wanted to let themselves, or each other, down. But it was all too apparent in the way everyone walked with leaden feet, often misjudging a length of jagged pavement or having to rest at the top of a slight incline to gasp for a shallow breath. They noticed each other's eyes, wreathed in blue, purple and green and the way in which small scrapes and minor scratches became easily infected and then took ages to heal. Endearing features such as plump cheeks and lively, bouncing hair began to sag and lay limp. When they stopped to chitchat with each other, they averted their eyes so their neighbour or friend wouldn't pick up on how the last eight months had aged them.

It was a long time to get by on little or no sleep or snatched naps here and there. It seemed to Joyce that nothing had changed in terms of the relentless German bombardment during all that time, and yet for her, everything was different. Each night when the siren sounded, her stomach began to grind against itself – it wound first one way and then the other, trying to find something that didn't feel raw to work itself against. When she was in the thick of it with the map, she could ignore the way it gnashed one way and gnawed another as if her insides consisted of rows of tiny, sharp teeth, but when the all-clear sounded she became more aware again of the scraping and mincing until she was home and knew Mum was safe, too.

Now, though, she was aware of another sensation, and it was more akin to the soft flutter of butterflies than the clash and clank of machinery. And the feeling of silky, expectant wings tumbling softly around inside her was to do with Derek. Hours would go by when he wouldn't enter her head and then, for a split second while she extracted a pin from her mouth, his face would flash in front of her and the insects or moths or whatever they were would rise up as if from a scented garden and tickle their way past everything else. Or she might recall, out of the blue, a joke he had told her or the way he placed his large hand on the small of her back when they crossed the road and she'd be invaded by hundreds of quivers again.

Of course, it didn't interfere with her work, she wouldn't allow that to happen. But it was a wonderful and unexpected diversion and one she liked to hug to herself. Everyone at Report and Control knew by now that she and Derek were dating and, much to Joyce's bemusement, none of them seemed in the least bit surprised. That she found hard to understand as she, herself, was most confounded that they had met at all, let alone taken to each other in such a huge way. *It's the war,* Joyce thought. *A man like Derek would never have looked at me twice if we hadn't been almost forced together because of these unwarranted circumstances.* But she was so glad they had been – and Derek seemed to be, too.

One afternoon, Mum leaned heavily against the sink while she was washing up and bathed her forehead with the grimy, greasy rag in her hand. 'Mum,' Joyce shouted, alarm prickling through her. 'Sit down this minute. Here, give that to me.' She plucked at the cloth and despite Mum's protests about Joyce having to meet Derek within the hour, forced her mother to sit and have a cup of tea while she waded through the dirty dishes.

'I'll stay with you, Mum,' Joyce said. 'You look a bit pale.'

'I won't let you keep poor Derek waiting in the rain and cold, thinking he's been stood up.' Mum said. 'Besides he'll be ever so worried about you if you do.'

'I can get a message to him at Regional Control later tonight,' Joyce said. 'He wouldn't want me to leave you feeling under the weather.'

'I'm no such thing, Joy love.' Mum swatted her with the tea towel. 'You have to go and give him that invitation for Sunday. You promised. Look, I'm back to my old self.'

Mum did have more colour in her cheeks and seemed steady on her feet, so Joyce sighed and resigned herself to asking Derek to tea. If she didn't, she'd never hear the end of it.

* * *

Joyce cringed when she passed on the message from Mum, expecting Derek to be taken aback at how quickly things were progressing. But she reminded herself that Derek had been the one to propel their relationship along at the pace of a run rather than a walk, so she took a deep breath and put the question to him, and he was delighted.

'Well,' he said, smiling so one side of his mouth pushed up against his cheek. 'I'd be honoured. What day and time and what shall I bring?'

'Is 4.00 on Sunday alright?' Joyce answered. 'And Mum will have everything in so please don't bring anything.'

As well as being inevitably well-prepared, Mum was beside herself with excitement, making the most of their rations to assemble a lovely, if innovative, spread. On top of a white starched tablecloth, she placed a large bowl of mock brain faggots, a platter of brawn sandwiches and another of Spam two ways, a plate of potato rarebit, a jar of piccalilli. Carrot squares and fruit shortcake were arranged on carnival glass dishes on the sideboard.

'Mum,' Joyce groaned. 'I've invited him just for tea just today, not every meal for a month.'

For a moment, Mum looked crushed, but she brightened when she justified herself. 'We want to make him welcome, don't we?'

'Of course we do,' Joyce said. 'But there's welcoming and then there's overwhelming. Promise you won't put another thing on this table except cups of tea. If you do, the whole thing will collapse. Look, it's buckling in the middle.'

The old, worn table did look as if it would cave in and take all the food down with it, but Mum ushered Joyce out of the room with a half-hearted promise to do as she was told and marched her upstairs. There she fussed about what to wear and wanted to help Joyce with her hair, the neckline of her blouse, the hem of her skirt, the shaping of her nails. Joyce laughed, telling her mother that she had been out with Derek a few times by that point and he seemed to like the way she dressed and groomed herself.

'What do I need to know?' Mum asked, slightly breathless. 'Tell me all about him. I don't want to put my foot in it, do I?'

That was unavoidable, Joyce thought, and something she was used to when it came to her mum. But she decided it was only fair to tell her the little she knew about her new beau. She shrugged. 'There's not much I can tell you, Mum,' she said. 'We've only known each other for a few weeks.'

'But you seem so keen on each other. And you've obviously told him all about us,' Mum said, sweeping her hands in front of her to encompass Joyce's bedroom, the house, all the food she'd prepared, the life they led.

'Yes,' Joyce said. 'Well, he's told me bits and pieces.'

'There you are then. Tell me the blasted bits and pieces he's told you.'

Joyce closed her eyes and smiled, allowing excitement at the thought of talking about Derek to override her reticence. She sat up straight, looked at Mum and said, 'Well, he's very tall.'

'Yes, you've told me that.'

'I know, but I mean exceptionally tall.' Joyce pretended to reach for a place far above her head. 'It hurts my neck to look up at him. And his back aches when he looks down at me.'

Mum thought that description hilarious and rocked back on the bed, holding her stomach. 'You sound like a good double act,' she said.

'And he's a bit older than me.' Joyce looked down at her hands, feeling almost shy about the age difference. 'He'll be thirty on his next birthday.'

Mum leaned up on one elbow and cupped her chin in her hand. 'It's quite nice to have an older man to look after you. As long as he hasn't been married before or has a wife and children tucked away somewhere already.'

Joyce felt her eyes widen with that sudden thought. 'I... I don't think so.' Then she shook her head forcefully. 'I've been given no reason to suspect that might be the case.'

Sitting up, Mum took Joyce's hand in hers and caressed her fingers. 'Then I'm sure it's not, Joy love. Trust your instincts not my silly fussing.'

Mum looked so upset that she could have made her daughter unhappy with such a preposterous idea, that Joyce felt sorry for her.

'What I know so far,' Mum carried on, 'is that he's ever so tall, has very dark hair and eyes, is nine years older than you and is high up in the Civil Defence – a Senior Regional Officer. But what about his job before the war? And what does his father do? Where do his parents live and does he have brothers and sisters? Does he like dogs or cats and what does he think about children?'

'Slow down, Mum,' Joyce wasn't able to stop herself laughing. 'You sound like a newspaper reporter or a detective.'

'I would have loved either of those jobs,' Mum said, with a hint of regret. Then she put her face close to Joyce's and inspected her.

'What is it, Mum?' Joyce began to feel self-conscious. 'Have I got smuts on my cheek?'

'No, my love,' Mum said. 'But are you going to put on a dab of lipstick and face powder?'

'I've gone off powder,' Joyce said. 'It's dry and itchy. But Flo helped me to choose a new lipstick.' She pulled on the drawer in her rickety nightstand, brought out a Max Factor bullet and twisted the tube with reverence. A brand new, glossy red stick of glamour was revealed. 'What do you think?' Joyce asked.

Mum exhaled slowly. 'Oh,' she said. 'It's gorgeous. Like something a film star would wear. And such a change from your usual. Try it on.'

Joyce jumped up and studying herself in the mirror, filled in her lips with the crimson colour.

'Oh, I say, Joy love, you look very sophisticated. It suits you.'

Joyce turned and smiled at her mum, her mouth feeling oddly heavy, coated as it was in the unfamiliar unguent.

Mum tapped her teeth.

Joyce stared at her and Mum pointed to her mouth again then touched a front tooth with her finger. 'You've got lipstick on your teeth,' she said.

Spinning back to the mirror, Joyce gave herself a smile then rubbed off the offending stain. When she turned back around, she said, 'Derek's father has passed away, like mine. He was injured in the last war and never really recovered. His mother has moved out of their house in Croydon and into their holiday home in Norfolk with Derek's older sister and her four boys. He still lives in the London house and the extra rooms are rented out to other officers in the Civil Defence who've come here from elsewhere. He took me there once, just to show me where he lives, and it's beautifully done out. But he doesn't think it proper for a young lady, his young lady, to be in a house with so many unmarried blokes. Like his father, he was an accountant before the war but joined the Civil Defence because the Forces wouldn't take him due to his chronic asthma. It's horrible to hear when he has an attack, but it's like water off a duck's back to him. I think he likes dogs *and* cats, and we haven't talked about children although he seems to be tolerant and patient with them if they get in his way. He's very easy going and laughs a lot. Do you want a smear of my lipstick?'

Mum blinked. 'Oh, well. Ta, Joy love. I probably know as much as you now.'

Joyce nodded and proffered Mum the golden cartridge.

'I'd love to, but it might look silly if we're wearing the same lipstick,' Mum said.

That made Joyce laugh out loud again. 'He might as well get used to our silliness from the get-go,' she said. 'Pucker up, Mum. Show us your best pout.'

As Joyce was bending over, one hand on Mum's forehead and the other applying the red paint, there was a loud rap at the door. Joyce froze. Derek was very punctual, but not usually by a good half an hour. 'I didn't expect him so early,' Joyce said.

Then voices drifted up the stairs along with the sounds of the coat cupboard being opened, shoes being taken off, crockery added to the belly flopping table and Auntie Cath's distinct shout. 'We're here, Maggie love.'

'Mum.' Joyce was disbelieving. 'You didn't. Yes, you did, didn't you? How could you?'

Mum looked very sheepish and knotted her hands together until the knuckles turned white. 'I just thought... that it would be better if Derek met everyone at once rather than in drips and drabs.' Her face had taken on a pink hue and the earlier excitement of new lipstick and getting ready and asking about Derek seemed to have evaporated. 'I'm sorry, Joy love.' She shook her head. 'I don't know what I was thinking. I just get carried away.'

That was the fact of the matter and that was why it was so

difficult for Joyce to be cross with her mum for long. She sighed. 'Is it just Auntie Cath?'

'No,' Mum looked as if she wanted to fold into herself. 'I asked everyone,' she said in a small, timid voice. 'Sorry. But we'll have a lovely time.'

Yes, Joyce thought. *We'll have to as there's nothing we can do about it now.* 'Come on then, Mum. We'd better get downstairs.'

Mum nodded then pointed to her mouth. 'Don't leave me looking like this, Joy love. Can you do my bottom lip, please?'

Together they made their way down the stairs, Mum going through her ritualistic monologue, warning Joyce to hold the banister, mind the edge of the ragged stair carpet, look where she was going. Then, two steps from the bottom, Mum grabbed Joyce's shoulder and asked her what they should call Derek. 'Officer Nicholls? Or Sir, perhaps?'

'No, Mum,' Joyce felt weary already. She pictured Derek being addressed with either of those monikers and the red cheeks and wide, mortified eyes she saw made her wince. Besides, she liked to call him Sir Derek when they were cuddled up together in a doorway or were pinned close against a tree in a quiet patch of Hyde Park with their hands roaming under each other's' coats – and that she was certainly keeping to herself. 'I'll introduce him to you as Derek and that's what you should call him,' she said.

Mum nodded and then threw her arms around Auntie Cath, Uncle Terry and Flo, who crumpled her face into a look of innocence to let Joyce know that none of this had been her doing.

Auntie Cath was about to plonk a huge bowl of something that looked like trifle on the table when Joyce raised the alarm. 'No, Auntie Cath – stop. The table already looks as though a

Jerry bomb's sitting on top of it and threatening to drop to the floor.'

Everyone laughed. 'Here,' said Uncle Terry. 'Where's that old wallpaper table? Come with me, girls.'

Joyce groaned inwardly at the thought of the wallpaper table in the house, but they had often used it to set food on or sit around when everyone was there, so she resigned herself to letting Derek see them, all of them, as they were. Following Uncle Terry to the shed, Joyce wondered if Derek might compare her house and circumstances unfavourably with his own. Then a feeling of shame engulfed her. She loved her family, they loved her, and she was proud of the way they laughed and took care of each other. She lifted her chin and told herself sternly that if Derek didn't like the effort everyone had put into meeting him and drawing him towards their generous warmth, then he could sling his hook. It would be good riddance to him and he wouldn't be deserving of a backward glance from her. But the thought of that potential outcome caused the blade of a knife to slice through the butterfly wings she was beginning to enjoy.

She needn't have worried, though, because from the minute Derek arrived, with a potted geranium in one hand and a small packet of sugar in the other, he seemed to fit right in. He appreciated each sandwich he ate, and he managed a good number of them, every cup of tea he was handed, every foul mock brain faggot he popped into his mouth and the many bowlfuls of mushy, stewed apple trifle that were forced on him. He laughed at all the jokes and family banter bouncing around and put his elbows on his knees, leaning close to Granddad to listen to the stories the older man told in his low, gravelly voice. He complimented Mum and Auntie Cath on how lovely they looked and put up with Nana peering at him closely through her thick spectacles. Flo, who he'd met on three previous occasions, was treated as a great pal.

There was no room to sit around the precariously laden table, so they balanced their plates on their laps. Mum commanded Joyce and Derek to sit next to each other on the settee and Derek took every opportunity to graze his leg against Joyce's or touch her arm when he spoke to her or give her his widest, most lopsided smile. There were only two incidents when Mum was embarrassing and by the end of the afternoon Joyce couldn't quite recall the details, so the tea was definitely a success.

'Now, lads,' Granddad rasped. 'The Moon Under Water for a jar or two?'

Uncle Terry cheered, but Joyce was disappointed with that proposal as she and Derek had hoped for a bit of time to themselves. Then Derek came to the rescue when he cleared his throat and said, 'Joyce and I get so little time to ourselves, do you mind if I postpone the invitation until another day so I can take her out for a quick drink?'

Joyce felt sure everyone could hear the thud-thud of her heart as it was about to burst. But Granddad, who craved company, turned down the corners of his mouth and Uncle Terry looked confused. 'Go,' Joyce said, covering Derek's hand with hers. 'I'll be here when you get back.'

Then it was Derek's turn to look disenchanted. 'How about a compromise?' he said to everyone. 'One drink with Granddad and Uncle Terry, then I'll come back and take Joyce out.'

Another cheer went up around the room and the men put on their outdoor clothes. Uncle Terry stood on one side of Granddad and Derek on the other and as they left the house together, it seemed to Joyce as though Derek had seamlessly become one of the family.

After they all made their plans to meet later in the underground, Flo was next to leave, saying she was meeting a friend from work. Joyce suspected she might have had a date but didn't want to say and leave herself open to the same microscopic scrutiny from the family. Mum helped Nana on with her coat and Auntie Cath said she would walk their mother home. As they said their goodbyes, they told Joyce how lovely they thought Derek was, how much they liked him and said, 'Well done, Joy love.'

Alone with the clearing up, Mum reiterated the same acclamation of praise. 'I think it's Derek who should be congratulated,' Joyce said, moving plates and cups to the kitchen. 'Or his parents. I haven't played any part in moulding him.'

'No, but you're to be congratulated for being such a lovely person that you've attracted a young man like that. That's what we mean.'

'Oh,' Joyce said, reddening a little under her collar. 'That's very nice of you, Mum.'

Mum pinched Joyce's cheek lovingly and wriggled the flesh about between her fingers. 'You're beautiful and you deserve the very best,' she said.

Joyce was pleased it had gone so well, but wanted to make sure Mum understood that she and Derek had not committed themselves to each other – nowhere near. 'Ta, Mum,' she said. 'But at the moment we haven't made any promises. We're in the process of getting to know each other, that's all.'

'And you should take all the time you can for that.' Mum dabbed at her mouth, testing the staying power of the lipstick that had been applied earlier. 'Did it last?' she asked.

'For a fair while,' Joyce said. 'I think I'll go upstairs and put on another layer so I'm ready when Derek calls for me. We won't have much time together before we have to be at our posts.'

'Alright, love,' Mum shouted above the noise of the kettle she was boiling to make a start on the washing up. 'I wonder when you'll meet his mum?' she called over her shoulder. 'Has he mentioned it yet?'

'No,' Joyce yelled back. 'Norfolk's a long way to get to and back in one day off.'

* * *

Alone in her room, Joyce leaned on the windowsill and took in the view of the garden below, the duplicates next door and those following on along the terrace. Each was the same size and shape and all backed onto the gardens of the houses in the next street over from Rabbit Row. As she pulled up the sash, a rush of May air slipped over her as softly as a square of gauze. Some neighbours had tried to maintain a few flowers, but most of them, like Mum, now devoted their patches of earth to vegetables. Once heady scents would have risen up to her, but now rose and sweet pea and lavender perfumes were an undernote, replaced by the headier, heavier aroma of radishes, carrots, runner beans, potatoes, the last of the cabbages and of course, the all-pervasive smoke – there was no getting away from that.

Turning from the window Joyce fiddled with the lipstick, turning the tube so the seductive colour appeared and disappeared from view. When she stopped and thought about it, she realised that Derek rarely talked about his family at all. Not as much as she did. There were no anecdotes from his childhood, no nicknames that he imparted, no references to aunts, uncles, grandparents or cousins. He had never mentioned receiving a letter from his mother or sister or said, with a hint of melancholy, that he missed them and his nephews. He certainly enjoyed hearing her stories about growing up, but didn't offer any of his own as most people do. She wondered if it meant he was not family-oriented, then told herself she was being ridiculous as his reaction to their teatime get together had been one of ease and contentment.

Joyce thought about Mum's question which seemed to be a reasonable one. Derek hadn't said a thing about them making plans to travel to Norfolk to meet his mother any time soon or in the distant future. And he hadn't given her any indication about whether his mother knew about her at all. *Perhaps,* she thought, *I've been running away with myself.* As she'd reminded Mum, she and Derek hadn't made any long-term pledges to each other. But when the soft, insistent beat of insect wings announced their presence, Joyce sometimes allowed herself to imagine a small, solid, bright, clean house somewhere in a Notting Hill that was clear of bomb damage and debris. Derek would use his own key to let himself into that house, Joyce would be wearing something other than itchy blue serge and children would be piecing together a jigsaw puzzles or turning the page of a comic. But that would never happen, not if Derek wasn't prepared to introduce her to his mother and family. Or if this blasted war blew all of their dreams and ambitions to fragments that could never be pieced together again.

She felt unsettled and sorry as her thoughts had put a damper on the afternoon. She sighed, peered in the mirror and drew on her stretched mouth with the lipstick. There was only one thing for it. When they were alone together she would ask

Derek, in as natural a way as possible, to explain away her doubts. Smacking her lips together, she nodded at her reflection and began to draft a list of questions in her mind.

'Lovely,' Mum said when Joyce smoothed her coat over the back of a chair, ready to make a quick exit with Derek when he returned.

'We can share the lipstick, Mum,' Joyce said. 'I'll leave it on the mantelpiece.'

'Oh, Joy love, what would I want with a colour like that down in the depths of the underground or queuing for rations? You keep it for yourself, love. It's the perfect colour for your complexion.'

Joyce carried another stack of crockery into the kitchen, plucked the tea towel from a hook and started to dry a few dishes. Mum was humming softly and Joyce joined in. It was warm and damp and felt uncomplicated to be close to Mum, her hands raw and pink from the hot water and harsh detergent. They smiled at each other and for a moment, Joyce wished they could stay like this – happy, content and rooted together in unequivocal love that expected nothing more than one washing and one drying. How lovely not to have to think about the war or rationing or tiny pins with lethal tales to tell. *Or how to phrase my worries to Derek about his family,* Joyce thought. Then the dust from the insects' wings stirred in her again and she knew that the cocoon with Mum and the kitchen wasn't enough to satisfy her and couldn't last for ever, so all she had to do to put her mind at rest was ask Derek the questions on the mental list she'd composed. She put her arm around Mum's shoulder and pulled her close.

'I love your hugs, Joy,' Mum said.

In reply, Joyce kissed her mother on her cheek hard enough to make sure the lipstick left a bright, sanguine mark.

'Oi,' Mum laughed. 'You've rubbed your lipstick off on me.'

'Have a matching pair,' Joyce said, seizing Mum and planting another kiss on the opposite side of her face. 'That'll give them something to talk about in the underground tonight.'

Then without warning, the front door slammed back on itself and made the whole house shake. Joyce recognised her shock mirrored in Mum's reaction. They stood transfixed, dishcloth and tea towel suspended, wondering if the Germans had decided to bring forward the starting time of their offensive.

'Joy, what should we...?' Mum began.

'I'll get you to shelter, Mum, then get myself to Report and Control.'

But before they could move, Uncle Terry stumbled into the kitchen, his breathing shallow and a thin stream of sweat making its way from under his cap and into his whiskers.

'What is it, Terry?' Mum ran towards him, wiping her hands on her apron in a frenzy. 'Is it Granddad?'

'Joy,' Uncle Terry pointed towards the front door. 'It's Derek. He's very poorly. I think he needs an ambulance, but he insists that he's...'

Joyce bolted down the hallway, followed by Mum and Uncle Terry. But from the porch she saw Derek, sauntering towards them next to Granddad.

'Have you lost your mind at long last, Terence Peters?' Mum asked, swiping Uncle Terry with the tea towel. She scrabbled for Joyce's hand and Joyce felt her shaking with fright. 'Look, what is that, a mirage?'

'But, Joy,' Uncle Terry pleaded. 'He was coughing as if he was going to explode. On and on it went. He couldn't stop and he couldn't answer us when we tried to help. Oh, Joy love, it was bad. If he'd let me get an ambulance, I'd have jumped in it with him, that's how close I was to the whole thing giving me a heart attack.'

Uncle Terry did suffer from a bad heart and Joyce felt terrible that she hadn't prepared him for the severity of Derek's condition. 'It's his asthma, Uncle Terry.' She heard the impatience in her voice. 'I told you about it and how it's put paid to him joining up.'

'I know you did, Joy love,' Uncle Terry sounded as testy as she felt. 'Same as my ticker's done for me. But to tell the truth, I don't have a clue about asthma and I would never have guessed it was so... so desperate.'

'Sorry, Uncle Terry,' Joyce said, her voice softening. 'I should have explained in more detail, but I didn't want to make too big a deal out of it in front of Derek.'

They stood and watched as Derek curtailed his long strides to match Granddad's as they crossed the road. Joyce waved and Derek raised his hand in return, his lovely, oblique grin taking over his face as if he hadn't a care in the world. Behind her back, Joyce heard Uncle Terry whisper to Mum that the attack had been startling and that he'd been frightened for both their poor old hearts.

'Now this is what I call a greeting party,' Derek said, standing back to let Granddad step into the hall before him.

Joyce felt grateful to Mum who, with grace, gathered herself together and said, 'We know how to make guests feel welcome, Derek.'

'I now know that to be true from happy experience, thank you, Mrs Cooper,' Derek said.

They stood, crammed into the narrow, stuffy hallway and Joyce wondered if she could get away with disappearing into the coat cupboard and pulling Derek in with her, then shutting the door tight on the rest of them. Granddad was asking Derek if his breathing difficulties were a result of a mustard gas attack during the Great War; Uncle Terry was mopping his brow; Derek was shifting and shuffling about as if trying to take up less space and Mum, after what seemed like ages, ushered everyone into the sitting room and asked who would like a cup of tea.

'I'm very grateful to you, Mrs Cooper,' Derek said. 'And thank you for the wonderful afternoon. But I would like to take Joyce out now for an hour or so before our shifts begin.' He turned to look at Joyce. 'That's if you'll still have me,' he said.

Joyce smiled and nodded, aware of a flush to match the colour of the lipstick spreading over her face.

'Of course she will,' Mum spoke up on her behalf. And Joyce had to restrain a frustrated groan from escaping her lips.

'Are you sure you're able?' Uncle Terry's eyebrows came together in a deep frown of concern.

'Oh yes,' Derek said. 'I'm more than able.'

If any of the others picked up on the innuendo they didn't let on, but Joyce felt her blush deepen and force its way to the surface of her face and then the tumultuous butterfly wings took flight again.

There wasn't an opportunity that evening to ask Derek about the childhood he seemed to avoid or if his mother did know about Joyce's presence in her son's life. The precious hour they had together was spent recapping the afternoon and talking about Derek's asthma attack in the pub which he described with great animation. He aped Uncle Terry's panic and the way in which Granddad struck him on the back several times, then called for whisky and hot water that he proceeded to down himself. Joyce cried with laughter at the antics of her family that she recognised all too well.

On the way to Joyce's Report and Control Centre, they spent a sweaty quarter of an hour at the back of a bombsite off the beaten track where the fragile wings of a Meadow Brown or Red Admiral or Cabbage White started to beat ardently again. And before she knew it, their time alone together was at an end.

* * *

Four nights in April had seen them almost on their knees from intense, heightened and strengthened Luftwaffe raids. The magnitude of the relentless caterwauling noises, levels of catastrophe, endless destruction and heartbreak the bombardments brought with them seemed to be never-ending; Joyce could not fathom how they continued to survive. Sleep, and the hope that it would overpower them when they could eventually lie down, was all they could think about.

For the next few weeks after that they enjoyed, if that could possibly be the right word, a time of relative peace and quiet. And whilst they sagged with relief and felt beyond grateful for the respite, it was as though they were living on a knife edge – they didn't dare to think Hitler was finished with them yet.

But thank goodness for the days getting longer, Joyce thought as a refreshing breeze touched her face and the heads of a few peonies and sweet peas nodded to her as she walked by. Despite the lull, she made sure she was at Report and Control, ready to go, before nightfall. She dragged her feet a bit in the spring air and who could blame her. Smoke lingered, of course, but there was also a note or two of something fresher, greener and more alive. It was imperceptible, but Joyce thought she wasn't the only one who sensed it. There was a purpose, not energetic but definitely discernible, to how people lifted their feet and swung their arms and in the tilt of their heads when they inclined them towards each other. Joyce thought they must all hope, like her, that with fewer dark hours to use as camouflage, the Luftwaffe would soon give up.

How foolish they were to allow themselves that morsel of hope or a sliver of complacency. Night descended and the Nazis returned in their savage planes and bombed them with the renewed energy that could only have accumulated from a three-week holiday. There was not one minute's reprieve, which would have been a blessing; they lived through every second in a state of profound, focused anxiety. From the minute the first bomb fell, Joyce had an ARPM1 in one hand and a pin in the other and within an hour she knew there would be no butterflies to think about that night.

No heating was on in the packed basement, but Joyce was doused in perspiration. Trickles that turned to streams ran down her back and made her hair stick to the nape of her neck. When she could, she wiped her hands on her skirt so the pins couldn't slither and slip from her grasp, then carried on with her work. Over and over again, Controller Davis wiped his incandescent face with a handkerchief he took from his pocket. He clumped across the room to view the map, a gang of uniformed men in tow. A drop of salty sweat that had been balancing on the tip of his nose lost its hold and landed with a dark stain on his shirt; if he noticed, he didn't say a word. If she hadn't already understood the seriousness of the raid, that brought it home to her – Controller Davis would have otherwise been mortified about such a scene in front of Joyce and his apologies would have been profuse.

Mrs Bertrand did the rounds with cup after cup of tea, her hands and wattles trembling more than usual; there was more dust and grime on the boy scouts when they dashed in, dishevelled and pale; wardens, unsteady on their feet, came in to have minor bumps and cuts bandaged and were then turned around and sent back out to get on with it; when he wasn't monitoring the map, Controller Davis had the telephone glued to his ear, a hot imprint of his hand shining on the receiver or he was talking to other senior officials, their faces pale and serious as they discussed strategy. Joyce created mountainous piles with the ARPM1 forms, most of them relating to houses, shops, buildings and families that she was frighteningly familiar with. She was never more grateful that Mum was in the underground and that she would hear, via the telephone, if anything happened to Derek. When she glanced at the hands on the clock, they seemed to have remained stagnant as if they were giving time away to the Luftwaffe.

Beyond the organised hubbub, Joyce was convinced she could hear bombs whistling through the air and exploding when they reached their targets. Not the kind of buoyant and bubbly whistle that would have once signalled Bill's presence, but a thin, cowardly whine that cut through the air like a weapon from a sneaky bully boy's slingshot. No one panicked; no one became hysterical; there were no shed tears. What choice did they have? It was either carry on or give up and what that boiled down to was no choice at all.

Joyce shook her tin, then shook it again and scrabbled amongst the contents for the ones with the lethal black heads. So many of the ARPM1 forms had the box denoting total destruction ticked, that she'd run out of the required pins. 'Mrs Bertrand,' she raised her voice.

The older woman walked back towards the kitchen without turning, so Joyce called her name a bit louder but it was too late, Mrs Bertrand hadn't heard her. Blast, as Mum would have said. Joyce let the Controller know she was going to collect a supply of pins and he acknowledged her by forming a circle with his thumb and forefinger.

She was brisk and efficient and couldn't have been more than three minutes, but when she returned there were five grubby, stained forms waiting, ink and mud streaked across them. They smelled too, of smoke and sweat and a whiff of fear. She picked up the first, recognised the place it referred to and plotted its location on the map with a yellow pin. Another boy scout stood in front of her and she pointed to where she wanted him to start another pile; he threw down the form and bounded out of the room. The library had taken it next and she pictured skipping there hand-in-hand with Flo, eager to claim a pile of books as their own for a few weeks. Now no children would be enjoying the same experience for a good while as the whole thing had been reduced to a purple pin. Then there were addresses she was less familiar with in Bayswater and Holland Park – totally destroyed.

Three more boy scouts looking like urchins stood in front of her, but she snatched up the one remaining form before she let them put down the ones they were clutching. She took in the address with one sweep of her eyes, but felt some kind of blockade drop into place and her mind refused to believe what she read. Her hand wilted at her side and she looked around at the Centre, packed and teeming with wardens and officers and boy scouts all going about their business in the same way they had been the minute before she'd picked up the form. So that proved it couldn't be true. If her little terraced house had taken a hit, why would the world and everyone in it still be behaving as if nothing had happened?

She steeled herself to read the address again and there it was – 27 Rabbit Row. Total destruction. 1K. Bile rose in her stomach. She crumpled the form in one hand and clamped the other tight across her mouth. Her house was gone. Obliterated. And one person had been killed. But there were only two people who had a key to their front door – she and Mum – and the pain ripping through her attested to the fact that she was very much alive.

'Someone get Mrs Bertrand to take over at the map.' Controller Davis was at her side, his orders clear and forthright. He tugged to free the form from Joyce's clammy fist, but she held onto it with a ferocious grip. The Controller relented, put one hand around her shoulder and the other under her elbow and guided her to the first aid room.

Joyce glanced back and hissed under her breath. 'I believe we're causing a scene for no reason whatsoever. Please, I must stay with the map. It's my duty.'

But Controller Davis limped through the room, intense and industrious, and murmured to Joyce that she mustn't worry, the map would be safe in Mrs Bertrand's hands for now.

Dizzy and sick, but not quite able to remember why, Joyce allowed herself to be edged down into a large, tatty armchair. 'Gladys,' Controller Davis said, 'Senior Warden Cooper is in shock. A cup of sweet tea, please.'

With pallid skin and bright feverish eyes, Gladys showed all the symptoms of shock herself, but she turned to the urn and began to ready a pot of tea.

Controller Davis drew up a chair and sat opposite Joyce.

'May I?' He said and pulled gently on the form. Joyce couldn't think why she was still holding onto it – it belonged with the others next to the map. She shook her head and chastised herself; it was unlike her to be so careless.

The Controller skimmed the details on the form, then held it up for Joyce to see. 'Is this your house, Miss Cooper?'

Joyce peered at the scrawled address and nodded.

'I'm so sorry, my dear,' Controller Davis said.

'Ta,' Joyce said in a clear, confident voice. 'But you needn't be. It's not correct.'

Gladys dragged over a small table and put down two cups of tea.

Controller Davis thanked her and turned back to Joyce. 'No, Miss Cooper. It's not incorrect. That rarely, if ever, happens.'

'Oh, I'm sure my house is no longer standing,' she said. 'I accept that. But there couldn't have been anyone inside. Mum goes to the underground every night and stays there. So, either this,' she pointed to the box on the form that trumpeted its terrible truth to the world, 'is wrong or the person killed was unknown to us. An intruder perhaps.' She made to get up, but the Controller put his hand on her arm and held her in place.

'I really do need to get back to the map,' she said and lowered her voice. 'You know what a mess it will be in no time at all if we leave Mrs Bertrand at it much longer.'

'I expect the all-clear in twenty minutes,' Controller Davis said. 'No real harm will come to the map in that period of time, none that you won't be able to sort out quickly at any rate.' He stood and looked down at her. 'I must get back and you must stay here.' He whispered something she couldn't hear to Gladys, then listed out of the room, taking the form with him.

Gladys came and touched Joyce's forehead, smoothing her hair when she was satisfied with her reading. Then she felt the pulse in her wrist and placed her hand with great care, as if it were made of glass, back on the arm of the chair. The older woman nestled a bowl on Joyce's lap and told her not to get up of her own volition. If she needed the lavatory, she was to ask for help. *What a lot of dither,* Joyce thought. *Hundreds upon hundreds have lost their homes.* She and Mum could stay with Nana or Auntie Cath. They could share a bed and talk late into the night about the things they'd lost – the one and only photo of Dad; the pregnant, bulging table; the new scarlet lipstick. She could hear Mum telling her that objects didn't matter – they had each other – and then together they'd slip easily into sleep, musing on that comforting thought.

She was cold. The skin on her arms felt clammy, but pools of sweat had gathered under her arms, at the back of her knees and rubbed against the waistband of her skirt. The walls tipped first one way and then the other and she had to clutch the bowl in her lap to steady herself. Of course the form was wrong, she knew that, but who could have been in their house? Could her brother have come home unexpectedly and used the key that Mum insisted he keep? If the 1K did pertain to Sid, Mum would be beside herself when she found out. Or perhaps someone could have seen Mum drop her key and then opened the door with it and rifled through their paltry belongings? Or used the house for shelter if they were frightened in the underground as so many people were? Mum hated the depths of the Tube, but she had promised Joyce... had sworn to her every night... The blockade slotted into place in her mind again. She tried to take a deep breath, but couldn't seem to inhale enough air. Around her, the urn and cups and biscuit tins and picture of the King on the wall were all in their rightful places and yet they stood out in sharp relief as if under the beam of a searchlight.

For a moment she closed her eyes but forced them open again when faced with an image of the form carved in stone in front of her. Joyce had lost all track of time, but was astonished to hear the sound of the all-clear. This time, it didn't bring a flood of relief as it usually did, but a vague unsettling feeling that there was something much worse she was going to have to face. Something ruinous and lamentable and woeful that would make a night of the Blitz seem like a walk in Hyde Park.

She wanted to get up and look at the map; she wanted to say goodbye to her colleagues and make her way home; she wanted to take note of the overnight bomb damage and admire May flowers and the light of dawn. She wanted to see Mum, hear her calling out, 'Hello, Joy love,' and smell toast and tea for breakfast.

But when she tried to stand, her arms would not lever her from the chair and she found that her legs were not made of bone and muscle. 'Gladys,' she called. 'Gladys, can I please go back to the map?'

No one replied, but there was a commotion in the main room and then Derek was kneeling next to her. He took both her hands in his and said over and over again that she'd had a terrible shock and that he was with her now and everything would be alright. It was lovely, but she didn't believe him.

Nodding, she allowed him to help her on with her coat and lead her towards the stairs. 'What about my map?' she asked.

Derek shook his head. 'The map can wait.'

When they stepped outside, Joyce could see an ambulance waiting in the misty rain. Derek guided her towards it but she held back, frightened that she was being taken to hospital for no reason she could discern. Derek shook his head. 'We're going to your Nana's house,' he said. 'It's too far for you to walk in your present state.'

She refused to lie down on a stretcher, but allowed herself to be strapped into a seat, Derek next to her. She couldn't understand why she was sweating but felt so shivery. Derek held her close and each time she looked up at him, he tried to bring his crooked smile into position, but was defeated at every attempt. Joyce was glad the windows were covered – she didn't need to see outside to know that the night had been one of the worst.

By the time they reached Nana's house, Derek had to support Joyce's every move through the narrow hallway and into the living room, so similar to the layout in Mum's house – their house. For the last few steps, Derek had to gather Joyce in his arms and carry her, no heavier to him than a spring fledgling fallen from its nest. Auntie Cath and Uncle Terry jumped up and smoothed the cushions for her. She heard one violent snivel from Flo and then the room was quiet.

Joyce looked at the mantelpiece; the coal scuttle; the newspaper next to Granddad's chair; the blackouts covering the windows despite the all-clear; the teapot; Nana's mending box; Flo, Derek, Auntie Cath, Uncle Terry, her grandparents. All of it so right and in its place, but with something missing which made it feel terribly wrong. 'Where's Mum?' she asked.

There was a pause and no one said a word. Then Uncle Terry and Granddad averted their eyes and Nana, Auntie Cath and Flo started to cry, tears running down their faces. They all turned to Derek who was kneeling on the floor next to Joyce, holding her hands; he shook his head.

Auntie Cath sat on the edge of the settee, took Joyce's

hands from Derek's hold and stroked them. When her wracking sobs died down to a shudder, she explained that Mum had left the underground half an hour before dawn as she'd been worried about some food she'd left out and uncovered – something she'd planned for breakfast.

Joyce could not believe what she was hearing. Anger forced its way past her dizziness and disbelief; she struggled to sit up. 'And you let her go?' she shouted, staring at each of them in turn, accusing them of duplicity. 'For a bit of bread or bacon or butter or milk?'

'Joy love,' Nana said. 'She wouldn't listen to any of us.'

'You know what she was like,' Flo added.

They all started to talk at once, their voices getting higher and louder as they tried to give their version of events. Joyce closed her eyes against the diatribe and felt the twist of a knife under her ribs, making it hard to breathe. The bit of food that Mum was worried about had been, she knew, for her. *Oh Mum,* she moaned to herself, *it wasn't worth it. I'm not worth it.*

For some reason, Joyce felt desperate to keep an aura of dignity and decorum, she tried to lie still and keep her tears in check. Then an overwhelming sense of how ridiculous she was swept over her and she wept hot, angry tears that soaked the lapels of Derek's blue serge tunic.

He patted her back, wiped her eyes, pushed the sodden hair from her face. But nothing he did forced the powdery butterfly wings to float up from where they lay, as heavy as a mound of rubble in the hollow of her stomach.

NINE

Hamlet House looked unremarkably similar to Cordelia Court and Macbeth Mansions, two other blocks of white, concrete flats with doors stained in primary colours that Mr Taylor had previously dragged her around. They walked from the street along a paved path, flanked on either side by imma-ture bushes and plants in freshly dug beds. Sunken lights were embedded at the edge of every third paving slab and Mr Taylor took great pains to explain that they were timed to come on at dusk, so residents could find their way home in the dark.

Joyce was not impressed; what could possibly astound her after that tour of London in an open-topped Spitfire Triumph? Not a box of residences named after one of Shake-speare's tragic heroes, that was for sure. Besides, for all his cosmopolitan manners and sophisticated people skills and contemplative nodding of his head while he listened to her, he really had no idea about how astute she was at getting around in Stygian darkness – how did he think she'd managed in the blackout?

Mr Taylor unzipped a small, brown leather folder and took out three brochures, each the mirror image of ones he'd given her on previous occasions and that she'd tossed in the bin at the first opportunity. 'These are the ones we're going to view today, Miss Cooper,' he said, pressing the papers towards her hand. 'One is on the ground floor, another on the first floor and the last on the top floor.'

'Mr Taylor,' Joyce said. It seemed now as if the adrenaline the jolly in the car had produced was seeping from her and she felt drained of energy. 'There is no need, really. Once I saw one brochure and one flat, I saw them all.'

'You must take them,' Mr Taylor said. 'You might want to refer to them later. And,' he continued, his tone slightly defensive, 'I know they look identical, but there are variations that might sway you one way or another.'

Joyce didn't want to appear rude so she took the brochures, folded them and stowed them in her handbag.

'This way, Miss Cooper,' Mr Taylor said, touching her elbow and guiding her towards the concrete monument to gentrification. Already a skewed crack ran diagonally across one of the paving slabs and soft plops of water from a down-pipe painted a yellow stain on the white exterior of the building. But Mr Taylor didn't mention those flaws or the hillock of bikes and buggies and washing baskets outside Malvolio Maisonettes, a larger, taller, noisier concrete block that housed young families across a patch of green from Hamlet House. Instead, he was forthcoming with his usual spiel about the double glazing and the boilers and the neat, clean lino on the floors. 'And don't forget,' he said, looking beyond pleased with himself, 'that the ground floor flats all have a garden. Even numbers have a garden at the front, odds at the back. I know you like a spot of gardening.' He smiled at her. 'I've seen your lovely efforts.'

A few small tubs positioned to get what little sun made it past the walls of the surrounding houses in Talbot Road could hardly be called gardening, she thought.

They arrived at a red door that was recessed back from the path. Next to it and jutting out so it seemed to be growing towards the walkway, was a shoulder-high white stone wall surrounding the garden next door. Whoever lived there could truly be called a gardener – not a putterer, like Joyce. Mr Taylor peered over the bulwark and Joyce stood on tiptoes to do the same. Hanging baskets filled with deep maroon cyclamen and purple and yellow pansies hung in lush layers from every corner of the space; a yellow and white honeysuckle filled the air with a sweet scent; a Christmas rose trailed up a trellis; there were pink Daphnes and bright aconites and mauve heathers in pots. Snowdrops danced across the rectangle of lawn, daffodils and tulips pushed their way up to join them through the blades of grass. Mr Taylor looked as pleased with the garden as if he had nurtured it himself. He breathed in through flared nostrils and said, 'See what wonders can be done with a small space. The garden in the house we're buying in Potters Bar is a blank slate, so we're going to ask Mr Norris,' Mr Taylor nodded to the backdoor of the flat, 'to give us some advice.'

'Lovely,' Joyce said, thinking about how difficult it would be to live next door to Mr Norris and have a scrubby, spartan, failing garden like the one she would inevitably produce or, worse still, have him poking his head round every five minutes with helpful hints.

Joyce lowered herself off her toes and crabbed the two

steps towards the red door. Mr Taylor followed her, produced a key from a large ring and unlocked the door not a minute too soon – Mr Norris's flat opened and Joyce heard the repetitive bars of that annoying song, 'Chirpy Chirpy Cheep Cheep' emanating on a loud, clear whistle. 'Oh,' Mr Taylor said. 'There's Mr Norris, it would be nice to introduce you as you might well be neighbours.'

Joyce couldn't think of anything less nice and waved away the idea. She checked her wristwatch to give the impression that there might be somewhere she had to be or something she urgently had to attend to. Stepping over the threshold, she waited in the narrow off-white hallway for Mr Taylor while he exchanged a few hurried words with Mr Norris.

When he re-appeared, apologising for keeping her waiting, Joyce began to open doors and peer into cupboards and turn light switches on and off. Mr Taylor followed her around, lauding the merits of the magnolia paint throughout, the integral flush on the toilet, the space on the kitchen counters. 'Look, Miss Cooper, at this.' He opened a drawer next to the sink and stood back for her to admire the interior. 'No need to bother with wooden cutlery boxes, there are compartments built right into the space.'

Joyce nodded and said she thought it a very handy addition to any kitchen. Marching ahead of him, she stuck her head around first one bedroom door then the other, bemused as to why she had been offered two-bedroom accommodation when there was no possibility of her ever having company to stay the night. When she mentioned that fact Mr Taylor shrugged and said, 'No singles were built.'

'And that's the thing, Mr Taylor.' Joyce stood in the middle of the small room that was described on paper as a living/dining room. 'They're all the same. Boxes within boxes within a larger box. There's no... I don't know... soul to them. Or depth.'

For a minute Mr Taylor looked defeated. 'That's the way all homes are built now. It's inexpensive. It gets people housed. Our new build is very similar to this, except the door cupboards will be teak. And that will be the same in all the houses on what will be our estate.'

'I think that's a great pity,' Joyce said.

Mr Taylor's bright, sparkling eyes looked at her with straightforward candour. 'So do I,' he said softly. 'But that's the position we're in. That's progress. And you have to bring your own depth to a place. Fill it with your own soul.'

Joyce wondered why she'd ever thought that Mr Taylor didn't listen to her when she talked. If she wasn't careful, tears would fill her eyes and the next thing would be Mr Taylor offering up his handkerchief and feeling sorry for her and she couldn't have that. 'I am trying hard, believe it or not, to imagine how I would go about that.'

Then Mr Taylor beamed again and said, 'I do wish you'd let me introduce you to Mr Norris. He'd gladly show you what he's achieved in his flat. He's put his stamp on the place as indelibly as he's done in the garden.'

But Joyce shook her head; if his choice of songs was anything to go by, she dreaded to see his taste in interior design.

'Perhaps another time,' Mr Taylor said to which Joyce made no comment.

Producing the ring of keys again, Mr Taylor unlocked the red back door and they stepped out into the garden of the flat. Inside the oblong space, there was a plot of loamy dirt surrounded by a slab walkway. The earth was rich and perfect for planting, like the soil she'd seen years ago in Norfolk.

'Miss Cooper?' Mr Taylor was talking to her. 'Do you want to have another look round?'

'No, ta,' she said. 'I've seen enough.'

'Well then, we shall proceed upwards.' Mr Taylor pointed to the identical abodes balanced on top of the one they'd just viewed.

Joyce opened the red gate with a click and there, coming out of his blue front door was Mr Norris, whistling the same sugary pop tune through puckered lips. This time there was no escape and Joyce's impeccable manners would not allow her to do anything but stand, with decorum, and allow herself to be introduced.

Mr Norris held out his calloused hand, which was undoubtedly scrubbed clean, but had the tell-tale earth of a gardener ingrained under the nails. When she returned the gesture, his hand was dry and his grip solid. His sideburns were long and grey and when he doffed his trilby, the hair on his head was sparse. He was in his sixties, but was wearing flared jeans, a maroon shirt with spiky lapels that matched Mr Taylor's and on his right middle finger he sported a ring in the shape of a serpent's head.

'How do you do,' Joyce said.

'Pleased to meet you, Miss Cooper,' Mr Norris replied, smiling generously. 'I see we may well be neighbours.' He enunciated each letter in every word, but still managed to sound like an amiable everyman or a hail fellow well met.

'Possibly,' Joyce said, not wanting to commit herself.

'Miss Cooper has three to choose from,' Mr Taylor added. 'All in this block.'

Mr Norris broadened his smile. 'Then we shall definitely be living in close proximity,' he said.

Joyce felt her low spirits move closer to despair. If Mr

Norris thought that living near him was in any way enticing her to feel enthusiastic about the prospect of moving to Hamlet House, he had the wrong end of the stick.

'I shall look forward to it,' he said, doffing his hat again. Then he turned to Mr Taylor and said something about not being able to hang about as he had a meet a few friends in the pub for a game of whist.

'This way now, Miss Cooper.' Mr Taylor led the way to the central staircase and up to the first floor. On the way, he regaled Joyce with the many hobbies, clubs and pursuits that Mr Norris was either involved in or was planning to organise or was soon to join. 'Oh yes,' Mr Taylor said, 'he's started a reading group, a monthly film night, outings to Southend, the MIA club, a walking group and he's taking a night class to learn Esperanto. Quite a lively character. There's so much for you to join in with around here.'

Joyce could feel the skin on her face sag with the thought of that. But she said, 'What on earth is an MIA Club?'

'It stands for Missing in Action.'

'I thought that much,' Joyce said. 'But how can that be a friendly hobby?'

'It's very interesting,' Mr Taylor said. 'Someone said they couldn't find the whereabouts of an old friend who'd moved to Canada right after the war so Mr Norris did a lot of research and got them back in touch. Remarkable. Now he's in the process of helping a few others to find relatives and friends.'

Joyce's thoughts immediately turned to Flo and then to Hettie, but she wouldn't allow a flicker of interest to cross her face.

'Of course,' he carried on. 'You don't have to join in anything if you don't want to. You can keep yourself to yourself if you prefer.'

They walked past a green door and stopped outside one painted yellow; number 6B. Inside, they followed the same course around the flat, except this time there was a balcony instead of a garden at the back and Mr Taylor sung the praises of being able to fill it with pots, baskets and perhaps a small table and a couple of chairs. Joyce felt the urge to remind him that she would not have the need for two seats, but she couldn't muster the energy.

Between each balcony there was a barrier fashioned from the same white stone that surrounded the ground floor gardens which gave the illusion of privacy and solitude. But although they served their purpose by blotting out any visual reminder of the inhabitants of numbers 5 and 7B, they were certainly not soundproof. From the left, Joyce could hear a man reading aloud from a newspaper about Rolls Royce declaring bankruptcy and being nationalised. A woman's voice, bored and resigned, interjected with grunts that sounded as if she were half-listening. And emanating from the other side, she heard the clashing cacophony of pots and pans being yanked out of a cupboard and soon, no doubt, the smell of bacon or chicken, cauliflower and potatoes would not be far behind.

Joyce sighed, but didn't need to say a word to Mr Taylor about how distasteful she found these surroundings – he was astute enough to pick up on that without any help from her. He looked embarrassed and fidgeted with the chain around his neck, adjusting it so it fell into the hollow of his throat. 'Onwards and upwards?' he ventured.

The final dwelling was behind a green door, tucked right up in the corner of the top floor. The layout inside was the same as the others apart from a few tweaks that Joyce knew she would forget by the time she got home. 'Each flat has its advantages,' Mr Taylor said in his best salesman's voice. 'The ground floor has a garden, the one on the first floor has two immediate neighbours and this one, a lone companion to your right. In other words, it's semi-detached. He laughed at his own silly joke and Joyce smiled at him for trying. Standing on the balcony, she couldn't hear a sound from whoever lived next door. Of course, he or she might have been out, but Joyce thought the peace and calm a good omen.

'I believe,' Mr Taylor said. 'That Mr Frenchay next door is quiet and contained.'

Propping her forearms on the balcony railings, Joyce surveyed the scene beneath her. A few people were walking along the designated paths; a man was guiding a child riding a three-wheeled bicycle; birds flew from tree to tree; a cat prowled towards a hedge. In the distance she could see smoke from chimneys, rooftops, the patterns of parks and green spaces, red buses and a couple of lofty cranes.

Mr Taylor joined her and together, without saying a word, they viewed Notting Hill from a height – Joyce's second new perspective of her world that day. 'How odd,' she said, talking as much to the vista as to the young man next to her. 'I've spent so many years looking up and now this,' she said, sweeping her hand through the air.

'Do you mean because you're so tiny in stature?' Mr Taylor asked.

Joyce laughed out loud, as she'd done in the car and decided she felt better for it. 'Well,' she said, 'that is so, but not what I meant. I've spent so long living in a basement, gazing up at passing feet and wheels on buggies and bikes and the bottoms of trousers and skirts, that looking down is a novelty.'

'Oh, I see,' Mr Taylor said. 'Of course.' And he stood up a

bit taller with what Joyce supposed was optimism that she might be about to succumb to her unavoidable fate.

'Mr Taylor.' Joyce turned to face him. 'Is it absolutely true that I must decide on one of these today?'

'Yes.' He nodded. 'There are no other flats I can offer you and if you don't accept one of these, it will, nevertheless, be compulsory for you to vacate Talbot Road in two weeks' time. Where you move to then...' Mr Taylor let his arms flop to his sides in a gesture of helplessness, 'would be up to you or the Emergency Housing Department.'

Something as hard and immobile as the concrete surroundings rose up in Joyce. She didn't like the ultimatum, but she'd been in similar situations before in her life when there were no other choices but to get on with it and that, she understood, was what was required of her now. In a small, soft voice she said, 'Then I'll say yes to this one.'

'Miss Cooper,' Mr Taylor turned to her, pale and unbelieving, 'can you say that again? I didn't quite catch it.'

'I'll take it. This one,' Joyce repeated.

Mr Taylor held her elbow and bundled her back into the flat. On a worktop, he opened his folder and spread out a contract. When he passed her a ballpoint pen, his hand was jittery. 'I'll use my own, thank you,' she said and took the Taperite from her handbag.

Watching her sign her name on the appropriate line, Mr Taylor beamed. 'Miss Cooper,' he said, 'welcome to 8C Hamlet House.' And her spirits plummeted again.

TEN

DEREK

July 1941

Two days after Mum was taken from them, Auntie Cath and Flo wanted to see the damage for themselves, saying they couldn't rest until they'd searched for any trace of their beloved Maggie, and Joyce insisted on going with them. Arm in arm, they clung to each other as they combed every inch of land the house had stood on. From time to time one of them veered off towards where the outdoor privy or the front porch or the back door had been, think their own thoughts, kick around in the mire and then walk back to join the others.

The neighbours on either side were doing the same on what had been their own patches of ground. They commiserated with each other over the invisible barrier where their fences had stood, but none of them intruded into each other's annihilated gardens. Both sides said how cruel it was that after they'd been attacked, there had been one last night of horrendous bombing and then the Blitz seemed to come to an abrupt end – Hitler had sent his manpower to the Eastern Front. 'One more night,' they said, 'if only Maggie could have held on for one more hour that morning, then one more night, she would have been here with the rest of us.'

Joyce gritted her teeth and let Auntie Cath take the lead in the monotonous, repetitive conversation, but inwardly she boiled with hot resentment. Of course, she knew Mum shouldn't have left the underground before the all-clear, but this wasn't Mum's fault and Joyce could not and would not hold her dear, loving, fussing and somewhat scatty mother to account. That would have been missing the point about where to point the finger of blame.

Politely, she took her leave and turned back to her hunt for a precious, comforting reminder of Mum to take away with her. There'd been a blue brooch that had belonged to Dad's mother; a tortoiseshell hair comb; the ticket stub of a day trip to Brighton; that one photo of Dad – all things she knew Mum had held dear, taken care of and squirreled away. She kicked through a pile of rubble, picked over a few bricks, wrung out more tears from what she thought was a dry well. She couldn't look at the neighbours knowing fresh blood was racing through their veins, their hearts pumping, their mouths moving, their stomachs rumbling, their hair, nails, eyebrows and lashes growing. If they were lucky, they would grow old and if they weren't, they had today and Mum had been robbed of that in the most definitive way possible. As they turned their backs and left the bombsite, Joyce realised with a terrible, frightening twist in her stomach that it would be easy for her to find another home, but Mum would and could never be replaced.

That evening, Joyce wanted to return to work but with

one voice Derek, Flo, Auntie Cath and Uncle Terry forbade her.

'You don't understand,' Joyce heard herself whine. 'Mrs Bertrand will ruin the map. It took me months to get it right and now that she's been let loose on it, I'll have to spend hours to get it straight again.'

'I don't think so, my girl,' Granddad said, his voice more croaky than usual.

Then they all chipped in.

'Joyce, my love, you stay right where you are.'

'You can't, Joy, you've had a terrible shock.'

Derek put his arm around her and eased her back onto the settee next to him.

Still she insisted until Auntie Cath told her, in no uncertain terms, that it was considered the height of rudeness to go about one's usual business until after the arrangements had been carried out. Of course Joyce knew that, but she'd forced it to the back of her mind. She felt mortified when she was reminded, but nodded her acquiescence and gave in to her grief, allowing the waves of disbelief and sadness and anger to engulf her.

During Mum's service, Joyce felt as if she were looking down on the proceedings as they were happening to someone else. Her knees trembled and her lips were numb and rubbery as she mouthed the prayers. Derek's hand under her elbow or around her waist was a comfort, but tears spilled from her eyes at the thought that for her, there was no comfort like that her mum had given her and she would never experience that again.

But somehow, they all managed to get through the day with dignity. Joyce stood above the mass grave, a bunch of stock poised to throw on top of the dust and dirt. All that held her back when a surge of panic threatened to push her into the hole to join Mum, was Derek holding the sleeve of her coat to steady her. She let go of the fragrant bouquet and watched the pale, fragile blooms dip towards the earth. Sid had sent money for a headstone which she would take him to see when he next came home.

The whole family spent the following day sardined together in Nana and Granddad's house, during which there was a bit of a tussle about who Joyce would live with. Their voices seemed to have a muffled edge to them, but were blaring at the same time. In her mind, Joyce covered her ears and screamed until they stopped.

But they went on and on or at least that seemed to be the case to Joyce.

'If Joy came to live with us,' Uncle Terry said, 'she'd be closer to work.'

'That's true,' Auntie Cath agreed. 'And she could bunk up with Flo.'

'That would be lovely,' Flo said. 'Wouldn't it, Joy love?'

Joyce nodded and thought it would probably be the best outcome under the circumstances. But she wouldn't describe sleeping anywhere or with anyone, other than her own bed in her own house with her own mum, as lovely. And that included Derek.

Eventually Nana said, 'We would love to have our Joy here. After all, she's been to this house almost every single day since she was born so really, it's like her second home.'

'And I suppose,' Auntie Cath said. 'Joy could give you and Granddad a hand, too.' She turned to Joyce. 'What do you think, Joy love?'

Joyce nodded, so they set about moving furniture, airing bed linen and towels and turning Nana's old front room into her new bedroom. They couldn't do enough for her and started immediately to refer to their house as her home.

Then she joined the hundreds of thousands of others who had to get back to their daily routines which were the same as they had been, but also changed beyond recognition.

* * *

'Senior Warden Cooper,' Controller Davis greeted her with warmth on her first day back at her post. 'It's lovely to see you back at your map.'

'Thank you, Sir,' she said. 'I'm glad to be here.'

He shook her hand and pressed it for a few minutes in his, but he'd already offered his condolences, as they all had, so nothing else was said on the matter of her loss. It was, from then on, business as usual.

As she'd feared, the map was a mess but less so than she had imagined. With Hitler busy elsewhere, the bombs were not as frequent so there were fewer pins to re-arrange.

'This whole area,' the Controller swept his hand above the road she and Mum had lived on and those surrounding it, 'has been completely wiped out.'

Joyce nodded. She was all too aware of that.

'But,' Controller Davis lowered his voice even though Mrs Bertrand wouldn't have heard, 'as you can see, there's only one black pin that's been placed in the middle to signify all the damage.' He sighed. 'That won't do.'

'No, of course not,' Joyce said. 'There wasn't just one ARPM1 was there?'

By way of reply, Controller Davis sighed and handed her a wad of forms. 'No, there was one for each hit, but Mrs Bertrand thought one pin and label would suffice.'

Joyce felt a giggle begin to bubble, but guilt caused an uncomfortable lump to take its place and she forced the laughter back down. 'You'd need a huge black knife to symbolise that amount of devastation in one go.'

'My thoughts exactly,' the Controller said. 'So, your first job is before you.'

'Understood,' Joyce picked up a form and placed her box of pins within easy reach.

Controller Davis stood next to her in companionable silence for a few moments, then before hobbling back to his desk he touched her sleeve and told her to let him know if it got too much. But it didn't. She worked her way through the ARPM1s and when she got to the one that told the story of her house and Mum, she drew back her shoulders, stuck in the pin with steely determination and moved on.

Life with Nana and Granddad took on some semblance of normality, although it was hard to get used to her bed that faced a window rather than a wall as it had done in Mum's house. The bedclothes, too, smelled slightly musty and they wrapped themselves around her arms and ankles when she couldn't sleep. Mum had always had strawberry jam and Nana liked raspberry. She and Mum had enjoyed their fish fried, when they could get a bit and Nana and Granddad liked theirs steamed. And when Joyce came in from work, she wasn't met with a waft of breakfast cooking, but instead put on the kettle and prepared the meal for her grandparents. They were inconsequential things she knew, things that should have been too pathetic for her to even think about. But it was those

small, everyday variations that made her life seem so monu-
mentally different.

Other aspects of life resumed, too. Derek loved Madame
Beaupre's Dance Studio and they often attended a lesson on
their days off, with or without Flo. They were competent at
the Foxtrot and the Jive, which made them laugh, but the
Waltz was taking a bit longer.

'Have you been to any dances yet?' Madame Beaupre
asked, breathless after a spin around the floor with Derek.
'You must as you are both improving with every lesson.'

'No, not yet,' Joyce replied.

'How about a tea dance, if you can't manage the evenings?'
Monsieur Beaupre asked. 'They're very accommodating for
people who work unsociable hours.'

'But, Monsieur Derek,' Madame Beaupre said, 'you will
have your work cut out for you what with Mademoiselle Joyce
on one arm and Mademoiselle Flo on the other.'

Derek cuddled close to Joyce's back, bent down and
circled his arms around her waist. 'I'm sure Flo won't have any
trouble getting a full dance card and as for Mademoiselle
Joyce, she's not dancing with anyone but me.' Derek held her
so close that she felt his warm, moist breath on her neck and
smelt his faint, lemony scent. For one fraction of a moment,
she felt happy and cocooned and radiant.

She thought a lot about Derek when they were apart and
she was happy with the way he'd been a solid, unshakeable
buttress through her dark, dismal days. They walked and went
to the pub and the pictures and the frantic half hours they
spent pawing at each other in secluded alleyways and on
hidden park benches took on a new intensity, as if they didn't
have a minute of life to spare.

In a different time, Joyce might have batted away Derek's

wandering hands and tongue that found their way beneath her undergarments with ever-increasing frequency. But now, having witnessed and experienced the fragility of life first-hand, she welcomed his advances. Well, apart from when she was anxious that he hadn't declared himself to her with a firm promise or when she was worried about still not having met his mother or sister.

When things settled back into something of a regular pattern, Joyce began to rehearse in her mind the many different ways she could approach the subject of his family with Derek, but each string of sentences reverberated with clumsiness or offence.

Walking through Hyde Park one afternoon, she at last decided that the only way to begin was to start. 'Derek.' She turned to him. 'Tell me about your mum. And your sister, of course.'

Derek removed his arm from around her shoulder and shoved his hands in his pockets. He stared down at his feet and seemed to shrink into himself. 'My mother? Celia?'

'That's all I really know, that you call your mother Celia instead of mum and your father Edgar, not dad.'

'Yes,' Derek nodded. 'We had fun with Edgar, from time to time. But he was busy with work and when he was at home he took his lead from Celia.' He seemed to soften and wound his arm around her again. 'He had pet names for us – I was Mustard and Cressida was...'

'Cress!' Joyce was happy to hear that anecdote.

'That's right,' Derek said. 'We thought it very clever.'

'And endearing.'

Derek thought for a few moments. He gazed down at the path again as if everything he couldn't say was written there.

'You hardly ever mention Celia or what your childhood was like,' Joyce prompted. 'It's very puzzling.'

'Celia,' he said, 'is not like your mum was and my childhood did not resemble yours.'

'Oh, Derek.' Joyce was acutely aware of the pain behind her lovely boyfriend's stoic statement. She guided him towards a bench overlooking the Serpentine and they sat down. Leaning close to him, she breathed in the smell of the citrus soap he used. 'Tell me?' she coaxed.

After a beat, Derek nodded and said, 'There's not much to tell, really. Or at least I don't know how to tell it. There was no cruelty, or not much, anyway... Just a... I don't know. Lack of warmth, I suppose. And a great many expectations. She didn't believe in spoiling children to the extent that she never cuddled us or praised us or showed any leeway when it came to us creating a mess or crying or feeling upset and hurt. So,' he shrugged, 'we tried not to. But when we didn't live up to her vision of perfection. Whack!' He pulled his hand back and swiped through the air with all his strength as if he were meeting a startled target.

Joyce couldn't imagine never getting cuddles and kindness and plaudits from Mum and being on the receiving end of a smack or a slap instead. Mum, who had been effusive in her endearments to the point of embarrassment. Although how Joyce longed to be embarrassed by Mum all over again. 'That must have been awful,' she said.

'We didn't know any better then.' Derek shrugged. 'But I do now and I try to be different. I want to feel and have empathy with others. Cress, though, can come across as haughty and I know she finds being affectionate to her own children difficult, especially in Celia's presence. And they're together all the time at the moment.'

He looked and sounded pitifully lost and Joyce's heart went out to him, a grown man with a responsible war job reduced to looking at his feet and rounding his shoulders in order to talk about his family. She wished then she hadn't raised the topic and said so.

'No, Joyce,' Derek said. 'You have every right to ask, and I should have been more forthcoming with you. But it's difficult and a bit shameful to explain to someone like you, who comes from a completely different kind of family.'

'Just because your people aren't like mine, doesn't necessarily mean one is right and the other is wrong,' Joyce tried to be fair. 'And you're not a bit like them.'

They sat so close that Joyce could feel Derek's lean, sinewy arms and legs pressed against her. Two small children ran towards the water with mouldy crusts of bread in their hands for the ducks, two women bustling after them and grabbing at their jumpers to keep them safe. One of the tots crammed a lump of bread in his mouth before his mother could stop him and Joyce and Derek burst into laughter, glad to have a distraction.

Then Derek's mood darkened again. 'Celia would never have tolerated that sort of behaviour,' he said. 'Even at that age. It was all about her damned impossible expectations,' he said, with venom in his voice. 'And how we were viewed by everyone else. Manners, studying, exercise, the structure of the day, who we spent time with, what we read, how we laughed.' He spat out the words as if they tasted of the green, fuzzy blight on the children's bread. 'Every minute was accounted for, every slight deviation from her strict orthodoxy questioned.'

Joyce sat and listened, not daring to interrupt now Derek was in full flow. But she was alarmed at the anger he felt towards his mother. 'Is that why you became an accountant, because your mother wanted you to follow in Edgar's footsteps?'

'Yes,' he said. 'Although I don't know what else I would have done as I was never given the opportunity to think about alternatives.'

'But you're high up in the Civil Defence and you live miles from Celia,' she said, nestling closer to him and caressing the lapels of his jacket. 'And you have me. You're free now.'

'Not quite,' Joyce heard Derek mumble under his breath. Then he turned, a grin on his face again as if he thought that was the end of the matter.

But Joyce couldn't let it finish there. 'What do you mean by not quite?' she asked.

The smile fell from his handsome face as quickly as one of Hitler's bombs dropped from the sky and his eyes, trained on the ground, were hidden behind shadows. 'There are other things to consider,' he said at last. 'Things to do with... inheritance and matters like that. Things I've presumed will be rightly mine in time.'

A horrible thought hit Joyce like a ton of bricks from a collapsing building. 'Oh.' She jumped up from the bench and backed away from him. 'So you have expectations of your own when it comes to the future. Is that why you haven't introduced me to your mother? Or even told her about me for that matter.'

Derek stood and faced Joyce, furrows deepening along his forehead and around his mouth. 'Joyce. My love.' He opened his arms to her, but she shook her head with a vengeance.

'Money.' Joyce said. 'That's what you're talking about, aren't you?'

Derek didn't answer.

'Aren't you?' She challenged him again, her voice shrill to her ears. 'At least now I know where I stand in your eyes. And that's behind your inheritance.'

'Joy!' Derek pleaded. 'It's not like that, Joyce. Please sit down and let me explain.'

They stood and stared at each other, Derek beckoning her closer, his hands waving gently.

Joyce felt insulted and in her mind she walked away, but Derek's pale, stricken face and the butterflies she'd felt so often when she was with him or thought about him, pulled her back. She plonked herself down on the opposite end of the bench to where he sat, her coat drawn tightly around her. Determined not to let him dive into an explanation first, she began before he could start. 'If your first consideration is money,' she said, 'I'm not sure we're right for each other.'

'It's not just about the money,' Derek said.

'In our family, family always come first. Taking care of each other. Sharing what little we have.'

'And they're my priorities, too,' Derek said. 'But try to understand. There are certain ways of living that I became accustomed to before the war, at any rate, that I would like to be able to provide for my own family in time.' He reached over, squeezed her hand and ducked to try to make eye contact with her. 'Our family, I hope.'

That made Joyce dart a look in Derek's direction. He smiled shyly and his face brightened, but Joyce could feel hers darken.

They were quiet for a few moments and Joyce felt Derek clench her hand tighter.

'But are you telling me that because I come from a different kind of family your association with me might stop you from acquiring your inheritance?'

'I'm saying nothing of the sort.' Derek was quick to defend himself. 'And I have written to them about you. I've told them you're the kindest, most beautiful, most thoughtful girl I've ever met and I went on to describe you as loving and caring and hard-working and trustworthy.'

Joyce was grateful there wasn't a swarm of flies buzzing past or they would have become trapped in her mouth that hung wide and slack. She could not believe what she was hearing, but repeated it to herself to engrave it in her memory.

'And I haven't taken you to meet Celia and Cress yet because the opportunity hasn't arisen,' Derek said with an edge of huffiness to his voice. 'We've been a bit busy what with your mum and the war and our jobs.'

Guilt surfaced amongst the other emotions Joyce felt and she turned to Derek and mouthed sorry at the exact moment he said the same word to her. They threw their arms around each other and as Joyce buried her face in Derek's chest, he snuggled his into Joyce's hair.

'There are one or two minor things to sort out with my family,' Derek said. 'But you're right, I have you and for me, that's the most important consideration.' He drew away from her as far as was necessary for her to see how sincere he was. 'You do believe me, don't you?'

Of course she did and she told him so.

* * *

In July, Derek had two surprises for her. He met her as she ascended the steps into stark, steely daylight from Report and Control, flicking two tickets backwards and forwards in front of his dappy grin. 'Guess,' he said, leaning down to kiss her lightly.

THE WOMAN WITH THE MAP

'Are we going to the pictures?' she asked. She hoped it would be *Love on the Dole* starring Deborah Kerr and Clifford Evans – she'd wanted to see that for ages.

Derek shook his head. 'This is much more exciting.'

Joyce's eyes widened and she felt the press of exhaustion lift from her. 'Don't tease,' she said. 'Tell me.'

'Two tickets. That's one for you and one for me to the First Night of the Proms. At the Albert Hall.' He was in raptures.

She'd heard about the Proms; Derek had been a regular attendee until the original venue, Queen's Hall in Langham Place, had been destroyed by a blasted Jerry bomb. He had been bereft as he'd so been looking forward to taking her with him to marvel at the whole experience. He'd described how uplifting the lofty music made him feel; how wonderful it was to be squashed amongst other young people equally enthralled with the showmanship of the conductor, Sir Henry Wood, and the aptitude of the orchestra; the reverent yet vibrant atmosphere. They'd read in the paper that other concert halls were being considered, but Derek hadn't held out much hope for this year. Then a decision had been made about the Albert Hall and now he was beside himself with excitement about the tickets he held in his hand for the following Saturday.

The pale grey dress she borrowed from Flo went beautifully with her soft, navy jacket and the black patent shoes and when they met outside South Kensington Tube station, Derek bent double to pin a sprig of lilac to her collar that was so heady, she thought she might get drunk on the scent every time she inhaled. He kissed her lightly and when they drew apart, she noticed a tiny shaving scratch on his cheek. Skimming her finger across her lips, she transferred the touch to the sore spot on his face and he smiled down at her.

She loved *The Marriage of Figaro* and Beethoven's 'Symphony No 5 in C Minor' and felt transported away from the war, what had happened to Mum, the map, the debris, rationing and as if she were flying somewhere peaceful far, far away on the wings of Elsie Suddaby's soprano. There was no doubt that she would always remember the night.

Then Derek announced he was planning a week's leave to visit his mother in Norfolk and he asked her to go with him. Joyce was thrilled and arranged for the same time off. Their train tickets were booked for 8.00 in the morning and Joyce sat on the small bed in what had been Nana's front room, staring at the old, battered suitcase borrowed from Uncle Terry, empty except for a washcloth and a chip of coal tar soap in a small washbag.

Spread out around her was what was left of her personal possessions – her uniform and the one outfit she'd safely stowed away in the Control Centre after a dance class with Flo and Derek which consisted of a pale duck egg blue blouse, a black fitted skirt, the navy blue jacket, a few bits of costume jewellery and the black patent shoes Auntie Cath had given her. She'd had every intention of taking the clothes and shoes home, but when her shift had ended there was no home left to take them to.

Joyce looked at that one exonerated outfit laid out amongst the things she'd borrowed from Flo. She caressed the raised blue and pink embroidery on the collar of a soft grey blouse, then let it fall back into position next to a brown skirt. Flo didn't have many clothes either, none of them did and whilst Joyce was grateful to her cousin for sharing with her, most of the garments were too long or too loose around her waist and hips. Auntie Cath and Nana had rummaged through a number of bags at the Women's Voluntary Service and found a few bits and pieces they thought might do; some of them did and some of them didn't but she wore them anyway as there was nothing else. It had taken ages to replace the ration books that had been lost, too and when she did receive her clothing coupons, she'd used them to buy much needed undergarments.

A deep, involuntary sigh forced its way up from her lungs, past her mouth and into the warm air of the room. That happened often, but the doctor said not to worry, it was a natural part of bereavement. That and the tears and the hoarse voice and the episodes when she stared into space. She heard Mum's voice too, calling her Joy love in the middle of the night and felt her hand on her arm or stroking her hair, but she only mentioned those episodes to Derek and Flo, frightened that the doctor would think she was going mad.

Standing, Joyce looked out of the window onto the road. A few passers-by hurried with umbrellas over their heads or the collars of their macs turned up against the summer weather that had been anything but seasonal. Instead of the long, sunny days and balmy evenings they all longed for, they had been served grey skies, thunderstorms, cold winds and a steady stream of lukewarm rain. She turned and surveyed again the sum total of her scant belongings and decided that what she would need more than anything were clothes to keep her warm.

She would have to start making decisions as she had one hour left before she had to start her last shift for a week. Underclothes of course would be needed. Opening a small wardrobe that had been nudged into the corner, she rummaged on the top shelf and brought down her spare brassiere, vest, knickers, hosiery and suspender belt; she was wearing the other set so that saved space. Into the washbag went a comb, toothbrush and the new make-up Flo had convinced her to buy – rouge, a block of mascara and lipstick in a slightly darker red than the one she'd shared with Mum. She'd dearly wanted a small bottle of rosewater or lily of the valley scent, but her money wouldn't stretch to it, so she made do with a sachet of crushed lavender that she nuzzled in between the folds of her underwear.

Her momentum fired into a frenzy and she threw in a tatty Fair Isle jumper, a pair of houndstooth trousers, a grey cardigan and a royal blue velvet dress so old that the nap was worn around the backside. *There,* she thought, *that should do it.* The only other things she would need were a coat, which she would wear and a nightie.

Then she didn't feel quite so sure. Perhaps she should reconsider the embroidered duck egg blue blouse or the dark green midcalf dress with short, puffed sleeves and what about the navy jacket?

There was a tap at the door followed by a yoo-hoo from Flo. 'I've come to see you off,' she said. 'Being as I won't be up in time to wave you goodbye from the platform.' She looked into the suitcase and grimaced. 'What's all that?'

'Oh, Flo.' Joyce bumped down on the bed. 'I don't want to complain. Or sound ungrateful. But nothing fits. None of it matches. And what do people wear in Norfolk?'

Flo tilted her head back and laughed, her soft, silky hair falling down her back and her chest jiggling with delight. 'Whatever they can get their hands on, I suppose,' she said. 'Like the rest of us. Come on, let's have another look.' She kneeled down next to the suitcase and flung everything onto the floor. Then she arranged outfits on the bed that Joyce could mix and match during the week.

'I'll need to be warm,' Joyce said.

'Yes, you will. So pop in your gloves and a scarf.' Flo answered. 'And you'll also need some glamorous changes for the evening.'

The idea hadn't occurred to Joyce that she might be on show for dinners and gatherings. 'Do you think so?' she asked. 'In the middle of nowhere?' She scanned her belongings again and couldn't see one sophisticated or elegant outfit amongst them.

Flo picked up a few things, scrutinised them, then let them droop back down as if touching them would taint her. 'I think you might have to feign a headache if a supper party is announced.'

'I might get away with that once, but I couldn't keep ducking out.'

'Alright,' Flo said, her eyes narrow and serious. 'How about these?' She picked up a bronze coloured blouse, paired it with a brown skirt and carried them to the light from the window. Together they did look rather striking. 'You could pin that golden peacock on the shoulder for a bit of pizzazz.'

Joyce fetched her cousin's brooch, wrapped it in the skirt and stowed them away in the case. Then she chose the embroidered blouse, held it up with a navy blue skirt and when they had Flo's approval she folded them with precision and laid them on top of the other garments.

'Those four items will interchange so do you think that will be enough? With the trousers for walks teamed with that off-white jumper.'

'I reckon so. And I will probably look so refined in the back of beyond that they won't know what's hit them.'

Flo laughed again and said, 'They'll think you've come straight from a fashion house in Paris, not from the common or garden squalor of Notting Hill. Besides,' she added, 'if anyone raises an eyebrow or passes comment along the lines of you being underdressed, just look them in the eye and tell them straight that you were bombed out and are dressing in hand-outs for the minute. They wouldn't dare say another word after that.'

'Of course.' Joyce stopped in the middle of folding and storing away the things she'd decided against and smiled at Flo. 'You clever girl. Why didn't I think of that myself?'

Flo huffed on her fingertips and brushed them across the lapel of her coat. 'Well,' she said, 'some of us have beauty, some have brains and a very few of us have both.'

Joyce catapulted the Fair Isle sweater at Flo who unwound it from her head, sniffed it and tossed it aside. 'I think this came from an old fish wife,' she said. 'It reeks.'

'Probably from someone who worked in the fish and chip shop on the high street. Do you want it, Flo?'

Putting up her hands as if to ward off evil spirits, Flo pretended to back away. 'When you get home I think we should spend a few hours weeding out what you don't want and taking the rest back to the WVS.'

'Good idea and perhaps bring home another bag to forage through.'

Flo picked over the clothes left on the bed, discarding some on the floor and putting others back in the wardrobe. 'Well,' she said. 'I'll leave you to it. Have a lovely time and I hope Derek's old battle axe of a mother doesn't make it too horrible for you.'

'She probably won't be as bad as we think,' Joyce said.

'We're just comparing her with our lovely mums. Yours and…'
Joyce's voice was faint and distant. 'Mine.'

Flo put her arms around Joyce and held her close. When
she pulled away, she turned to the door and said she was going
to say goodbye to Nana and Granddad then go home. 'Make the
most of the break,' she said. 'And say hello to Mustard for me.'

'Oh,' Joyce said. 'I wish I'd never told you that.' She aimed
the Fair Isle sweater at her cousin again, but Flo was too fast
and ducked out before it reached her. 'Mustard,' she mumbled
under her breath and shook her head.

* * *

Liverpool Street Station was cold and draughty, and Joyce
stood hunched inside her coat opposite the platform where
she and Derek had arranged to meet. The entire glass roof had
been shattered in an air raid and was boarded up, making the
station more dreary and grey than it needed to be. The huge
West Side hanging clock in its wooden box had been taken
down and was being used as an enquiry desk, but it continued
to tick away and now read 7.53. Joyce was weary from her
shift, but too agitated to relax. She looked first one way up the
concourse and then the other. Behind her the clock ticked
again and she felt her stomach begin to convulse at the
thought that something might have happened to Derek.
Perhaps he'd changed his mind – if that were the case, she
would deal with it later but for now, she just wanted to know
he was alright and not lying somewhere having a terrible
asthma attack or nursing a broken leg or worse. She picked up
her suitcase and paced away from the platform, but the clock
marked the passing of another minute with a loud click and

she turned back, thinking that Operation Norfolk was a hopeless lost cause.

Then she saw him, running through the milling crowds, a suitcase in one hand and the other waving to her as if he were carrying the Union Jack in a parade. 'Joyce,' he called.

She walked towards him but shook her head.

He shook his back and swooped down on her without slowing his pace. He took up her suitcase with his free hand and told her to run. She did, as fast as she could, but it was hard for her short legs to keep up with his elongated pair and as he flung himself into the nearest carriage, she heard the guard blow the whistle.

'Derek,' she gasped. 'I don't think I'm going to...'

But shoving the cases into the corridor with his foot, he caught her under her arms and lifted her up to where he kissed her on the mouth. 'You're as light as a feather, Senior Warden Cooper,' he gasped.

They found their compartment and flopped into their seats, exhilarated from the excitement of their run. Every time they glanced at each other they laughed again, pleased with themselves that they had somehow cheated the clock.

No one else was in the compartment, although two empty seats were reserved from Ipswich. Before either of them could say a word Derek started to cough, his breathing the agonised wheeze of a bagpipe. Joyce touched his sleeve lightly, but knew by now that she should let him be until the episode reached its natural resolution.

When it did, Derek wiped his mouth on his handkerchief and smiled his unbalanced grin, his mouth trembling with the effort. 'Breakfast,' he said. 'Shall we make our way to the restaurant car?'

Joyce was thrilled at the thought. 'Oh, yes please,' she said.

'I've never eaten anything on a train before other than Mum's jam sandwiches.'

Derek opened the door of the compartment for her and the rhythmic scream of the wheels connecting with the ties filled her ears. 'Well,' he said, 'don't expect too much, Great Eastern is on rations, too.'

Sitting opposite each other on plush, dark red banquettes in the dining car, Joyce took in the little table lamp that cast a low, amber light on the starched tablecloth; the serviettes folded with precision; the clean, gleaming cutlery. Then she looked out of the window and felt shame at the disparity between their surroundings and the scene that rushed past outside.

The glimpses of London she caught from the valley of a railway cutting or the bridge above a road were sorry sights. Grotesque gaps stood in between buildings left standing; splintered windows blinked blindly at her; fences lay in puddles; wasted water spurted from mains; construction workers swarmed over larger bombsites while smaller ones lay dormant, waiting their turn to be patched up.

It was the people, though, that fascinated Joyce. Most of them walked with determination and purpose as they moved around fallen bricks and roofs and windows as if it was the most natural thing in the world. Perhaps by now it was or maybe having three months of relatively calm and peaceful nights had put a renewed spring in everyone's steps. *How easily we adapt,* she thought. *And hang onto the most fragile thread of hope to give us comfort.*

While they waited for their meal, they touched hands under the table and Derek's fingertips traced the curve of Joyce's thigh, sending a shiver slipping and sliding along her spine. They turned to each other and smiled, but Joyce quickly averted her gaze when she thought the heat she felt from his touch might show on her face and give them away.

They talked about what work had been like and how much they were looking forward to their first holiday together. On and off, Joyce felt a swell of anxiety about meeting Derek's family and wished she could find a way to ask him for reassurance, but she didn't want his mood to take a dive like it had when they'd discussed Celia a few weeks previously.

The food arrived and they tucked into powdered scrambled eggs, a rasher of streaky bacon, three shrivelled mushrooms and a spoonful of stewed tomatoes. There was toast, margarine, jam and a pot of tea. They ate in silence for a couple of minutes, hungry after working all night.

The train stopped at Ingatestone where a few passengers alighted into the rain and a few others got on and shook out their umbrellas. London was far behind them now and the views of open countryside mesmerised Joyce; she was so unused to seeing farms and cows and sheep, copses and meadows. She glimpsed a man walking around a field and she envied him the fresh air and the quiet companionship of the two dogs scampering at his heels.

'I can feel my eyes going,' Derek said. 'This would normally be the time we get our heads down, if paperwork allows.'

'Yes,' Joyce said. 'It's going to be strange having a whole week of keeping regular hours.'

And then as if he could sense her unease and the cause of it, Derek said, 'This is our first holiday together, Senior Warden Cooper, and by golly we're going to enjoy it. Don't you worry about Celia. She will be charming, amiable and very welcoming. Both she and Cress will love you.'

Joyce hoped that would be the case.

Back in their compartment, they closed the doors behind them and Joyce felt as if they were in the insulated refuge of the little house she'd imagined in detail for them. Derek opened the vent and said Joyce must tell him if it was draughty, then they snuggled up together. 'I've never seen such lovely countryside,' Joyce said. 'Look how green the grass is. And the trees. There are so many of them.'

Derek chuckled at Joyce's fervour and pointed out streams and herds of cows and crops and fields of sunshine-yellow rape.

'Tell me about Norfolk,' Joyce asked. But Derek refused, no matter how she cajoled. 'I want you to discover it for yourself without any prompting from me.' He smiled rather smugly. 'All I will say is it's beautiful. You will be smitten.'

They napped, read the papers, enthused about the changing scenery and the shoreline they glimpsed at Manningtree, Joyce saying she could smell the salt water. When the two reserved seats were occupied by a middle-aged couple at Ipswich, they pulled away from each other, sat up straight and talked in low whispers about the big sky and the soil that was as dark and rich as clumps of treacle toffee until they reached Norfolk.

There, they had a quarter of an hour's wait for the two-carriage Bittern train that would take them to where Celia and Cressida lived in Cromer. It was crowded and noisy and Joyce could not make out what people were talking about, their dialects broad and alien to her ears. There was no dining car but there was a great deal of coming and going. Some people got off at Salhouse and another few got on; then a few alighted at Worstead and five more came on board; two of those got off at Gunton but three others got on at Roughton Road and then more than half of the passengers,

Joyce and Derek included, made Cromer their destination. And when Derek handed her down onto the platform, she could truly smell the sea and hear the forlorn cry of gulls, too.

Outside the tiny station, Derek took both their cases, told her to hold onto his arm and said it wasn't far to walk, they would be there in time for a quick wash before lunch. The red brick and pebble stone town was charming despite the wind and cold. They passed a few pubs, a tea shop, a small cinema and dance hall, an imposing church, a bakery, a hotel incongruously named the Hotel de Paris, a fish and chip shop.

'Has the pier taken a packet?' Joyce asked. 'The middle's missing.'

'No,' Derek said, shouting above the wind. 'Engineers came along right at the beginning of this damned war and took out the middle section. That's when shows stopped in the Pavilion that's right at the far end, more's the pity. It would have been lovely to have taken you there to see something like Ronnie Brandon's *Out the Blue*.'

Joyce was shocked. 'Did Celia take you?'

'Oh no,' Derek said. 'That would never happen. Once Cress and I pooled our pocket money and went to a matinée while Celia thought we were collecting shells or some other such nonsense. Shh,' he put his finger on his pursed mouth. 'It's our secret.'

At each narrow road they crossed, Joyce peered towards the sea and was rewarded with a postcard view of waves and sand and endless sky. She'd had one day trip to Brighton with Mum and another to South End with Nana and Granddad and Flo, but now she had an entire week to explore and paddle and breathe in good, clean air and it felt as if she could almost forget Notting Hill and the map; bombs and incendiaries and broken sewer pipes; powdered egg and clothes that didn't fit; heartbreak and the whole blasted war.

They walked up an incline that led to the cliffs and the houses became more spread out, larger, darker and brooding. The sea crashed beneath them and on either side of the sand-packed path, spindly grasses twisted in the fierce wind. 'It's fresh,' Joyce shouted.

'Yes indeed,' Derek answered. 'They'll be no cobwebs left on us by the time we go home. There it is,' he said, pointing to a huge, double-fronted house made darker than its neighbours by the overarching shade of an enormous pine tree that stood just inside the black, wrought iron fence. When Derek had said it was a holiday home she'd imagined a chalet, but this, she thought, would house a family of twenty in Notting Hill, and all their relatives and friends to boot.

Joyce couldn't believe Derek had to stand, ring the bell and wait; no key, no mum or sister waiting at the door. He squeezed her hand and she smiled up at him, but when he focused back on the door, she had a quick look around. Peeking from the corner of the house was a motorcar, of all things, standing outside a large wooden shed with windows. Joyce was astounded.

'Ah,' Derek said. 'I see you've spotted the old dear.'

'Celia?'

'No,' Derek said, lowering his voice and laughing. 'The car.'

'Does it work?'

'Oh yes,' Derek said. 'But I'm not allowed to drive. Because of my asthma.' He patted his chest.

After what seemed an uncomfortable length of time, the door was opened by a woman in a maid's uniform. 'Mary,' Derek said. 'How lovely to see you.'

The woman smiled, what was once a dimple disappearing into an engraved line on her cheek. She was slim with a black and white cap on top of a knot of grey hair. Varicose veins undulated beneath her thick stockings. 'And you, Mr Derek,' she said.

'This,' Derek said, beaming, 'is my young lady, Joyce.'

'Joyce,' Mary said with fondness. She took Joyce's outstretched hand and held it tight. 'I'm pleased to meet you.'

'Pleased to meet you, Mary,' Joyce said.

Mary ushered them into the high-ceilinged hallway. A spray of flowers was arranged on a polished table and the parquet floor shone. 'I hope your journey wasn't too tiring?' Mary asked.

'Well, we both worked all night so we were quite tired to begin with. But I think we're alright, aren't we, Joyce?'

'Good,' Mary said, bending to pick up their cases. 'Now, Mr Derek, you'll be in your old room and Miss Joyce will be in one of the spares. Follow me.'

Derek snatched up the suitcases before Mary could grab the handles and said, 'Is Celia in?'

Averting her eyes, Mary said, 'She asked me to tell you she would see you at luncheon and Miss Cressida has gone to fetch the boys from school.' She began to climb the stairs, Joyce and Derek following behind. 'Shall I tell cook you'll be ready in twenty minutes? Is that enough time?'

Joyce nodded to Derek and he translated that into a yes for Mary. There was a picture window at the top of the landing looking out over a large, clipped lawn and tidy garden. Another pine grew in the corner and from it hung a child's swing, moving backwards and forwards in the squall. The stairs turned a corner, and they scaled another set then two more until they were on the second floor. Despite the carpets and rugs, paintings on the walls, the mirrors and vases on occasional tables, the house was chilly and Joyce was glad she'd packed her hat, scarf and jumper. There were no cooking aromas, either, which had been the first thing to hit Joyce whenever she walked into her home with Mum, but perhaps they were having cold or the house was so big that the smell of frying or roasting or boiling was contained in the kitchen.

Mary pointed to a door just off the landing and said, 'Those are the facilities, Miss Joyce.' But they marched on without stopping until she opened a dark door at the end of the corridor and beckoned Joyce to go in; Mary followed but Derek stood on the threshold. Despite the brisk breeze, the window was open and the net curtains billowed inwards. Mary pushed down on the sash and the room was quieter and calmer. A perfectly smooth, unwrinkled yellow counterpane was draped over the bed, one door of the double wardrobe stood open and empty, a dressing table with a triptych of mirrors was against a wall, there was a blue washstand in the corner and the carpet was an intricate pattern of red and blue worsted wool.

'There's an extra blanket in the wardrobe and of course, I'll pop a hot water stone in your bed every night.'

Mary waited for Joyce to respond and after a moment she said, 'It's lovely. Thank you.'

Nodding, Mary went to shut the door behind her but Derek leaned over her head and said, 'I'll come for you in fifteen minutes, Joyce.'

And then the door closed and she was alone. She felt shell-shocked and abandoned and cemented to the floor. A rush of nerves curled in her stomach and she wished more than anything she hadn't come. She wanted to be back in Notting Hill with Flo and the rest of her family. And more than anything she wanted her mum. Tears welled in her eyes but she staunched the flow, scared that if she started to cry she might never stop and she didn't want to give Celia the satisfaction of knowing she'd been tearful all alone in her room. But really! What kind of a welcome was this? No meeting; no introduction; no greeting or warm embrace. If this was Celia being charming and amiable, as Derek said she would be, Joyce would have hated to see her when she wasn't. They might as well have shoved her in this room and left her to rot.

Joyce flung her case on a chair, opened it and rummaged for her small bag of toiletries. Her hurt and bruised feelings gave way to frustration and anger, and when she saw the clothes inside that weren't really hers, the crying started in earnest. She rubbed at her tears with her handkerchief and sniffed so loudly that she wasn't sure the noise she heard was a tap at the door. Curling her hair behind her ear, she listened intently and the rap came again followed by Derek whispering her name.

She flew to the door and pulled Derek in by his sleeve.

'Joyce,' he said, bending down to look at her face. 'You've been crying.'

'I'm missing Mum,' she sniffed. 'And... this isn't quite what I...' she sobbed. 'Expected.'

For a beat, Derek's dark eyes flashed. He raked his hands through his hair. 'It will get better once they meet you. Celia in particular is just trying to prove a point.'

'What point is that?' Joyce snapped back. 'That she's a very rude woman?'

Derek strode to the window and looked out at the empty swing in the tree. It was awful to argue, especially at the start of their first holiday together.

'I'm sorry.' Joyce conceded. 'For saying that about your mother. It was cruel of me.'

Derek turned and a glimmer of a crooked smile crossed his face. 'The thing is, Celia wouldn't see her behaviour as rude. This is how visitors are greeted in her circles. It's not until you see how other people live that you learn there's a warmer way to behave.'

Joyce went to him and let him put his arms around her. 'But where are you, Derek,' Joyce said. 'What if I need you in the night?'

'Why, Senior Warden Cooper,' Derek's voice was playful, 'might you need me in the night? That sounds rather thrilling.'

She had been harbouring thoughts about sleeping with Derek and imagining where and how it would happen caused butterflies to beat their wings in her stomach again. But she cuffed him on the arm then looked up at him and said, 'Not now. And definitely not here.'

Derek looked disappointed. 'Anyway,' he said, there wouldn't be a chance of anything like that as Celia will be listening for any and all movement during the night. She'll be like some kind of one-woman radar system, believe me. Now,' he wiped his finger under her eyes, 'have a quick wash and we'll go down to the dining room. I'll show you where my room is on the way.'

The thought of meeting Celia at last made Joyce's skin bristle and she wished she and Derek could stay in this room, gazing out at the back garden and listening to the wind and the sea for the entire week.

* * *

Celia did not look like the tall, elegant, sophisticated woman Joyce had conjured up in her mind. Everything about her was average; she was of medium height, with medium brown hair pulled off her face in a French pleat; her eyes were a nondescript shade of brown and the make-up she wore was neither too much nor too little and she wasn't under or overweight. Her clothes, though, were impeccable. She wore a dusky pink costume which was cut to fit her curves and the collar on the jacket was edged with dark brown velvet. There were no mends in her stockings and her shoes looked as if they were made of soft, brown leather. She had been standing at the head of the table when Joyce and Derek joined her and she advanced towards them, smiling and with her hand outstretched. Joyce took it, but had to fight not to shudder when she imagined the rigid palm drawing back to strike Derek for some imagined misdemeanour or another.

'Miss Cooper,' she enthused. 'I am so pleased to make your acquaintance. How lovely of you to spend time with us in the sleepy backwater of Cromer.' There was one, brisk shake of their hands and then Celia released her hold.

'Thank you for inviting me, Mrs Nicholls,' Joyce said, forcing herself to hold Celia's gaze. But Joyce broke the eye lock first, intimidated by the woman she'd been led to believe was dictatorial and authoritative; the huge, elegantly set table; the chandelier and the candlesticks on the sideboard.

'Derek,' Celia held out her hands, which Derek took in his, and offered her cheek to be grazed by her son.

'Sherry, Miss Cooper?' Celia gestured towards the sideboard without looking at it. 'Derek, will you do the honours?'

'Of course,' Derek said, taking the stopper out of a cut-glass decanter that caught the light as hundreds of tiny, fractured crystals.

Joyce was incredulous. She'd seen scenes like this at the pictures, of course, but had never experienced anything like it. At home, they had a nice cup of tea with their lunch and sherry was for Christmas, if they were lucky. It was as if Celia were playing the role of someone for whom the war and working and scrimping and making do had not touched. Joyce brought her glass to her lips and listened to Celia talking about how dreadful it must be for them in London and what she had heard on the radio that morning about Roosevelt and Churchill signing the Atlantic Charter. So, Joyce thought, she isn't as cut off from the real world as she gives the impression of being.

Joyce's stomach tied itself into a knot when Celia turned to address her, but she was saved by Cressida rushing into the room, breathless and windblown. She smoothed down her hair and apologised, saying one of the boys had fallen and it had taken her a few moments to calm him. Joyce's first reaction was to ask if the little fellow was alright, but Celia made the introductions without enquiring about her grandson.

'Miss Cooper,' Cressida said, adopting the same manner and intonation of voice as her mother. 'So pleased to meet you.'

'Nice to meet you, Mrs Martin,' Joyce said.

'Won't you excuse me?' Celia said, leaving the room by another door. Derek poured his sister a sherry and while the three of them made small talk about the weather and how the house in Croydon was faring, Joyce was able to discern how much the siblings looked like each other. Cressida was tall and slim with dark hair, eyes and brows like Derek's and the crooked smile was there, too, although not as pronounced or warm as her brother's lopsided grin.

When Celia returned, she said the soup would be served

soon and Derek held out the chairs for each woman. There were no places set for the boys and Joyce wondered where they were and who was watching them. It was on the tip of her tongue to ask the question, but the situation didn't seem unusual to any of the others so Joyce supposed the children ate somewhere else under the guidance of someone else – Mary, perhaps, or the cook. *What a strange situation,* Joyce thought, remembering the times each and every one of her family had squashed around the rickety wallpaper table so they could share a meal together.

It would not have entered any of their minds to feed the little ones in another room or at a different table or with a minder. But maybe it was for the best, Joyce reasoned, if it kept the boys out of the way of Celia's raised hand and Cressida's for that matter, if she followed her mother's lead where discipline was concerned.

Mary and a young girl brought out bowls of onion soup and set them down in front of each of the assembled in turn. When the steaming broth was placed on Joyce's mat, she smiled up at Mary and said, 'Thank you very much.' Then to show her appreciation she inhaled deeply and added, 'Mmm, smells lovely.'

There was no sign of recognition or response from Mary and Joyce was bemused as when they'd met no more than an hour ago, Mary had shaken her hand warmly. She realised that none of the others had smiled or said thank you and were acting as if they'd never laid eyes on Mary or her young helper before. Looking from one to the other, Joyce saw that Celia's eyes were glued to her soup, her nostrils flaring and a high point of colour in each of her cheeks. Cressida, too, stared into her bowl as if it held the exact formula to how the Allies could win the war, but it was obvious she was finding it difficult to stifle a fit of the giggles.

So, she'd made an awful mistake and would have dearly loved to bolt for the door. But Derek was smiling at her across the table. He tipped his head almost imperceptibly and, finding her foot with his, gently stroked her ankle. Celia was aware of that nod and must have seen it as a small act of solidarity on Derek's part because her lips pursed with annoyance. But she was a model of containment and picked up her spoon, as did Cressida, and started sipping at her soup. Joyce hesitated but Derek pointed to Joyce's bowl with his eyes, willing her to begin so, with a slightly trembling hand, she managed her first spoonful. Only then did Derek start on his.

'How was your journey?' Celia addressed her question to Derek.

'Ghastly, I imagine,' said Cressida.

'No holdups,' Derek said. 'Were there, Joyce?'

'No, none,' Joyce answered, looking down at her clothes every few seconds, petrified she'd spilled a drop of soup on her blouse.

'And we were tired coming straight from work, but had a rest after we'd eaten breakfast which was rather tasty. Wasn't it, Joyce?'

'Yes,' Joyce said. 'It was.'

'I see,' said Celia.

'The journey from London is so tedious and flat,' said Cressida. 'There's not much else to do except eat and sleep.'

'We talked a lot,' Derek said. 'And admired the scenery. Didn't we, Joyce?'

'Yes,' Joyce agreed. 'We did.'

Mary must have been watching through a crack in the door, because the minute they all placed their spoons in their empty bowls, she and her assistant appeared to whip the used crockery away. This time, Joyce kept her eyes straight ahead and didn't acknowledge Mary in any way. But how that went against everything she'd been brought up to understand as polite and kind. Mum would have been appalled at how quickly she'd acquiesced to Celia's will, but how could she do otherwise in a house where she was a guest? That would be ill-mannered, too.

Lord Woolton's Pie with gravy was next on the menu and although it was lovely, the pastry stuck in Joyce's throat and she had a hard time chewing the root vegetables. At home she would have told everyone about that and they would have teased her or insisted she pass her plate to one of them – they'd soon polish it off. Here there was no laughter or quips or repartee. The clock ticked loudly, all four of them tried to muffle their chewing, Celia coughed into her serviette, Joyce felt as if she was sitting in a pool of sweat, or perspiration as Celia and Cressida would no doubt have referred to it.

Say something, she willed Derek and as if he could read her mind he said, 'Any news of Michael?'

Joyce knew that Cressida's husband was an officer in the RAF and she replied, a rather vacant look in her eyes, that as far as she was concerned he was holding his own. There was no hand on her heart or hint of anxiety in her voice.

A prune and marmalade pudding and watery custard was served for afters and at that moment in time, Joyce's dearest wish was that there wouldn't be a cheese course or coffee as she didn't think she could stand to be in the airless, cheerless, icy room for one more minute.

Celia chose the moment Joyce had taken her first spoonful to say, 'Derek tells me your mother has been killed, Miss Cooper, and your house razed to the ground.'

'Celia,' Derek said. 'I don't think this is the time to...'

But Celia ignored her son and watched Joyce, her features soft with fabricated compassion. Joyce thought she was going to have to spit the pudding back into her bowl, but Derek came to the rescue with a glass of water. 'Celia,' he said again, sterner this time, 'this is very raw for Joyce.'

But Celia turned to Derek with a look of innocence and confusion on her face.

'I merely wanted to offer my condolences,' she said. 'It would be terribly wrong of me if I didn't. Wouldn't it, Cressida?'

'Yes,' Cressida said, answering her mother in the exact way Joyce had replied to Derek throughout the meal. 'It would.'

They were cruel and heartless, but Joyce decided that she would not stoop to their level – she owed that to Mum. 'Thank you,' she said when she'd composed herself. 'I'm grateful for your sympathy.'

When the meal came to an end at last, Joyce felt drained, her shoulders and neck rigid with tension.

'The boys,' Cressida said, 'are going to come in to say hello before I take them back to school.'

Joyce thought that would probably be the highlight of the meal.

There was a timid knock at the door to which Celia said, 'Yes.'

Four little dark-haired lads filed in and lined up in descending height order. They ranged in age from ten to four and all wore matching grey shorts, navy blue blazers and striped ties. Their faces were scrubbed and their hair was combed. 'Boys,' Celia said, 'this is Miss Cooper.'

Joyce knew she must offer her hand first and each of the

boys took it and gave it a formal shake. They didn't smile, no one did, and Joyce felt so sorry for them, standing as immutable as miniature soldiers frightened of offending their sergeant major. Then something gave way in her and she no longer felt as if she had to watch her every move or try hard not to make a fool of herself in order to impress Celia and Cressida; Derek liked her the way she was and that was good enough for her. So she smiled broadly as she repeated their names: Edwin, Norman, Alexander, Michael. 'I'm so happy to meet you,' she enthused. 'Your uncle Derek has told me lovely things about all of you.'

They looked uncomfortable, but didn't fidget or shuffle about. The eldest peeked at his mother and grandmother for a hint, Joyce supposed, about how to react, but neither woman chipped in to help. 'I hope,' Joyce ploughed on, 'that your lunch was as scrummy as ours.' She patted her stomach. 'I for one enjoyed mine.'

'Yes, thank you,' Edwin answered for himself and his brothers.

'Now,' Celia addressed Derek, 'you and Miss Cooper must do as you please and I will see you for supper at 7.30. Boys, your mother will take you back to school now.'

The boys' sense of relief was palpable as they filed back through the door. Joyce, too, was weak with the thought that emancipation from the dining room was imminent and she hung onto that one glimmer of confidence she'd felt a few moments earlier when she resolved to be herself – that was what her mum would have told her to do.

'Shall we walk with you,' Derek said to Cressida. 'It will give Joyce a good introduction to the delights of Cromer.'

But Cressida marched after her sons and when she did look over her shoulder at her brother, she could not meet his eyes. 'We haven't time to wait,' she said in a clipped voice. 'The boys hate to be late.'

'Right you are,' Derek said breezily, but Joyce could hear the hurt and bewilderment in his voice.

'I could do with a walk,' Joyce said. 'Just give me a minute to get my things.'

Then Cressida looked Joyce up and down, her eyes coming to rest on the black patent shoes. 'They won't do here. Derek, show Miss Cooper the wellingtons near the back porch. She can borrow a pair.' And before Joyce could thank her, she was gone.

Wrapped up against the battering elements, Joyce and Derek made their way down the path they'd climbed a few hours earlier and Joyce asked Derek for an explanation about Celia and Cressida's hurtful behaviour during lunch.

'Manners,' Derek said in a sullen voice. 'Expectations, appearances and manners, that's all that Celia is really bothered about.'

'Is it good manners to make a guest feel uncomfortable in your home?' Joyce was fuming.

'No, of course not,' Derek sounded exasperated. 'But Celia wouldn't see it like that. All she would think is that she was sticking to the rules of etiquette.'

But Joyce wasn't so sure. She thought Derek's mother knew perfectly well she was being provocative and vindicative and that Derek was somewhat blinkered as he so wanted the visit to go well.

In silence, they walked into the compact, flinted town. They looked in the windows of the bookstore, the bakery, the fish shop, the haberdashery and a gift shop where Joyce saw a few little polished shells and postcards, a trinket box and a lipstick clip that she might take back for Nana, Auntie

Cath and Flo, depending on how she could eke out her money.

Derek was quiet, his dark features sombre and melancholy and it wasn't until Joyce exclaimed about the lack of rubble tumbling onto the pavements, how calming she found the roar of the measured waves, the mouth-watering aroma of fresh fish and chips, the twisty cobbled lanes, buckets and spades for sale, that Derek seemed to come-to out of his reverie and allow her enthusiasm to rub off on him. 'Shall we do our best to have a good holiday?' he asked. 'I have plenty of things planned for this week.'

Joyce thought for a minute or two then decided that she might as well try to make the most of it. 'Tell me about them.' She entwined her arm through his.

'There's the museum, the church, the pub, dinner at the Hotel de Paris, sandcastles, swimming in the sea, and the pictures, for a start.'

Joyce laughed and shook her head, the fresh wind whisking strands of hair across her forehead. 'They all sound lovely, except the swimming. I don't think I can manage that.'

'Senior Warden Cooper,' Derek said, 'I believe you can do anything you put your mind to. Don't forget I've seen that map of yours. And we will have a day in Norwich, viewing the cathedral and wandering around the market. We'll have a high tea and... something else. Can you guess?'

What Joyce knew about Norwich could be written on the back of a postage stamp. Stuck out on a limb and a place that no one ever passed through to get anywhere else was the sum of it, so she wondered what secrets it could possibly harbour. 'Tell me,' she said. 'I'm terrible at guessing.'

'A tea dance,' he said, beaming. 'At a dance hall called Samson and Hercules, believe it or not.'

Joyce refused to believe it. 'What a name for a dance hall,' she said. 'What's wrong with the Palais or the Palladium?'

'And it's a very good fit for our theme of swimming as it used to be an indoor pool. Boards have been laid over it now, but the water is very deep, so you have to make sure you don't dig your heels in too hard when you undertake a turn or you'll go right through to the depths.'

Joyce stood frozen to the spot and stared at Derek. 'That,' she said, 'cannot be true. Even for the back of beyond that's Norfolk.'

Derek grabbed her hand and they ran down a narrow lane towards the beach. 'It's all the truth except the pool is now empty. Come on, let's walk back along the shore.'

It was such a filthy day that apart from one or two dedicated dog walkers, they had the sands to themselves. They walked into the wind, holding onto their hats and scarves. There was no point in talking, their voices wouldn't have been heard above the wind and the relentless buffeting waves. Joyce was mesmerised by the thrashing tower of grey water as it drew back into itself and then culminated in fingers of white foam at their feet.

A solitary figure came into view ahead of them and Joyce thought she recognised Cressida's stooped, forlorn back receding in the direction of the house. She looked to Derek for his reaction and he pulled back, letting time and distance come between them. 'Your sister looks so alone,' Joyce said.

'Yes,' Derek said. 'She seems to be, doesn't she? Poor Cress.'

Dinner that evening was a repeat of the lunch ritual except with a different menu and more sherry along with wine and lit candles on the table. Joyce was glad of the peacock brooch she'd pinned on her blouse as both Celia and Cressida wore sparkling necklaces and earrings to complement their elegant dresses. The boys, Joyce presumed, had eaten earlier in some other part of the house and had been put to bed. But one thing was different and that was Joyce's attitude. She remained polite and unassuming, but spoke with confidence about whatever subject came up – the war, the Civil Defence, rationing, her first impressions of Cromer.

But there was no getting to know Joyce, which Derek had said was the whole point of the trip. Neither woman asked about her family or her job, her hobbies or hopes for the future. And neither of them mentioned Mum again. That pattern was then set for the week, and she felt as though she had been asked along for a jolly little holiday treat and nothing more.

Derek, though, was true to his word. They visited all the places of interest in Cromer and had a wonderful day in Norwich, a city that proved to be much livelier and more sophisticated than Joyce had imagined. They stumbled their way through the tea dance, laughing and resetting their feet and handholds numerous times and couldn't wait to tell Madame Beaupre that they'd danced in public at last and enjoyed it.

Other than a few minutes when they played in the garden before their tea, Joyce never really saw the boys again. On one occasion, she opened the glass door to go out to them, but Celia told her that playing on their own for half an hour encouraged independence and they must be let alone. Joyce felt her face burn, but stood at the door and waved to them instead.

Once or twice while Joyce was resting in the afternoon, she thought she heard Derek and Celia's raised voices, but when she asked Derek whether he and his mother had been arguing, he changed the subject and told her about the next walk they would take or another teashop they would visit. On the Friday before they left, Derek said he had business to discuss with Celia and suggested she take a walk along the beach to the town where he would meet her later. Although intrigued about the nature of the business, she didn't mind walking on her own and thought she might have time to buy those few souvenirs so her family would know she'd been thinking of them. The wind was howling again and seemed to be coming off the sea and the land at the same time, if that were possible. Sand as rough as an emery board stung her face and the waves she had come to love churned grey and frothy at her feet. She was disappointed with the way the week had gone in terms of Celia and Cressida and thought they had treated her abominably, but for every ignorant slight they had shown her, Derek had stepped up and his attention had become more fervent and loving. So, she had a dilemma. Could she let herself be increasingly serious with Derek, knowing his family thought her no better than a smear of dog's dirt inadvertently brought into the house on someone's shoe? She would never come back here again and if, when the war was over, Derek's family moved back to London, she could choose to see them for a mere hour or two when she absolutely had to and Derek might decide to do the same. Now she longed for London, as damaged and dangerous as it was, and the train tomorrow morning couldn't come soon enough.

When she reached a familiar inland cutting, Joyce turned and headed for the town. As she stepped off the sand and into the lane, she came face to face with Cressida. She looked up, Cressida looked down and for a beat they stood facing each other. 'Cressida,' Joyce bellowed above the wind and surf. 'It really is wild. Shall we find somewhere and have coffee? The lounge of the Hotel de Paris perhaps?'

'No, thank you, Miss Cooper,' Cressida answered, but didn't give an explanation as to why she couldn't spare the time.

'I'll carry on then.' Joyce made to move around Cressida. 'I want to take a few little things home for Auntie Cath, Nana and Flo.'

But Cressida put up her hand to stop Joyce's progress and from nowhere that Joyce could fathom said, 'He'll never marry you, you know. He won't be allowed.'

Joyce couldn't believe what she was hearing. The woman had hardly spoken two words to her all week and now this. It beggared belief. Tears welled in her eyes, but she thought of how her mum would want her to react and kept them in check. 'Who would be able to stop a grown man from marrying whoever he wants to marry?' Joyce bellowed above the bombast of the waves.

'Celia,' Cressida roared back. 'Celia will disinherit him if he marries you. Or anyone else she thinks unsuitable. And he's due a sizeable amount that he won't want to throw away on a...' She clamped her mouth closed.

The hammering in Joyce's ears rivalled the pounding of the waves. She felt cut to the bone. Was she so inadequate? Was her family so uneducated and common? No, she didn't think so. 'I think,' she said, 'that Derek will be the judge of that.'

Cressida chuckled without humour. 'Besides, it would make a mockery of me.'

'I'm afraid I don't understand.'

'Ah, so Derek hasn't told you. I was in love once, too.' Cressida stepped closer and lowered her voice. 'He was a music teacher, but not from the right kind of family, so Celia put a stop to it. She introduced me to Michael and I agreed to marry him when I was at my lowest point.'

'Oh, Cress.' Joyce's hand flew to her heart. 'I'm so sorry for you.'

Now it was Cressida's turn to ebb her tide of tears.

Joyce went to put her hand on Cressida's arm to comfort her, but the wretched woman shifted her stance and moved away. 'I don't want your pity,' she said. Then, stumbling across the furrowed sand, she made her way to the shoreline without looking back. Joyce stared after her, trying to piece together everything that Cressida had told her and feeling nothing but a deep ache of compassion for Derek's sister. And for herself.

By the time Derek walked into the Lifeboat Café, Joyce was sitting at a corner table, her second cup of tea in front of her. Despite his slant of a smile, Joyce could see Derek was agitated. He ordered coffee and, as Joyce had decided to do, she confronted him with Cressida's story straight away.

'I am ashamed of my mother and sister, truly ashamed.' He reached across the table and placed his hand over hers. 'I had hoped that by the time we departed for London, Celia would have grown to love you and I planned to tell you all about Cressida then.'

'But?'

'But it hasn't worked out and, as I feared, Celia has threatened to disinherit me if we marry.'

Joyce snatched her hand back and curled it against her chest. 'Derek,' she said, 'I've never felt so... shocked and insulted.'

Derek nodded, his head hanging. 'I feel terrible on your behalf, Joyce, my love,' he said. 'And told my mother so in no uncertain terms.'

'But what conclusion have you come to?' she asked. 'If you think more of your inheritance than you do of me, then...'. Joyce took a long, deep breath, 'there's nothing else for it but that we part company.'

Derek looked down at her, the pupils of his dark eyes large and searing. 'But I want to marry you, Joyce. More than anything.' Then he clenched his jaw and his voice took on an edge. 'But I also want my inheritance. It's rightfully mine and I've earned it by putting up with this snobbish nonsense all my life, Joyce.' He held her gaze. 'Putting Celia and Cressida to one side, do you think you would consider marrying me?'

Joyce managed to pick up her cup with a shaking hand and took a sip of tea. 'I would have,' she said. 'Before this revelation. But Celia and Cressida are not going to be easily put to one side. You know that.'

Derek grabbed her hand again and kissed it. 'Please don't give up on me, Joyce,' he said. 'Give me – us – until the end of this damned war. Celia will change her mind, I'm sure she will. And if not, then when it's all over I'll make you Mrs Nicholls and to hell with them.'

Joyce wasn't sure what to do. She looked into the leaves floating in the bottom of her cup, then towards the windows, clammy with condensation and wished more than ever that Mum were here to help her. She tried to imagine life with Derek and without him and despite the circumstances, the first image was more vivid and the one she wanted to hold close. She nodded her head slowly but knew that when she spoke, her voice lacked conviction. 'There are many things to consider, Derek. Like the fact that we have no idea how long the war will drag on and I can't wait for ever on a promise.'

'I understand that, Joyce,' Derek said, his head nodding in agreement. 'I truly believe the war will end sooner rather than later, but let's just say that you'll give me a year to iron all of this out. Please, Joyce. I love you dearly.' When Joyce looked up at him, she could see a slick of sweat on his upper lip and hear a growling rasp in his chest. He grabbed for her hand again and mouthed, 'I'm begging you.'

So Joyce agreed and the decision, when she played out the options in her mind, felt like the right one. She bought her souvenirs and then they trudged up the hill to face one last night with Derek's closest relatives, who to Joyce did not seem anything like a family at all.

ELEVEN

Monday 25 February 1974

When Joyce told the girls in the office that she had to be out of her flat in two weeks' time, she was amazed that their first reaction was to offer their help. She didn't consider them friends, although they were all friendly with each other within the confines of work. But despite the fact that they had families and responsibilities of their own, they had been so enthusiastic and generous with their invitations to assist that she had trouble fending them off.

Elaine and Barbara wanted to come to the flat and help with the packing. Alison offered her husband's van on the day. Sandra insisted on being present in the new flat to help unload boxes and arrange furniture. Audrey said she would do whatever needed to be done. It was all rather touching.

'No, ta,' Joyce said, polite but firm. 'I wouldn't dream of taking you away from your families at the weekend. Besides, by the time I've had a good clear out there'll hardly be anything left to pack up.'

She was grateful, but knew she wouldn't have been able to bear her work colleagues picking through her belongings, holding up an old tin opener or shoehorn, packet of hair pins or the red lipstick she'd worn until pale pink became the rage and asking her if she wanted to keep them or dump them. They might well be surprised at how little she had to show for her years in the flat and how little of it was worth anything. They might whisper amongst themselves about the number of tins of custard and peas and pilchards that were in the cupboard and why she still used Vitapointe and Drene shampoo. Then they would try to guess at the reasons why she kept a yellowed train ticket or a First Night of the Proms programme from many years ago. They might come across Auntie Cath's black patent shoes wrapped in tissue paper that she'd pushed to back of the wardrobe and want to know about their history and really, there was not much of a story to tell. And if they insisted, she might get upset and then there would be questions and clumsy hugs and pity, and it would all be insufferable. No, it was too personal an undertaking and one which she would be better off confronting on her own. That way she could take her time, make sure she was thorough and stop for tea whenever she wanted without having to cater to others.

Barbara did, however, tell their manager about the move and Mrs Browne said she would book two days of annual leave for Joyce – the Friday before the moving date and the Monday after. She said Joyce would need the time so she should take it and by then, Joyce was so weary of arguing against people's best intentions that she agreed.

She accepted the recommendation of a moving company. from Mr Taylor and every evening she headed home with as many boxes as she could carry and set about ordering the sum total of her life into cardboard crates labelled bathroom, bedroom, kitchen or living/dining room.

* * *

Sitting amongst the packing cases, some taped and ready to go, others open and gaping, she shuffled through a mountain of *Woman's Realm* magazines going back years and asked herself why she'd kept them so long – she didn't knit so would never use the patterns; sometimes she tried one or two different recipes but in the main she kept to her tried and tested meals; the problem pages and serials were engaging, but once read she never looked at them again. Perhaps the girls at work would like them, they were always passing weeklies back and forth, but then she thought the dated books could only possibly have an amusement or curiosity value so threw them into a box of rubbish.

She would, of course, keep all her kitchen utensils, her clothing, what was left of the food she was trying to use up, curtains, bedding, her few rusty gardening tools, towels and toiletries, the neatly ordered salary slips from Bourne and Hollingsworth, her library card, her personal papers in the bulldog clip. But gone were the old ration books, the sausage dog draught excluder and the picture of Big Ben that had been on the kitchen wall for years. When she unhooked it, the bare, ghostly imprint of where it had hung remained. She stared at that stark, empty square and thought it somehow symbolised all the homes she'd lived in and the people she'd shared them with – now mere shadows where once there had been something concrete and real and tangible. That thought took her breath away and made tears spring to her eyes, something she hadn't allowed to happen for years. For a beat she held the picture and wondered if she should put it back in its place and let it be pulled down with the rest of the building, but with sudden determination she binned it, knowing that the void she felt in the pit of her stomach was nothing to do with whether the bare space on the wall was occupied or not.

After that, she refused to give in to sentimentality. After all, this wasn't the first time she'd emptied a flat or seen the rudiments of her life, or the lives of others, spread out around her. During the war all manner of people's personal things would lay strewn about the streets until someone claimed ownership or they were cleared away. She could still remember how grateful a middle-aged woman had been when she'd stopped and helped her retrieve a petticoat that had caught in a tree. Grey, tattered undershorts; diaries; Post Office savings books; letters; telegrams; knickers; vests; bits of skin and shattered bone; swimming caps; toenails; spectacle arms; tankards; all the intimate paraphernalia and detritus of life exposed to the scrutiny of passers-by who had untold miseries of their own to contend with.

Often, she had wondered where all those unclaimed possessions had disappeared to and she imagined them turned over and buried beneath the footings and walls of the new houses, shops, restaurants, bakeries, pubs, bridges and coffee houses that had gone up since the war. Even now, some unsuspecting digger driver might see the glint of an engagement ring or the horror of an empty-eyed doll or a shred of a sandal caught in the mud he'd excavated, deaden his machine and call over one or two of his workmates to stare at the treasure he'd found. They might find a fragment of one of the tea towels that Mum had always had in her hand, shrug their shoulders, then throw it back into the depths of a chasm where it would join the repository of lost life and limb that was helping to gentrify a new London. There was some sort of comforting, poetic justice in that, but the thought made her shiver.

Years ago, she had realised that structure to her hours, days, weeks and months held back the tidal wave of introspection that could so easily engulf her. Her rigid schedule made her feel secure and gave her purpose and without it she was apt to become morose and unsettled. As she emptied the last of the drawers in the sideboard and labelled the piece of furniture so it would end up in the new living/dining room, she knew that was what was happening to her now. Quickly, she sized up what there was left to sort out and checked her watch to see if she could reclaim some part of her usual Saturday schedule – if she hurried she could get to the library and return her books so they didn't get misplaced in the move, purchase a custard tart from the bakery, pick up her weekly *Woman's Realm* to read later.

Yes, that was what she had to get on with, so she took off her tabard and brushed the dust from her skirt. But when she caught sight of feet walking on the pavement above her, she covered her mouth with her hand and dropped down onto the settee. This reassuring view she had of the world would soon be changing for ever. She'd learned to confront, grapple, endure and survive her life by feeling a connection to the lives of the people who owned the shoes and trousers and coats, prams and bicycle wheels that paraded by each day. Through them she had lived vicariously without having to take a place amongst them, something she knew to be a drain on emotions and resources. Twenty-nine years ago she'd found a place and a situation here where she felt at ease and now she couldn't imagine how she would be able to recreate that feeling from the second storey of a block of flats on a new estate.

In a rush, she found her library books and took them into the hallway to put on her coat and shoes. The letters marked Urgent were still on the table under the coat hooks and she tore them to pieces, ready for the rubbish when she returned. She smoothed her hair, checked her bag for her keys, grabbed the books, closed the front door behind her and climbed the steps. At street level she stopped and looked down towards her front room, a film of anger and hurt clouding her vision. This, she thought, is what all those people getting on with their own lives could see when they looked down at her flat – nothing. To them her life was nothing more than the void on the wall where the picture of Big Ben had hung.

She took a deep breath, reminded herself that she'd been through much worse than this paltry move, turned and nearly stumbled against Mr Taylor. Really! The man had no idea about the proper time and place.

'Miss Cooper.' He beamed at her. His chain was again gleaming between his collarbones, his flared jeans at least as billowing as they had been the previous weekend and the points of his collar were, if anything, more tapered and lethal. 'I've come to see if you're getting on alright.'

'Thank you, Mr Taylor.' Joyce could hear her stiff, formal reply. Well, better that than let him know she had been unsettled and tearful a few minutes earlier. 'Quite alright.'

'Can I help you with anything?' He looked down at her and creases appeared around his mouth and eyes.

It took all Joyce's well-mannered upbringing not to tell him to leave her alone and barge him out of the way. 'I appreciate your concern,' she said, 'but I'm on rather a tight timetable to get to the library. If you'll excuse me.' She smiled thinly and hurried past him.

'You will let me know, Miss Cooper,' he called after her, 'if I can be of any assistance?'

Without turning, she looked back over her shoulder and dismissed him with a wave of her hand. 'Yes, yes, much appreciated,' she said.

Half expecting him to come after her, she walked with her head down until she was forced to look up to cross the road. There, on the opposite side, she saw the little green sports car and in the passenger seat she glimpsed a lovely young woman with fair hair, black flicks across her eyelids, a Liberty scarf wound around her neck. The thought that Mr Taylor and his fiancée had given up part of their Saturday together to check up on her made her chest ache when she took a breath. She could go back, apologise for being so abrupt and invite them in for a cup of tea. Then she looked down at the books in her hand, knew the library and bakery would be closed soon and marched on without a backward glance.

TWELVE

SID

September 1941

When Joyce arrived home from the ill-fated trip to Norfolk, Nana couldn't wait to tell her that on Wednesday, the siren had screamed at them on and off all night and they'd had the chance to try out the Anderson they'd decided to build. 'And how was it in there?' Joyce asked.

'Cosy,' Nana said. 'Your Derek would have ended up with terrible neck ache. But, oh, we were pleased you'd made us build it.'

Joyce felt exonerated and a bit smug to hear that. When the nightly screech of air raid sirens had stopped and people began to tentatively feel safe enough to spend nights in their own homes again, she'd worried and nagged and pleaded with them saying that Report and Control was as good as an underground bunker, but she couldn't bear to think of the rest of them as vulnerable targets in their own beds.

'Let's build an Anderson,' she'd said. 'Or a Morrison. I

don't mind which, but there must be a shelter all of us can use.'

So Granddad and Uncle Terry got all the materials they needed free from the council and together with Joyce and Flo they'd spent a day putting it together and burying it in Granddad and Nana's garden. Auntie Cath made them tea and Nana studied the structure through her thick spectacles and said she knew what she was going to plant on top of it after it was in the ground and covered with soil.

There were fourteen panels that needed to be bolted together and being the smallest, Joyce had been sent up onto the roof to make sure the seams met. Uncle Terry had made a joke about not trusting Joyce to have the clout to make sure the screws were tight enough to save them from Jerry bombs, but Joyce had known that her determination to keep her family safe would give her the strength she needed. Granddad had hung the door on upside down and Joyce said they should have let her get on with the whole thing by herself. When Derek turned up to help and had to squeeze his height into the small space, they had been limp with laughter again. What should have been a dismal undertaking turned out to be one of the best days they'd had as a family for ages and Joyce went to work that night knowing that if the siren suddenly sounded, her family would be somewhat safe.

'Thank goodness it wasn't the night Sid and Hettie were here,' Nana said. 'We would have had to stay in there until you got home and let us out with a tin opener.'

Joyce couldn't believe that Sid and Hettie had been in London for two days – of all the bad luck. She hadn't seen her older brother or his wife for over a year and now they had missed each other and who knew when they might have the chance to meet up again.

Nana bustled around the kitchen much as Mum had done, but she was slower on her feet and her eyesight was so bad that she missed crumbs and dust in the corners when she was wiping down the sides; she tired easily, too. Joyce took the cloth from her grandmother's hand and said she would finish the chores. Nana tried to argue, but puffed a sigh of relief when she flopped down in one of the hard, rickety kitchen chairs.

'If I'd known,' Joyce said. 'I wouldn't have gone to Norfolk.' *And it would have been just the excuse,* she thought, *to save me from the heartbreak of meeting Celia and Cressida.*

'He only had five days off, Joy love,' Nana said. 'Survivors' Leave. Again. That boy must be a cat who's rapidly using up his nine lives.'

The cloth in Joyce's hand stopped delving for grease and grime around the sink. She could hear her pulse pounding against her ears and her stomach began to churn. This was the third time Sid's ship had gone down in the middle of a cold, forbidding ocean. Once when Sid had been home on leave, Mum had been worrying about how he'd survive on a minuscule rubber dinghy if the vessel he was working on sank.

'Mum,' Sid had laughed out loud. 'A lifeboat isn't anything like a Lilo. It's a proper, sturdy, seagoing vessel.'

But Mum hadn't been appeased and when Sid signed up for his next ship, he'd sent Mum a postcard of a lifeboat, men sitting along either side of the interior of the well-built, high-sided craft, pulling on solid oars. Joyce couldn't believe that a huge boat like that was one of a number stored on a ship to save the crew if it went down. A picture of the waves flailing against the beach at Cromer came into Joyce's mind and she knew they were docile and benign in comparison to the hostile swell beyond the horizon that had hypnotised her. And no matter how happy and relieved Mum felt when she saw the comforting proportions of the lifeboat, it was nothing more than fragile driftwood when pitted against an enormous expanse of ocean.

But Sid had been lucky again. Joyce had been lucky, too, as she could so easily have lost her brother as well as her mother in the space of a few months.

'So he and Hettie,' Nana was talking on, 'decided to come here for one night and then go on to see the little ones in Oswestry.'

Joyce put on the kettle and thought about her niece and nephew and hoped they had experienced a better reception from their host family in Shropshire than she had from Derek's family in Norfolk. The poor little things, away from their parents and their school and all their familiar landmarks. Joyce had only met the children twice and they would have little recollection of her, but she sometimes sent them a note and they wrote back saying they were happy and they had seen lambs and played hopscotch in the road. But it was a blessing they were away, no matter how brutal it seemed, as when Hitler had turned his attention away from London and towards the Eastern Front, he had also decided to target Liverpool and they had taken it there in a most devastating way.

'I expect Hettie was glad to have him with her for a few days,' Joyce said.

'Oh,' Nana said, 'she couldn't get enough of him. I said to Granddad there'll be another baby there soon enough after this leave.'

'Nana.' Joyce giggled, but pretended to be shocked.

'It's only natural,' Nana said. 'The world has to go round.'

'Come on then, tell me everything they told you.'

Nana stretched out her legs and rubbed the back of her

left calf, where Joyce knew she had developed a distended, purple varicose vein. 'Well, you know Hettie's living with her sister now and she said she's very grateful to her for making room, but how she misses her own place and her own things and she hates feeling like an intruder or a visitor all the time.'

Joyce was glad her back was to Nana so the sudden surge of tears that gathered in the rims of her eyes was not on display. But Nana must have noticed something or been stung by the insensitivity of her own words, because after a moment Joyce felt her grandmother's arms around her shoulders and they stood side by side and cried together. 'I'm sorry, Joy love,' Nana said. 'I was about to add that I know it's the same for you, but I could see I was too late. Do you feel like that, Joy? Like you're a guest here?'

Nana poured them each a cup of tea and brought out a tin of broken biscuits from the back of a cupboard. 'I've been saving these,' she said. 'For an emergency and I think this is it.'

Snivelling, Joyce reached into the tin and brought out the corner of a custard cream. Her mouth started to water. 'Lovely. Ta, Nana.'

They sat at the table and Nana asked Joyce again if she felt like an outsider in her new home. Joyce knew what Nana wanted to hear – that she was completely at ease in the house she'd frequented on an almost daily basis for as long as she could remember. So that was what she said because how could she tell her beloved grandmother that there was something so different about the ingrained smell of the rugs and curtains, the irritating way in which two of the windows stuck at the bottom, the creases in her blouse from the way Nana bunched garments together on the clothes horse, the fact that there was no longer her own home to return to after a fun afternoon of baking or painting or learning to knit with Nana.

'I feel happy here, Nana,' she said. 'But I do miss my own things in all their places and cubbyholes. And,' she tried to gulp down her grief, 'I miss Mum.'

'I know, love.' Nana swallowed hard as if she, too, were trying to cram her sadness back into a hidden place from where it couldn't surface. Everyone was so thoughtful about Joyce, offering her all their kindness and support, that it was easy to forget that Nana and Granddad had lost a daughter who they had doted on and Auntie Cath had lost her only sister. With a start, Joyce thought that perhaps she had been behaving in a self-absorbed way and was lost too often in her own private depths of melancholy when she should be offering her consolation and help to the others who shared Mum's loss with her. Inwardly, she shook herself and resolved to be more gracious in her grief.

'But Nana,' she said, 'let's go back to Sid and Hettie. I know poor Hettie was bombed out and she's living with her sister, but what else?'

'Sid spent two days on a life raft in the middle of the ocean with a crowd of other seamen and do you know who rescued them?'

'No. Who?'

Nana looked over her shoulder to the door that led to the sitting room. She took two steps across the small kitchen and pushed the door closed then lowered her voice. 'Careless talk costs lives,' she said. 'Mr Hitler wants to know...'

Joyce sighed. Nana wouldn't move on until she'd recited the whole slogan. 'He wants to know the unit's name,' she continued. 'Where's it's going, whence it came. Ships, guns and shells all make him curious.'

'I can hear you,' Granddad called out from his chair by the window. 'But silence makes him simply Fuhrerious.' The kitchen door flew back on itself and Granddad walked in, paper and teacup in his hands.

'The enemy.' Nana pointed her finger at him. 'A spy in our midst,' she berated. 'See how easy it is to give the wrong information to the other side, Joy love?'

'Oh, give over, woman,' Granddad said, pretending to bat her out of the way with his paper. 'Did I hear the rattle of the SOS biscuit tin?'

'You did, but I don't know what you've done to deserve one,' Nana said.

'I am going to sit here and tell Joy everything that Sid told me when we went to the pub, as you don't seem to be passing on much of the news,' he said in his rasping voice. 'And that warrants a bit of biscuit in my eyes.'

Once again, Nana took the top off the box of hallowed sweet treats. They sat around the table with their cups and crumbs of Garibaldis and Bourbon creams and Granddad told Joyce that Sid had been rescued by a U-boat of all things. Joyce could hardly believe what she was hearing. 'And they didn't take the men as prisoners?' she asked.

Granddad shook his head. 'It wasn't that simple. The U-boat surfaced, and someone asked the men in broken English if they had food and water.'

'"A bit," the British said, holding up what little they had left. "But not much, thanks to you blighters." Then the Jerries threw over watertight bundles of dried food and water and said they would alert the authorities to where our lads could be found and rescued. And true to their word, they were picked up by a rescue boat within hours.' He shook his head.

'I don't care if the captain of that U-boat is the enemy, he deserves a medal for showing such mercy. Without him our

Sid and the whole boatload of men would be lying on the bottom of the ocean right now.'

Nana nodded in agreement. They sat in silence for a few minutes and Joyce would have taken bets that Nana and Granddad, like her, were thinking about how different things might have been for their family if it hadn't been for an implausible act of compassion.

'I've never heard anything like it,' said Joyce. 'Won't the captain be court-martialled by the German authorities?'

'No,' Granddad said. 'It happens a lot, according to Sid. They're more interested in bombing or setting fire to the cargo than they are in capturing the men, who they take pity on and think of almost as comrades at sea.'

'Do the British do the same for the Germans?' Joyce wondered.

'No idea.' Granddad looked thoughtful. He smoothed his moustache into place, gyrated his cup and peered in at the whirlpool of dregs he'd created. 'But I like to think there's some rapport amongst them,' he said. 'Don't you?'

'I suppose,' Nana said. 'In that instance. But when I think about all the upset they've caused. Our Maggie gone. All the dead and hurt. All the mess everywhere. I can't see how it'll ever get sorted.' Nana was getting more and more agitated, her face puce with rage. She pushed a hanky under her spectacles and wiped at her eyes.

'Alright, Ada love,' Granddad said, placing his gnarled hand tenderly on top of his wife's fist. 'We've done it before, we'll do it again.'

'But the last one wasn't as bad, Reg, not over here at any rate.'

The three of them sat and listened to the incessant noise of machinery trying desperately if not to rebuild, at least to make good. From somewhere close by, a man's whistle split the air and the picture in Joyce's head of Sid on a huge expanse of merciless sea changed to one of Bill, steering his pushbike with one hand, his chest puffed out with pride. At least she didn't have to add a last image of her brother on a life raft, hungry and frightened and vulnerable to the gallery of horrors she carried around with her.

Granddad wandered back to the sitting room and Nana began to clear away the tea things, making sure the lid was tight on the biscuit tin. 'Anyway, Joy love, me and Auntie Cath took them to the your mum's grave and Sid was pleased with the headstone. But he was a bit worried about you.'

'We're all worried about each other,' Joyce said.

'No, about Derek. He said he doesn't know much about your fella, only what you've told Hettie in your letters and as your older brother he feels he needs to know more and give his consent or at least his approval. So he said can you please send him a letter and tell him all about your young man.'

Like being rescued by the captain of a U-boat, that was another unexpected twist in Sid's life. He'd struggled with reading and writing at school and always said that letters were a jumble on the page. Mum had been patient, sitting with him and trying to help him untangle the hieroglyphics, but Joyce could remember him getting so frustrated that he'd bolt out the door and not come home for ages. The school said they were helping, but Joyce didn't know how being made to face the wall in the dunce's corner would encourage a child to be literate. But when his teacher said Joyce had all the brains, Mum had been livid and reminded her of the skills Sid possessed – woodwork, numbers, geography and singing and then said she would not allow the school to cuff him around the ear or throw board rubbers at him or keep him in at dinner time, but Joyce thought his teachers found other ways to humiliate him.

Clouds scurried across the sky and cast checkerboard shadows of light and dark on the kitchen table. A quiver of guilt passed through her, as it had done occasionally when she was growing up, at the thought that reading and writing had come to her so easily. She could remember feeling full of childish remorse at the thought that perhaps she had unfairly acquired part of Sid's brain and she would squeeze her eyes closed during Sunday School and pray to be able to give them back to him. But of course she hadn't been able to manipulate that prowess for Sid and he'd left school the minute he could and joined the Merchant Navy hoping never to have to read and write again.

Mum worried about him understanding the letters she sent him, though, but Sid said he gave a mate a cigarette to read them to him and another to write a reply. That was until Hettie came along and perhaps because he was older or she loved him in a different way, she was able to teach him the rudiments of how literacy worked and they could write uncomplicated letters to him and receive simple replies.

Most of the news, though, went through Hettie but there had been no need to tell her all the particulars, as Nana and Auntie Cath would have written to her about Derek in great detail. Joyce loved Sid, but because he lived elsewhere and there was quite a big age difference between them, she didn't feel as if she knew him very well. But she had always harboured the hope that they would become closer and since Mum had been gone, she thought it was a necessity. Now, Sid had specifically asked that she write to him and she wanted to set about it straight away.

'Have you got washing to do from your trip?' Nana asked. 'Shall I do yours with Granddad's things?'

'No, ta. I'll do mine, Nana.' Joyce jumped up right away, desperate to avoid rinsing her new undergarments in the same water used for Granddad's tatty vests and underpants.

Nana went to fill the copper with a sprinkling of soap flakes, but Joyce took over and said if Nana gathered her dirty clothes together she would see to all the laundry. Nana was very grateful. 'You are a good girl, Joyce Margaret,' she said.

Heat gathered around the base of the copper and Joyce heard the ping of bubbles as they burst against the metal interior. In a hurry to get through her chores so she could write to Sid before she had to leave for work, she set out the copper dolly and arranged the mangle on the flagstones outside the back door, just as Nana did.

'Granddad,' she called into the sitting room. 'What time is it, please?'

There was a creak as Granddad got up from his chair and a scrape as he turned the clock towards him. '3.05, my duck,' he said.

Joyce did the calculations quickly and figured that if she hurried she could get the washing done by 5.00, take an hour to write to Sid, return Uncle Terry's suitcase and say hello to Flo and still be at Report and Control in plenty of time before dusk descended. The schedule left no time for a nap, which she knew would benefit her before the long night ahead, but the longer she left writing the letter, the longer it would take to get delivered to Sid and she so wanted to build an affinity between them.

The water in the copper built to a furious crescendo. Gingerly, Joyce lifted the lid, turned her face away from the steam and lowered her blouses and skirts, scarf and gloves into the cauldron and gave them a stir. While they were agitating, she washed hers and Nana's underclothes in the sink and pegged them on the line where they would dry in no time. Then back to the copper where she lifted out her clothes and dropped Granddad's things into the roiling water. By the time she'd mangled and hung everything to dry, she was hot and bothered; her sleeves were rolled up above her elbows, her curls had turned to frizz and she could have done with that lie down. No wonder Nana refused to allow a fire in the house on washdays and insisted on opening the kitchen window and back door. Wiping the film of sweat from her top lip, she knew she could not allow Nana to do the laundry any longer and she would take over that task for all three of them.

She found some writing paper, tiptoed past Granddad who was asleep in his chair and shut her bedroom door softly behind her. The window was open a crack and she could hear Nana nattering to the woman next door about powdered eggs, then she heard Sid's name and hers but couldn't make out the details. Leaning back against her propped-up pillow, she spread the paper out on her lap but had to get up again when she realised she didn't have a pen. There were a couple of blunt pencils in the sideboard which would make her letter look as though it had been torn from a child's copybook or a dip pen somewhere in the sitting room that would be so painstaking to use her hour would be up before she started. Then she remembered the Taperite that Derek had asked her to stow in her handbag after he'd finished the crossword on the train home and she thought about how lovely it would be to form letters with it and sign her name with a flourish in its jet-black ink. Derek wouldn't mind, she knew that about him now and he would probably insist she keep it if he thought for a minute that she longed to feel the heft of it in her small hand.

The pen didn't disappoint, it sat elegantly between her fingers and thumb and when she began to write, the ink flowed in a perfect, steady stream across the page.

Dear Sid love,

I could not believe it when I got home from Norfolk and Nana told me you and Hettie had been to visit. If only I'd known that you were coming to see us I would have changed my plans so I could have spent time with you.

She wanted to let him know how important it was to her that they stay close, but she didn't want to overwhelm him with sentiment or lead him to think she was lonely or unhappy. She also wanted the letter to sound natural, as if she were sitting talking to her brother, and not contrived or formal in any way. It was a fine line to tread and she brought the pen to her mouth to nibble on its end, as she did with pencils at work, then started when she realised what she was doing. She would have to watch herself as she dare not put a chip or dent in such an expensive writing implement.

It's important for me, she carried on, *that we keep in touch now that it's just the two of us. I know it's never going to come to that, or to one of us being on our own as we're very lucky to have Nana, Granddad, Auntie Cath, Uncle Terry, Flo, Hettie and your little ones to call family. But you know what I mean, now that Mum's gone and there are no other brothers or sisters. So I was delighted that you asked me to write directly to you with all my news of Derek, who will be most upset at having missed the opportunity to meet you.*

Derek and I haven't known each other for long, but we are becoming closer and more serious as every day goes by. He's very kind, he's very funny and he's very tall. Mum loved him and approved of us seeing each other and he has been wonderful to me and the whole family since Mum was killed.

Now, I'm not sure if I should tell you this as I don't want you to worry unnecessarily, but there are two shadows that hang over us, one named Celia – also known as Derek's mother and the other is his chronic asthma. I can't say his mum doesn't like me as she hasn't done me the courtesy of getting to know me, even though I spent a week with her in her home in Norfolk.. I think it would be fairer to say she had a different type of woman in mind for her son – one who always says thank you, not ta and has more than one pair of going out shoes. That I believe we can deal with as Derek seems determined we continue with our friendship despite his mother's lack of enthusiasm. His asthma, though, is another matter. He is very level-headed and dismissive about it and I suppose I'm learning to follow his lead, but as a warning for when you do meet him, his attacks are alarming and it's a case of standing by and waiting until it's over as there's nothing anyone can do to help when he's in the throes of it.

All of that, though, is nothing compared with what you have had to endure time and time again. I cannot imagine how awful it was when your ship was destroyed and you had to wait to be rescued from the unpredictable elements. Granddad said you told him that sometimes after ships are torpedoed or bombed, the fuel or chemicals on board spill into the water and the surrounding sea is left ablaze. How you can possibly swim or row away when flames are licking around you is beyond my comprehension. You are very brave, but please don't be too brave as I would rather you were safe than courageous.

Reading back over this letter, I can see that some of it may well not get past the censors, but I will seal it and send it to Hettie who knows the best way of getting it to you.

With love from your little sister,

Joyce XXX

P.S. Please write back straight away.

Joyce bought a stamp at the post office which was temporarily trading from a side door of The Pelican then hurried to Auntie Cath's house to return Uncle Terry's suitcase. The Luftwaffe must have continued to be occupied elsewhere as London was still getting off lightly, although Joyce had heard on the wireless that coastal towns were taking hit after hit and the poor people in Portsmouth and Southampton were now living through raids like the ones Londoners had experienced for months on end. Controller Davis said that there was now a sophisticated radar system in place that gave the RAF time to meet the Jerries head on before they reached British shores. Even so, some German planes slipped the net and when they'd had enough of tormenting Brighton and Bournemouth, they used up the last of their bombs on London.

It had been easy to get used to blessed calm and respite after four months without a proper raid, but there was no room for complacency, Joyce knew that. Despite government reassurances that the Germans were through with them for now, who knew when they might return. It could be today, tonight, tomorrow, the middle of next week. Perhaps they would strike when Joyce was threading a shirt through the mangle or when she and Derek were entangled on one of their secluded park benches or when she was trying to master the intricacies of the Jitterbug with Flo.

But the breather was giving London a chance to get back on to a wobbly footing. And more than that, it was a delight to walk through streets whose aspect hadn't changed for weeks before she went to Norfolk. How reassuring it had been to find so much untouched by bombs and incendiaries when she walked up the steps from Report and Control and into the early morning light. If that continued to be the routine, she promised herself she would never tire of it.

Joyce breathed deeply, savouring air that wasn't thick with smoke. Paving stones on the corners of roads were smashed and crumbling, but they had been that way for weeks and she knew how to manoeuvre around them; five months ago, something red and slimy had appeared on the brickwork of the half-demolished hardware store, but it had been scrubbed clean and not only that building but all the pavements and houses and shops left standing had been free of stomaching-turning gore since the middle of May. They all knew what happened during a war, but none of them wanted to be faced with the flagrant reality. Mum was never far from Joyce's mind, and she shivered when she thought that although they'd found no trace of her, that was so much more bearable than what they could have had to deal with.

From across the road, Joyce saw Flo coming out of her front door. 'Flo,' she called and waved to her cousin.

'Joy,' Flo smiled and beckoned to Joyce that she would cross to meet her.

They threw their arms around each other as if, as Mum used to say, they'd been apart for years. And this time, during which so much had happened, it felt like it.

'How did it go, Joy love?' Flo asked.

Joyce groaned. 'It was memorable, Flo. For all the wrong reasons.'

'Oh,' Flo's eyes widened. 'That bad?'

'And worse. But if you want to hear the whole story and not the abridged version, it will have to wait until we have a good hour or more to chat.'

'The ABC tomorrow lunch-time?'

Joyce nodded. 'It's a date,' she said.

'I'll walk with you,' Flo said, twining her arm through Joyce's. 'I have some news.'

'More news!' Joyce said. 'How intriguing. I thought the big story was Sid and Hettie coming home.'

'It was so lovely to see them,' Flo said. 'Too bad you missed all the fun for a visit to Her Royal Haddock, Queen of Norfolk.'

'Don't let Derek hear you say that,' Joyce said. 'Although he would probably agree. Hang on.' She wriggled her arm free from Flo's rather firm hold. 'I'll just take the suitcase in to Uncle Terry.'

'He's at work,' Flo said without missing a beat and clutched at Joyce's arm again. 'Doing an extra shift.'

'Is he allowed?' Joyce asked. 'I thought he could only do so many hours a week because of his heart.'

'It's just sweeping and cleaning. Gentle stuff. He'll be fine.'

'I hope so.' Joyce shrugged. 'I'll give it to Auntie Cath then.'

'Give it to me,' Flo said, tugging on the handles.

'Steady,' Joyce said, puzzled at Flo's strange behaviour. 'It wasn't in the best condition to begin with but I don't want Uncle Terry to think I've bashed it about.'

'He won't look at it twice. Now please, Joy, let me have the case and I'll give it to Dad later. Come on,' she pulled at Joyce's sleeve.

Joyce could see now that her cousin was in a bit of a state, so gave up possession of the shabby suitcase and let herself be led away. 'What is it, Flo? You're beginning to worry me.'

They cut through Westbourne Green, Joyce almost running to keep up with her cousin. 'Slow down,' Joyce said. 'You know my legs are shorter than yours.'

Flo stopped and, breathing heavily, put her hand out to Joyce. 'Sorry, Joy love,' she said.

'But whatever is the matter? Are you ill? Pregnant? You'll have to tell me now because I'm due at work soon.'

Flo stopped and a huge grin lifted her face. She squinted against the late autumn sun and the light that sifted through the trees caught her light brown hair as it moved around her shoulders. *She really is lovely,* Joyce thought. And so full of fun and life and anticipation of something that neither of them would be able to properly explain if asked to do so. Despite the atrocities of the bombs and chandeliers of incendiaries, losing Mum and her home, she sometimes still felt a heightened sense of expectancy about... she could never find a word for it. Something elusive and intangible that never quite seemed to come to fruition.

'I'm joining the WAAFs,' Flo said and saluted smartly.

Joyce stood inert and stared. 'Well,' she said at last. 'Is their uniform good enough for you?'

'Better than *that* old thing.' Flo ran her eyes up and down Joyce's dull serge.

They linked arms again and marched down the path, matching their footsteps with precision . 'Good for you,' Joyce said. 'But I didn't know you'd been thinking seriously about it.'

'Old Lady Neville did the dirty on me. Out of the blue she signed apprenticeship papers with her niece who's a lazy, simpering girl who hasn't got a clue about the difference between a permanent wave and a pin curl. The first day she was in the salon she ordered me to make her a cup of tea and sweep the floor. So I took off my tabard, put on my coat, walked out the door and didn't look back.'

'Good on you, Flo.'

'Ta, Joy love,' Flo said in a matter-of-fact tone of voice.

'Then I remembered what you'd said about war work so I carried on walking straight to the Employment Exchange and signed up for the WAAFs. I leave on Friday for basic training in Innsworth.'

'Innsworth?' Joyce echoed. 'Where's that?'

'Gloucester,' Flo answered. 'It sounds like a long way away, doesn't it?'

Joyce nodded. Until she'd been to Norfolk, she'd never been far from Notting Hill and neither had Flo. Gloucester might as well have been the other side of the world.

Suddenly, Joyce felt a sharp stab of regret at having encouraged Flo to join the Forces even though she would have been conscripted before too long. But coming so soon after Mum passing away and Sid narrowly cheating death she felt as though she were losing her beloved cousin, too. Despite knowing she was being irrational she heard herself whine, 'Why can't you be stationed at West Drayton so we could still see each other?'

Flo shook her head. 'I did ask, but was told I didn't have a choice and would have to go where I was told. I'll get leave, though, after I've finished the basic training. Then I could be posted any number of places.'

The prospect of not knowing where you would be living and working in a few months' time filled Joyce with dread. The transition from her home with Mum to Nana and Granddad's house had been hard enough. And yet, if she had been in Flo's position, she thought she might feel a tiny fizz of excitement alongside the trepidation. 'I'm going to miss you,' Joyce said. 'But we all have to do our bit and I'm proud of you. You'll make a fabulous WAAF. I bet you'll be promoted to Air Commandant in no time.'

They turned the corner and Flo tightened her grip on Joyce again. 'Come with me,' she said in an urgent whisper.

Joyce stopped and looked at the modest house that had been requisitioned for Group 1 Report and Control, the paraffin lamp in its makeshift box and the smashed billboard outside. Then she studied her brown lace-ups, thick stockings and the coarse blue uniform. The twinge of excited expectancy she'd imagined Flo must be feeling dissipated and she knew that unless forced to, she would find it difficult to leave her duties in Notting Hill. 'Are you worried about going away on your own?' Joyce asked.

'No, I don't think so,' Flo said. 'Well, maybe a little bit. I just thought it would be an adventure.'

'Too much of an adventure for me. Besides, there wouldn't be any guarantee we'd be together.'

For a moment, Flo's eyes clouded. 'No, I suppose not,' she said.

'Look, I must go,' Joyce said. 'See you tomorrow afternoon.' She made for the door to take her to the basement that she knew would be buzzing with activity. Then she remembered the suitcase. She called after Flo and asked why she'd been reluctant to let her hand it in to Auntie Cath.

'Mum and Dad were a bit shocked at my decision.' She shrugged her shoulders up to her ears, then let them drop. 'I didn't want them to talk you into talking me out of it.'

Joyce laughed. 'I shouldn't think there's any fear of that,' she said. 'And I'm sure they think you've done the right thing.'

The crooked nail holding ARPM1 forms was in the same position on the wall; the stairs were as dark as they had ever been; the tea urn was babbling; Controller Davis said how pleased he was to see her back; her colleagues asked her about her holiday; her map had not been tampered with. She took off her coat and smoothed her hair and uniform, checked the pins and labels and flicked through the pile of filing teetering on the table. Despite the harrowing nature of the one and only reason that a Report and Control Centre existed and she was working in its depths, it felt secure and warm and as it should be. It greeted her as if she were coming home and held her there in its warm embrace.

* * *

One rainy afternoon, after a visit to see what was left in the British Museum, Derek curtained them under his umbrella, bent low, fixed his raven black eyes on hers and asked if she wanted to spend the hours left before they started work in his bedroom. It had been the last thing Joyce had expected him to ask and she pulled back, her hand on her throat. The colour rushed to and then from her face and she wondered if he'd read her mind, because part of her had been willing him to make a move in that direction. But now something – decorum or fear that if they took this next step he would never give up his inheritance and marry her because why would he if he had everything he wanted? And then where would that leave her?

Derek took her hand from her neck, held it gently in his and waited. But she could see a fevered flash in his eyes as he held her gaze. 'Shall we?' he asked softly.

'It seems so sudden,' she said. Then at the same minute they both laughed out loud. They knew they'd been building up to this for months. Through the steady stream of rain, Joyce watched curators and assistants tending the museum gardens that were now being used as allotments. An earthy smell of turned-over mud, marl and compost lingered. Her mind went back to the day Derek had asked her to be his special friend and how she had decided, against her character, to take a chance and be impetuous. She hadn't regretted that decision. And what had changed? Nothing, except they were more deeply entrenched in a war that could extinguish one or other or both of them at any minute. And then how sad not to have savoured each other to the full while they could.

'Yes,' she whispered. 'Yes. Before any more time passes. But I'm frightened.'

'Of me?' Derek was genuinely puzzled.

Joyce shook her head. 'Of you growing tired and leaving me to miss everything about you.'

'I think,' Derek said, 'that I'm the one who should be worried about that happening. But if I promised you it never would?'

'A promise like that, Sir Derek, would make everything okay.'

Derek laughed and they did their best to walk nonchalantly until they couldn't bear the wait and ended up almost breaking into a run when the house came into view. As luck would have it, Derek's friends were out although it did occur to her later, with a blush, that the chances were he had engineered the situation.

Under a replica of the yellow cover that had adorned the bed in her room in Norfolk, she felt naïve and timid which was, she reminded herself, exactly what she was. Perhaps because he was older, Derek seemed to know what he was doing and when she felt brave enough to open her eyes and look at him, she saw him studying her with nothing in his eyes but tenderness and the will to please. It was all so much lovelier than she had imagined and when they lay close together, talking about Celia, what their work might have in store for them that night, how wonderful life was, she languished in the protective feel of his long limbs wrapped around her.

They stayed in that tableau until the last possible minute then tidied themselves, dressed and made a dash for the Tube. Reluctant to prise themselves apart, they huddled together on the platform, laughing and talking and oblivious, for a few blissful minutes, to the stark reminders of a war going on around them. Joyce couldn't stop smiling and refused to think about anything other than how lucky she was, until her optimism and abandonment were pulled up short by Derek suffering the worst asthma attack she had witnessed.

* * *

Flo wrote to everyone on a regular basis, but between her and Joyce letters were endless, often crossing so that their news was disjointed. She said the camp was a series of long, low, forlorn-looking huts and she was in number nine. She and the other girls who'd started at the same time were given their fetching uniforms, a white kitbag, gas protection and their irons, which is what they called their cutlery, plate and mug. Then they'd been checked for infection and given a series of inoculations and marched around under the orders of their officers. According to Flo, they ate a lot of cabbage which was unlucky for her as she hated the stuff but by the end of each day she was nearly dropping from exhaustion so was glad of it.

What Flo had to tell was novel and interesting and Joyce was well aware that her letters related nothing new or different. She wrote about dancing lessons with Derek; Nana's sore leg; the coughs and colds everyone seemed to be dragging around with them as summer was turning into autumn. It would have been unethical to write about the map or the few air raids they were experiencing or how the rebuilding was coming along but she conveyed, without giving away details, that in London at least they were managing without any major catastrophes.

As for her private life with Derek, that she kept to herself. Although if Flo were to ask her about it, which she probably would when they next saw each other, Joyce would no doubt tell her the truth of the matter.

But the frequency with which Flo's letters arrived highlighted the time passing without a reply from Sid. Nana and Granddad said she mustn't worry as correspondence to the Merchant Navy crew could sit for months on a wharf anywhere in the world waiting for their ships to dock and then, for any number of reasons, miss being put in their hands. They'd all heard from Hettie, though, who had received one letter from Sid and seemed to be in reasonable spirits. Her big news was that Nana had been right and there was another Cooper baby on the way.

But it niggled at her. When she tried to sleep, a vivid picture of Sid alone on the sea, the skin on his face and arms rubbed raw by salt water and whipping winds, came to her as relentlessly as those of her mum, Bill and the young mother in Ladbroke Grove. During the long nights with the map, when she was up to date with the pins and the filing, her stomach would suddenly feel like a clenched fist and she willed a letter to be on the mat in the next post. But she should have known that her will could not control anything. If it could, the blasted war would never have started.

At the end of November, Auntie Cath was waiting for her at the top of the steps leading to Report and Control. Joyce knew right away that something was wrong as that had never happened before. With wardens pouring out of the basement to wearily make their way home and a thin pink stain streaking across a slate sky, Auntie Cath handed her a telegram and whispered, 'Oh, Joy love.'

Joyce stared at what she knew was the culmination of her anxieties clamped between her aunt's fingers. She refused to take it but asked, 'It's Sid, isn't it?'

Nodding, Auntie Cath put the telegram in her pocket. 'You can read it later. I'm sorry, love. Let's get you home.'

Auntie Cath put her hand under Joyce's elbow and they turned towards Nana's house. When Mum had been killed, she had refused to believe it had happened. But this time she knew that Sid was gone. With chilling clarity, she realised that the bombs and torpedoes and infernos and cruelty could seek anyone out at any time; the war had no respect for the fact she'd already lost people dear to her. If he'd been the cat that Nana had suggested, she thought ruefully, Sid might have had a few lives left. But he'd been a vulnerable human target who'd had his one precious life swept away from under him as if he'd been no more than a shred of flotsam or jetsam.

THIRTEEN

Friday 8 March 1974

Plans Joyce made for the evening before the move consisted of last-minute packing, double checking that the milk and papers had been cancelled, a tea of cheese and potato pie followed by a vanilla slice and then one long, last bath before bed. But of course she should have known, better than anyone, that the more solid the plans set down, the more likely they were to go awry.

First, Joyce was short of one box. She hunted around the echoing rooms, peering into crates and cases to see if she could possibly transfer a few items from one container to another. But she had been too organised and conscientious and couldn't find the smallest space in which to cram or slot the last few items she wanted to take with her. So she pulled on her mac, twisted her hair into a knot and headed out to scrounge a cardboard box from Portobello Market. How often in the twenty-nine years she'd lived in the flat had she popped out to the market or one of the shops close by for some little thing or another. And the hub of the high street close by had always been such a comfort when the isolation and routine she thrived on shifted into loneliness and she felt the need, quite unexpectedly, to be out amongst people.

The new flat wasn't far away, but it was out of range to make a quick dash out and back. That was another of the grumbles she had about the move – the new estate was part of a large residential area with one shopping parade that housed a fish and chip shop, a newsagent, a convenience store and a bookie's. No outdoor market, no library or doctor's surgery, no butcher or baker, gift shop, ironmonger or chemist. Shopping would have to be planned and if she forgot an item, she would have to do without or pick it up another time.

Hyde Park, which she knew well enough to consider her personal garden, would be further away and there would have to be considerable thought put into the walk there and back every time she wanted to make use of that open space. No matter how Mr Taylor and the girls in the office insisted, this was not a simple move for her but amounted to an almost complete re-ordering of her lifestyle. A way of life that she knew wouldn't suit a lot of people, but one that had been dependable and had sustained her.

So this, she thought, was the last time she could leave her flat without being prepared for every eventuality. After tomorrow she would have to cart around an umbrella, a list, gloves, a scarf, a sturdy shopping bag, don a pair of stout walking shoes, have another bag ready to put her warm things into if the weather turned and enough money to pay for what she needed plus any spontaneous purchases so she wouldn't have to make the trek back again later. And although she craved the peace and quiet that transcended when she locked and bolted herself into her flat, she couldn't imagine living without the knowledge that a lively racket was hers to listen to should she choose to open her front door.

A sharp blast of wind caught the hem of Joyce's mackintosh and she drew her collar up around her neck. For the thousandth time since she'd signed that blasted contract, she reprimanded herself by remembering that she had been faced with much worse circumstances and soldiered through them with dignity and resilience. But that was part of the problem – she'd done her bit and was thoroughly fed up with the thought of having to go through the same upheaval yet again.

As she rounded the corner, Joyce could see the striped awnings that covered the market stalls standing out in bold relief against the grey sky, the frills that hung from them sashaying in the wind. An odd concoction of greens on the turn and fresh citrus fruit whirled towards her and her mouth started to water. The six years of wartime deprivation had taken their toll and the smell or sight of any food caused the same desperate, habitual reaction. Rummaging in her pocket, she clasped her hand around a coin and smiled. She would buy herself an orange to eat later and let the sticky juice run down her chin and over her fingers.

Stallholders called out as they packed up, their lingo barely decipherable. All Joyce could make out were fragmentary words such as 'get your' or 'pound' or 'lovely bunch' or 'the last few'. One of her favourites, a stocky man named Ken who ran a stall with his burly teenaged sons, was building a tower from wooden crates and breaking down cardboard boxes. 'Hello, my lovely,' he said when he saw her. 'Bit blowy for you, ain't it? You'll get lifted off your tiny feet in this.'

Joyce laughed. 'No fear of that,' she said. 'It would take more than a breeze to make a kite out of me.'

'Good on ya, girl. What can I do you for?'

'Well, I'm on the cadge for a box, please. If you have one spare.'

The greengrocer indicated his horde with a sweep of his hand. 'Take your pick, lovely. And I won't even charge you.'

'Bless your heart,' she said. 'Perhaps I could take two off your hands just in case?'

Joyce could feel Ken watching her as she picked over the boxes, looking for the sturdiest with well-fitting lids. 'Having a clear-out?' he asked.

'Of sorts.' She nestled one box inside another. 'I'm moving tomorrow.'

'Oh,' Ken said, genuine interest in his voice. 'You're leaving us? Where are you off to, then?'

'I'm not going too far,' she said, although it seemed like the end of the earth. 'The Shakespeare Estate.'

'Oh yeah?' Ken stopped what he was doing, folded his arms and seemed to be settling himself down for a long chat. 'The Missus' auntie is there. We helped her move in.' With a lift of his chin he indicated his sons who were busy on a van that had been nudged close to the tarpaulin walls of the stall.

'It's not my choice,' Joyce said. 'I am, in effect, being evicted to make way for the demolition crews.'

'Same thing happened to Auntie Maude,' Ken said. 'And about time, too. She couldn't wait to leave her damp old flat. It smelled of something rotting under the floorboards and it was a death trap, too.' He shook his head. 'Whenever she put the geyser on to run a bath or wash up, she said it sounded like a doodlebug with her name on it ratcheting through the sky. So you must be pleased to be going somewhere modern, like she was?'

Searing tears threatened to flood Joyce's eyes and embarrass her. She clamped her mouth shut so Ken couldn't see how her lips trembled. Pretending to consider the seams of the boxes in her arms, she gathered herself together. 'I've lived in my flat for almost thirty years,' she said. 'And I... well... I like it. It's my home.' She admonished herself for giving such a vague and insipid explanation.

Ken seemed stupefied. 'Thirty years,' he echoed. 'Time for a change, then.'

He didn't come across as insensitive, but she thought his reaction was flippant. She was fed up with change and had been since 1945. But what would he know about that? He'd been a child during the war and like everyone else who couldn't really remember those years he yearned for change, for adventure, for a break from the day to day. Perhaps that wasn't his fault, but his wife's aunt should know better.

'How much for a cauli?' A woman with a headscarf knotted so tightly under her chin that she moved her mouth like a ventriloquist, pointed to a few brown-tinged cauliflowers on the edge of a trestle table.

Ken jumped towards her, eager to get rid of the decomposing produce. 'Three pence to you, my lovely. And for an extra two I'll throw in this head of cabbage.' Ken held up a gnarly leafed green vegetable as if he were offering the woman an emerald.

'That's on its last legs,' the woman said.

'So am I, my love,' Ken quipped. 'But you wouldn't say no to me, would you?'

'Oh, go on then,' the woman said. She and Ken laughed with salacious delight.

As Ken peeled a bag from the hook above his head, Joyce took the opportunity to slip away unnoticed. The orange would have to wait for another time.

All day the wind had whipped across the clouds, revealing

capricious patches of bright blue lurking behind them. Now the grey won out. The sky became a heavy blanket; a crack of thunder was followed by a firebolt of lightning; sleet and rain draped towards the pavement in front of Joyce's feet and splashed back up onto her legs and coat.

Caring more about the boxes than herself, she dived into the nearest doorway to wait out the worst of it. It came down in vicious, icy needles and there was nothing that Joyce could do but stand and watch. Before long, the relentless deluge caused rivers of filthy water to stream down the street, bits of tomato and onion skin and pear stalks caught in the slipstream.

A lot of people would be pleased to get rid of the sights she stood and watched, but she felt hollow and homesick already at the thought that this was the last time she could say she lived a matter of minutes away from the market. Taking a deep breath, she swallowed the lump in her throat like she'd taught herself to do years ago when she'd lived with deeply unsettling feelings daily.

The thrum on the roof slowed to a steady drip; a cleft of light opened in the sky and was followed by another. Joyce kept her head down so she could avoid the worst of the puddles and within minutes she was home, boxes dry and intact. But there was Mr Taylor, his back to her and his nose pressed against her window. She hesitated, wondering if she should circle the streets in the hope that he would get fed up and leave. Then again, she knew from experience that Mr Taylor did not give up easily and was apt to wait for ages if he got it into his mind that he wanted to see her. Really, where were his manners? She'd signed the contract and agreed to the eviction, so surely he should move on to bothering someone else.

She shifted the boxes from one arm to the other and that was enough for Mr Taylor to start, turn, and greet her with an almost senseless smile on his face. 'Miss Cooper,' he bounded up the steps. 'Let me, please. Did you get caught in the downpour?' He reached for the boxes. 'Oh, that's so silly of me. I can see you managed to avoid it.'

Where did he get his interminable energy from, Joyce wondered. She could almost see his tail wagging he was so eager to please. Well, perhaps he should be after she'd caught him peering through her net curtains.

'I'm alright, really,' Joyce said. 'Besides, a drop of rain never hurt anyone.'

She unlocked the front door, gave it good kick at the bottom and took the boxes from him. Then they stood and stared at each other. After a beat or two during which Mr Taylor looked awkward and gangly, he said, 'Have you still got much to do? Can I help?'

'Bits and bobs. Then I must get an early night.'

'Yes,' Mr Taylor said. 'It's the big day tomorrow.'

As if she needed him to remind her.

He shuffled a bit and then, as always, Joyce felt sorry for her unwelcoming demeanour, relented, and asked him if he wanted to come in.

'Thank you,' he said. 'For a few minutes.' He picked up the boxes and strode down the hallway. 'Which room shall I put them in?'

'Leave them in the kitchen, please,' she said, trotting behind him.

'My goodness, you've done a great job. Everything looks so bare.'

Again, she didn't need telling. She'd been rattling around

in the ever-increasing emptiness for more than a week. 'Tea?' she asked, holding up the kettle.

'Yes, please. A quick cup.'

It really was getting to the point where everything she did, each step she took, every feeling of safety these walls and ceilings and floors had bestowed on her would be the last and she wanted to savour these moments as she had spent most of them in this flat – on her own. But all she could do was wait for Mr Taylor to tell her, when he saw fit, why he was there.

'I'm sorry,' she said, putting a cup down in front of him. 'I haven't a biscuit to offer you. I've been running food down and I didn't expect callers.'

'Don't apologise, Miss Cooper,' Mr Taylor said. He patted the bright blue shirt over his stomach. 'Jacqueline and I are going out for dinner later so I'm saving myself.'

'Lovely,' Joyce said and hoped he wasn't going to wait for his date in her flat.

'I just wanted to make sure all was well for tomorrow. I wondered... you know... if I could do anything.'

'No, thank you, I believe I'm well-prepared.'

Mr Taylor smiled and for a moment, when she could see beyond his long hair, whiskers and sideburns, an inkling of what Jacqueline might find attractive about him shone through. Not for the first time she noticed the similarities between him and her Derek – his height; his long legs; his easy manner; the way he would do anything he could to help others; his shy confidence; the disregard he had for his own good looks. Joyce had to turn her head away for fear that he might be embarrassed by the softness in her eyes or the smallest hint of an upward tilt to her mouth.

Mr Taylor went to say something, but then seemed to think better of it and sipped from his cup instead. No doubt he had been going to spew another of his stock phrases about why the move was the best thing for her; how much she would love her new flat; how she would enjoy her new neighbours and their silly MIA Club. She'd heard it so many times before and didn't want to hear it again. Hoping to create a diversion she said, 'Actually, now you're here, perhaps there is something you could do.'

Taken aback, Mr Taylor spluttered and choked on his tea. He looked as delighted as a child who'd been asked to set out the copybooks for his teacher. 'Anything, Miss Cooper. Lifting, packing, labelling? Shall I take down your curtains?'

Joyce shook her head. 'I'll do that early tomorrow morning. It wouldn't feel right in here tonight with bare windows. But here,' Joyce handed him a roll of parcel tape on a contraption with a serrated-edge. 'Can you please take this and tape all the boxes I've written on? I'll pack the last few things myself then I can't blame anyone else if things get broken, can I?'

Jumping up with enthusiasm, Mr Taylor set the chair he'd been sitting on into a rattle, steadied it, then clamoured for the tape dispenser. She pitied Jacqueline when the time came for them to move into their new house but then again, perhaps his eagerness and boyish charm were what she found endearing about him.

They worked companionably in separate rooms – Joyce in the bedroom stowing away anything left lying around and Mr Taylor roaming from room to room in search of unsealed boxes. The sound of tape being torn against a cutting edge was the only noise that bounced around in the almost empty flat until Mr Taylor started to whistle. Joyce shoved the last of her costume jewellery into a plastic bag, burrowed it deep inside a pink knitted toilet roll cover and sat on the bed. Mr Taylor's whistle was a bit scratchy, not full-bodied and hearty, so she had to listen carefully to discern the tune he was aiming for. After a few more bars she realised it was 'Billy Don't be a Hero', which was better suited to a reedy whistle than one that was robust.

'Any boxes ready to go in here?' Mr Taylor brandished the dispenser as if it were a weapon.

'The last two are just there, thank you.'

'And I do apologise for whistling, Miss Cooper.' Mr Taylor lined up the flaps of the boxes and taped them. 'I know that some people think it's the height of bad manners and I know you're a stickler for etiquette.'

'Good manners don't cost a penny and make everyone happy.'

'Yes, I absolutely agree,' Mr Taylor said.

'But I don't mind whistling,' she said. 'I never have. It reminds me of...' Joyce broke off, aware that she was bringing to mind things that had been buried for a long time and which were better off staying that way.

Mr Taylor sat back on his haunches and smiled. 'Who do I remind you of?' he encouraged. 'An old matinée idol? Jacqueline thinks I look like Guy Madison who played Wild Bill Hickock in a film many years ago. Do you know who I mean?'

Joyce studied him for a minute. 'Yes, I suppose you do, a little bit. But it was your whistling that reminded me of someone I once knew.' She felt as if she were in a dream, with all the edges of the pictures she conjured up blurry and imprecise. 'Not Wild Bill Hickock, but another Bill. A Bill more like the Billy in your song – a hero.' The images in her mind swam together then became as crystal clear and luminous as stills from a film.

Standing abruptly, Joyce smoothed the wrinkles out of her

bedcover and thought about how she could tell Mr Taylor, as politely as possible, that it was time for him to go.

But Mr Taylor showed no signs of departure. 'I'd love to hear about this Bill,' he said in a soft voice. 'I'll bet it's a fascinating story.'

'Yes,' she said. 'Yes, it is. Fascinating in retrospect, tragic at the time.' Then for some reason she couldn't fathom, she told Mr Taylor all about Bill and how his whistling had been cut short. She thought the act of retelling might make her feel ashamed, as if she'd let the side down in an undignified way. But apart from being wrung out, she felt relief. 'And that, Mr Taylor, was that,' she said. 'Now I really must get organised for an early night, if you don't mind?'

Staring at her as if in a trance, it took Mr Taylor a few moments to come to. 'Of course, how thoughtless of me.' Then he stopped and for one dreadful beat Joyce felt sure he was going to hug her. 'I'm so sorry about your friend Bill,' he said.

She shrugged. 'One of many. I'm sure your parents and grandparents have stories about that era, too.'

'Oh, yes, they have. But none of them quite so poignant or... heartfelt.' He did put his hand out then, to touch hers, but she accepted the gesture as an offer of a handshake and dismissed him with a quick 'goodnight'.

Jaded, Joyce demanded she pull herself together and that involved not thinking about the story she'd related to Mr Taylor or about the blasted move tomorrow. She put the cheese and potato pie in the oven, heated a tin of peas and ate her dinner at the kitchen table. When she'd finished she washed the dishes, dried them and packed away everything except the kettle, the teapot and one cup and saucer which she would need in the morning.

Next, the long-awaited soak in the bath. But click and turn

as she might, the geyser refused to splutter into life. She hit it with the flat of her hand, but all that achieved was a stinging palm. The thought that she would have to take a detour in the morning to leave a note in the landlord's door passed through her mind, then she remembered there was no need. She rested her head on the geyser and the metal felt cool on her forehead.

She had a quick wash instead with cold water and got into bed with a cup of tea and a copy of *Woman's Realm* on the bedside table next to her. When her eyelids grew heavy, she settled down for what she hoped would be an uninterrupted night. But she fidgeted and fussed and the sticky, bothersome bedclothes wound themselves around her legs and arms as they hadn't done since the first few weeks after her mother was killed and she'd moved in with her grandparents.

FOURTEEN

DEREK

March 1942

In the months before Flo joined up, she had been unhappy and unenthusiastic when she talked about her job and had seemed, to Joyce, like a drifting, untethered hot air balloon. That image was very apt as that was what she was involved in now and she was full of it.

After her initial training with the WAAFs, there were a number of roles she could have chosen to pursue such as aircraft mechanic or parachute packer, telephonic or telegraphic operator or meteorologist. But not Flo. She'd opted to be part of a Barrage Balloon Squadron and had been sent for training to the Number One RAF Balloon Training Unit at Cardington. Next up had been a position in the Number Four Balloon Centre in Surbiton and as she got on so well, she'd been seconded back to Cardington as an Operational Training Officer, for which she was due to report for duty the next day. She'd earned a stripe and Joyce thought the way Auntie Cath boasted about her daughter, the WAAF Section

Officer, could have rivalled her own mum's bragging about her.

'Whatever made you decide on balloon handling?' Joyce asked her cousin. She and Flo were sitting on Flo's bed in Auntie Cath and Uncle Terry's house. The bedroom window was open despite the earlier rain and the warm smell of drying pavements drifted in. From a distance, they heard the tinkle of the rag and bone man and the sturdy clop of the milkman's horse making its way back to the dairy. Then a sudden crash and the insistent bell of an ambulance broke the almost bucolic aura. Once upon a time they would have reacted, but neither girl started and Joyce felt both sad and self-satisfied that they'd become so stoic.

'I can't imagine the uniform you wear for taming a barrage balloon is glamorous.'

Flo laughed. 'No, it's definitely not,' she said. 'It makes your scruffy old serge look like the height of fashion. We have to wear dungarees that have dark sweaty stains under the arms and are permanently spattered with mud.'

'So what was the attraction?'

'There was just something about it that fascinated me,' Flo said. 'Initially, I could not believe that we were being allowed to train for such important, heavy work and then I thought, why not take the blokes up on it?'

'Good on you,' Joyce said. 'I do believe there are some wardens who think to this day that women shouldn't be allowed in the Civil Defence.' The thought of that poster asking for men to join the ARP still made her hackles rise.

'When we stood to attention at the end of our first day of training, one of the girls heard an officer whisper to another, "Good God, petticoats in the RAF." And his friend replied, "These damned women are everywhere." "And a good job, too," my friend Ellen said. "Or none of us would be here, would we?"'

'That's a fantastic story.' Joyce said.

'Then,' Flo had continued, 'at the end of the three weeks, I'll be blowed if one of the same officers didn't congratulate us by saying he was most impressed.'

'Do you think he meant it?' Joyce asked.

'We all thought he was sincere. He certainly seemed to be.'

Flo seemed excited and a bit agitated about the posting. Stuffing the last of her possessions into Uncle Terry's old suitcase, she turned to Joyce and said, 'Let's go underwear shopping.'

Joyce was taken aback by the statement that seemed to come from nowhere. 'Why?' she asked. 'Have you saved enough coupons to buy something new? I know I haven't.'

Flo plonked herself down next to Joyce and sighed. 'No, probably not. But don't you ever want something to just happen?' All of a sudden she looked defeated and downhearted. 'I don't know.' Something. Anything,' she sounded exasperated.

'Well,' Joyce said. 'It seems to me that you don't have to look far to see that there's an awful lot happening.'

'I don't mean the war.' Flo pushed Joyce's shoulder. 'In fact, anything other than the war. Something nice that doesn't involve putting on a uniform or making your way to war work or counting rations or waiting for the next bomb to drop.' She looked at Joyce expectantly, as if she desperately wanted her cousin to understand.

And of course, Joyce did. She longed to be able to toss aside her scratchy, irritating uniform and wear a dress made of some kind of shiny, clinging material. To meet Derek, too, at a reasonable time in the evening and sit with him without fear of a raid making them fall to the ground for cover. Or not to live with the constant anxiety that one of your loved ones' houses might be the next to take a packet. And to have the business of Derek and his inheritance settled one way or another so they could be married and sleep with each other whenever they wanted to in their own bed.

'So, let's do something fun and spur of the moment. If we can buy a little something then we will. But if not,' she shrugged, 'well we can dream, can't we?'

Caught up in Flo's whirlwind, Joyce said, 'Yes. Alright then. Oxford Street here we come.'

So they spent a carefree couple of hours discussing the pros and cons of a bit of lace here and a tiny bow there and Flo did manage to find a pair of rather functional knickers in some kind of silky, peach-coloured material that made her smile before she had to say goodbye and run for her train.

* * *

Letters flew back and forth to and from Flo, and Joyce sat next to Nana on the old settee, each of them absorbed in the correspondence they'd received in the first post. Granddad was yet again dismantling the wireless in an attempt to get the antiquated model to pick up a signal. 'What does she say, then?' he asked in between grumbling about the tiny screws he was finding troublesome to keep between his fingers.

'She's home on leave tomorrow,' Joyce and Nana said at the same time.

All three of them laughed and Nana squeezed Joyce's hand. 'Jinx,' she said.

'That will be lovely,' Granddad said, his voice tremulous.

'If we get to see her as she'll be off out with you and Derek most of the time. As usual.'

'Oh, don't begrudge them their fun, Grumpydad,' Nana said. 'And I hope you're not getting grease on my chair covers. Can't you do that in the shed?'

Granddad looked offended but pocketed the screws, picked up the radio and headed towards the garden.

'I only see Flo during the day when she's home,' Joyce defended herself. 'Derek and I are at work every night. Except for a night off once in a while.'

'Oh, don't mind him.' Nana patted Joyce's arm. 'And don't you worry, we see as much of Flo when she's on leave as we did before she joined up.' She peered at her letter through her thick, black-rimmed spectacles. Then she took them off and tried to read without them. 'Your letters are always much longer than mine. What else does she say?'

Joyce was never sure how much Flo told her parents or Nana so she picked through the gossip from her cousin as if she were censoring an important document. 'Well,' Joyce scanned through the letter, playing for time. 'She writes quite a lot about her daily routine and about the other girls in her Balloon Squadron.'

'Yes,' Nana nodded. 'They sound like good fun.'

'And about the grim food they're given. She says she's tired because they train and work hard but she doesn't mind that and as always, she misses us and can't wait to be home.' But there was a paragraph in the letter that Joyce didn't want Nana to see, so she folded the pages and pushed them back into the envelope before her grandmother asked to have a look.

'That's exactly what she wrote to me,' Nana said. 'Perhaps her handwriting's bigger when she writes to you so she uses more paper.' Nana looked at Joyce from the corner of her eye and smiled knowingly. She popped her spectacles on again, massaged the back of her leg, tucked her own letter behind a vase on the mantelpiece with all the others and said she was going to scrape a few carrots and potatoes for dinner. 'Are you sure you don't want some, love? With a bit of Toad in the Hole?'

'Oh, that's my favourite,' Joyce said. Rationing made sure that breakfast didn't fill her up like it used to and now the thought of sausages in batter with a bit of watery gravy made her ravenous.

But she was meeting Derek for lunch, then spending a few hours at his house before they started work, something they did now whenever the opportunity arose and hang the fellows who lived in his spare rooms. She checked the clock and found she had a few minutes, so nudged Nana away from the sink, took the knife from her and pared away at the vegetables. They were past their best, but they were used to that and she saved as much as she could by peeling the skin very thinly.

Nana measured a tiny bit of milk into a bowl, added water, flour and a shake of powdered egg and beat the lot together for the batter. Working with Nana in the kitchen hadn't been easy for Joyce at first, but she'd gradually come to appreciate the feelings of closeness and comfort that reminded her of being safe with Mum. Now she took every chance to help her grandmother in that small sanctuary which was pivotal to the necessities of life. It also made her think about how Nana had divided up household duties with Mum and Auntie Cath when they were young girls and how Nana's mother had probably done the same with her – all of them benefitting from the snug proximity to each other and the purpose they pursued. And that, Joyce thought, was the only godsend when it came to the endless cycle of women's work.

Nana stopped beating the Yorkshire pudding mixture and wiped her forehead with the back of her hand. 'We never hear about a young man, do we?'

'What are you on about, Nana?' Joyce said. 'I talk about Derek all the time and he's round here more than I am.'

'No, not your fella. A bloke for Flo.'

'Oh.' Joyce bent over the potatoes. 'Sliced or quartered?'

Nana deliberated. 'Sliced I think, love,' she said. 'I'll fry them with a bit of onion for a change.'

'Right you are,' Joyce attacked the potatoes with force to distract Nana from the topic of conversation as Flo had written that she might bring a manfriend home with her. But it was to be a surprise as she didn't want a repeat of Derek's initial introduction to the family.

'Excuse me, my girl,' Nana looked over at her. 'Mind my best knife. And those are English potatoes. They weren't grown by the Jerries, so no need to treat them harshly.'

'Sorry, Nana, I've just got one eye on the time.'

'Well,' Nana said, laying out a few gristly sausages in a roasting tin. 'It can't be for lack of good looks or personality. She's got both in droves. So I suppose she'll get a fella when she's ready, won't she?'

Joyce hated not telling the truth, even if it was lying by omission. She held up a slice of potato for Nana's inspection and asked, 'Is this thin enough?'

'Perfect, my love,' Nana said. 'Now I guess you have to get going.'

'Yes,' Joyce said. She kissed her grandmother and told her to tell Granddad she would see him later. 'I hope he gets his wireless sorted,' she shouted from the hall.

'Fat chance of that,' Nana yelled back. 'See you in the morning. Love you.'

'You, too, Nana,' Joyce called out. And she really did mean what she said.

Out in the fresh air, Joyce breathed a sigh of relief. It had been a close call not to betray Flo's trust as Nana had a knack of knowing when something was up. But this was the first time in ages that Flo had brought a young man home and Joyce didn't want to ruin the moment for her cousin. Besides, what she'd told Joyce was inconsequential – his name was Vernon; he was stocky; he was older than Flo, but she didn't say how much older, and he was in the Australian Air Force but posted to Bedfordshire. That, Flo said, was the most exciting bit. He was lively and fun and had the most charming accent. Joyce could picture Vernon from Flo's scant description of him as having sandy colouring and blue eyes; because of his age and exposure to the Australian climate, she added the attributes of a weather-beaten, lined face and a dusting of freckles.

Last night Paddington had taken four hits, Shepherds Bush one and Notting Hill three. That low count struck Joyce as a miracle after the hundreds they'd endured a matter of months ago. But she immediately berated herself for being so glib – one was too many and the few dropped on them should engender a state of utter shock and unacceptance instead of complacency. One of those evil devices had taken the side off a house she passed and gouged a sizeable hole in the street. She'd given the damage a light red label and pin and now a group of men peered into the crater to assess how to go about repairing the serious damage. All five of them stood in a circle, their heads almost touching, staring into the abyss. Then as one they drew back, burst out laughing and bowed their heads again to survey whatever it was they found so funny. Joyce was tempted to cross the road, tell them she knew of this hole in the ground almost as soon as it had happened and ask to be let in on the joke, but behind them two women and an elderly man were dragging what was left of their worldly goods onto the path at the front of the bombed house and she changed her mind. It wouldn't be respectful. Her eyes passed over their precious items – a colander; a singed rug; an armchair without arms; broken plates; a badly battered hearth tidy set; what looked like a dog bowl. A sad and sorry accumulation of life, but much more than was left of Mum's pile of nothing.

There was warmth in the air and a blue sky, a few flowers cautiously proclaimed spring amongst the debris and Joyce decided to walk to meet Derek outside the British Museum, one of their favourite haunts. She decided she'd had enough of feeling maudlin, although it was difficult not to let dark thoughts take over when faced with the effects of war wherever she went. Instead, she occupied her mind with plans for Flo's week of leave.

There would be dance lessons at Madame Beaupre's, perhaps an actual tea dance, a walk through Hyde Park or Holland Park for a change, a matinée at the Coronet to see *Bob's Your Uncle* or *Coastal Command* at the Electric and of course, the inevitable round of visits with Nana and Auntie Cath. But this was all supposing Vernon, if he did accompany Flo, wanted to dance or sit in a cinema seat. He might have other ideas as it could well be his first trip to London. If that were the case, he would probably want to see the sights, or what was left of them, and he might not want Joyce and Derek hanging around while he and Flo explored.

That realisation pulled Joyce up sharp. Although she maintained nothing had changed when she and Derek had met and become a couple, Flo had said that Joyce was different, not better or worse but certainly changed. She'd added that her job as a Bomb Plotter had altered her, too. On reflection, Joyce agreed although she did think that every day changes a person, let alone when major events occurred so she was wise enough to know that Vernon might want Flo all to himself and that Flo might allow that to be the case. She would have to wait and see.

Approaching the British Museum, Joyce realised that she hadn't formed any clear plan for the time Flo was home, but given she didn't know what Vernon would want to do and that she was eager to see Derek, she thought she could leave it for now. Besides, thinking about it had served its purpose and she'd been pleasantly distracted from the raw sights and sounds and smells and offences of the bombed-out streets she'd walked through. Of course, her ruminations meant she'd missed any number of other things that might have served as a diversion – oily rainbows in puddles; the children who had returned home in droves from evacuation in the country; the smell of tea and toast being sold from the ruins of a café; Canadian soldiers jostling each other along Bloomsbury Street.

As soon as she turned onto the walkway and could see the steps that led up to the Roman columns outside the stately building, she knew something was wrong. The gardens were eerily devoid of the assistants who usually swarmed over the vegetable patches they tended; instead, they had congregated in a huddle on the steps where a brouhaha was in progress. She squinted towards the fuss and walked faster, thinking she might be able to offer some assistance. Then she made out a pair of long, lanky legs sprawled haphazardly down the length of six or seven steps, one trouser leg pulled up to expose a white shin and a sagging argyle sock. Forgetting decorum, Joyce hitched her skirt, pumped her arms and ran towards where Derek lay awkwardly against the rough concrete.

'Derek,' she threw herself next to him, laddering her stockings and skinning her elbow.

Derek's face was puce, his breath an off-key accordion. All he could do was shake his head and claw at the air near his windpipe. His rescuers had opened his coat, loosened his tie, undone his top button and were trying to pin him back against the steps. 'No,' Joyce shouted. 'He must sit up.'

'I don't think so,' a middle-aged woman said.

'Someone's gone for the nurse,' a man said. 'Let her decide.'

'No,' Joyce insisted. 'I'm his girlfriend. I know what to do.' She put her hands under his arms and pushed him forward until he was bending from the waist and coughing into the empty space between his knees.

The crowd stood back and watched, evidently impressed by her competence.

'What's the matter with him,' someone asked. 'Bronchitis? TB?'

'Asthma,' she said, keeping her arm around him in what she knew was a gesture of possession, but she was here now and she knew what to do. Except as Derek's back and chest strained to expand in his fight to take a breath, some hidden force squeezed against his jarring attempts. She could feel his ribs swell to their full capacity beneath her hand and then instinctively labour for another inch, but his poor, scarred lungs would not respond. Not for the first time Joyce marvelled at how such a tall, energetic, powerful man could be lumbered with a weak, feeble chest.

Joyce began to sweat. This attack was not taking the same trajectory as the others she had witnessed – instead of the convulsions receding in waves they were escalating and she was frightened, but she continued to rub Derek's back in circles. He dragged his head up to look at her and for the first time she saw a startled panic in his red, watering eyes, as if he were an animal cornered in a trap.

The nurse was taking too long so Joyce turned to a woman behind her and mouthed, 'Call an ambulance. This is now an emergency.'

The woman dropped her trowel and ran for the museum. Joyce saw her stop and talk to the nurse who was hurrying from a side door and she willed them not to delay with lengthy explanations and descriptions. The nurse bustled down the steps and said they should try to move Derek into the museum where they could boil kettles and get him to breath in the steam. Derek shook his head and waved his rigid hands about in front of his mouth. On and on he coughed until Joyce was sure he would bark up his lungs in front of her there on the steps of the British Museum.

'He hasn't got croup,' she said. 'He suffers from asthma. Steam won't help.' She stood and tried to will the ambulance into sight or hearing. It must come quickly – all the times she'd organised one for someone else and now that she needed help there didn't seem to be one available. Help for Derek, she knew that's what had to happen. He was fading fast, in front of her eyes. She raked her hands through her hair and they came away wet and sticky; she bent to him and tried to find soothing words. 'It's alright, Derek,' she said, grasping his hand. His eyes were wild, his hands writhed and pulled at his throat. 'Help's on the way. Hang on. I'm here.'

Never before had she felt so helpless, so underprepared, so desperate. Then she heard the hopeful clatter of lifesaving bells. Crouching next to Derek, she whispered that the ambulance had arrived. 'Breathe with me' she said, placing his hand on her sternum and instructing him to expand his chest with hers and let air fill it smoothly and calmly. He tried; he really did. But his agonising attempts told her he was past her amateur doctoring. His eyes bulged and his tongue hung distended between his teeth. The ambulance stopped at the bottom of the steps and Joyce ran to meet the crew. A frantic hope that she would know them passed through her mind, but she didn't, as far as she could tell in her muddled state. 'Quickly,' she said, sure they were dragging their heels. 'He has asthma. But this is the worse attack I've witnessed.'

'Please stand back, Miss,' the thinner of the two ambulance officers said. 'And the rest of you can do the same.'

'But I'm...'

She was dragged a few feet back with the rest of the crowd, then jostled her way to the front where she could see and hear everything that was happening.

Derek had his pulse and heart checked; his lungs listened to.

'Please,' Joyce said. 'He needs the right medication.'

The crewman with the bald head smiled at her. 'Yes, Miss,' he said gently, 'that's why we're taking him to hospital. Are you this young man's girl?'

'Yes,' she said, allowing herself to feel a tiny ray of relief that these men knew what needed to be done to help Derek and that they were going to do it. They were going to make him better.

An oxygen mask was placed over Derek's face, which alleviated his symptoms enough that he closed his eyes. They carried him on a stretcher to the ambulance and Joyce jogged behind. But when she put one foot up and tried to follow Derek into the van, she was told she would have to make her own way to the hospital and meet Derek there. When she hesitated, they said there was too much equipment on board; they couldn't accommodate her; they had to hurry.

'Of course,' she said. 'Derek,' she called through the closing doors, 'you're in the best hands now. I'll be with you soon.'

One of her stockings was torn and flapped against her leg; her bag drooped at her side; her elbow was bleeding. Then she stood and watched the ambulance carrying a hideously breathless Derek through the gates of the British Museum. It stopped for a moment, set its bell to clang and turned the corner on two wheels. Plans for the afternoon and the week with Flo had been forced out her mind as surely as the breath had been crushed from Derek's lungs. And she knew that this time, there was nothing she could call on to distract from the excruciating images left behind.

Joyce looked at the crowd still gathered on the steps, turned and followed the progress of the ambulance until it was out of sight, then like a fool focused on the people behind her again. She felt dazed, like she did when Mum had been killed, sure she wore the same bewildered look on her face that she'd seen on so many others caught up in one disaster or another. At least this catastrophe couldn't be put down to the war, but wasn't the war enough? Must the haphazard nature of disease and illness bear down on them, too? *Or,* thought Joyce, *weren't the natural tragedies of life enough to contend with, without bringing a war into the mix?* Anyone who had control over these things should be made to think about that.

When the nurse broke the invisible cordon around the bystanders and came down the steps towards her, Joyce felt ashamed that she hadn't thanked these good, thoughtful people. 'Thank you, Nurse,' she said. 'For helping Derek.'

The nurse, a plump middle-aged woman wearing a

uniform that was too tight, shook her head. 'They'll be taking him to University College,' she said. 'You can catch a bus or there's the Tube.'

'Yes, ta,' Joyce said, aware that the crowd was beginning to disperse. 'I did want to thank you and everyone else before I left. Thank you,' she called out in a thin, timorous voice. 'Thank you for your help.' She raised her palm towards them. 'I'm most grateful.'

The nurse reached out, put her hand on Joyce's shoulder and peered closely at her. Her eyes were hooded and lined. 'I think you should have a cup of tea and a rest. Let me have a closer look at that elbow. You might be going into shock.'

But Joyce declined. 'I want to get to Derek,' she said. 'I'll ask at the hospital if I think I need treatment. I've been in shock before. Haven't we all? I know the signs to look out for.'

'Alright, my dear,' the nurse said. 'Mind how you go.'

Feeling stunned and a bit unsteady on her feet, Joyce walked back down the path she'd walked up twenty minutes earlier. Then she'd been happy and optimistic and so looking forward to the day with Derek, now she was on her way to see him in hospital. The thought of how tenuous life could be and how much of it she took for granted, even after what had happened to Bill and Mum and Sid, made the ground shift beneath her.

When she rounded the corner towards Tottenham Court Road, she seemed to leave her disoriented state behind. Instead of feeling as if she were floating and gazing down on herself, she was right back in the thick of it. A few people stared at the state she was in, but she wouldn't meet their gaze in any kind of apologetic way. They must have seen sorrier sights than her these past two and a half years and if they hadn't, well perhaps they should think about joining the Civil Defence.

The usual hubbub at the entrance to the Tube station greeted her as she moved through the throng towards the Northern Line. People following arbitrary paths crisscrossed in front of her, determined to get where they needed to go but Joyce was steadfast and, whilst she didn't quite knock anyone out of her way or bowl anyone over, she kept her focus.

Luckily, a train was pulling in. There were plenty of vacant seats, but she knew that if she sat she would fidget and want to stand again immediately, so she clung to a pole near the door instead. Goodge Street came and went and the next stop on the line was her destination. She made her way through the thick, fetid air of the platform, and up the escalators. Mum had hated being down there for hours every night and Joyce could understand that. Whenever she emerged from the underground it was always a wonderful feeling to take that first deep gulp of fresh air and she wondered if Derek, poor Derek, ever had the capacity to enjoy that sensation.

Once inside the hospital, she had no idea where to go. First, she was directed to the General Ward, but Derek wasn't there. Then she followed corridors with low ceilings and grey walls that smelled of antiseptic and cabbage to the Men's Respiratory Ward. There the Ward Sister told her that Derek could very well end up with them but was probably being treated and monitored in the Emergency Department. Sister was tall and commanding and had a row of tiny moles along her cheekbone. 'Come with me,' she declared with such an air of authority that when she turned on her heels and led the way Joyce followed without question.

Trotting along behind Sister's efficient heels, Joyce tried to match her clipped, smart stride. She felt relieved that someone who knew their way through the maze of wards and stairwells and medical equipment was taking her to Derek at last. But no, Sister pulled back the curtain around a bed at the end of the ward, demanded that Joyce sit, donned a pair of surgical gloves and began to inspect the wound on Joyce's elbow, now encrusted with dried black blood. 'Really,' Joyce protested, 'I'm quite alright.'

'And we want you to remain that way, don't we?'

Joyce wondered who the 'we' referred to. 'I'm a Senior Warden in the Civil Defence and I've been privy to much worse than this.'

'Well, your station will expect you this evening in one piece, won't they? And that's how we'll deliver you to them.'

Sister moved Joyce's elbow around and Joyce could have kicked herself when the sudden movement made her flinch. 'It's not broken but it will be badly bruised in the next day or two,' Sister said. 'The most important thing is we get it cleaned up and covered. This is a hospital and you have no idea how many germs there are flying about.' She looked up and Joyce was struck at how calm and serene the woman appeared to be, her face smooth and unlined without a scrap of make-up covering her skin.

'But I'm worried about Derek,' Joyce said.

'And do you want to give him the extra worry of seeing your elbow bashed about?' She left and returned with a small bowl of soapy water and set about dabbing at the wound until it was clean. 'There. It looks much less serious now, doesn't it?'

Joyce had to agree that it did.

With precision, the Ward Sister taped a rectangle of gauze over the sore spot. 'How does that feel?'

'So much better,' Joyce said and shimmied down from the bed.

'I'm sorry I can't do the same for that ragged stocking. But take them both off, please.'

'My stockings? Here?'

'Yes, here,' Sister said in the same authoritative, matter-of-fact voice. 'I'll dispose of the damaged one in the bin. Put the other in your bag.'

Joyce did as she was told but said, 'Sister, surely you understand I can't go about with bare legs, it just...'

'I'll be two ticks,' Sister said, leaving the cubicle with a swish of the curtain.

When she returned, she handed Joyce a brand-new pair of thick, uniform stockings. 'Have these,' she said. 'They might not be very elegant, but my goodness they will last.'

'Thank you, Sister,' Joyce said, fumbling for her coin purse. 'Let me pay you for them. You mustn't be out of pocket on my behalf.'

'I won't hear of such nonsense,' Sister said. 'This is my ward and I get to decide what happens to supplies. Now pop them on and I'll show you the way to the Emergency Department.'

Joyce sat on the edge of the bed and rolled the soft, taut stockings up to her suspender belt. Perhaps it was an accumulation of the day's events, but the Sister's brusque show of kindness touched something inside her and tears welled in her eyes. When she stood, Sister tore a length of soft paper from a roll and handed it to her without saying a word.

Then she led her to the end of a corridor and told her to turn left, then right, walk down a flight of stairs to ground level where she would find the Emergency Department. Before

Joyce had a chance to thank her again, the Ward Sister was halfway back to her empire.

At last Joyce found the right place and yes, Derek was on the ward, but there were strict visiting hours and she would have to wait thirty minutes before she could see him. There was a canteen if she wanted a cup of tea, but she decided that now she'd found her way through the hospital labyrinth she would not chance her luck a second time. As the clock inched towards three, a few people gathered and waited with an undercurrent of impatience and trepidation.

The doors opened on the dot and a nurse led her to Derek's bed, giving her instructions to sit with him calmly and quietly as he was not well and needed time to recover. Joyce didn't know what to expect – Derek sitting up in bed smiling his lopsided grin with shaky lips? Derek hooked up to machinery breathing for him? But when she saw him, he was propped up on three pillows, strange equipment around him, his eyes closed, breathing softly and steadily. A tiny cry escaped her, but it was enough to wake him. He reached out a hand, which Joyce grabbed and held close and they sat, neither saying a word, until Joyce had to leave to take up her duties.

* * *

Report and Control felt like a haven that night. She told Controller Davis what had happened to Derek and he telephoned through to Regional Control so they wouldn't be alarmed when their Senior Regional Officer failed to turn up. Then she got on with her job. The relative lull of the last nine months meant that she had completely cleared the backlog of filing. All incidents were recorded in logbooks; every single

ARPM1 and ARPM2 was duplicated, with one copy sent to Regional Control and the other catalogued and stored in date order in labelled cabinets. When she stood back and studied her map, she could see why the Controller described it as a work of art, but that seemed like a jarring term in light of the subject matter that had created it. When she stepped closer, she could see the countless flaws and faults on the canvas – those little pins, like arrows tipped with poison that had struck almost every road and street, avenue and lane in her West London stamping ground.

'So sorry to hear about Derek,' Mrs Bertrand said, placing a cup and saucer and the regulation digestive biscuits on the table next to Joyce.

'Ta, Mrs Bertrand, he's on the mend, thank goodness.'

'Eh?' Mrs Bertrand cupped her ear and strained towards Joyce.

'He's getting better,' Joyce enunciated every syllable.

'Funny business,' the older woman said. 'What causes it? Smoking? Upset?'

Joyce shook her head. 'Derek doesn't smoke and he's not the type to let his nerves get the better of him,' she said in a raised voice. 'It's probably a disposition. You know, a weakness.'

Mrs Bertrand took a cup of tea to Controller Davis, a puzzled look on her face, which Joyce could well understand. Asthma was a disease she found hard to fathom, too. And although there was no question of her wanting to marry and build a life with Derek, she worried about how living on the knife edge of waiting for the next attack would affect him and her.

A warden rushed in, her tin helmet slipping on her head and a smear of muddy dust across her cheek. Joyce stood to attention and waited while the warden handed an ARPM1 to Controller Davis. From across the room she watched his eyes flicker backwards and forwards as he scanned the form, taking in all the information he needed. His bottom lip curled down and without looking up, he dialled a number on the telephone and held the piece of paper out towards the Warden who passed it Joyce. When she read through it, she could see what had caused the look of consternation on the Controller's face – a basket of incendiaries, a horrible weapon they hadn't seen for ages and had hoped never to see again, had floated down through the murky sky and set the roof of Gold's dress shop alight. Nana loved Gold's and so had Mum, but according to the message in her hand, none of the local women would be using their clothing rations there in the near future.

Of course, that conflagration spread and first the newsagent on one side and then the tobacconist on the other were in flames. Report after report arrived of the ferocious candelabra landing on houses and shops throughout the area. Controller Davis was on the telephone to the Fire Service without a break until, two hours after the first attack, other senior officials joined him and he was able to take the receiver from his ear and talk to his colleagues in person. Joyce read the reports, wounded her map with more pins, filed the forms then started the process over again. She wondered where these firebombs had come from after such a long absence. Had they been manufactured recently or had they been found at the back of some warehouse or hangar in Germany and loaded onto Luftwaffe planes in an attempt to keep Londoners on their toes?

Each and every ARPM1 reported an incendiary and the wardens who brought them into Report and Control were covered in soot and smelled of fire. The reeking stink of smoke had only recently been cleared from Joyce's throat, her coat, her hair, the washing on the line, her nostrils. And the haze that drifted below the clouds had only recently lifted, but now it was descending again.

Westbourne Grove took a fair few flames and Joyce was relieved to see that Madame Beaupre's had been spared, until another report appeared and she had to label and shoot the dance studio through with black. Joyce looked at the clock and knew that at that time of night no classes would have been in progress, but she hoped that Madame and Monsieur Beaupre hadn't been on the premises. Pictures of the elegant couple passed through Joyce's mind. She felt for them viewing their beautifully designed studio after it had been reduced to blistering ash and for herself and Derek and Flo who'd spent happy hours there trying, as the owners had achieved so admirably, to rise above the madness for a few short periods of time.

When the all-clear sounded, everyone was more exhausted than they'd been for months. A pile of reports towered on a table, but Joyce decided she would go home for breakfast before making her way to see Derek, then aim to get back into work early to catch up on the filing. After all, who could say what the upcoming night might bring.

Again, the streets were scorched and smouldering. Fire trucks and ambulances raced from one sorry sight to another; silent families huddled close together. Joyce pulled a scarf from her bag and wound it around her face to filter out the worst of the fumes. At least Derek was in hospital and not trying to breathe his way through the cloying vapours.

Taking the long way home so she could walk past Madame Beaupre's, Joyce was disappointed that neither of her dance instructors were surveying the damage. But perhaps they hadn't been informed or if they had, maybe they'd convinced themselves that no such thing could happen to the oasis they'd created. She would try to contact them in some way if their paths didn't cross.

* * *

When Joyce arrived at the hospital, Derek was pale and clammy but looked much better; his breathing was laboured but he was managing on his own without the help of an oxygen mask. She'd been warned again that he must remain calm and quiet but she had no intention of exciting or alarming him in any way, so they held hands with a light touch and Joyce could feel Derek's weak fevered pulse fluttering in his wrist. He asked her to tell him about the night before and if Regional Control knew he'd been unwell.

'Does Celia know?' Joyce asked, the name almost sticking in her throat. 'Would you like me to contact her?'

'Oh,' Derek rasped. 'Do you know, I hadn't even thought.' Speaking those few words seemed to tire him and he closed his eyes for a moment. 'No, I'll be leaving hospital tomorrow or the next day so there's no need. She'd only want to come to London and take over. Then she might never leave and we don't want her hanging around the house for weeks on end, do we?' He made a huge effort and gave her one of his crooked smiles, doing his best to make it flirtatious.

She smiled back, but knew that it would be quite a while before they could resume their passionate assignations in Derek's bedroom. 'Well, let me know if you change your mind. It wouldn't take me a minute to drop her a note.'

Derek shook his head as if the thought of his mother added to his weariness; it certainly did to hers.

'Flo's coming home on leave,' she said. 'And she might be bringing someone named Vernon with her.'

'That sounds intriguing,' Derek's voice scratched and scraped. 'Tell me all about it.'

Not expecting a reply, Joyce filled him in with the few details she knew. 'And I was worried about plans for them, but now Flo will have to do all the entertaining as I'll be with you. And there will be no dancing as Madame Beaupre's took a packet last night. Sorry,

I forgot to tell you.'

Derek shook his head from side to side. 'Oh no,' he managed to say. 'I can't believe it. Can it be repaired?'

'No, I doubt it,' she said.

'Anyway, I'll be out in time to have a drink with Flo and this Vernon chap, if he turns up. Or a trip to the cinema or tea at Auntie Cath's.'

But Joyce doubted it when she was told by a nurse that visiting time was over and there were four doctors waiting to join Derek in his cubicle.

* * *

Two incendiaries were dropped the following night and after that, the nights became relatively quiet again. So Joyce thought that perhaps she'd been right and the fountains of flame had been discovered behind a pile of other things and used up for the sake of it.

Fewer bombs during the nights meant less paperwork during the day, so Joyce used the respite to visit Derek and spend time with Flo, but she didn't get the chance to meet Vernon as he hadn't been able to make it after all. And Flo, she could tell, was not happy with the situation. Auntie Cath,

Uncle Terry, Nana and Granddad must have thought Flo was distracted with tiredness as they didn't know any better about her disappointment, but Joyce felt sure her cousin's altered demeanour had something to do with Vernon or with the lack of his presence.

When they met at the ABC for an early lunch, Joyce and Flo ordered their usual, found a table and spread out their fare. Flo looked brighter than she had done since she'd been home and Joyce wondered if she'd had a letter from her new beau, but her cousin wasn't forthcoming.

They exchanged pleasantries about their respective jobs, then Flo itemised all the ways in which the war in Bedfordshire was different from the war in London. 'It's still apparent,' she said. 'But it doesn't hit you in the face like it does here.'

'Probably a lot slower in general,' Joyce observed. 'It was like that in Norfolk. There was the blackout and rationing and men and women in uniform but nowhere near as many signs of damage as there are here.'

'Have you had to suffer Celia or Cress again?' Flo placed her cup on its saucer and wiped her mouth with a serviette.

'Celia's been to London once since our trip to Norfolk. She had some business to attend to so stayed in the Croydon house overnight. Sadly,' Joyce put her hand on her heart and blinked hard a few times, 'I was working and couldn't get the time off. Honest.'

'I don't suppose you can sidestep her for ever, though.'

'No, of course not,' Joyce said. 'I will probably have to see her next time, but I do believe it suits her as much as me that we avoid each other whenever possible.'

Flo nodded, but looked more interested in the quarter of potted tongue and ham sandwich left on her plate.

'Why couldn't Vernon make it this week? I was looking forward to meeting him.'

Flo sighed. She looked fed up and on the edge of tears. 'He had his leave cancelled at the last minute.'

Joyce wasn't sure she believed that explanation. Flo's reaction to what was an everyday occurrence was too extreme and emotional. 'It must be disappointing,' she said, 'but cancelled leave happens all the time. To all of us. There's always the next time.'

There was no response from Flo other than a sulky stare down at her tea, so Joyce ploughed on. 'Tell me what you like about him, so I'm prepared when we do meet.'

Such a bright pinpoint appeared in Flo's eyes that it could have been mistaken for the beginnings of a fever.

'I think it might be easier for me to list what I don't like about him.'

'That's a good start,' Joyce smiled.

Flo moved closer and glanced over her shoulder, as if she expected her Mum or Dad to be listening. 'He's a bit older than me,' she said in a low voice.

'I know that much,' Joyce said. 'And I won't hold that against him. After all, Derek's older than me and nobody's said a word about it.'

'But he's quite a lot older than Derek,' Flo said. 'Which makes him... I don't know.' She looked up at the ceiling for inspiration. 'Mysterious, maybe? Certainly sophisticated and worldly wise.'

Mum's initial niggle about the difference between her and Derek's ages came back to Joyce and she wondered if Vernon had a wife and family in Australia and that was what was making Flo anxious and unhappy. 'How much older, Flo?' she asked. 'Uncle Terry or Granddad's age?'

'Nineteen years older,' Flo said, an embarrassed glow creeping over her face. Then she lifted her chin and looked Joyce straight in the eye.

Joyce quickly did the sums in her mind but Flo beat her to it. 'He's forty-three,' she said.

To Joyce that sounded ancient and she thought it was a good job Vernon hadn't been introduced to the family as Uncle Terry would go mad at the idea of a middle-aged man courting his Flo. But she couldn't say that out loud, not when Flo was so forlorn.

'He's funny, gentlemanly, hardworking, ambitious, smart,' Flo was going on about Vernon's attributes.

Joyce felt positive there was more to the puzzle that was Vernon than Flo was letting on, so she decided to try to unearth the missing pieces. 'Tell me what he did in Australia and how he landed up here.'

Flo fussed a bit with her plate, moving it an inch one way and an inch back again, then stared past Joyce's ear at a potted plant that stood askew behind her. 'He worked on a farm he owns with a business partner. But the arrangement soured between them, so Vernon joined up and asked to be posted here to give himself a chance to get things sorted out.'

It was an implausible story. If Vernon needed to get his business affairs in order he would have stood a better chance of accomplishing that by staying put. So Joyce concluded that he was either married, as was her first theory, or bankrupt and running away from debtors. Or possibly both.

The little glint in Flo's eyes and the few buoyant minutes while she'd talked about Vernon passed and once again she was miserable and listless. Joyce wondered if Flo had been hoodwinked by Vernon's story or if she knew the truth, whatever that might be, and they had cooked up this yarn between them.

Usually at this point in the many lunches they'd shared, they would have ordered a second cup of tea to have with their buns, but this time, a thin skin formed on the cups they hadn't finished and their cakes were untouched. Flo didn't offer any further information, so Joyce reached out and clasped her hand. She knew she must give Vernon a chance, but felt a surge of anger that he was making Flo so wretched and worried. Any other man would fall over himself to see her laughing, smiling and carefree.

'Our tea's stone cold,' Flo said suddenly, as if it was a national disaster akin to a Jerry invasion. She smiled at Joyce. 'Shall we order two more cups and dig into our buns?'

Joyce nodded. 'Good idea,' she said.

Then as quickly as it had appeared, Flo's smile faded and she started to cry. Joyce shuffled her chair next to her cousin's and put her arm around her shoulder. She could only guess how upset they looked as several people made it their business to keep glancing over at them. 'Listen, Flo love, I'm not putting myself up as a pinnacle, but if Derek didn't make me happy I would finish it without a backward glance.

'But Vernon does make me happy,' Flo blurted out, dabbing at her eyes with a balled, soggy handkerchief.

Joyce sat back and crossed her arms over her chest. 'This is you happy?' She scratched her head in an exaggerated manner. 'I must have been getting the signs of happiness and heartache mixed up all these years. You're upset and worried and it's turning you into someone else.'

Flo nodded and then in a barely audible whisper said, 'I know.'

They sat quietly for a few moments, then Joyce ordered

them each another cup of tea and they nibbled on tiny pieces of their cakes. When they'd finished, Flo reached into her bag, retrieved her lipstick and expertly re-applied it. 'I know I haven't heard the last of it,' she said, 'but can we change the subject for now? I'm exhausted.'

'Me too,' Joyce said, slumping against the back of the chair. And she felt it. Her limbs ached and her stomach pitched as if it were on a roundabout. 'But I just want to say one final thing. I love you dearly, Flo love, and I'm on your side.'

For a beat, Joyce thought Flo's tears would start again. But she kept them under control and closed her lipstick with a click. 'Ta, Joy,' she said, giving Joyce a cheeky grin. 'But I have to correct you. That's two things, not one.'

And Joyce was so pleased to see some life in Flo again that she had to fight to stop a flood in her own eyes.

By the time Flo left for Bedfordshire, neither of them had said another word about Vernon, but she seemed much jollier. There had been one trip to the cinema and several times Flo had been waiting outside Report and Control at dawn for Joyce to emerge and the brisk walk home did both of them good.

* * *

Derek was strong enough to be discharged the day after Flo's leave was up, so the three of them weren't able to have a drink together which Joyce was pleased about as she didn't want Derek to do too much and set himself back.

True to his nonchalant and resilient character, Derek refused to take any more time off to fully recuperate, but insisted on getting back to work straight away. 'And you, Joyce, have done enough. I don't expect you to nurse me while I lounge around the house in Croydon.'

Joyce would have been happier if he had, as he'd lost quite a lot of weight and was sometimes wracked by fits of coughing that were violent enough to jar bones. But the more she insisted, the more Derek put his foot down until there was nothing for it but to drop her pleading and let him get on with it; she knew him well enough to understand that he wouldn't be dissuaded.

But whilst Derek slotted back into his life with ease, Joyce could not relax. Whenever they were together, she found herself waiting for his next attack and when one started, as was inevitable, she willed it not to escalate but was on the verge of panic that it would. No one could predict how each terrible bout would play out – not even the doctors.

Neither was there any respite when they were apart except when Joyce was engrossed in her work. It had been the same after Mum and Sid had been killed, she'd found solace and distraction and comfort not in the actual work or the reason for the existence of the work, but from knowing what she had to do and doing it as if she were on a production line. There were times when she was so entranced with carrying out the finer details of her job with conscientious precision, that when the telephone jangled she would be jolted out of her reverie and immediately think someone was ringing to let her know that Derek was unwell again. Of course, she chastised herself, her first thought should be about what bomb damage had occurred and where, or if the Jerries had found another cache of hidden incendiaries and were raining them down on Notting Hill or if water mains had burst or gas been released. But initially, her anxiety was directed at Derek. She knew that would be difficult to explain, but she'd been there with him when he was at his worst and the images were hard to dismiss.

But as the weeks went by, seeing Derek improve a little each day became an expectation rather than a flimsy hope. She didn't think she could ever take his good health for granted, not after she'd seen him at death's door, but she began to trust that the frightening episode had been an anomaly rather than the norm.

Letters arrived from Flo in which the only mentions of Vernon were superficial – they'd been for a walk together; he'd treated Flo to the biggest cream bun imaginable; they'd learned to jive at a local dance – nothing about whether or not he was any closer to sorting out his problems in Australia, whatever they might be.

Then during the night of the 23rd of April, when Notting Hill was taking it at a relatively slow pace, Controller Davis took a telephone call that made his eyebrows meet above his nose. When he hung up, he limped over to Joyce and studied her map. 'Apparently,' he said, 'an attack on Exeter has come out of the blue.'

'Exeter?' Her own eyebrows strained towards each other. She thought back to her schoolgirl geography. 'In Devon?'

'Yes,' the Controller nodded. 'It's most peculiar as there's nothing there of importance to interest Jerry.'

'Perhaps the Wehrmacht lost their way?' Joyce offered.

'Very logical conclusion, Senior Warden Cooper, but there were too many of them for it to be a mistake. No, for some strange reason, Exeter was their target.'

'How bad is it?' Joyce feared the same destruction and numbers lost as they'd endured in London at the start of the war.

'Not as bad as it could have been were it not for cloud

cover.' The Controller shook his head as if he couldn't understand the lack of reasoning that had gone into the planning of the raid.

Percy presented an ARPM1 to Controller Davis which he read and passed to Joyce to deal with by means of an orange incision and Joyce, for one, forgot about the strange incident. But the next morning, Derek told her the bombing of Exeter was being called a Baedeker Raid.

'Where does that name come from?' Joyce asked, turning to Derek and tucking his scarf around his neck to keep out any breeze that stirred.

'Baedeker is a German tourist book of British cities and because we've done such a neat job on Lübeck, the damned Jerries have sworn to bomb every city in Britain marked with three stars in the guide. The bastards.'

Derek indicated a small café where they often had greasy spam rolls for breakfast. 'Shall we?'

Joyce nodded. 'Yes, please. I'm famished. But how do we know all of this,' she asked.

'It's been leaked,' Derek lowered his voice although they were the only customers in the rundown restaurant. 'By a spokesman for the German Foreign Office. A propogandist named Gustav Braun von Stumm.' He snorted with derision. 'He'll be in for it now from Hitler et al.'

But the Wehrmacht didn't let that hold them back and the following night, winging their way through clear skies, thirty to forty German aircraft bombarded the Devonshire city again. This time, instead of five people killed there were over eighty dead, with street after street reduced to devastating rubble and for no other reason than the city was of cultural and historical significance. *Tit for tat,* Joyce thought. *That's all war is. A deadly game of tag in a children's playground.*

After that night of bombing, Derek was one of many to put his name forward to travel to Exeter and confer with the city's bigwigs to find out what they had done so admirably that led them to be commended by the government. He was one of a handful chosen and Joyce was over the moon that his hard work and diligence had been recognised. But pangs of trepidation overwhelmed her; he wasn't about to let the first words he spoke to the Regional Commissioner in Exeter or the landlady of his digs be about the severity of his asthma, so what would happen if he had another acute attack?

They had lunch on a bench near the Serpentine during the afternoon that Derek was due to leave, then spent a couple of hours under the lemon-coloured counterpane in his bedroom. Whether it was because Derek's near-miss asthma attack had left both of them vividly aware of each precious minute they spent together or because they didn't have a clue when their next opportunity to be alone might arise or simply because they felt the ease that comes with being a more established couple, their lovemaking was less frantic but more passionate than it had ever been. They took their time, savouring the way they covered each other with light, butterfly wing kisses. Joyce traced the hills and hollows of Derek's back and chest, willing her fingers to memorise the shape of him that she could then recall during his absence. She no longer kept her eyes closed but held his intense gaze and their slow, deliberate, considered movements made her feel as if her and Derek's connection was deeper and more intimate than it had ever been.

But Joyce ruined the last precious hour by trying to come up with a way to tell Derek she didn't think he should go and then rejecting every explanation she played out in her mind as being overprotective or henpecking or unreasonable. And was she prepared to hold him back from any opportunity for the rest of their lives in case another attack befell him whilst they were apart?

That thought was absurd and she refused to humiliate him by restraining him on a short leash. So when they said goodbye on the station platform, Joyce held Derek close enough to hear the rattle in his chest but said nothing other than how much she would miss him.

'I will miss you, too, Senior Warden Cooper,' he said, his oblique smile wide and buoyant. 'But it's not for long and I'm looking forward to the challenge.' He shook his head. 'I still can't believe I was given the job.'

'Well, I can,' Joyce said, although in her heart she wished he'd been overlooked.

Derek boarded the train, the whistle blew, they held onto each other's hands until the acceleration of the train tore them apart, then Joyce waved until long after the last carriage disappeared.

Bath took it next and Derek was sent there straight from Exeter. Then it was Norwich and Joyce wondered if he would have the time or inclination to contact Celia and Cress. After that, he chased the Luftwaffe to York and when no telegrams arrived informing her he'd had a bad turn, Joyce felt calmer and settled down, like so many girls, to life with men away in the Services. Postcards of cathedrals and parks and winding streets began to arrive and Joyce lined them up on her dressing table in Nana's old front room. Each time she looked at them she felt sad that some or all of the depicted pride and joys of those cities no longer existed as they had done a week or two earlier.

On the third of May, the German sorties returned to the 'jewel of the West' as Exeter was described in the Baedeker guide and Derek followed in their wake. But despite the Jerries going on to bombard Cowes, Norwich yet again, Hull, Poole, Grimsby and Canterbury, Derek was unable to pursue them. Joyce's most outlandish fears had come to fruition when he suffered another brutal asthma attack and no one had been able to help him in time.

FIFTEEN

Saturday 9 March 1974

When the first chink of light breached the bedroom curtains, Joyce was wide awake and ordering a mental list of the jobs she had to get through. Take down the curtains and rails; strip the bed; check every nook and hidey hole for anything she might have missed; turn off the gas and lights; instruct the removal men not to forget the few pots in the garden; wait for everything to be loaded on the van; lock all the doors; post the keys as she'd been told to do.

And of course she must be up and dressed before there was a knock on the door at 8.00 and the evacuation began. But still she lay there, sure now that she could turn over and fall into the sort of heavy, peaceful sleep that had eluded her for the entire night. Everything about her felt weighted and leaden – her eyelids, her arms and legs, her will. She pictured herself moving from one item on the list to the next; overseeing each step with a bustling calm that would not allow her time to dwell on how reluctant she felt about the finality of the day. Reaching above the bed, Joyce pulled on the curtain and looked up through the window at the slate grey sky, bulked out with more rain or sleet or hail.

Her wristwatch, propped against last night's cold, half-empty cup of tea, read 7.15. She could grab fifteen minutes and feel better for it, but knew she shouldn't as she might drift off and not wake up until there was a pounding on the door. But once she sat up and put her feet on the floor, she was aware that the day would gather a momentum of its own. It would run away from her and the last few hours here, in her beloved flat, would become nothing more than a blurred memory. Experience told her she didn't have the power to stop the inevitable; if she did, she would have rerouted her life many times over so she wouldn't have such an intense desire to do so now.

Joyce's feet found her slippers without her having to look down. She shivered and shrugged into her dressing gown, but there was no point in putting on the electric fire as the jobs she had to get on with would see her warm and sweaty. Almost every previous Saturday morning for twenty-nine years she'd enjoyed a lie-in, but today she shuffled to the kitchen where she filled the kettle and lit the gas under it. She would have a last cup of tea while she was getting ready. She washed quickly, brushed her teeth and hair, dressed in sensible, house-work clothes – all for the last time in this basement haven. Then she asked herself if there was a point to her constant reminders that each small act was the last; they only served to torture her. Besides, she knew no good came of sentimentality and that was why she hadn't indulged in it for years. Better to steel herself, rise up tall and get on with what needed to be done. So that was what she determined to do.

At 8.05, three hulking men rapped on the door. 'Morning,

love,' they said and introduced themselves as Brian, Kevin and Jon. 'Any chance of a cuppa?'

They propped open the front door so they could trail backwards and forwards to the van which was parked at the top of Joyce's steps. 'I'm afraid I didn't think,' she said. 'I've packed all my cups bar one. But I can wash it and you can share that?'

'Don't you worry, darling,' the one called Jon said. He disappeared into the van and came back with an assortment of plastic cups that had once belonged to various flasks.

That made Joyce laugh, which helped to lift her mood. 'How enterprising,' she said.

'Got an extra one for me?' Mr Taylor appeared in overalls, solid boots and wearing a cap on his unruly hair. There were a few moments of friendly jostling and teasing amongst the men which seemed to centre on Mr Taylor's lack of formal attire. The moving company had been his recommendation, but how did he know these men well enough to banter with them so freely? Everyone Mr Taylor met seemed to become one of his best mates – Mr Norris at the new flats; these removal men; people he waved or nodded to on the street. She could understand how his charm and consideration, his energy and easy manner ensured he was well-liked, but surely she wasn't the only one who often found him irritating, too?

Brian found one more scratched cup and Joyce fired up the gas again and made another pot of tea. 'How are you this morning, Miss Cooper?' Mr Taylor had followed her into the kitchen.

'Fine. Very well, thank you.' She set the cups out in a row. 'I didn't expect to see you today. Shouldn't you be with Jacqueline?'

All of Mr Taylor's features turned gooey at the mention of

his fiancée's name. 'She and her sister are shopping today,' he lowered his voice. 'For ladies' things.'

Joyce hadn't heard of any female relatives trawling the shops together for undergarments for years, but she remembered the giddy fun she and Flo had had when as girls they'd visited Oxford Street to do the same. For a few hours, it had seemed as though not even a war could detract from their excitement. 'That's lovely for Jacqueline,' Joyce said. 'And her sister.'

'Yes,' Mr Taylor agreed. 'They'll be giggly for the rest of the weekend.'

'But don't you have something you'd rather be doing?' Joyce poured milk into the cups.

Mr Taylor shrugged. 'I was going to wait at your new flat with the keys, but as I had a couple of hours to spare I thought I'd look in on proceedings here. Shall I get the curtains down?'

Joyce thought he might as well. 'I'd be very grateful,' she said. 'But Mr Taylor. Do you do this for everyone forced to move? Or is it just that you don't trust me to be good to my word?'

Colour spilled past Mr Taylor's sideburns and spread onto his face. 'That's not the case, I assure you,' he said. 'I trust you implicitly. And I do help some other clients, but only if they're amongst my favourites.'

Joyce laughed again. 'Flatterer,' she said.

'It's just that…' Mr Taylor trailed off, as if he thought better of what he was going to say. He picked up the steaming, plastic cups. 'I'll take these to the lads,' he said.

'Just what, Mr Taylor?' Joyce insisted. 'You only offer your assistance to the most stubborn or reluctant?'

'Not at all.' Mr Taylor's voice softened. 'It's just that most people have someone who can help them. You know, look out for them.' He took a sip from one of the cups.

'I thought you could do with a friend. Here we are, chaps,' he called out to Jon, Brian and Kevin. 'The cup that cheers but does not inebriate.'

Mr Taylor and the three removal men filled the tiny flat with their shoulders, their thick arms and necks and their loud, cheerful ribbing. They were ever so careful with her old, tatty furniture, as if they were moving royal heirlooms from Windsor Castle to Balmoral. Mr Taylor took down the curtains then carefully taped the screws that had held up the poles to the sides of the wood so they could be hung again at the other end. Joyce took off the bedding, folded it and put it in a bag. Although she felt timid at the thought of using the washing machine that had been installed in the new flat, she'd bought a small box of washing powder from the corner shop so she could try it out. It was either that or go back to washing everything by hand, as carting all her laundry back and forth to the laundromat in Notting Hill would be too much of a chore.

There was more tea, then Joyce pointed out the pots she wanted from the garden. She rinsed her cup and the teapot and pushed them into a box. Brian said he thought they were good to go, if she agreed. 'Yes, ta. There's nothing left now.' She had to gulp to stop her voice from fracturing.

'Right you are then, love. Are you going to get on the van, too? There's room up front for a little one.'

'Oh,' Joyce was alarmed at the thought. 'No, I think I'll walk,' she said.

'Or you can come in the Spitfire with me,' Mr Taylor said.

They all waited and watched, but she stood her ground. 'You're all so kind,' she said. 'But I would really like the walk.'

'We'll start putting up your bed, then,' Kevin said. 'And taking in the boxes.'

The three movers piled into the van and beeped their horn as they pulled away from the kerb. Mr Taylor hesitated in the doorway. 'Are you absolutely sure, Miss Cooper? I could wait for you in the car until you're ready.'

Not for the first time Joyce wondered how someone so kind could also be so very annoying. 'I would like to walk, Mr Taylor,' she was direct and confident. 'Thank you for your help. And I'll remember to post my keys back through the letterbox.'

Mr Taylor shook his head. 'That was if I wasn't here,' he said. 'I'll take them from you later.' He put his hands in his pockets and, looking dejected and reluctant from behind, climbed the steps to the street.

For a moment, Joyce rested her forehead on the door and wondered whether she should pick up her bag and mackintosh and leave the flat quickly, or take one last nostalgic walk around the empty rooms. Bracing herself, she decided for the latter. In the kitchen, a white envelope with her name across it stood to attention against the empty worktop. She thought it might be a moving out or moving in card or some such nonsense. Had those been invented during the war the manufacturers would have made a fortune. She tore it open and pulled out a thick, rough card printed in gold cursive lettering with silver horseshoes around the border. She traced the raised writing with her finger as she read out loud.

Mr and Mrs Anthony Carstairs request the pleasure of your company at the marriage of their daughter, Jacqueline, to Mr Paul Taylor at All

*Saints Church Edmonton on Saturday 20 April
1974 at 2:30 p.m. and afterwards at the Six Bells
Public House.*

RSVP Mr and Mrs Carstairs

There then followed an address and telephone number.

The last wedding she'd been invited to was Hettie's in
1945 and that had been on a lined bit of paper cut from a
school copybook. Joyce turned the beautiful card over in her
hand and felt a stab of tenderness towards Mr Taylor and
Jacqueline; she had to admit they'd been kind to think of her.
She could imagine what the day would be like from stories the
girls in the office had told her and she saw in her mind the
monochrome of the happy couple's outfits against the guests'
colourful clothing, the bunting and presents wrapped in
bright paper. She heard the speeches and the music and
laughter of grandparents and small children and she smelled
vanilla when the cake was cut and fresh, fragrant flowers – she
would have chosen lilacs if she and Derek had made it that far.

Looking around the barren kitchen, she knew that she
could manage this move because she had to, but she didn't
have to go to a wedding, or any social occasion and sit next to
someone she might quite like talking to and then never see
again. She might enjoy the dancing and watching the little
ones skid around with balloons in their hands and being
served food she hadn't prepared for herself, only to return to
her flat without any hope of the experience being repeated in
the future. No, it was better not to get involved in the first
place than to go through the pain of being left on her own all
over again. She shook her head to rid it of such melodrama.

Besides, she reminded herself, she wouldn't know what to wear or how to get there or what to say except please and thank you and really, there's no need to bother on my behalf.

Putting the invitation in her bag to reply to later, she took that one last sentimental tour of her empty flat. Twenty-nine years, she thought, as the tread of her sturdy shoes reverberated around the desolate, soon to be abandoned rooms. For all that time it had been her and the walls and the ceilings and the floors and the feet going by above her – no one else. The largest number of people to have ever been in the flat with her had been the four men helping that morning. And these rooms hadn't meant anything to anyone except her, but to her they had meant everything.

She allowed herself to cry a little, then dried her eyes, gathered her things, drew herself up from the crown of her head and locked the door behind her. For the last time.

SIXTEEN

NANA

June 1942

Joyce would have been none the wiser about the arrangements for Derek's funeral had it not been for the Regional Commissioner informing Controller Davis, who in turn very kindly told Joyce she could take off all the time she needed.

'Miss Cooper,' he said in the tone of voice she imagined her father would have used to relay anything that might have upset her. 'You should have mentioned this sooner. Surely you know the Service would not expect you to stay glued to your map and miss such a solemn occasion.'

Joyce, barely able to keep her balance on the sheer cliff of grief, could not believe what she was hearing. For the best part of two weeks she'd waited for news about where and when Derek would be buried. Nana and Auntie Cath told her to write to Celia, which she did. Then Flo said she should send a telegram. Neither brought a response. Twice she'd visited the house in Croydon in case Celia happened to be in residence, but there hadn't been an answer at the door.

'Derek's mother hasn't told me about the funeral plans,' she faltered, embarrassment at being given the news in such a demeaning way flooding her ashen cheeks with a crimson flush. To have been so blatantly and deliberately insulted by Derek's family, when they were well-aware of her place in Derek's life, filled her with a hot sense of injustice.

Controller Davis frowned as Joyce stuttered and stumbled over her words, wondering what she could say to save face. Then all of a sudden she didn't care what was thought of her; she was the wronged party and it was Celia and Cress who should be ashamed, not her.

'Oh, my dear,' Controller Davis stared at her. 'I... I don't know what to say. What a terribly cruel outcome for you.' He waited, the map between them, with a look of horror and pity on his face which made her decide to tell him all the details.

'Derek's mother didn't approve of me as his choice of girl-friend,' she said in a rush. 'But she only met me the once, when we went to Norfolk. Do you remember?'

The Controller nodded.

'And she made it quite plain she thought me beneath her son. So much so that she threatened to cut him off from his inheritance if he married me.'

'She sounds frightful,' Controller Davis said, shaking his head. 'Like a matriarch from the Dark Ages. Doesn't she know how the world's changed?'

'Yes,' Joyce agreed. 'She was ever so inconsiderate. My family might be a good few rungs beneath hers on the social ladder, but none of us would treat anyone so rudely.'

'I expect Derek was mortified,' Controller Davis said.

The reverent way the Controller spoke Derek's name made tears press against the backs of Joyce's eyes. 'Yes,' she said. 'He was most upset. And I'm sure this latest slight would have made him seethe.'

The telephone reverberated around the room and Controller Davis limped towards it. Relatively few bombs and incendiaries had been scarring the area, but that had changed with the Tip and Run raids on gasholders, prominent buildings and coastal towns in Essex, Sussex, Hampshire and the West Country that then found their way to the Docks in East London and, probably because they could, to other districts like Notting Hill, Paddington and St John's Wood. And the Jerries no longer confined their audacious attacks to blackout hours, but they dared to drop their bombs during the day as well which meant there was often a pile of ARPM1s waiting for Joyce when she started her shift. But now the map was up to date; all reports had been written; the filing was done; tea had been served and Mrs Bertrand was napping in the first aid room. The Controller signed off the call and told Joyce that a dodgy roof on a bombed-out warehouse in Paddington had collapsed. No one had been hurt, but he had been asked to send a few of their crew members to make it temporarily safe.

When he'd set that in motion, he dragged himself back to sit with Joyce at the table she used to organise her paperwork. 'I cannot understand how anyone would be unwilling to allow you to marry their son,' he said.

'Ta, Sir,' Joyce said. Her head throbbed and her nose and throat were thick and itchy from crying so she was reluctant to resurrect the conversation where it had been left off.

But Controller Davis persisted. 'The woman cannot be anything other than an absolute snob not to see how you would grace any family.'

'A snob. That's what Derek said she was.'

'It wouldn't be good for your well-being not to attend,' the Controller said. 'So you must go.'

'Where?'

'To the funeral.'

'Oh, I couldn't possibly.' Joyce wondered if the Controller had been listening to her at all. 'As I said, I haven't been notified or asked.'

Controller Davis put his palms flat on the table and leaned towards her. 'You don't have to be. Funerals are open to the public and anyone can attend. Of course the reception afterwards is a different matter, but I imagine you want to pay your respects to Derek, not hobnob with the likes of his mother.'

The next morning, Joyce asked Nana and Granddad what they thought and they agreed with the Controller, so she booked the time off work and looked into which train to get there and back, but dreaded making the journey on her own. It seemed like such a long way to go and every mile of it would remind her of Derek and how he'd tried so hard to make their first trip away together memorable. Then what if Celia or Cress were awful to her face and she had to get herself home without anyone to lean on or talk to – she couldn't imagine how she would manage. But from nowhere, a letter arrived from Flo saying that if Joyce wanted her to, she could get two days compassionate leave, meet Flo in Norwich and they could travel back to London together after the ceremony. *If* she wanted that to happen. Joyce could not believe her cousin had read between the lines of her letters and picked up on her anxiety. She held the letter to her chest, closed her eyes tight and felt less alone than she had since first Mum and then Derek had been taken from her. She sent a letter back by the next post saying how grateful she was and telling Flo they should meet under the Norwich station clock at eleven thirty.

* * *

Although it was chilly, Joyce was grateful it was spring and not the height of summer so she couldn't compare every scene beyond the carriage window with the ones she and Derek had commented on when they travelled to Norfolk together. She knew she wouldn't be able to bring herself to eat alone in the dining car, so had packed a flask and a couple of rounds of bread and dripping. An elderly woman sitting opposite said she wore her uniform well and they talked on and off about the war, the woman's grandchildren and why on earth censors sent on letters to recipients with nothing but a hole in them.

As the train approached Norwich, Joyce's heart started to thud and her legs felt feeble. Suppose there had been a complication and Flo didn't show up; what would she do if Celia or Cress ignored her completely or even more horrifying, vilified her during the service; who would help her if she fainted; what if she could not bear to see Derek's coffin and had to run crying from the church. But she remembered Controller Davis's words about how she needed to pay her respects and she reminded herself that was the one and only reason she was here. *But oh Derek*, she thought with a new emotion that felt very close to anger. *I know none of this is your fault, but how could you have left me like this?*

She retraced the steps she and Derek had taken together along the platform and she could almost see him striding along, carrying both their cases as if there was nothing in them, offering her his arm to hold, wheezing into the sleeve of his coat.

And then, there was Flo, stamping her feet and clapping her hands to keep warm. They spotted each other at the same moment and ran into each other's arms. Joyce drew back first and smoothed her cousin's hair away from her face with her hands. 'I can't thank you enough,' Joyce said, looking straight into Flo's eyes. 'If it weren't for the thought of you waiting here for me, I would not have made it.'

Flo squeezed Joyce's arm. They both knew they would not cry or cause a scene here or anywhere else in public if they could possibly help it – if they gave into that, the streets, trains, buses, pubs and shops would be teeming with blubbering people and what good would that do anyone. Instead, Flo curled her lip and said, 'Norfolk. Of all places. You owe me.'

Joyce giggled. 'For this and a lot more.'

Derek must have been saddened by how heavily Norwich had been bombed when he'd trailed there behind the Luftwaffe's Baedeker Raids. Thank goodness the report she'd read hadn't mentioned the market or the Samson and Hercules, where she and Derek had spent an almost carefree evening trying to look as though they knew what they were doing on the dance floor. But when those thirty aircraft dive-bombed the city relentlessly, they'd destroyed a hospital, two churches, Caley's Chocolate Factory and a number of lovely, old terraced houses. She'd seen the proof of businesses being able to start up again or trade from the ruins of their premises whilst waiting for repairs to be undertaken, but apart from the loss of life and limb, it was the flattening of houses and flats that caused her the most upset. It seemed heinous that in the midst of all the upheaval, uncertainty, terrible food and deafening noise, people had to lose the anchor of their shelter and comforting possessions, too.

The Cromer train crawled out of the station at such a snail's pace that Joyce was able to make eye contact with several people shoring up the brickwork on the outside of what used to be their living rooms or kitchens. She tried to tell them with her eyes how much she felt for them as she'd lost her home with Mum, too, but they stared straight through her before averting their eyes back to the onerous task they had to get through.

When they alighted, Joyce tried not to peer down every side road and passageway to view the sea as they made their way to St Peter and St Paul's Parish Church. She knew that every glimpse of the grey, churning waves, the flint stones on the beach and the endless sky would only take her straight back to how she'd felt when she'd first seen them with Derek. She'd been excited then, with little idea of how difficult their week in Norfolk would be. There was no hiding from the cadenced inhale and exhale of the sea, though, as it hit the shore and drew back on itself into the depths again. For a moment she was comforted by the steadfast rhythm and the knowledge that the ebb and flow would carry on regardless.

There were crowds of people filing into the church and when Joyce saw them she pulled Flo to the other side of the road. 'How do I go in?' she asked.

'You put one foot in front of the other and hold your head up high,' said Flo. 'Watch me.' She made to lead the way.

'No, wait.' Joyce tugged on Flo's sleeve again. 'I don't want to be the cause of a scene, even if it's not of my doing. I'd like to slip into a pew at the back and slip out again at the end.'

Flo set her lips in a line and looked a bit disappointed. 'Well, I think you should confront old Celia and her dried-up daughter.'

But Joyce was adamant. 'I won't have that, Flo,' she said. 'I will not give Celia the evidence to tell her friends how right she was all along about me and my family.'

A cold blast of air whipped around the corner and turned Flo's pale, wintry complexion to a translucent blue. Her lips shivered, but she nodded and said she hadn't seen the situation from that perspective and agreed. Clutching each other, they kept their heads down, sidestepped the shuffling crowd and found two seats right at the back next to an older couple wearing dark clothes that smelled of mothballs. Cross stitched kneelers hung from little hooks underneath shelves that held hymn books; a marbled christening font stood behind them; wisps of candle smoke spun towards the ceiling and boards were nailed to the windows where a few years ago stained-glass depicting the lifeboat crews of Cromer would have let in the leaden light through a stream of colour.

The organ started up a dirge, the vicar walked slowly down the middle aisle, a hush fell over the congregation and everyone stood. Joyce's knees buckled, but Flo caught her and propped her up with a tight hold around her waist. Off key voices soared with the first hymn and Flo held open a book at the right page so she and Joyce appeared to be joining in. Joyce was unable to lift her eyes from the kneeler in front of her, but for one moment she lapsed and caught sight of the shiny black pallbearers' shoes, stepping in time with each other and then felt compelled to take one swift look at the scene. But she immediately wished she hadn't as there was Celia following right behind the casket. When she was level with Joyce her eyes flared with defeated recognition before she gathered herself together and nodded to someone on the other side of the church.

Cressida read from the Bible, the vicar said a few words, more hymns were sung and a man who Joyce presumed was

Cress's officer husband, Michael, read the eulogy. He mentioned that Derek had been an exemplary son, brother, uncle, accountant, friend, colleague, Senior Regional Officer in the Civil Defence but not boyfriend or intended or lover. When he folded the sheaves of paper he'd been referring to and sat down at the opposite end of a pew from Cressida, the four dark heads of their sons in between them, Joyce's tears started. Not for the awful slight, but for the children she and Derek would never have.

Still grasping each other, Joyce and Flo sidled out past the receiving party in the covered porch, but Joyce wondered why they'd bothered as she knew they wouldn't be stopped and introduced. The eldest of Derek's nephews eyed her quizzically, but was soon distracted when told to shake so-and-so's hand, and the cousins escaped into the fresh air.

'Let's get a bun and a cup of tea over there,' Flo pointed to the Lifeboat Café.

'Not that one,' Joyce said and led Flo to a tea shop she hadn't visited with Derek.

Flo ordered for both of them and while they waited to be served, she asked Joyce if she thought it was a good thing they'd attended.

Joyce smoothed the tablecloth, tracing dainty pink embroidered flowers with her finger. 'Not a good thing,' she said. 'But perhaps the right thing.'

The waitress brought them tea, cheese on toast and two pieces of Norfolk shortbread. 'Ta,' Flo said. There were a few moments of silence, then she continued. 'I think it will help you in the future.'

Joyce felt so miserable and drained that any thoughts of the future, other than tomorrow and perhaps the day after at Report and Control, were beyond her imagination. All she could do was pick up her teacup with trembling hands and shake her head forlornly.

Flo reached out and touched her cousin's arm. 'I know it's difficult now,' she said. 'But there will be a future. I promise you.'

'I wish I could be so sure,' Joyce said.

They didn't talk much on the long train journey back to London. They snuggled together for warmth, napped on and off and Flo finished Joyce's sandwiches. When they arrived home, Flo wanted to tell Auntie Cath she would be spending the night with Joyce at Nana's house, but Joyce insisted she'd done enough. As grateful as she was, all Joyce wanted to do was crawl into her own bed, sob her heart out for Derek and lick her wounds.

* * *

Every thought of Derek was raw and the fluttering in her stomach that thinking of him used to create was replaced by an aching void. Concentrating on the minutiae of her map to take her mind off images of him, she jumped when she heard Controller Davis call her name.

'Senior Warden Cooper,' he said. 'The Regional Commissioner is here to have a word with you.'

Joyce was bemused, but she saluted and followed the Commissioner to the first aid room which was unoccupied except for Mrs Bertrand, who raised her eyebrows and edged away.

Joyce felt nervous and wondered if she'd filled in one of her reports incorrectly and hoped the officer would accept bereavement as a good enough reason, although she knew it couldn't be an excuse as they were all in that boat together.

'How are you, Senior Warden Cooper?' The Regional Commissioner smiled at her. He was older than Controller Davis and when he took off his hat, his mottled scalp shone through his thinning hair. One of his eyes was bloodshot and his wiry, white eyebrows were thick and unruly.

'I'm well, thank you, Sir,' Joyce answered.

The Commissioner coughed drily. 'I'm so sorry about Senior Regional Officer Nicholls,' he said. 'We all miss him terribly as I'm sure you do.'

'Yes.' It took all the discipline Joyce had not to let herself down by showing her emotions. She looked at her hands on the table, the intertwined fingers white with tension.

The Commissioner dug into his greatcoat pocket and took out a small parcel which he pushed across the table towards her. 'I want you to have this.'

'Shall I open it now?' Joyce asked without picking it up.

'Yes, please do.' The officer watched as Joyce unwrapped a sheet of brown paper and a few layers of tissue to reveal a small, maroon box. Inside, pinned to a piece of white card, was a red and gold plastic badge in the design of an upright sword balancing on a wreath and topped by a crown. There was no space for the beneficiary's details, but Joyce touched the inscription that read For Brave Conduct.

'A King's Commendation for Derek,' she said. 'Ta. Thank you very much.'

'We thought it was well-deserved.' The Commissioner coughed and uncrossed his legs, then thought better of it and crossed them again. 'Derek was courageous and never let his debilitating condition stand in his way,' he said. 'But knowing what we did, we should never have let him go.'

'I'm afraid you wouldn't have been able to stop him,' Joyce said. 'You know that as well as anyone.'

'Do you read the *Gazette*?' asked the Regional Commissioner.

'No.' Joyce shook her head.

'Ah, then you will have missed this.' He unfurled a newspaper cutting and showed Joyce Derek's name on a list with others who'd been awarded the medal the previous Thursday. It was a long list and Joyce was struck by the fact that one of a similar length must appear daily without fail, each name representing someone else's broken heart.

Joyce carefully folded the clipping and put in the red box. 'I'm not Derek's next of kin,' she said, not wanting to take the medal unless it was legitimately hers.

'Well, Miss Cooper,' the Commissioner lowered his voice as if they were conspirators. 'Mrs Nicholls paid me a visit at Regional Control and asked for Derek's effects. I handed over the few personal things he kept at work, but this hadn't yet been issued.' He coughed again. 'And even if it had... I think you should have it.' He stood to leave. 'If anyone should try to take it from you, refer them to me or Controller Davis. Do you understand?'

'Yes, Sir,' Joyce managed. They shook hands and she thanked him again. Then she nestled the precious box at the bottom of her bag before going back to her map. At home the next morning, she pushed it into the toe of one of the black patent pumps where she kept the Taperite pen for safekeeping, but the following night at work she realised how foolish that decision had been when reports of Tip and Run bombers once again caused her to pockmark the map. After that, she kept her valuables with her in her bag so that if she took a blast, they would be blown away with her.

* * *

Joyce was grateful to have her job. But because it was quieter than it had been, a few Junior Wardens left to join the Land Army or the WRENs or to be conductors on the trains or work on the tools. Flo asked again in a letter if Joyce would consider swapping the Civil Defence for the WAAFs, but Joyce could not imagine giving up the job and the map she knew so well.

Every evening she reported to Report and Control an hour before blackout. She checked every detail on the map, making sure that if anything happened to her someone else could read it without difficulty. Then she dusted the table she used, set out the pins, labels, a pencil and pen, had a cup of tea with the Controller and waited to receive the first ARPM1 that might or might not materialise. The telephone rang on and off all night, whether Notting Hill took any hits or not, with requests from other Report and Control Centres asking for assistance with burst water mains, gas leaks or emergency services and she assisted Controller Davis in co-ordinating the necessary help. Of course, there was no telling how the night would pan out so there was no insulating structure to cling to with that, but unless they took a direct hit, the framework remained rigid and that gave her a sense of security.

Every morning, she took Nana and Granddad a cup of tea in bed when she got home and then made all three of them breakfast. She slept; she wrote to Flo; she read and walked and spent an ever-increasing amount of time with her grandmother. A few girls she vaguely knew asked her to the pub, but she wanted nothing more than to wash dishes or clothes in the kitchen next to Nana or carry her bags to and from the shops or sit next to her on the lumpy settee.

Poor Granddad tinkered endlessly with his old, clapped out wireless but could never get it working long enough for them to listen to an entire news or music programme. Joyce thought it would be good for all of them to have a radio, so saved money every week until she had enough to buy a second-hand set from the pawn shop. Granddad, in particular, was delighted with the purchase and Joyce had some good conversations with him about aspects of the war they could not have gleaned from articles in the newspaper.

Whenever news of the Warsaw Ghetto Uprising was broadcast, their ears were stuck to the set. Joyce could not believe that those brave people had imprisoned themselves behind barricades and were fending off the Germans with makeshift weapons. She couldn't imagine living through the sort of war that must have felt like being in the grip of an iron fist. In comparison, they were experiencing a kid glove grasp and that was bad enough.

'How can they manage that, Granddad,' Joyce asked. 'They must be so cold and hungry and frightened. And if they can do it, why can't others?'

'That's the six-thousand-pound question, Joy love,' Granddad answered. 'But I suppose some people are too hungry or too scared or don't know where to start. If you can't imagine it, then that must be the same for most other people, too.'

That made sense to Joyce and she liked to think about that and all the other things she and Granddad had listened to and talked about while she walked backwards and forwards to work. It stopped her thinking about Mum and Derek and Sid and wallowing in self-pity, if only for short periods of time.

Every time Flo came home on leave, she tried to drag Joyce out for a drink or to the cinema or a dance, but Joyce could not be persuaded until one weekend in July when the thought of having a shandy filled her with a long-forgotten sense of buoyant anticipation.

Flo could not believe the turn of events and insisted on collecting Joyce from Nana's instead of meeting her outside The Mitre in Holland Park. Joyce wore her navy jacket, a brown skirt, a dusty pink blouse and the black pumps, then she smoothed her curly hair, put on a bit of make-up and found she had enjoyed getting ready.

Men and women in uniform were spilling out of the pub, all of them making the most of a balmy summer's day despite the crater in the pavement they had to avoid to get into the premises, the air raid siren staring down at them from the top of a wooden pole and the obliterated buildings across the road. Joyce and Flo managed to find two chairs at a tiny table squashed in the corner next to the hedge that surrounded the courtyard and Joyce sat while Flo fetched a port and lemon for herself and half a shandy for Joyce, who gawped around her. 'Ta, Flo love,' she said and took a sip of the golden liquid that instantly lifted her spirits. 'It's so... busy.'

Flo threw back her head and laughed. 'Well, don't forget you've been out of it for ages,' she said. 'A year and more.'

For a split-second, Joyce felt disloyalty towards Derek wash over her, but another gulp of beer quashed that. Besides, everyone told her Derek wouldn't want her to sit in on her own for ever and she was beginning to think that was good advice.

Flo looked as lovely as usual in a charcoal skirt, cream jumper and green cardigan. She leaned across the table, careful to avoid the tacky rings left by numerous beer glasses. 'So,' she said, 'what made you decide to venture out today?'

Joyce thought about that. Closing her eyes, she took a breath of fragrant summer air deep into her lungs. 'A combination of things, I suppose,' she said. 'The weather, suddenly missing being out, wanting to hear laughter. Thirst.' She pointed to her glass.

'Whatever the reason, it's a good sign.'

Joyce nodded, but wondered what it was a good sign of. Putting the past behind her? Carrying on regardless? Having a stiff upper lip? Being ready to move on? Or any of the clichés people dispensed to make themselves feel as if things were getting back to normal.

A guffaw of laughter erupted from the table next to theirs, followed by the heavy clink of glasses being pounded on wood.

Joyce turned her head discreetly and was greeted with a wink from a soldier sitting with a crowd of his mates. Swivelling her head back just in time to catch Flo winking back, heat spilled over her face and she fumbled for her drink. 'Granddad's enjoying the wireless,' she said. 'And so am I. I've learned so much about what's happening. For instance, all of the Allied activity in Italy.'

Flo took a cigarette from her bag and lit it, which was, in Joyce's opinion, nothing more than an affectation. 'Have one?' Flo asked.

'Not for me,' Joyce said. 'I'd never have been able to afford the radio if I smoked. Besides, Derek hated...'

'I'm glad you're enjoying the new set,' Flo said, shreds of smoke fading into the air around them. 'We have a wireless in our common room and some girls listen to all the news but mostly we like the music.'

Joyce nodded. '"Music While You Work" is lovely,' she said. 'Nana listens to it most days.'

The lads at the table behind them burst into laughter again and called out to another group walking past. For a few minutes their loud voices made it difficult for Joyce and Flo to talk. When the hubbub died down, Joyce asked Flo if the wink meant she'd finished with Vernon.

Flo's face darkened and her mouth turned down, but only for a beat. 'No,' she said, 'of course not. A wink's nothing more than that.'

'You don't mention him much in your letters,' Joyce said. 'And why haven't we met him?'

Their glasses were empty and Flo said she'd refresh them at the bar, but it was Joyce's turn to order so she went into the pub instead. When she returned, Flo was smoking another cigarette and the soldier who'd caught her eye was sitting next to her. Joyce felt like a piece of fruit – a lemon or a gooseberry – and hovered with the glasses in her hand until the young man said she must sit down. He bowed from the waist in a theatrical way and went back to his mates.

Joyce mouthed, 'What about Vernon?'

Flo shrugged in reply. 'There's nothing wrong with having a chat. I suppose he talks to lots of girls when I'm not about.'

'You suppose or you know?' Then Joyce suddenly became exasperated with her cousin. She'd never been devious or artful or anything other than candid and Joyce put the change down to Vernon. 'Why are we talking in riddles?' she asked. 'We've always been straightforward and told each other everything.'

A few clouds passed over the sun and Joyce pulled her jacket close. From a tree came the sound of birds squabbling and she hoped that wasn't a bad omen for her and Flo, who had never quarrelled before.

Flo sighed. 'Vernon is married,' she said, waiting a few moments to let that piece of information sink in.

Joyce was surprised rather than stunned and a lot of things

fell into place now she knew that. 'Well,' she said. 'I suppose I should have guessed given his age. Is he separated? Divorced?'

'He's in the process,' Flo said, her voice flat and fed up. 'So I'm waiting until that's resolved before I introduce him to Mum and Dad. Can you imagine the inquisition otherwise?' She mimicked a man's voice. '"When are you going to make an honest woman of my daughter, Vernon?"' Then her mum's, '"What's his situation, Flo love, and tell me the truth."' She shook her head. 'I couldn't bear it.'

'It's because they care about you,' Joyce said. 'We all do.'

'I know,' Flo drew out the last vowel like a petulant child. 'But they won't see Vernon like I do. They'll be blinkered to everything good about him by the one fact that he's married. So I want to have our concrete plan ready to tell them before I break the news. You understand though, don't you, Joy love? You've been in the same position, after all.'

Joyce wasn't sure she did understand as her and Derek's situation had been completely different from Flo's. 'Derek wasn't married and living thousands of miles away from where he could get his divorce sorted out,' she said.

The way Flo looked away made Joyce understand that she'd come to that same conclusion herself. When she turned back, her features were harder than Joyce had ever seen them. 'I know that,' she said with venom. 'What I meant was you didn't have a smooth ride either, what with Celia and Cress hanging over you and Derek like a wet weekend.'

That was true, Joyce thought and although she wasn't persuaded that their experiences were similar, Flo had always offered her sympathy and solidarity and Joyce felt ashamed that she'd failed to do the same for her cousin. Mum and Derek were gone and she'd didn't want to lose Flo to a silly disagreement about a man. When she'd asked Flo what she liked about Vernon over a year ago, Flo had given her some vague answer about him being funny, gentlemanly, hardworking, ambitious and smart, with no examples to back up those alleged attributes. Perhaps she could ask Flo to elaborate, but she decided that she'd got her to admit Vernon was married and she should probably drop the subject for today.

The crowd of men left without giving them another glance and the sun came out again. Joyce smiled. 'I really am glad I came out for an hour or two.'

Flo cheered up and said, 'Strike while the iron's hot. Let's go for a dance.'

'That,' Joyce said, 'is a step too far. Besides I'm working tonight.'

'A tea dance tomorrow then.'

Joyce closed her eyes and shook her head.

'A lesson then.'

'A lesson. Where?'

'At Madame Beaupre's, of course.'

Joyce was sure she'd told Flo about the dance studio being bombed out. 'You're going mad,' she said. 'Don't you remember Madame Beaupre's took a hit?'

'I'm not the one who's crazy,' Flo said. 'Haven't you seen the notice tacked to a post on the bombsite?'

Joyce hadn't been along Westbourne Grove since she'd looked for her old dance instructors in those first few days after Madame Beaupre's had been razed to the ground. 'No, I haven't,' she said.

Flo's eyes sparkled and she sat up straight; she was beside herself with excitement. 'They're giving lessons in the Church Hall.'

When they'd first met Madame Beaupre, Joyce had been awestruck at how adept the dance teacher was at rising above the terrible circumstances of the blasted war they all found themselves a part of. Now that admiration intensified and she wanted nothing more than to see the older woman and tell her how proud she was that she'd managed to bounce back.

'In that case, then yes. Tomorrow before lunch at the ABC?'

Flo grinned and Joyce hoped it was not only with anticipation for the dance lesson, but that she'd pushed thoughts of Vernon to the back of her mind.

* * *

A group of chattering women was waiting outside the dance hall in the morning. Joyce and Flo tagged onto the end of the queue and whilst Flo was excited about the lesson, Joyce was more keen to see Madame Beaupre. The two women in front of them, who were dressed in bib and braces ready for some kind of manual work, started to mimic the way Madame Beaupre moved in and out of a French accent. 'Yes, your left hand goes just there,' said the one with pancake make-up stuck fast to a crop of spots on her chin.

'I mean *Oui*, your left hand goes there,' her companion laughed.

Joyce and Flo shared a look that meant they knew better. Madame Beaupre was much deeper than her spurious accent and manner would have everyone believe, if only they would take the time and trouble to dig. She presented herself in that artificial light because that was the sophisticated way she truly perceived herself to be in the midst of such a coarse and base war. And Joyce, for one, thought they could all learn from the dance instructor's attitude.

'When we go in, shall I take Madame Beaupre to one side and tell her about Derek?'

'Ta, Flo love,' Joyce said. 'That would help. But I want to speak to her, too, and say I'm sorry about the studio.'

A key scratched around a rusty lock and the wooden doors were flung open with a flourish. '*Bonjour mes demoiselles. Entrez s'il vous plait,*' Madame Beaupre greeted everyone.

When it was Joyce and Flo's turn, Madame Beaupre's eyes widened and her face lit up with a smile. 'Mademoiselle Joyce and Mademoiselle Flo!' She threw her arms around them and Joyce could feel her quick, birdlike heartbeat through the whalebone stays. 'I've missed you both so much.'

'I came looking for you and Monsieur Beaupre at the site of the old studio on many occasions,' Joyce said, 'but I never timed it right.'

'We could not bear to look at the ruins at first,' Madame Beaupre said whilst ushering in a few women waiting behind them. 'But now Monsieur Beaupre has started making enquiries about whether it's worth renovating.' She shook her head sadly and Joyce could see how she'd aged – her face was gaunt and her lipstick bled into the lines around her mouth. But most noticeable was the way her shoulders slumped and her once still, serene, perfectly manicured hands fidgeted and fluttered.

Flo steered Madame Beaupre to the side of the hall and Joyce took that as her cue to join the others on chairs lining one wall. A mop and bucket standing in the corner hadn't done their job very well because dust and grime blackened the edge of the floor. Instead of the huge mirrors that had lined the studio, one sorry full-length looking-glass was propped up next to an old, second-hand gramophone.

Madame Beaupre pointed Flo towards the chair next to

Joyce and chose a record from a depleted stack, turned to the learners and announced they should choose their partners and prepare for a waltz. She placed the needle down with her thumb and index finger, then made her way straight to Joyce. Sweeping her up, Madame Beaupre placed one hand on top of her head and the other where her waist met her ribcage and drew herself up until she seemed at least an inch taller. 'You must do the same, Mademoiselle Joyce,' she said. 'Rise up from the crown of your head and from the middle of your being. Rise up. Lift your head and look the world in the eye.'

Joyce did as she was told and something close to a miracle occurred. Instantly, she felt taller, shielded and almost impenetrable. She thought it was the best advice she'd been given in a long time.

* * *

Nana's eyesight had always been poor and the optician had tweaked her spectacles until he said he couldn't do any more to help and he'd referred her to Moorfield's. Joyce went with her to every appointment, helping her grandmother on and off the two buses each way, guiding her around obstacles that appeared overnight; she read aloud the writing on posters, notices in shop windows and on newspaper hoardings, warned Nana to mind herself on loose paving slabs and saved her from knocking into other people.

Joyce hadn't realised how much sight Nana had lost until they were away from the house and streets Nana knew so well and she asked her granddaughter to describe what was going on around them. Joyce was shocked at the request and, at first, took the task seriously. She reached up towards Nana's ear and detailed everything she saw until, for some reason or another, she felt like being silly and started to speak in the King's clipped English. 'I say,' she said in a guttural tone, 'that rather tall chap over there is dashing along with his paper under his arm and a black umbrella swinging by his side.'

It was so good to hear Nana laugh that Joyce kept it up until Nana cuffed her and said, 'Give over, Joy love, my sides ache.'

When Joyce did as she was told, Nana batted her on the arm again and asked her why she'd stopped the funny voice. So Joyce attempted as many different dialects as she could and that kept them amused for quite a while. She wondered what kind of comments someone passing would make about them. A short older woman hanging onto an even shorter, younger woman. Both very slight but not rake thin. Enough similarities between them to make it obvious that they were grandmother and granddaughter. The older woman wearing spectacles as thick as the bottom of stout bottles and the younger with a good head of curly, dark auburn hair. And she hoped they'd go on to note how easily they laughed and enjoyed each other's company.

When they sat side by side in the waiting area, the smells of disinfectant and greens boiling in vats of water reminded Joyce of that long week when Derek had been so poorly. And the paint on the walls must have been purchased as a job lot because it was the exact match for the muddy shade she'd sat staring at while she waited to see him on the ward at University College.

In the examination room, Joyce sat in a chair in the corner while doctors carried out test after test on her grandmother. They all looked unpleasant, but the only time Nana grumbled was when a yellow dye was put in her eyes and she said the specialist had made her eyesight worse, not better.

Granddad went with them when the doctor said he would have some news and the three of them sat in a row facing the specialist's desk. Nana rubbed the sore spot on the back of her leg, Granddad fidgeted in his ill-fitting best clothes and Joyce could feel her stomach gnawing on nothing. The doctor placed a model of an eyeball in front of him, turned it around and explained that Nana had cataracts at the backs of her eyes and that was why she saw everything as if through an opaque veil. 'Can you do anything about these cataracts, doctor?' Joyce asked.

'There is an operation,' he said, his voice as posh as the one Joyce had used to make Nana laugh.

The colour drained from Nana's face. 'I'd rather take tablets,' she said.

'I'm afraid, Mrs Stanbridge, that medication won't help your condition.'

'Stronger spectacles?' Granddad suggested in his gravelly voice.

'I have a pair ready for you,' the doctor said and produced the thickest, heaviest pair of glasses Joyce had ever seen. 'They should help a bit in the short term, but only the operation will restore you to good sight.'

'When can my grandmother have the operation?' Joyce asked.

'Well,' the doctor sat back in his chair. 'I'm afraid this bl— war has changed everything.'

'Blasted war, we call it,' said Nana.

'That's one word, certainly,' the doctor said. 'I can think of a few more. You've seen the state of the building, haven't you?'

They all nodded. The entrance held up with lengths of wood; the cordoned off steps reduced to crumbling lumps of concrete, the right-hand side covered by tarpaulin; a makeshift reception desk next to a pile of broken furniture were all hard to miss.

'The eye patients who need to be admitted for some time have been evacuated and this hospital is now used for more general surgery.'

Nana looked at Joyce, her poorly eyes wide with alarm. Joyce reached over and took Nana's hand. 'Will my grandmother have to go away for her operation, doctor?'

Nana shook her head.

The doctor opened a large book and ran his finger down one page then another. 'If you don't mind waiting, Mrs Stanbridge, I should be able to accommodate you here. Would that suit you better?'

Joyce would have preferred Nana to have the operation straight away, but Nana and Granddad were so profuse with their thanks that she didn't try to change their minds.

The doctor stood, buttoned his white coat, positioned the new glasses on Nana's nose and stood back to admire his handiwork. 'I say,' Nana said. 'These do the trick.' Beaming, she turned and for a split-second Joyce drew back in horror. Nana's eyes were huge and distorted behind the lenses and they seemed to wobble around like the studs used for eyes that were sewn on teddy bears.

Joyce looked to the doctor for affirmation that a mistake hadn't been made, but he was nonplussed, so the spectacles must have been as intended.

'What they're doing is magnifying everything, Mrs Stanbridge and nothing else. But they should help for now. Please be careful until you get used to them as they can make the ground appear curved and warped when you look down.'

Of course Nana had to try that out. She stood, gazed down

at her feet and started to laugh. 'Oh, it makes me feel like a drunken, seasick sailor,' she said.

The doctor chuckled and said he was going to use that description when handing out similar spectacles to other patients.

For a few weeks, Joyce worried about Nana bumping into things or tripping over ragged rugs or uneven paving slabs. And she wouldn't have dared to leave her all night if it wasn't for Auntie Cath taking over the reins when she was at work.

But one early evening she was left alone. Not for long, but long enough for a gas explosion at the other end of the terrace to hew a path to Nana's house and send it up into the skies and back down again in a heap of bricks, mortar, glass and wood. Joyce heard the blast on her way to work, but didn't find out the details until a few hours later when she was handed the ARPM1. Granddad and Uncle Terry heard it from The Ladbroke Arms where they'd gone for a quick pint. Auntie Cath heard it and saw it from the corner she'd been hurrying around to get to Nana and the woman across the road told Joyce that Auntie Cath tore through the rubble with her bare hands calling, 'Mummy! Mummy!' until she'd been pulled away.

Something broke in Joyce when she heard that. It felt as if everything substantial around her turned to jelly and she wondered how much more they could take. Then she drew herself up, stood as tall as possible and willed what had been broken inside her to be shored up. There was nothing else she could do as Auntie Cath and Granddad were in shock and paralysed with grief. Uncle Terry helped to organise the arrangements, but Joyce knew that the day to day running of the new household they now shared in Auntie Cath and Uncle Terry's ground floor flat was dependent on her. Besides, it was easier for her this way. She no longer had time to dwell on anything other than being methodical, logical, and structured in how she took care of the basics at home and at work.

Flo came home right away and on top of everything else, she dared to bring Vernon with her. Joyce was livid. What a time to introduce him to the family, but Joyce suspected it had been a considered move, although she could not get Flo to admit it. They walked together through Porchester Square and after they'd spoken in soft voices about their grandmother, Flo asked Joyce what she thought of Vernon. Joyce was astonished. She stood quite still and unpeeled her arm from Flo's. 'Vernon is the last thing on my mind right now,' she fumed. 'I, for one, cannot believe that Nana is gone. And poor old Granddad and Auntie Cath need a lot of taking care of. Then there are all the things that need to be done so we can live together reasonably comfortably.'

To her credit, Flo looked mortified. 'I... I'm sorry, Joy love.' She made a grab for Joyce's hand.

But Joyce had started and she couldn't seem to stop. 'And if you really want to know, he's nothing like you described him. When he isn't laughing at his own jokes, he looks bored, as if we're beneath him. He says all the right things but he's not really interested as he never remembers what he's been told from one hour to the next. He's arrogant, too, although what he's got to be smug about I have no idea. And the worst thing is, you've lost your candour and walk around with an imperious attitude, too.' Joyce stopped, aware that she'd gone too far. Her legs were shaking, she was breathing heavily and Flo's mouth hung open with disbelief.

Joyce dropped down on a bench and Flo sat at the opposite end, lit a cigarette and inhaled a lungful of smoke. Joyce felt sick. Everything she said was true, she just hadn't said it the way she should have. But she couldn't bear the way Vernon's foot twitched and fidgeted when he wasn't getting Flo's full attention. Or the way he languished on the settee next to Flo, his arm flung over her shoulders and his knees so far apart that no one else could squeeze in next to him. He gave the impression he owned everything he surveyed, including Flo, and her cousin couldn't see any of it. All she saw was what she wanted to see and she looked at Vernon as if the sun rose and set at his bidding.

'Why now, Flo?' Joyce asked. 'It seems to me you've used this opportunity while we're all so terribly distracted to allow Vernon to wheedle his way in. Then you think that Uncle Terry, Auntie Cath and Granddad will just accept him with no questions asked.'

Flo stared at the ash hanging from her cigarette, then at the trees on the other side of the fence. She didn't say a word in self-defence.

'I'm sorry, Flo,' Joyce said. 'But I can see what's happening and I don't think you're being at all fair.'

Flo took the last puff from her cigarette and ground out the stub with her toe. 'I'm upset, too, Joy and wanted my boyfriend with me during this horrible time. Just because you can't have Derek with you doesn't mean I have to suffer, too.'

Joyce felt as though she'd been slapped first on one cheek then the other. 'Flo,' she managed at last, 'how could you say that? Yes, I'd give anything for Derek's arm to lean on, but jealousy isn't why I'm upset.'

When Flo turned to look at her, her face was so hard and rigid that Joyce was startled all over again. 'You're right,' her tone was cold and flippant. 'In that I would love for Vernon to be a part of the family without too many questions asked, but I have not used our Nana's passing away as a means to do that. Nothing could be further from my mind.'

* * *

Over the next few days Joyce's outburst preyed on her mind. She thought she was right to have said her piece, but she was ashamed that she'd gone about it in such an indecorous way; she felt as if she'd let herself down badly. Every time she thought about it, sickening bile rose from her stomach and sweat prickled her neck until she promised herself she would never again be so ill-mannered – it would be better to bite her tongue next time, rather than have to feel guilty, like she did now, about her rude outburst. Full of remorse, she spent a lot of time devising a way to apologise to Flo for how she'd handled the situation.

Then Flo and Vernon spent three days away from the house, gawping at Downing Street and Buckingham Palace and Trafalgar Square and Joyce was left to co-ordinate meals, new ration books, clothing, beds, linen, keys, crockery, cutlery, sleeping arrangements, washing and cleaning for herself and everyone else as they squashed in together in Auntie Cath's flat. She and Flo barely spoke for the remainder of the time Flo was home and when she and Vernon left for Bedfordshire, their goodbyes were cursory.

Auntie Cath and Uncle Terry had their bedroom, of course, but this time around the front room had to be kitted out to accommodate Granddad. Joyce bunked down on a camp bed in Flo's room where once she would have been cosy and comfortable and content, but now she felt as if she were an intruder in a space belonging to someone she hardly knew. The wireless was gone and Joyce hadn't the heart or the money to replace it so it was back to newspapers and hearsay. Superficial letters arrived from Flo, with never a mention of Vernon, which Joyce answered in an equally perfunctory, polite style. She went to work, cooked breakfast for everyone when she got home, read, walked, bought food with Auntie Cath and did her best to fit in with her aunt's ways in the kitchen.

During September, an official letter arrived for Nana that had been diverted from her old address. It was from Moorfields and when Auntie Cath opened it she started to cry. 'Oh dear,' she said. 'Poor Mum. She would have loved being able to see without those horrible spectacles.' Then she put her arms around Joyce and cried, mumbling something about 'the blasted war' over and over again. Joyce returned Auntie Cath's hug, but waited until she was alone in Flo's room to shed her own tears. Then she put on her uniform, pulled herself up from the top of her head and readied herself for another long night with her map.

SEVENTEEN

Monday 25 March 1974

The idea of buying a cork board to put in the kitchen and pin reminders on had occurred to Joyce, but she'd blanched at the thought of using the necessary thumb tacks. She'd had enough of those little lethal spears and could not face holding and aiming them ever again. At work, a noticeboard every bit as large as her old map covered one wall, but she always managed to finagle her way out of using it. 'While you're pinning yours,' she'd say to Sandra or Elaine or Audrey, 'would you mind putting this up for me?' Or else she would leave her notifications where she knew one of the other girls would find them, think she'd forgotten about them and pin them up for her.

Instead, she bought a blackboard on an easel, a pack of coloured chalks and an eraser so she could keep a running shopping list plus a note of everything she needed to take with her when she left the flat. It was working well and helped her to feel prepared and organised and reminded her of the metal grocery list that had hung from a piece of string in Nana's kitchen.

That morning she read what she'd written the night before: milk, tea, sugar and coffee which she bought for the office; sandwiches; shopping bag; a reminder to buy a chop for tonight; half a head of cabbage; two carrots and a packet of digestives. Then at the bottom, in capital letters, there was one word in bright pink chalk – KEYS.

Mr Taylor had explained to her in great detail that the lock on the front door wasn't like the one at her old flat. There, the door couldn't be locked without using the key from the outside. But here, where everything was new and modern and allegedly more efficient, the door locked when it was closed, key in hand or not.

But outside the front door she fumbled with her coat and bags and umbrella. She put the keys down in the hall, for one minute, to reach for a circular she wanted to throw in the bin when a breeze slammed the door shut. She stood frozen to the spot for a minute, her belongings pooling around her ankles, not able to believe she'd been so foolish.

In frustration she tried the door, rattled it a few times, then laid her forehead against it and kicked it with her toe. 'Blast, she said. She had a spare key, of course, but that was in the kitchen drawer and not in a deep recess of her handbag where she knew to keep important things. She picked up the circular and tore it into tiny pieces.

Taking a few steps backwards towards the balcony, she wondered if she could ram the door open with her shoulder like Steve McGarrett and Danno Williams in *Hawaii Five-o*, but didn't entertain that idea for long. Then she began to search her bag and pockets for a hair pin or any object she could use to turn the lock, but even if she could find such an instrument she wouldn't know where to start when it came to breaking and entering. No one was about to ask for assistance; the mothers were drinking coffee in each other's maisonettes after taking their children to school and the older people were not yet out for their walks or shopping. She looked at her watch and worried that if she missed her bus, she wouldn't make the connection and she'd end up late for work, something that had never happened before and filled her with horror.

She heard a scrape from the other side of Mr Frenchay's door and looked towards it in anticipation. He might telephone the Housing Department for her, and Mr Taylor could leave a spare key at the council reception desk that she could collect later. But she realised that Mr Frenchay was watching her through his spyhole and when it scuffed again without him making an appearance, she knew he'd gone back into the confines of his flat. She hadn't seen him once since she'd moved in and she wasn't going to see him this morning either. That was the way she wanted things to be, but common courtesy should have made him ask her if she was alright, at least.

Checking her watch again, she decided there was nothing else for it but to leave for work and once there, phone a locksmith to meet her at the flat when she got home. Then she heard the jovial whistle of that irritating 'Wombling Song' and before she could duck down to collect her bags, Mr Norris called up to her. That, she thought, was all she needed. 'Good morning, Miss Cooper,' his brash voice rang out. 'How are we today?'

She loathed the incorrect use of the pronoun 'we' and whenever anyone used it when addressing her, she had to hold herself back from looking over her shoulder and asking who else they were referring to. But she smiled, waved quickly and made her way down the stairs where, much to her annoyance, Mr Norris was waiting for her.

He doffed his hat and asked her if she was settling in.

'Yes, thank you,' she said. 'I hate to appear rude, but I have a bus to catch for work. I daren't be late.'

'Ah, yes,' he smiled and released a slow, self-satisfied sigh. 'I forget that not everyone in this block is retired.' She wouldn't have been surprised if he'd started to miaow like a contented cat. 'Although I keep myself busier than I've ever been.'

'I'm sure you do. Thank you, Mr Norris. Good day,' she said.

'But I'm not too busy to help a new neighbour,' he continued. 'You must let me know if I can do anything at all for you.'

It was a heartfelt statement and Joyce wondered if this once, and only this once, she could ask him to arrange a spare key for her. Blushing and stammering she quickly told him her dilemma and said she would reimburse him for any phone calls he made.

'My dear Miss Cooper,' his tone of voice was dramatically offended. 'I would not dream of taking payment from you. I did the exact same thing a few weeks after I'd moved in.'

Joyce didn't know whether to believe him or not.

'Now, off you go and be confident that I will see to everything.'

Really, he was too charming to be plausible, but Joyce thanked him profusely and when she was sitting safely on the bus and thought about it, found she did have faith he would sort out the awkward situation by the time she returned.

The girls in the office were exchanging news of their weekends when she arrived and Alison turned to her, as one of them always did and asked how she'd spent the two days off. She grumbled a bit about having to walk so far with heavy bags of shopping and gave them the latest instalment of not being able to work the washing machine.

'Well, if you'd bring in the instructions like we keep asking you, perhaps we could help out,' Elaine said with a touch of annoyance.

'I'll write that on my chalkboard tonight so I remember in the morning,' Joyce said quickly so as not to offend.

'Oh, you write your reminders on a blackboard?' Elaine sounded impressed. 'What a good idea.'

The others agreed and thought they might try the same rather than writing lists and notes to themselves on scraps of paper. It was Barbara's week to make the hot drinks and she asked all the women if they wanted their usual. While she waited for the kettle to boil, she fluffed up her beehive hairdo with a pencil and asked Joyce about any other handy household items she'd invested in.

'I bought an electric kettle like the one here and a plant for the balcony, but I can't get an outdoor table and chairs as I couldn't possibly carry them home.'

'The new Argos store will deliver for a bit extra,' Alison said. 'We had a bookcase delivered last week.'

Then they all started to jabber about things they'd bought at Argos and Joyce was glad to be able to set out her pens and pencils, ruler, stapler and ledger and sip her cup of tea. When she removed the first stack of payroll slips from the safe and started to transcribe them into her book, she lost the thread of the conversation until Sandra said, 'How about it, Joyce?'

'I beg your pardon,' Joyce said, looking up.

'We'll go to Argos in the lunch hour and show you how to order something.'

'Oh no, really,' Joyce said. 'I don't like to think I'll be taking up your time.'

'You won't be,' Elaine said. 'It'll be fun.' And so it was settled.

Every time Joyce thought about the key incident during the morning, prickly heat tiptoed along her skin and she had to grab a piece of paper and waft it in front of her face.

Sandra lifted her eyes from her calculator. 'Hot flush, Joyce?'

'Worse than that,' she said. 'I've embarrassed myself terribly.'

Her five colleagues stopped what they were doing and waited. 'Tell us about it,' encouraged Alison.

Normally, Joyce would have kept such an excruciating tale to herself but she felt as if she'd been caught out, so she sighed and told them the whole sorry story. She expected them to either exchange knowing looks about how silly she was or try to give her the same nonsense as Mr Norris with his account of having done the same. But they started to laugh. All of them. 'Joyce,' Audrey said. 'You are funny.'

'That sounds like a scene from a sitcom,' Barbara managed between snorts of laughter.

Joyce didn't know whether to be offended or compli-mented. But when she thought about it, she supposed it was quite amusing and didn't mind too much that they were laughing at her expense.

On the bus home, one small patio set poorer, she could not revive that light-hearted attitude when she thought about facing Mr Norris and asking for her key. Her bag was heavy with the meat and vegetables she'd bought in a mad dash between buses and her feet hurt from the longer walk to the flat from where the bus stopped.

With apprehension, she knocked on Mr Norris's door and while she waited for him to answer she grew her extra inch from the crown of her head and determined to keep the handover short and simple. 'Miss Cooper,' Mr Norris said, throwing his door wide. 'Come in.'

'Thank you, Mr Norris,' Joyce said in a clipped tone, 'but I am exhausted and have a number of things to do this evening. So...' She stopped herself short of holding out her hand.

'You can rest here for half an hour while you have a much-needed cup of tea.' Mr Norris indicated the interior of his flat with an open palm. Behind him, Joyce could see swirly brown, yellow and orange wallpaper, a purple lava lamp, an aquarium, a stereo and a wall lined with books. Beyond that were the doors leading to the garden with its abundance of plants pressing themselves against the glass in their fight to get inside.

But Joyce stood her ground. 'I'm afraid I must take my shoes off, Mr Norris, and I couldn't possibly do so in your flat.'

Mr Norris looked crestfallen, his jowls wobbling a bit when he shook his head. 'Well, I can't force you,' he said. 'One minute.' He sorted through a bowl in the middle of the table and re-appeared with a key on a blue plastic ring. 'Paul dropped it round,' he said. 'I mean, Mr Taylor.'

'I can't thank you both enough,' Joyce said. 'You have been lifesavers. And I will do my utmost not to do the same thing again.'

Mr Norris shrugged. 'It wouldn't matter if you did,' he said. 'It wasn't difficult to resolve.'

Thanking him once again, Joyce turned to take her leave but almost let out a cry when Mr Norris grabbed her bags from her.

'Let me take these,' he said, holding them in one hand,

putting his door on the latch and ushering her up the concrete steps. There was no arguing with him, she knew he would not take no for an answer.

'That's what I must remember to do when I step outside,' Joyce said by way of conversation. 'Latch my lock.'

'It's a helpful devise,' Mr Norris said. Joyce unlocked her door with the new key and Mr Norris placed her bags in the hallway. Before she had a chance to thank him yet again and say goodbye, Mr Norris said that one good deed deserved another.

For a beat Joyce was taken aback and wondered what on earth he meant. 'I beg your pardon?' she said.

'In return for sorting out your predicament, you must arrange to take tea with me or allow me to have tea with you. Or come along to the MIA Club or film night. At your convenience of course,' he said as if it were a done deal.

Then he jogged towards the stairs whistling another pop song and Joyce gawped after him, but could not bring herself to call him back and refuse his rather forceful invitation. She was much too well-mannered for that.

EIGHTEEN

GRANDDAD AND UNCLE TERRY

June 1944

Everyone agreed that war was wicked, Joyce felt sure of that. Politicians on both sides of any conflict would probably be the first to swear to that being their belief even if their country had declared war upon another in the first place. They would rationalise their decision by saying the first move had been self-defence or a justified retaliation for some previous slight or disagreement. There was no doubt that in the case of this blasted war they were living through, the Allies declaration on the Axis had been warranted and the morally right thing to do, but she would have taken bets that Hitler still maintained he deplored combat and the Allies were nothing more than vicious warmongers.

Stark evidence against the Germans ever being able to prove that came to Britain on the 13th of June in the shape of the V–1 flying bombs. And they brought with them a whole new meaning to the word wicked. In the early hours of the morning, four of the evil things glided across the Channel and one of them found its way to Grove Road in Bow where the behemoth's staccato pulse stopped and it fell silently to earth, killing six people including a young mother and her eight-month-old baby. When Joyce heard those details she thought again about that poor mum in Ladbroke Grove, whose first thought had been for her children and not the crown of flames encircling her head.

The ARPM1 for the first doodlebug attack must have landed in the hands of Joyce's counterpart in the East End, but she heard about it from Controller Davis who heard about it from Regional Control. Joyce froze in the act of organising her pins, hot waves of alarm coursing through her stomach.

'The Regional Commissioner reported that the weapon was unmanned,' the Controller said. 'He warned we must be prepared.'

'Yes, Sir,' Joyce said, wondering how on earth they could prepare themselves for an attack by a weapon they knew nothing about.

Over the next few weeks, though, they learned a lot more about the bombs but wished they'd been spared the horrific knowledge. Besides being called doodlebugs, people named them buzzbombs because of the insect-like noise they made. They could be heard from a long way off and the rattle, as well as the air raid sirens, had everyone running for shelter all over again. But actually hearing one was a comfort, especially if it droned away from your house or factory or the shop or Control Centre you were in. It was when the clanking vibrations stopped that the fear started as the depraved thing would either fall straight down in eerie silence or drift first and then plummet, as quiet as a feather, to earth. Once there, it could blow a crater in the ground of up to one hundred feet in every direction.

Joyce gleaned this information on the new second-hand wireless she and Uncle Terry had clubbed together to buy. At first, she'd been against the idea because she thought it would remind her too much of Nana, but Uncle Terry pointed out that Granddad would benefit as he had from the one they'd previously owned and he promised they would never tune in to Nana's favourite – *Music While You Work*. And although they enjoyed the General Forces Programme, Joyce and Granddad soon resumed their habit of listening to the news together, with Uncle Terry and Auntie Cath joining in when they could.

One late afternoon, Churchill was due to make a speech about the latest bombing campaign. Up until then, the government had not said anything concrete about what was happening, but after more than one hundred had been killed during a morning service in the Guards Chapel at St James's and a Children's Home in Crockham had taken a packet killing twenty-nine defenceless mites and seventy-four had gone down at the US Army Living Quarters in Sloane Court, the newspapers started to demand an explanation and Churchill had been forced to comply. When he started with his humming and hawing, Granddad mimed smoking a cigar and downing a shot. Joyce rolled her eyes at him and tried to look cross, but it was rather funny.

'Terry,' Granddad called, his voice low and scratchy. 'Cath love, Winnie's going to put us all straight.'

Uncle Terry came in from the garden and stood in the doorway and Auntie Cath motioned for Joyce to budge up so she could squeeze in next to her. Auntie Cath was warm from the kitchen and it felt good to be pressed against her soft, round chest. Joyce laid her head against her aunt's shoulder and let it rest there, then she remembered that it didn't do her any good in the long run to get too close and cosy, so levered herself away. Churchill started in earnest by telling them that so far 2,752 people had been killed by the innocuous sounding doodlebugs and 8,000 had been detained in hospitals. Despite the RAF constantly bombarding the Jerry launch sites in France and Holland, somewhere between 150 and 200 V–1s were being hurtled at them every day. He ended his announcement by saying there was no guarantee the bombs could be prevented until the soil from which the attacks were mounted had been liberated. Not very hopeful, Joyce thought, but perhaps it was better to know the truth.

'Well,' Uncle Terry said, 'that's the end of the pipe dream that this blasted war is nearly over.'

'Yes, Terry love,' Auntie Cath said. 'Seems like we're back to square one. It's the Blitz all over again.' She wedged herself out of the chair and followed Uncle Terry through to the kitchen.

'I'll put the kettle on in two minutes,' Joyce called after them.

'Oh, you are a good girl, Joy love,' Auntie Cath said. 'Ta very much.'

Then the presenter continued by explaining that the vengeance weapons were Hitler's retaliation for D–Day, the Allied victory the week before the first flying bomb had been launched. 'Shoo, buzz off.' Granddad swotted the air in front of his face. 'Tell us something we don't know.'

'Shush, Granddad,' Joyce chastised. 'It took us a while to put two and two together.'

Granddad looked a bit put out and smoothed his moustache over his top lip, but couldn't argue Joyce's point.

'The weapon,' the presenter continued, 'is a bomb with wings and causes devastating damage.'

Granddad raised his eyes skyward while this piece of old news was related. Then he sat up and leaned towards the set when the presenter began to question whether or not the conventions of war had been broken by the use of this fierce new flying bomb. When the commentator finished his spiel, Joyce said she didn't know there were any rules about staging a war.

'Yes, there are some, Joy love,' Granddad said. 'But they're mostly about how wounded and sick soldiers are treated on the battlefield. Not really to do with civilians.'

Joyce was dumbfounded. 'That's absurd,' she said.

Granddad frowned. 'Is it?' he asked in his croaky voice. 'I think it's rather a good thing.'

'Oh, yes, of course. What I meant was, if people can sit down and draw up a charter about war conventions, why can't they come up with a way to stop wars altogether?'

Granddad gazed at Joyce for a few moments before she realised that he looked immensely proud. Then he sighed and said, 'Joy love, you ask questions that should be raised in Parliament and that I have no answer for. Much as I wish I did.'

On her way to Report and Control that evening, Joyce thought about the anomalies of war. How applying rules to what was in reality a killing spree reduced it to nothing more than a game of draughts or rounders. Kids' play. She wondered again why more people weren't up in arms about it and then she looked around at the old wounds waiting to be healed on half-demolished building sites, the new scabs gorged into roads by the V–1s, long queues for a bit of fatty pork or spam or a spotted apple, the ghosts of those lost, like Billy and Mum,

Derek, Sid and Nana and she knew everyone was too exhausted from trying to get by on a daily basis to think of anything else.

Then as if to prove the point, the sirens sounded and Joyce thought it a wonder there wasn't a rising moan from every last person in London to rival the wail. Instead, women abandoned their quests for food and hurried towards home, men working on mains finished as much as they could, downed tools and headed for shelter. Then she heard it, they all did. The ratcheting of an overworked engine struggling uphill. Joyce put her head down and walked as fast as she could without running towards what she hoped would be safety, intent on making it without having to throw herself face down under cover of a shop doorway as she'd had to do a few days before.

The beastly noise seemed to be above her head and whichever road she scooted down it followed her. In a blur she was aware of people ducking into Anderson and Morrison shelters, gathering children and bedding under their arms and making their way to the underground. She wanted to cover her ears with her hands to block out the rasping din. Sure that if she looked up she would see her name written across the underbelly of the faceless thing, she took her eyes off her feet for a split second and glimpsed what looked like a blind, overfed grub through the low cloud.

Gasping, she took two steps backwards and ricked her ankle on a broken paving slab. 'Blast!' she muttered. A tear trickled down her cheek and angry with herself, she swiped at it roughly. Then as if suddenly bored with taunting her, the deafening noise changed direction towards the west and relief made Joyce's arms and legs wobble. A reprieve for her, but not for those beneath the bomb when the racket suddenly stopped. In the unnerving quiet that followed, Joyce could hear her own heart thrumming in her ears, then that was silenced by an almighty explosion as the device tore into whatever it had landed on. One repercussion after another ripped through the ground and Joyce stared as a dark angry plume of smoke danced above the rooftops. Mesmerised by the scene, she took a couple of steps backwards, wrenched her ankle again then limped as fast as she could to Report and Control.

She must have looked very pale when she hobbled down the stairs and into the main room, but at least she could blame that on her twisted ankle. Mrs Bertrand wrapped it in a bandage for her and made them all a cup of tea and no one was any the wiser that the sight of the doodlebug, so close and menacing, had spooked her. 'There must be an ARPM1 any minute for that hit,' she said to Controller Davis.

'Not ours,' he said. 'It struck somewhere near Daffodil Road. In White City.'

'But...' Joyce had been convinced it was closer than that. 'It was right overhead. I saw it.'

'Yes, I'm sure you did.' His voice was grave. 'But the distance they travel is pre-set. Once the rocket reaches that point, the power cuts out and it goes into a deep dive, so we were lucky. This time. Senior Warden Cooper,' he said, 'you look very waxen. Would you join me in a sherry to steady our...?'

Suddenly there was nothing Joyce would have liked more than a glass of sticky, uplifting sherry. 'A small one would be welcome. Ta, sir.'

The Controller dragged his leg to a filing cabinet, opened it with a key, took out two glasses and a bottle of dark, red liquid and poured them each a finger. When he passed Joyce her glass, she noticed that there was not the slightest tremor in his hands. *The man must be made of steel*, she thought, although he had referred to both of them, not just her, as being alarmed.

'I ought to offer Mrs Bertrand a glass,' Controller Davis said, a mischievous grin spreading across his face. 'The fact that she probably didn't hear a thing is beside the point.'

Joyce laughed and that, plus the spreading warmth of the sherry made her feel much better.

When he shuffled back from Mrs Bertrand's haunt, Controller Davis said they needed to make contingency plans. 'Jerry's so brass-necked he's dropping these buzzbombs day and night. I'm afraid we're going to have to up our game. It will be the same for all Report and Controls in London and the South.'

Joyce rested her foot on a chair. 'Goodness,' she said. 'How will we go about that?' For almost five years they'd worked every night and then squeezed in administrative duties during the day when necessary and she couldn't see how they could do much more. Not unless they took up residence in the basement.

'What I propose is all senior personnel – that's me and you – be available here for twenty-four-hour shifts, with other competent wardens on duty with us during the day and then swapping with others for the nights. Does that seem fair?'

It probably was fair, Joyce thought, but she'd just got used to sleeping in Auntie Cath's flat and hated the thought of the upheaval. 'What about sleep?' she asked. 'We couldn't possibly go without kip for a week.'

'I've ordered two cots to be delivered tomorrow morning,' the Controller was matter of fact about the whole arrangement. 'Yours can go in the first aid room and mine will squeeze into the walk-in cupboard. Look, I've drawn up a rota.'

Controller Davis produced a few pieces of crossed out, cross-referenced paper. 'Can you help me with them, please?' he asked, sheepishly.

Joyce cleared her table and while she was transferring the information onto a larger, clean sheet she noticed that they were to be given a few hours the next morning to sort themselves out, then their new regime would begin. She tried to find some gung-ho attitude and reminded herself that despite this new bombing campaign, D-Day had been a great victory and that must count for something. But she couldn't help herself – she felt miserable. 'Sir,' she said. 'What about taking a walk or seeing our families and making sure they're alright?'

'Of course we'll make opportunities for those things,' he said, shaking his head. 'But we must be prepared to do our utmost during this latest bombing campaign. Beastly as it is.'

The Controller looked at the clock then opened his filing cabinet again. 'We won't make a habit of this, but could you do with another drop? I know I could.'

Smiling, she told him that one more finger wouldn't hurt.

Granddad and Uncle Terry thought asking a slip of a girl, especially one with a swollen, bruised ankle, to sleep on a cot in a basement was too much. 'The blokes should see to that,' Granddad said. 'And let the girls work days only.'

'That's right, mate,' Uncle Terry agreed. 'Joy's been on night duty since the beginning, so I say she's done her bit.'

They were sitting around the table eating the toast and watery porridge Joyce had prepared. 'There aren't enough men left who can manage it,' she said. 'All the younger ones have joined up so that leaves Percy, who has a bad heart...'

'I know what that's like,' Uncle Terry patted his chest.

'Horace has arthritis or rheumatism or something like that and Alan dare not leave his wife alone at night. That leaves the Controller and me with Gladys, Mavis, Jean, Mrs Bertrand and a few others to help on the twelve-hour on and off shifts.' She pulled herself up tall. 'And as for my ankle...' She lifted her foot to show them the purple and green streaked skin. 'It looks worse but it's much better. So the girls have to continue to do their bit.'

'Hear, hear,' Auntie Cath said. 'Good on you. Look, there's a bit of this pear and apple compote left if you want it to cheer up your porridge, Dad?' She leaned across the table to pass Granddad the bowl and Joyce noticed the slack skin on her aunt's once plump arms. The sight made her say she wasn't hungry and she gave what was left in her bowl to Auntie Cath.

'You mark my words,' Auntie Cath continued.

'That's all I've done for the last twenty-five years,' Uncle Terry interrupted.

'And you'll continue if you know what's good for you, Terence Peters.'

Granddad and Joyce laughed at what was a regular exchange of repartee between Auntie Cath and Uncle Terry. 'Go on, Cath love,' Granddad said. 'Treat us to your words of wisdom.'

'After this war men will be competing with women for the jobs they stepped into and got on with very well to boot.'

'Ooooh,' Granddad shook his head until his cheeks quivered, 'I don't think so, my love. Bless you. The men will get their jobs back and the women will get their kitchens and their washing and their shopping back full-time. You,' he pointed at Auntie Cath, 'mark my words.'

Auntie Cath rolled her eyes in Joyce's direction and

started to clear up the breakfast things. Joyce gathered the cutlery together and followed her aunt into the kitchen. 'Auntie Cath,' she said. 'Would it be alright for me take in a set of bedding and one towel tonight? I'd rather use my own things. I mean, your things.'

'They are yours, Joy love,' Auntie Cath said. 'They belong to all of us and yes, of course you can.'

'Ta,' Joyce said. 'I'll wash them when I get the chance.'

Auntie Cath folded her tea towel and sighed. 'You're doing a good job,' she said. 'I'm so proud of you. But I'm worried, too. Being down in that basement all day and all night is just too much to ask. It will be so strange for you to live like that.'

Not as strange as living without Mum or Derek or Nana or Sid, Joyce thought. 'I'll get used to it, Auntie Cath,' she said. 'We all will.'

'We've got no choice in the matter anyway,' Auntie Cath said sadly, turning back to the sink.

In Uncle Terry's old, battered suitcase, Joyce packed her bedclothes, a threadbare camel-coloured blanket, a towel, her toothbrush and tooth powder, a bar of soap, her comb and a change of undergarments. Turning over *Forever Amber* in her hands, she debated whether she would have time to read and if she did, she would probably be better off trying to get some sleep. She would, after all, be at work and not on leave, so she left the book on her bed.

* * *

That first shift was no different from many of the others she'd spent in Report and Control, except it was V-1 damage being recorded rather than incendiaries and high explosives, but the difference in terms of destruction was frighteningly huge. Paddington took one hit that landed on a parade of shops; another came to rest on a church and school in Kensington and one took the corner off a row of houses between Bayswater and Notting Hill. When Joyce got that report in her hand she set her mouth in a line, looked at it quickly to get it over and done with in case it was in the vicinity of Auntie Cath's flat, then reached for her pins.

'One minute, Senior Warden Cooper, if you please.' Controller Davis had his hand cupped over the telephone speaker.

Joyce was puzzled but stood to attention and waited for him to complete his call.

'We've had an edict from on high,' he said, shuffling towards her. 'We're to mark the V-1 hits in a different manner so they can be monitored.'

'So, a different colour?' Joyce asked.

'No, a very small black circle surrounding the site of the blast.'

Joyce thought that small was a less than precise instruction. And she wondered what on earth she could use to draw the circle accurately. Then she remembered something she'd seen in the store cupboard. 'A compass,' she said. 'Just the thing.' She rummaged through the boxes the Controller had moved to make way for the cot, found what she was looking for and took it back to her table, feeling triumphant.

'You are a wonder, Senior Warden Cooper,' the Controller congratulated her. It transpired that an exact measurement had been decreed, so Joyce set the compass and practised on a piece of paper until they were both happy with the size of the small circle then she carefully aimed the point at the location of the hit and drew around it in black pencil.

After that she reinforced the mark with black ink and stood back to take in the effect. The lone spot looked odd, but she hoped it would be the only out of place mark amongst the myriad of coloured pins and labels. Three more times that night the siren keened and V-1s could be heard overhead. Everyone in Report and Control instinctively looked up, as if they would be able to see the bomb through the many ceilings and the roof in between them and the sky. They felt it, too, rocking the foundations of the building and making the black-out-covered windows in the floors above shiver. Joyce's whole body vibrated as though she had no control over her limbs, which in effect she didn't. Not for the first time she thought about how small and insignificant and vulnerable they were.

After each lethal lump of metal passed over them, they waited for an ARPM1 telling them where the flying bomb had landed, but no others hit their sector that night. News dripped to them of other areas that had taken the brunt, the East End getting the worst of it again, and they felt sorry but relieved it hadn't been them.

In the morning, Controller Davis instructed Joyce and Jean to take a walk together in the fresh air. Joyce was reluctant to leave her post, but the Controller said she must and he would take a turn around the vicinity with Percy when she returned. 'Please do not wander too far and report back immediately you hear the siren,' he said.

Joyce and Jean donned their coats and climbed the steps. Once again, the fresh air that should have greeted them was contaminated with the sting of sulphuric smoke. Both women took scarves from their pockets and wound them around their faces. They walked in silence for a few minutes until Joyce said she didn't think they would come across much damage in their area.

'Not unless we stride out to Bayswater, where we took that hit early last night,' Jean said.

Joyce glanced at Jean, bundled up in her scarf and coat. She didn't know her well, but had sat next to her on a few occasions during the daily briefing and noticed how thin and birdlike she was, with a soft bump on her nose and shoulder blades that poked through her uniform. She was older than Joyce, probably by about fifteen years and seemed to be a bundle of energy.

'You want to see the destruction?' Joyce was bemused.

Jean shrugged. 'It is rather fantastic, in a repelling kind of way. Didn't you stand outside during the Blitz?'

'No,' Joyce shook her head. 'I was in the Report and Control basement most nights that I can remember and if I hadn't been I don't think I would have wanted to see the spectacle more than I had to. Why, did you?' She'd heard about people climbing onto rooftop terraces or standing in their gardens watching the show provided by searchlights and barrage balloons.

'I'm afraid I was one of those that took every opportunity to catch the display, terrifying as it was.'

'Did you enjoy it?' Joyce asked in a deprecating tone of voice. She rather disapproved of treating the bombing as if were an act of theatre.

Jean turned to her, her scarf falling around her neck. 'That's certainly not the right word,' she said. 'I suppose it was more of a compulsion. We will, after all, never get to experience anything like it again.'

'Won't we?' Joyce turned on her colleague. 'What about last night then?' she spat. 'And tonight? And next week or year? You might rue the day you thought you'd never see anything like the Blitz again. The V-1s should be testament enough to that.'

Jean didn't come back with anything and Joyce hoped her colleague felt suitably chastised.

They walked around the streets of Notting Hill, gazing with surprise at people who suddenly stepped out from houses that appeared to be boarded up and abandoned. Pots with tomatoes or runner beans or peas growing in them stood on every available inch of front garden.

Then Joyce realised she'd been thinking about what the bomb site in Bayswater might look like and wondered if seeing it would be better than imagining it. They turned down a few more streets, crossed a road and Joyce steered them towards the exact spot where the V-1 had come down.

Describing what they saw as a damaged corner was an understatement. The unseeing, unhearing, unfeeling bomb had made a concertina of the row of terraced houses for as far as they could see. The back stairs of a bus were hanging from their frame by a thread and two inspectors were looking up at it as if they didn't know where to start with their repairs; wardens swarmed through the debris, some on their hands and knees; water fountained from a crater in the road; an elderly woman balanced a soot-streaked toddler on her hip and a man bent over a dog, patting it with long, loving strokes. And over everything hung a pall of dust. Joyce and Jean drew up their scarves again. 'We must get back,' Joyce said. 'So we can deploy some of our wardens to help.'

* * *

Learning about Jean's predilection for chasing bombing raids made Joyce think she wouldn't get on with that particular colleague. But as the weeks went on, she found there was more to Jean than that.

Jean told Joyce that her husband had fought in both battles for El Alamein, but now she thought he was somewhere in France – Caen perhaps. They had twin daughters in their early teens and both had been evacuated to New Buckenham in Norfolk. That gave them a lot to talk about as Jean had taken her girls on a trip to Cromer once when she'd been to visit them. Despite being on her own, Jean seemed endlessly busy. When she wasn't working as a warden, she was baking for the WVS or knitting for her twins or cleaning her mother's house or writing in her diary or keeping a scrapbook for her husband and children when they came home.

'It makes the time fly,' Jean said. 'How about you? What do you get up to?'

'When I'm not on this new twenty-four-hour duty, all I can think about when my shift finishes is breakfast and sleep.'

Jean looked up from the knitting she'd brought with her. Her brown eyes were bright and alert. 'I know what you mean,' she said. 'And I've always thought working on that map of yours must be draining.'

'I like to get it right. But I don't suppose it's any more demanding than being up on the streets, waiting for a raid.'

'It's all of a oneness,' Jean said, then she laughed with a delighted tinkle. 'Telling people to put their lights out is the most tiring.'

'I did that for a while,' Joyce said. 'Right at the beginning and I didn't find it too difficult.'

'As time's gone on, people have become a bit lackadaisical and they've blamed us for their fines when we've had to report serial offenders.'

'That must make you feel awful,' Joyce said.

Jean laughed again. 'I had some little blighter follow me shouting "put that light out" in a silly, singsong voice. But when I turned on him like this...' she screwed up her face and clawed her hands, 'he soon went crying to Mummy. So what else do you do, besides organising food and sleeping?'

Not much, Joyce thought. It was all what she had done with Derek or Mum or Flo and not what she did now. 'I like to read,' Joyce said. 'I'm in the middle of *Forever Amber*.'

Jean jumped up, went to her bag and came back holding a copy of the same book, a beam of solidarity across her face.

Their chat was disrupted by a telephone call after which Controller Davis had to sound the siren. They then had to man their stations, hope they wouldn't be attacked, deal with the ARPM1s when they appeared and wait for instructions to sound the all-clear.

When it was Joyce's turn to nap, she tried to sleep but turned first one way then the other, her legs tangled in her sheets and her mind working overtime. She felt defensive that she'd been asked to justify what she did in any spare time she had, as if it was Jean's or anyone else's concern. She could have gone straight out and found another fellow, but a simple replacement was not what she wanted and there was no earthly way she could find a substitute for Mum, Nana or Sid, even if she wanted to. Besides, she did her best to plump up her flat pillow, she knew what was best for her and that was sticking to her methodical, regimented schedule as much as possible.

An hour later, Jean crept into the kitchen to make a cup of tea and saw Joyce awake and staring at the ceiling. 'Can't sleep?' Jean asked.

Joyce propped herself up on one elbow and shook her head.

'How about a cuppa?'

'That would be lovely, ta,' Joyce answered.

When Jean put the cup next to Joyce's makeshift bed she handed her *Forever Amber*, too. 'I always go straight off when I read for a bit,' she said. 'Can you remember where you were up to?'

'Yes,' Joyce said. 'Chapter nine. Are you sure you don't mind?'

'Not one bit.' Jean tiptoed back to the Control Room and Joyce fell asleep before she'd read two pages.

The weeks began to take on some sort of pattern, Joyce manned her map, carried out administrative duties, organised rotas, took short bouts of exercise and called in on Auntie Cath to see how everyone was faring, and tried to sleep. But everything was dominated by the sinister shape of the V-1s. Day and night the bombs continued to lacerate the skies, but few culminated their journey in Notting Hill and because Joyce didn't go far from the area, she didn't see much of the end result. She heard about it on the news, though, and from Jean who wandered all over London when she had the opportunity.

'Not chasing the bombs,' she said. 'But I go to see old school friends in Bermondsey or Fulham and then there's my sister in Battersea.'

'Do they come to see you sometimes?'

'Yes, we love to go to dance classes together.'

'Here in Notting Hill?' Joyce asked. 'I used to go to Madame Beaupre's.'

'That's where we go,' Jean was excited. She loved to make connections between people. 'Why not come with us?'

'Oh, no,' Joyce replied. 'I wouldn't want to intrude on your arrangements. Besides, I'm on continuous duty here.' She was glad to have an excuse not to take Jean up on her invitation as she couldn't imagine dancing with anyone other than Derek or Flo.

Jean looked crestfallen. 'Of course. I know that. But what a shame. My sister would love to meet you.'

Joyce hoped that was the end of it, then Controller Davis announced that they could stand down and revert to their previous schedule of manning Report and Control from dusk to dawn and returning to the basement during the day to complete paperwork when necessary. 'And as always,' he added. 'You must return immediately if you hear the warning siren.'

Joyce couldn't believe it when the first thing Jean said was not how relieved she was, but that Joyce could now meet her at Madame Beaupre's for a dance. And what could she possibly use as an excuse to get out of it now? That she had to buy rations or cook or finish *Forever Amber*? She didn't want to appear rude, so she agreed.

Jean's sister was a slightly younger version of Jean, with the same coiled hair, soft brown eyes and small swelling on her nose. She radiated the same nervy energy, too. Madame Beaupre chose Joyce to dance with first and the instructor told her that she and Monsieur Beaupre hadn't been able to salvage their old studio but, she said with glee, they were going to move to Paris when the war was over and that city had been liberated. Joyce smiled and nodded and thought she hid her irritation well. Why did everyone keep talking about the end as if it were in sight? She knew that was what they were being led to believe, but really, was that feasible with the V-1s causing such chaos?

She danced with Jean, who was very good and her sister, but avoided going for a cup of tea with them afterwards on the vague pretext of having something else to do and knew that she would never go to Madame Beaupre's again, not even with Flo.

Seeing Jean and her sister enjoying themselves together made Joyce decide that perhaps it was time to at least try to make amends with Flo. There had been several letters from her cousin and, when she arrived home from the dancing lesson, another was waiting for her on the mantelpiece. 'Alright, Joy love?' Auntie Cath called from the kitchen. 'A letter from Flo. We got one, too.'

Joyce took off her outdoor things and slit open the envelope; since they'd argued there was only ever one page and this letter was no exception.

Dear Joyce it started

I hope you are well. I am being redeployed to --------- Flo should have known better than to think that would get past the censors. And I'll be stopping for a night with Mum and Dad on the way. If you're not on duty during that time, I hope we can share my bedroom without a sour atmosphere. Mum, Dad and Granddad shouldn't have to worry about our silliness on top of everything they've been through already.

Perhaps I'll see you next week.

Flo

No kiss; no love; no mention of Vernon.

Auntie Cath smartened the flat and baked prune flan, Uncle Terry tidied the garden and pulled up some lettuce and tomatoes and Controller Davis allowed Joyce a night off to see her cousin. Granddad said he hoped Flo wasn't going to bring that odd friend of hers with her. Auntie Cath raised her eyebrows and exchanged a look with Uncle Terry and

Granddad said, 'What? He was very peculiar, wasn't he? Not the sort I ever thought Flo would take to.'

Then all three of them looked at Joyce. 'Is Vernon coming with her?' Auntie Cath asked. 'She tells you everything, Joy love.'

That would have been the perfect opportunity to tell all of them that she and Flo had bickered about Vernon but Joyce thought it was up to Flo – not her – to be honest with her parents and tell them the whole story. So she shrugged and said she knew as much as they did.

Uncle Terry scratched his five o'clock shadow. 'How old is this Vernon chap? His visit was a bit of a blur what with your Nana just passing. But he didn't look much younger than me.'

Again, Joyce evaded the question with a shake of her head, saying that week had been hard for her, too.

'And what's he doing over here from New Zealand?' asked Auntie Cath.

'Wait a minute,' Granddad said. 'New Zealand pilots are our main defence against the V-1s what with our RAF lads busy elsewhere.'

'I believe Vernon's Australian,' Joyce said. 'And I think he volunteered to come here, but you'd have to ask Flo about that.' Again a look passed amongst them and Joyce excused herself saying she needed to get the bedroom ready for Flo's visit. When she closed the door to Flo's room behind her, she leaned against it, shut her eyes and made up her mind to have it out with Flo one way or another.

An almost imperceptible sigh of relief passed through the flat when Flo arrived by herself. There were hugs, kisses and cuddles although those between Joyce and Flo were short and not too close. They had a dinner of cheese, tomato and potato loaf with salad followed by the flan, then Uncle Terry and

Granddad announced they were going to the pub for a pint. 'I suppose you two girls are going out somewhere,' Granddad said. 'Up town or to a dance.'

Joyce stood and began to clear the table. 'And leave Auntie Cath with all this?' she said. 'Not likely.'

'Why don't we all go for a drink together?' Flo suggested. 'Then Joy and I can help with the dishes when we get back.'

Auntie Cath stared at her daughter with wide eyes, then a broad smile split her face. 'That would be lovely, Flo love,' she said. 'I can't remember the last time I went to the pub.'

'Shame on you, Dad,' Flo said. 'Come on, let's get ready and go.'

'Hang on one minute.' Uncle Terry crossed his arms over his chest. 'Granddad and I were going to our regular. Now we'll have to find somewhere that's clean and fancy.'

'Then you'd better hurry and have a wash and change your collar,' Joyce joined in.

'Or you girls could go to your lah di da place and we'll go to our usual,' Granddad said, sliding his hand over his moustache.

But Flo insisted and Joyce wondered if she had some other motive for wanting them all together in a public place.

Auntie Cath disappeared and came back with combed hair, pencilled eyebrows and wearing a smear of lipstick. She'd changed into a funny, flowery dress and was holding a dark brown bag with a fake pearl clasp. 'Oh, Cath love,' Uncle Terry said, helping her on with her fawn coat. 'I'm glad I tidied myself up so I can be seen out with you.'

It didn't take them long to put on their shoes and walk to the nearest decent pub, Auntie Cath's arm linked through her husband's.

Flo was twitchy; she sat, then stood up and said she would

get the first round as the outing had been her idea. Granddad and Uncle Terry let out a cheer. Joyce watched her cousin as she repeated each order and counted them off on her fingers. 'Joy?' Flo asked.

'I'll come to the bar and help you,' Joyce said.

'There's no need,' Flo said, not making eye contact with Joyce. 'Just tell me what you're having and I'll...'

Joyce took Flo's elbow and marched her to the bar. They stood side by side, their eyes straight ahead. As soon as the landlord appeared, Flo began to reel off her order. While the drinks were being poured, Joyce told Flo in her most polite, controlled voice, that she knew what she up to.

'Whatever are you accusing me of now? Flo snarled.

'The only reason you've asked everyone out is to tell your parents and Granddad what you've been hiding about Vernon and you know they're too well-mannered to ask awkward questions or get angry while they're in the pub. So you're going to upset them, but won't allow them any recourse. Then you'll leave them anxious and worried when you go first thing in the morning.'

When Joyce turned to catch her cousin's reaction, Flo's nostrils flared and her hands were trembling. 'Joy. Love,' she spat out in such a sarcastic voice that tears threatened Joyce's composure. 'I don't think they'll be at all upset when they hear my good news.' She picked up three drinks and pointed with her chin to the one left on the bar. 'Order whatever you like,' she said. 'It's on me and bring Granddad's with you, if you please.'

Auntie Cath's excitement about having a few hours in the pub made for a party atmosphere round their table. Flo regaled them with stories from Bedfordshire and Joyce thought no one could be having that much fun during the blasted war. 'So,' Granddad lowered his voice and looked around. 'There were huge holes in your letters. Can you tell us where you're going and why?'

Flo softened her voice to a whisper and they all put their heads together. 'The South Downs,' she said.

'Sounds like a holiday camp to me,' Uncle Terry said.

'It won't be when we get there.' Flo shook her head. 'There's to be a barrage line of defence against the V-1s all along the South Coast.'

Auntie's Cath's hand flew to her throat where it twisted and pulled at her top button. 'Oh, Flo love,' she said. 'You are so brave. But I shall be so worried about you.'

'Proud, that's what we are, aren't we, Joy love?'

Joyce hadn't said much, but now felt forced to reply. 'Yes, of course. The WAAFs are marvellous.'

'All you girls are.' Granddad smiled at Joyce and put his hand on top of hers. 'Here, Terry,' he said, taking a handful of coins from his pocket. 'Can you get another round in for me?'

'Let's go halves, Reg mate, like we always do.'

They all had the same again and when they were settled, sipping their drinks, Flo lit a cigarette and cleared her throat. 'There's something I want to talk to you about,' she said.

Heat crept over Joyce's skin as she waited for Flo to begin.

'I'm sure you remember Vernon?'

Granddad let out an involuntary huff which he tried to cover up with a cough.

Auntie Cath took a surreptitious peek at Uncle Terry and said, 'Your Dad and I were talking about him last night, Flo love. How we couldn't remember him too well or what you'd told us about him as we were all so busy sorting out dear old Nana.'

No, Joyce wanted to correct Auntie Cath, *we were not all busy organising Nana's funeral and the rest of the family's living arrangements.* Flo and Vernon hadn't lifted a finger to help out, they'd spent the time swanning around London. But she remembered how remorseful she'd felt the last time she was rude to Flo and how, deep down, she wanted to remedy what had gone wrong between them, so she kept her mouth closed.

'What about this Vernon chap?' Uncle Terry said, trying to take control.

Flo cleared her throat again and lit a fresh cigarette from the stub of the one she'd just finished.

'Whatever is the matter with you, Flo love.' Joyce could see that Auntie Cath had turned ashen and lines of concern puckered around her eyes and mouth. 'You know you can tell us anything.'

'Vernon's gone back to Australia,' Flo said at last.

'I thought he was from New Zealand,' Granddad said.

'Now?' Joyce could not hold her tongue any longer. 'Just when he's needed here to fly against the doodlebugs? He's nothing but a...'

Flo turned to Joyce, her face smouldering with rage. 'Dare to say it,' she threatened.

'Girls!' Auntie Cath hissed. 'What's got into you? Stop it before you make a spectacle of yourselves.'

No one said another word for a few moments, then Uncle Terry spoke up. 'Right, Flo love, start at the beginning and tell us everything.'

In a quiet, more refined voice, Flo told them how old Vernon was, that he was married but had gone back to Australia to divorce his wife, extricate himself from the farm he owned with his father-in-law and send for Flo when their path to getting married was clear.

Uncle Terry clenched and unclenched his fists, Auntie Cath was pale with shock and Granddad looked as if he were still unsure of Vernon's nationality. None of it, except Flo moving to Australia, was news to Joyce, so she sat and waited for the dust to settle but that wasn't about to happen yet. 'I forbid it,' Uncle Terry growled.

'On what grounds?' Flo whispered.

'I don't like the bugger,' he hissed.

'You just said you could barely remember him.' Flo didn't miss a beat coming back with what she thought was a clever reply.

'I remember that much,' Uncle Terry said. His lip curled as if he'd bitten into something rotten. 'And I can fill in the blanks.'

Now that Flo had unburdened her situation, she showed no contrition for the upset she was causing. 'I'm afraid those days are over, Dad,' she said, cool and confident.

'We've only met him the once and that was under dire circumstances,' Auntie Cath said. 'And now we won't get the chance to meet him ever again before you... you...'

A hint of wheedling compassion crept into Flo's voice at last. 'I'll send for you when I'm settled,' Flo said. 'You'll love it. Vernon says Australia is lovely.'

'Not as wonderful as New Zealand, so I've read,' Granddad said.

'Send for us?' Uncle Terry could barely get the words out. 'Australia is the other side of the world.'

Auntie Cath had turned a pasty, yellow colour. 'The other side of the world,' she murmured. 'I wouldn't make it. And I couldn't leave Granddad and Joy,' she said.

'I shall never leave Notting Hill, so count me out.' Granddad raked through his moustache and shook his head.

'And I can take care of myself,' Joyce said, stretching upwards. 'And Granddad.'

But Auntie Cath had the last word. She looked at Flo with a mixture of disbelief and betrayal and said, 'If and when you go Flo love, I will never see you again.' She turned to Uncle Terry. 'Take me home, Terry, please.'

They all stood and put on their coats except Flo, who stayed in her chair and lit another cigarette. 'Will you keep me company for another drink, Joy?' she asked in a subdued voice.

'No, ta,' Joyce replied tersely. 'I'd better go home and see what I can do for Auntie Cath.'

At the last minute, Uncle Terry leaned over his daughter and whispered harshly, 'You haven't heard the last of this, my girl.' Flo kept her head down and didn't look at any of them.

For the first time in Joyce's memory, Uncle Terry announced he was making a cup of tea. They sat around the kitchen table with Auntie Cath's tin of broken crisis biscuits and questioned Joyce for an hour or so. She told them everything she knew, why she'd kept the information from them and that she and Flo had fallen out about it.

But the one mystery she couldn't clear up for them was what Flo saw in Vernon. 'He must have some kind of hold over her,' Auntie Cath said, fidgeting with the collar of her dress. 'Do you think she might be pregnant?'

'Catherine!' Uncle Terry was shocked.

'It happens, Terry,' Auntie Cath said.

'Not to our Flo.' Uncle Terry dismissed the idea. 'Or Joy.'

Looking from one confused, sad face to another, Joyce wanted more than anything to lift their spirits. 'Do you know what I think might happen?' she said.

They all stared at her as if she were Churchill about to change the direction of the war in their favour.

'During the time it takes Vernon to sort out his affairs, Flo will meet someone else and forget all about him.'

She didn't believe what she'd said for one minute, but Auntie Cath clutched at the idea. 'Oh, I do hope so,' her aunt said, fiddling with her collar again and looking relieved enough for Joyce to take herself to bed.

An hour or so later Flo tiptoed into the room, changed into her nightclothes and slid between her sheets. Joyce couldn't think what to say that wouldn't start an argument, so lay tense and knotted in the dark. After a few minutes, Joyce heard sniffling and snuffling from Flo's bed which she couldn't ignore. She turned over and asked if there was anything she could do to help.

Flo blew her nose, sniffed again and whispered, 'You could take my side, that would help make peace with Mum and Dad.'

Joyce gazed at Flo's shadow on the wall, the silhouette of her hand moving backwards and forwards to her nose each time she wiped it. 'I could,' Joyce said, 'but I won't. It wouldn't be right.'

'I'd do it for you,' Flo said.

'I wouldn't ask.' Joyce turned away and closed her eyes. She needed her rest to cope with whatever the week threw her way in Report and Control.

As a steely dawn broke, Joyce saw that Flo's bed was empty. From the sitting room she heard her cousin and Auntie Cath's sharp, muffled voices rising and falling. Then the latch was lifted on the front door and Joyce sprang to the window, drew back a corner of the blackouts and watched Flo, head down and marching smartly, until she disappeared from view. When Joyce ventured from her room, Auntie Cath was sitting in the armchair, crying quietly into a handkerchief. The curtains were closed, the house was cold, no tea was brewing; her aunt seemed to be shrouded in loneliness.

Joyce stood and watched her for a beat, then put her arms around Auntie Cath's neck. 'Love you, Auntie Cath,' Joyce said.

'Love you, too, Joy love,' Auntie Cath answered, but although Joyce knew that to be true, she also knew it was Flo, as she'd been in the past, who her aunt wanted.

* * *

One Wednesday evening towards the end of July, Controller Davis came down into the basement with a frown on his face. 'Senior Warden Cooper,' he said.

Joyce turned from her map.

'Your aunt is outside, but try as I might she refuses to come in.'

'Auntie Cath?' Joyce said. 'Outside?'

'She seemed at bit agitated and asked me, most politely, to fetch you.'

Joyce bounded up the stairs to where Auntie Cath was waiting, a headscarf tied under her chin and her hands thrust into the pockets of her fawn coat. They'd had a close miss that afternoon when a V-1 struck the crossroads of Kensington High Street and Earl's Court which had sent Joyce scuttling back to her post. It couldn't have affected Auntie Cath's flat, though, but something wasn't right, Joyce could sense it. Perhaps it was a letter from Flo telling them she had a date to sail to Australia. She took a minute to take a deep breath and rise tall from the crown of her head, then asked Auntie Cath what was wrong. When her aunt turned, she looked haunted, with purple stains under her eyes and pallid, sunken cheeks.

'I wouldn't bother you unless I had to, Joy love,' Auntie Cath said.

'It's not a bother,' Joyce answered. 'What is it?'

'Terry and Granddad haven't come home.' Auntie Cath did up the top button of her coat, then unbuttoned it again. 'And I can't help it, Joy love, but I'm ever so worried.'

The doodlebug in Kensington flashed through Joyce's mind and she knew there and then what must have happened. 'Come with me,' Joyce said and led her aunt into the depths of the Control Centre where she sat her down, made her a cup of tea and bit by bit got the whole story from her. Uncle Terry had been due to finish work mid-afternoon and Granddad had decided to walk part of the way to meet him and then, perhaps, they would have a pint together on the way home. 'But they haven't come back.' Auntie Cath wiped her palms on her coat. 'And their dinner's stone cold.'

Controller Davis asked Auntie Cath if she'd looked for them.

'I followed the route they would have taken,' she said. 'But when I got to Ken High Street, where it goes into Earls Court, I couldn't go any further because of the cordons. There's nothing left of Lyons, Joy love. It's as flat as this table.' She ran her palms over the piece of furniture in front of her.

The Controller had spoken to Kensington earlier so they knew that the V-1 had not only razed the café, but had ripped an abyss into the High Street and ploughed through the surrounding area, turning over everything in its wake.

Joyce took Auntie Cath's hand and softly told her that it was more than likely Uncle Terry and Granddad had been caught up in the explosion as nothing short of a V-1 flying bomb would have stopped them coming home to her.

'I know, Joy love,' Auntie Cath said, patting Joyce's hand over and over again.

* * *

Joyce took Auntie Cath to look at the crater and kick through the debris for any particle of hair or skin or shoes or clothing that would give them proof of what had happened. When they looked down into that deep, dark depression, they could come to no other conclusion than it had swallowed up Granddad and Uncle Terry and spat them back out as dust.

Flo came back for three days, sat in a chair and did nothing but cry into her sleeve. And this time, Joyce had every sympathy for her as she knew her tears were as much for the last angry words she'd had with her father as they were for the fact she would never see him again.

NINETEEN

This was to be Joyce's first Saturday in the new flat without some pressing errand or chore to attend to and she hoped to establish what would be her routine. She'd allowed herself a lie in with a cup of tea and the *Mirror*, then managed to wash her hair in the shower without flooding the bathroom and now she was sitting on the balcony, waiting for her curls to dry, writing out her shopping list for that afternoon.

It was as close as possible to the schedule she'd kept in her basement flat for twenty-nine years, except there had been no shower there and she'd had to wash her hair over the bathtub with the help of a jug. The spray of warm water had overwhelmed her at first and she'd spluttered and swiped at her face to keep the shampoo out of her eyes, but she had to admit that once she adjusted the temperature and pressure, it was much more convenient, and the shower tray was easier to clean than her old enamel bath. The girls in the office told her about something called shower gel she could use instead of soap or bath salts, and they said it came in lovely scents like lemon or vanilla; Sandra's favourite was mandarin and Barbara's was horse chestnut.

After the shower, Joyce put her towels in the washing machine and set the cycle. The first few times she'd tried it out she'd taken a book and chair into the tiny utility room with her and sat next to the contraption, sure it would explode or go up in smoke or swamp the flat with dirty soap suds. But Alison told her the whole point of an automatic was that you could wash your clothes while you got on with other things. Gradually, Joyce had tested that by inching the chair further away, then into the next room and finally by chopping vegetables or dusting while the machine went about its business. Elaine said she put on a load before she left for work in the mornings and it was washed, rinsed and spun by the time she arrived home, but Joyce didn't think she could ever get to that stage of confidence.

But by far the biggest change that Joyce had to negotiate was looking down, rather than up, at people passing by. If she sat tall and craned her neck, she could see the hair and heads and hats of mothers and fathers ferrying their little ones to football or ballet, teenagers carrying LP records, children laughing and nudging each other off the path and the various prams, wheelchairs, shopping trolleys, bikes, trikes and umbrellas they had in tow. Beyond the trees that marked the boundary of the estate she could see double decker buses, tower blocks and if the clouds were low, she thought she could reach out and push them away. And it would be lovely to watch the landscape change according to the season.

Sometimes she would scoot her chair up against the concrete wall, lay her chin in her hands on the chrome railing and watch the goings-on below, confident she wouldn't be caught surveying the scene. Once a young lad, his arm around a girl, had thrown back his head with laughter and spied her, spying on him. He waved and Joyce, cringing in case he thought her voyeuristic, had returned the gesture.

Earlier, Joyce had moved the second chair that came with the patio set to a storage cupboard as she wouldn't need it unless the one she used broke, inspected her plant which was doing well and sat down to see what was going on outside. In her old flat she could estimate the height and build of individuals by the size of their shoes and shape of their legs under trousers or tights. Here, from the third floor, that was more difficult. Often, she would see the same couple walking to and from Malvolio Maisonettes and she'd convinced herself they were like she and Derek had been – the woman petite and the man uncommonly tall. But one morning she had come face to face with them and the difference in their heights was much less dramatic than she had imagined it to be. Unless someone bent to tie their shoelaces, features had been impossible to glimpse from her old flat, but from on high she could sometimes make out a person's age or the style of their hair which she enjoyed being privy to. As far as toddlers were concerned, the opposite was true. From her basement flat she could watch the little ones as they trailed behind their parents or held hands with an older brother or sister. It had been endearing to catch sight of a pair of Bambi-like eyes and fine, floppy hair and to watch them grow until all she could see of them, too, were their shoes and legs. Now she could only make an educated guess at their age, hair colouring and size of their eyes.

Joyce wondered if she would feel like a prisoner during the colder months when it was too dark and dismal and raw to sit on the balcony. She didn't like to think the only option she would have to be around other people at the weekends, if she wanted to, was to go out. Perhaps for that reason it would have been better to have nabbed the downstairs flat, but then she would have had no escape from the blasted Mr Norris and that would have been unbearable.

Half a pound of mince; potatoes; a steak and kidney pie; one chicken thigh; six eggs; bread; sugar; washing powder; a small cauliflower; two apples; two plums; sliced ham; her Saturday afternoon pork pie and vanilla slice supper, shower gel and the library books to exchange. She would definitely need the new pull along shopping trolley she'd invested in after Barbara's suggestion.

Noise reached her ears differently, too, as it drifted up rather than flowed down. At Talbot Road, the traffic not only sounded like thunder as it passed by, but agitated the foundations of the flat with noisy vibrations. Shouting, laughter and conversations had come to her in sudden bursts that were then cut off as abruptly as they had started. Here, she was aware of buses idling in the distance and cars slowing down as they turned into their allotted parking spaces, but they never reached the culmination of their mechanised power in her hearing. Apart from parents shouting at a child or the whoop of children playing, voices started off faint and indistinguishable, became muffled as they passed close by, then faded away in the opposite direction. It had been disconcerting at first and there were times she'd felt disorientated, but despite the fact that she would have done anything not to have moved from her beloved basement flat, time and experience told her she would adapt as she'd done many times before and she congratulated herself on how well she'd managed so far.

Sitting back, she closed her eyes for a moment and enjoyed the sun on her face. She patted her hair and thought it wouldn't be long before it was dry and she could make her way to the shops. Zoflora – she reminded herself to add the cleaner to her list. It came in new scents, too, she'd noticed, like Honeysuckle, Hawthorn and Violet and she thought she might try one of those rather than her usual Bouquet.

Then she heard the racket of what sounded like a crowd of men leaving the pub; she'd never heard such a noise since she'd moved, so stood and looked out towards the source. And she was right, coming down the path in the middle of the estate, in the middle of the day, was a huddle of four blokes, two sporting Queen's Park Rangers scarves. They were jostling and clapping each other on the back and right in the centre was – she should have known – Mr Norris. With – she would never have guessed in a million years – his arm around Mr Taylor's shoulders.

Jumping back into the shadows, Joyce put her hands to her head and a blush crept over her face when she thought they might have seen her with her hair in such a state. But from the snapshot she'd seen, they'd been too wrapped up in their jokes and jibes and camaraderie to have noticed her at all. Their hoots got closer, then there were a number of rattles from Mr Norris's gate and all was quiet again as they disappeared into his flat. *Probably either a football match,* she thought, *or one of Mr Norris's clubs, for men only.*

Peering in the mirror, she decided her hair had set rather well and all she would need to do was pull a dot of Vitapointe through the curls, twist it into a knot and she would be ready to face the long walk to the shops. She put on her sturdy shoes and lightweight coat, gathered together her trolley and umbrella and double-checked her bag for the spare key, although now she always kept it nestled in the depths of a special zipped compartment.

Then she heard the clink of the letter flap and stood quite still. The postman had been, so what could this be? Her heart thumped when she thought it might be Mr Norris, come to pin down a date for that blasted cup of tea, then she relaxed when she reasoned he would be too busy with his pals today to bother with her.

It was probably one of those pamphlets advertising the new Co-op that had opened in the opposite direction from where she did her shopping or what was on at the pictures in Bayswater. But there was a yellow envelope on the mat, obviously hand delivered because there was no stamp in the corner and nothing but her name was scrawled across it in black ink.

Slitting it open, she suspected it was something to do with Mr Norris and pursed her lips in readiness. She was puzzled and curious, but more than anything she hoped it wasn't an invitation she would have to fib to get out of. It contained one sheet of paper in bold, neat handwriting.

Dear Miss Cooper

I must apologise for not giving you advance warning that I was having a few friends around today. We are all in my flat at the moment and I hope we're not disturbing you too much. Shortly we will be heading out to a football match and then after a couple of pints we'll be back for a takeaway curry which I hope won't become too raucous.

Thank you for your understanding, but do feel free to bang on my door tonight and tell us to keep the noise down if we get too loud.

Kind regards,

Ken Norris

PS Paul wants you to know that it isn't too late to change

your mind and join us for the big day next Saturday. He says
you would be most welcome.

Joyce read through the letter again then let it fall from her hand to the kitchen table. This was the first personal letter she'd received in years and she was not happy. She did so wish Mr Norris and Mr Taylor would refrain from trying to pull her into the social life of this estate, surely they knew by now that she was quite content to keep herself to herself.

But there was something about Mr Taylor's insistence that touched a raw nerve she would much rather have kept unexposed. She remembered receiving the initial invitation when she was vulnerable and sensitive on the day she moved and being momentarily seduced by thoughts of heady flowers and dancing and people crushed together in celebration. Of course she wished a happy day for Mr Taylor and Jacqueline, but she would definitely not be there to see their smiles. She would be enjoying the quiet in her flat with a custard tart and a new library book.

She threw the letter in the bin then left the block of flats quietly and quickly as the last thing she wanted was to be intercepted by what was probably by now a very merry Mr Norris.

TWENTY

AUNTIE CATH

September 1944

The Jerries must have thought that the horrific V-1 responsible for killing Uncle Terry and Granddad and hundreds of others was lacking in cruelty and it was necessary to invent something that gave a whole new meaning to the words evil and wicked and destruction.

The first time Joyce heard the strange double-crack, followed by the rush of something heavy overhead, she and Jean had been walking along Westbourne Grove.

'Whatever was that?' Jean asked.

'A damaged doodlebug?' Joyce said, although that piece of wild speculation didn't fool her.

'I don't think so,' Jean answered. 'There's no rev of a motorbike about that sound.'

They stood riveted to the spot, listening to the deathly silence that ensued. Then the earth shook so violently that Joyce felt no more significant than a toy in a dog's mouth.

A split second later an explosion more powerful and deafening than they'd heard yet caused them to turn to each other, eyes bulging with contained panic. Everyone tried as hard as they could to portray a calm, dignified exterior; anything less would be letting each other down and those in uniform thought it part of their duty to exude an aura of capability and decorum and look as if they knew what was going on and what they were planning to do about it. Jean grabbed Joyce's arm and waited for her to give an order, but Joyce was as alarmed and confused as her colleague.

'It's something new,' she said, shaking off Jean's arm.

The siren howled and Joyce said they must get to Report and Control straight away, but then she decided to do something she'd never done before. Ordering Jean to return to the Centre and tell Controller Davis she'd been detained for a few minutes, she detoured to Auntie Cath's, let herself in, wrenched open the door of the understairs cupboard, reassured herself that her aunt was cowering in the shadows with her knitting, commanded her to, 'Stay there!', then marched to her post as quickly as she could, ready to face the fact that she'd disobeyed a command for the first time since the blasted war had started.

Controller Davis was on the telephone when she arrived, hot and out of breath. He, too, was bright red with a shiny film of sweat on his forehead. Joyce positioned herself near the map, checked her equipment and waited for an ARPM1.

When the Controller finished what sounded like a frenetic conversation, he dragged himself towards Joyce with such a stern look on his face that shame washed over her and she had to avert her eyes to the floor. 'Senior Warden Cooper,' he said.

'Yes, Sir.' Joyce met his intense gaze at last.

He lowered his voice, but his eyes remained as hard as

flint. 'What do you consider to be more of an emergency than the boom of a new weapon over London?'

There was no excuse; there wasn't even a rational explanation for what amounted to her abandoning her post – Joyce knew that. But she offered up the only reason she had.

'I went to check on my aunt,' she said in a small voice.

The Controller's tone softened. 'If it weren't for the fact that I know your personal circumstances, you would be facing disciplinary action.'

Tears threatened to roll down Joyce's face. 'I'm so sorry, Sir,' she murmured. 'I give you my word it won't happen again.'

'I know you well enough by now to be assured of that. We'll never speak of it again.' He turned on his heel and limped back to his telephone which pierced the wail of the siren again.

Trying hard to disguise her trembling hands and hide her face, throbbing with heat, Joyce arranged her equipment and waited for an ARPM1 or further orders. It was right that she was mortified, but her overwhelming feeling was one of relief that Auntie Cath was, at least when Joyce had seen her, safe in the shelter she'd swept clean and kitted out with a blanket, a pillow, a candle in a storm lantern and an old chamberpot.

Then the Controller limped towards her again with the snippet of news he'd been given. 'It's a rocket,' he said. 'And it's unmanned like the V-1s, but it's much bigger and faster and is being referred to as a V-2.'

Eventually, they learned that like their still operational predecessors, the new rockets were blind, deaf, dumb and numb to feeling, but not rudderless as the streamlined weapon, as tall as a four-storey building, had four of those on its tail to guide it through the sky as smoothly as if it were a warm knife cutting through the butter they all craved.

Orders arrived to mark V-2 hits on the bomb map with a black circle smaller than the ones used to denote the V-1s. Again an exact diameter had been pronounced, again Joyce practised on paper with her compass and again she stood ready to ring any areas plundered in their sector. One by one, the information on ARPM1s was transferred to her map with accuracy and although the rockets that landed in Notting Hill were few and far between, Joyce thought it would have been easier on the eye to symbolise the havoc caused by this latest weapon with a square or triangle, some shape that would make it stand apart from the rings that symbolised the V-1s.

Either side of Christmas, the doodlebugs and rockets flew through the sky like inelegant flocks of birds migrating for the winter and dropped suddenly, landing on the poor old East End in droves as well as on Islington, New Cross and Kent. From hits in Lancaster Gate and Hammersmith they saw what looked like thousands of tons of material being sent sky high and Auntie Cath was forever telling Joyce about this one or the other who knew someone else who had been hit on the head by debris that had been hurtled at them from miles away.

When she should have been catching up on precious sleep, Joyce fidgeted and fussed instead while images of Mum or Nana or Sid or Derek or Granddad or Uncle Terry or the young mum from Ladbroke Grove darted in and out of her mind. She turned one way, huffed and turned another then grew more and more anxious about what kind of weapon the Jerries were developing at that very moment to torment them with next.

And that wasn't all she worried about. She felt so sorry for Auntie Cath, alone every night and often during the day, too, in the flat they'd all squeezed into not many months ago. Now it echoed around them like a bare, cavernous space. Where once they'd had to manoeuvre their way through doorways and wait in turn to use the bathroom and outdoor privy, they found they had much more room than they knew what to do with and often one of them had to wander about to find the other.

Auntie Cath asked if she could sleep in the spare bed in Joyce's room until she thought she could face the double bed she'd shared with Uncle Terry for so many years. Of course Joyce said she could and the sight of dark tear stains on Auntie Cath's pillow made her stomach twist with pity. Each of the occasions she'd slept in the same bed as Derek had created a memory she could recall in vivid, sensual detail, so how much more painful must it be for Auntie Cath to have lost her life-long partner.

But they continued to take it, although it was getting harder. So many people were ill with bronchitis or influenza or ulcerated sores where they'd banged their arms or legs on something in the blackout. Auntie Cath had a hacking cough that linctus didn't help and Joyce had blisters in her mouth that wouldn't heal. She was also sporting an infected whitlow on the tip of her thumb which she supposed was a conse-quence of pushing so many tiny, coloured bayonets into her map. Everyone was hungry; everyone was cold. They all had spots or skin the colour of the pall of smoke that hung over the city and stomach upsets and earaches and missing fingers and swollen joints and Joyce hoped, like everyone else, that if they just held on for another little while, what they were told about the end being in sight would become a reality.

* * *

An uneasy truce had fallen into place with Flo and when Joyce first showed her cousin the amenities in the understairs cupboard, Flo had been impressed. 'This is excellent,' Flo enthused. 'You've done a great job.'

It had been so long since Flo had praised her for anything, that Joyce felt ridiculously proud of the compliment. 'You must get in, too,' Joyce told her cousin. 'If the siren goes while you're on leave.'

'Oh, I will,' Flo said. 'It looks lovely and cosy.'

Flo told them that the line of barrage balloons was of little or no deterrent to the V-2s, but they were a hindrance to the V-1s so she and her crew would be staying on the South Downs for as long as necessary. 'What will stop those blasted rockets?' Auntie Cath asked, her fingers fluttering around her neck. 'Anything?'

'Bombing the life out of their launching sites, which our lads are doing every day and night,' Joyce assured her.

'And we're letting the Jerries know in a roundabout way that the rockets are landing well off the mark,' Flo said. 'So they adjust their setting on the weapons and then they really do miss their targets.'

The three of them were sitting together waiting for the *Forces Programme* to start on the wireless. Watery winter sun filtered through the window and projected a stream of dancing dust motes into the room. Auntie Cath or Joyce cleaned every day, but an hour after finishing with the rag, a coating of powdery grime covered all the surfaces again.

'Do you mean to tell me we're talking to Jerry?' Auntie Cath could not believe what Flo had announced.

'No, we let them know through agents,' Flo explained. 'You know, spies.'

'Spies?' Auntie Cath echoed. 'Here in England?'

'Should you be talking about this, Flo?' Joyce said.

'Yes, Mum, spies for both sides are everywhere and no, I probably shouldn't be telling you but...' she shrugged. 'You won't go to the papers, will you? And Mum, you mustn't tell the neighbours or I'll never trust you again.'

'Right you are, Flo love,' Auntie Cath said. 'My lips are sealed.'

They enjoyed the programme, clicking their fingers or beating time on the arms of their chairs, although Joyce noticed that Auntie Cath seemed agitated, fidgeting with the collar and buttons of her cardigan; she kept looking over at Joyce, too, as if Joyce should have been aware of a secret between them. Then Flo started to jitterbug and she grabbed Joyce who soon picked up the movements, laughing at how fun it was to be thrown around the room as if she were a puppet. Flopping back down, Joyce pointed at Auntie Cath and Flo pulled on her Mum's hand.

'No,' Auntie Cath protested. 'I can't match your steps.'

'Course you can, Mum. Just go where I shove you.'

For a couple of minutes they tried their best, until their feet, legs and hands became tangled and they both staggered back onto the settee.

'Oh, Flo love,' Auntie Cath was out of breath. 'That was such a laugh.'

'It reminds me of when we used to Charleston with Mum and Nana when we were little. Do you remember, Flo?'

'I do, Joy love,' Flo said. 'And what a state our dancing was then.'

'Not much improved now,' Joyce said.

'Oh, I don't know,' Flo said. 'You haven't mentioned Madame Beaupre in your letters for a while. Have you been to any more lessons?'

Joyce shook her head. 'I can't face it,' she said. 'It's all so... sullied now.'

'Where it used to be shiny and new and polished,' Flo agreed.

'It was nothing more than an illusion though, was it?' Joyce asked.

'No, it was real enough at the time. But I suppose that time's gone.'

The cousins looked at each other, both knowing they were referring to things other than dancing.

'Shall we go for a drink?' Flo brightened up. She leaned across to the sideboard and turned off the wireless. 'Oh, what's this?' She held up a rather grubby envelope that had been resting behind the radio.

'It came this morning.' Auntie Cath glanced distractedly at the letter in Flo's hand.

'I think it's from Hettie. I was saving it for when we were sitting down together.'

'Well, here we are all together,' Flo said. 'Shall I open it?'

'I hope Hettie and the children are okay,' Joyce said. 'We haven't heard from her for ages.'

Auntie Cath nodded. 'Read it to us,' she said.

'It's just one small page of lined copybook paper,' Flo said, holding up the scrap for them to see.

'*Dear Everyone,*' she read. '*I hope you won't be upset, but I am getting married again on the 27th of March. The lucky man is Seamus Malloy...*'

'Well, I never,' Auntie Cath said.

'... and he's in the army this time, not the Merchant Navy, like Sid.'

A wave of grief caused Joyce's stomach to somersault when she heard her brother's name.

'He's the widow of an old school friend of mine who took a packet in a raid. Their children are gone, too. No one could ever replace my lovely Sid, but Seamus is kind, funny and he loves the children. Please give me your blessing. And we would be very happy if you came to the wedding. Please let me know. Love from Hettie and the little Coopers.'

'Goodness,' said Auntie Cath. 'I wasn't expecting that.'

Joyce drew herself up and said, 'I'm pleased for her.' But she also felt an overwhelming sadness for what Sid was missing out on, followed within a beat by a twist of jealousy that she would never have any of that with Derek.

'I wouldn't be able to get enough leave to go,' Flo said.

Joyce nodded. 'And I've had so much time off, I daren't ask for any more.'

'We shouldn't travel that far if we don't need to anyway,' said Auntie Cath. 'We'll send a telegram on the day, then she'll know we're happy for her.'

Flo put the letter back where she'd found it on the sideboard.

'The pub then?' Flo asked again.

'Not for me,' Joyce looked at the clock. 'I'm on duty soon.'

'Mum?'

Auntie Cath's finger found her top button, unfastened it, then did it up again.

'I want to talk to you first, Flo,' Auntie Cath said, and Joyce was surprised at how firm and confident her aunt came across.

Flo sighed on a loud breath out. 'I can guess about what,' she sounded sulky.

'Well,' Auntie Cath shuffled until she was sitting on the edge of her seat. 'Your father and grandfather aren't here to ask the right questions, so it's down to me and Joyce.'

Flo narrowed her eyes and shot Joyce an accusatory look. Joyce would have liked to defend herself by saying she had not had any conversations with her aunt about Flo, other than asking each other if they knew how she was getting on and when she was next coming home on leave. But she would not contradict or disrespect Auntie Cath so let her aunt continue.

'Two things you just said have got me thinking that I must say something to you now.' Auntie Cath held up two fingers.

'What were they?' Flo frowned.

'First, you said I must not tell the neighbours about spies or you would never trust me again. Well, I don't think I quite trust you.'

Flo gasped sharply and Joyce's eyes widened.

'Mum,' Flo said with hurt in her voice.

But Auntie Cath held up her hand. 'And the second,' she continued, 'was something about things being an illusion, which to my mind amounts to trust, too. Or things not being what they seem. Or not adding up.'

Oh, Joyce thought, *Auntie Cath and Mum were definitely cut from the same shrewd cloth.*

Flo pursed her lips and looked as if something unsavoury was underneath her nose. 'You're not being very straightforward yourself, Mum,' she stated.

'Flo, that's quite enough,' Joyce said. 'Don't be rude to your Mum. Say sorry.'

Sour silence hung amongst them. 'Sorry, Mum,' Flo said at last. 'But why don't you just come out with it and ask me about Vernon.'

Vernon – Joyce thought she'd heard that name enough to last her a lifetime.

'Yes,' Auntie Cath said. 'Vernon. And to answer your question, we don't ask about him because when we've done that in the past you get defensive and moody and clam up on us altogether. Doesn't she, Joyce?'

There was part of Joyce that still hoped for a reconciliation with Flo, but she knew, as Flo had intimated earlier, that the time when they could be as close as they had been in the past was gone. If they were able to be comfortable friends again, it would be on a different footing. 'Flo,' she tried to sound conciliatory, 'Auntie Cath and I haven't been talking about you and Vernon. Not for a long time now. But I know your Mum worries about you. And so do I.'

Now it was Auntie Cath's turn to dart a look of betrayal Joyce's way. 'And your dad,' she said. 'He worried about you every minute of the day and night since you told us about this Vernon bloke.' Her face was red and bloated, her eyes almost popping out of her head. The top button of her cardigan broke from its thread and fell to the floor with a jangle. 'I wouldn't be surprised if he walked right into the path of that doodle-bug,' she shouted. 'Because he was thinking of you and your situation and not minding where he was going.'

Flo's hands flew to her face where they covered her eyes and she released one dry sob. 'Don't say that, Mum,' she whimpered. 'Please.'

Joyce felt as if she were stuck fast to the settee cushions, at a loss for something to say that would help. But she couldn't say nothing. Life was too precarious to leave that statement hanging. What if... she could hardly bring herself to finish that thought. Then she faced it – the truth that Auntie Cath was talking about. They all lived their lives knowing that at any second one or all of them could be blown away. What if Flo was left and had to remember those harsh words as the last her mum had spoken to her. Or Auntie Cath had to live with knowing the last thing her daughter had heard from her was a cruel accusation about Uncle Terry's demise. Or if Joyce was suspended in this moment for the rest of her life, knowing she should have said something to ease the situation between her cousin and aunt. 'That's not true, Auntie Cath,' she offered at last. 'What happened to Uncle Terry and Granddad is not Flo's fault. Please take it back.'

She watched both women turn their heads away from each other, both sure they were in the right. 'Let's stop this now and talk to each other reasonably. Like we think the Allies and the Axis should have done years ago,' she pleaded.

Auntie Cath must have felt Flo's eyes boring into the back of her head because she turned and apologised. Like Joyce had been when she'd rowed with Flo, Auntie Cath was sorry not for what she'd said, but how she'd let it come out of her mouth.

Flo dried her eyes, gave her mother a hug and said, 'Shall we go to the pub now and talk about something else?'

'No,' Auntie Cath shook her head. 'I regret what I said about Dad, Flo love,' she touched the place over her heart. 'But I want to know what is going on with Vernon. I have a right to know. So does Joyce.'

As they waited, the light through the windows changed and a bank of clouds, heavy with snow, settled across the sky. There was never a fire in the grate until after the blackout and Joyce pulled her cardigan tight around her shoulders.

Flo concentrated on her fingers and picked around one or two of her cuticles. When she looked up Joyce was taken aback to see the bitterness and disappointment engraved on her face. There were lines where a minute ago there had been soft, plump skin; her eyebrows were drawn together in two angry smudges and her pale grey eyes were as hard and cold as the ice bound in the steely clouds.

'Alright,' she said, lighting a cigarette. 'You want the truth so I'll give it to you.

I haven't heard from Vernon since the day he left for Australia.'

Without thinking about Flo's feelings, Joyce and Auntie Cath let out an audible sigh of relief. 'What a rotter,' Joyce said. She knelt next to Flo and hung onto her neck. 'To leave you in the lurch like this without even writing to tell you it's over.'

'Yes, Flo love,' Auntie Cath said. 'What a coward. I've a mind to send him a white feather in the post if you give me his address. At least now you can find someone else.'

Flo brushed Joyce's hug aside and flapped her hand about, dismissing what Auntie Cath had said. 'It's not over,' she emphasised each word.

'I think you'll find it is,' Auntie Cath said. 'On Vernon's behalf anyway. Or else he would have been writing every day to keep you up to date on his news.'

'The post is notoriously slow, especially from abroad, we all know that.' Flo stubbed out her cigarette in Granddad's old ashtray. 'And Vernon's not a great writer, so he's probably waiting until he can send details of when I can travel out to him. Or his wife and father-in-law might be making things difficult for him – for us – and he doesn't want to worry me with the details.' She said all of this in such a reasoned tone that Joyce was sure she had convinced herself that was the truth of the matter.

Auntie Cath rested her head against the embroidered anti-macassar on the back of the chair and closed her eyes. 'So you insist on carrying a flame for him?' she asked.

'Always,' Flo said. 'That is what I promised.'

'But why Vernon?' Auntie Cath was exasperated. 'What's so special about him?'

Flo thought for a moment, then said simply, 'He's everything to me.'

There was nothing else Joyce or Auntie Cath could say against such determination, so Auntie Cath brought in a few sheets of old, scrunched-up newspaper and some dried twigs Uncle Terry had left in the shed.

Joyce jumped up and took the bundle from her aunt. 'Let me do that before I leave, Auntie Cath,' she said.

Flo didn't look at either of them. She lit another cigarette and asked again, 'The pub, Mum?'

'Not this evening,' Auntie Cath said in a flat voice.

After Flo had left the following morning, Joyce and Auntie Cath didn't hold their tongues as they'd done in the past but talked about what had transpired. 'She's a silly, stubborn girl,' Auntie Cath pronounced her judgement. 'Goodness knows what will become of this. Nothing, I'll warrant, and she will have wasted her precious time.'

Joyce wondered if Auntie Cath thought she was doing the same, spending all her free time in the flat with her aunt. But her circumstances were different, so she didn't take the comment to heart. 'Perhaps there is something between them deep down,' Joyce said.

Auntie Cath shook her head. 'I don't believe so,' she said. 'Flo was nothing more to him than a distraction while he was here. But she won't listen to us, so she'll have to reach that conclusion by herself.'

'Let's not ask her anything else until she does just that. She'll tell us when she's good and ready.'

Auntie Cath liked that plan and they agreed not to mention Vernon to Flo in letters or when she was home on leave, unless Flo brought up the subject herself. And whilst Joyce felt defeated by her cousin's attitude and frustrated that Flo and Auntie Cath had been rude and exchanged unkind words, she was relieved that she had brokered an uneasy truce between them.

* * *

In Report and Control they heard the labouring engine and braced themselves, standing to attention and waiting for the hateful racket of a V-1 to stop and the sinister silence to fill the air as it fell, found a target and exploded. A trickle of sweat followed the path of Joyce's spine; she felt a forceful twitch in her eyelid, but she would not allow her face to betray the icy cold running through her veins. Would it pass them by? She hoped so, but that was wishing the blasted thing on someone else. She pictured Flo with her crew of barrage balloon handlers, swearing as this one broke through their cordon. Then she thought if she conjured up a strong enough image of Auntie Cath in the cupboard that was where her aunt would be, perhaps with a cup of tea and her knitting pins.

The surrounding sectors must have wished harder than Joyce had in Notting Hill, because the wretched noise cut out and the next thing they heard was a blast violent enough to cause ringing in their ears for days.

The first ARPM1 that found its way to Joyce's hand told her that a doodlebug had floated down onto the roofs of a terrace that, on the map, was nowhere near where she lived with Auntie Cath, so the circle she drew around the hit didn't encompass her aunt's flat. But the buzzbombs and rockets didn't care a jot for maps or for confining their devastation to an area the size of a sixpence. What they were interested in was spreading the destruction they caused as far and wide as possible.

The telephone jarred; the room filled with men in charge of fire, rescue and ambulance services, a woman from the WVS, wardens and first aiders. Other forms came in rapid succession and they reported damage reaching out like poisonous tentacles in all directions from the site of the V-1 blast – down, up, north, south, east, west, left and right. They named familiar roads and streets and mews and crescents that had been burrowed deep or blasted into the heavens. Controller Davis gave orders that wardens could check on their own houses and families as part of their duties. From one ARPM1, it seemed that Jean's terraced house might have taken it, so she decided to patrol in that direction; Percy went to find his sister, whose road had been hit; there had been no news from Mrs Bertrand's vicinity so she stayed with her tea urn and Controller Davis lived near Shepherd's Bush, but would not have abandoned his post even if the bomb had landed on his roof with his wife and Bonzo inside.

The night wore on and with the arrival of each report naming a street progressively further away from Auntie Cath's house, Joyce shut her eyes for a minute and imagined, again, her aunt safely under the stairs with the other flats in the big, old house standing around her. Perhaps this time they would get away with it. And why not? She knew of some people, Mrs Bertrand for one, who hadn't lost anyone or anything. Her frail husband refused to take shelter and, according to his wife, stayed put in his chair through every raid, reading his paper with the light from a torch. Their grown-up children had gone unscathed, too and their grandchildren were home from evacuation, running in and out of their grandparents' house all hours of the day and night. Of course, she chastised herself, she didn't want Mrs Bertrand to lose any of her family or the china tea set her mother had left her or her cat or windows or porch. But she didn't want to lose Auntie Cath either, or the home they shared together and she thought, petulantly, that there should be some way of making sure war casualties were spread out amongst families more fairly.

The Controller placed another ARPM1 on Joyce's table and when she picked it up, she knew she would never again think that she was owed a break or that there should be justice in the world. Before Controller Davis reached his desk, she called after him. 'Sir,' she said.

Controller Davis turned. 'Senior Warden Cooper?' he said.

'May I have permission to stand down briefly?' She held up the report. 'Leinster Gardens, where I live with my aunt, has been damaged.'

Joyce watched as the Controller seemed to disintegrate on the spot as if everything solid about him had evaporated. 'Miss Cooper,' he said, coming towards her with his arms open. 'Let me send someone with you.'

'No, ta, Sir,' she said. 'I was expecting it.'

And as she walked quickly towards home, she realised that she had been waiting for it all along. Why else did she carry her ration books, the Taperite pen and Derek's medal everywhere with her in her bag? She hadn't willed it to happen, in fact the opposite was true, but now it seemed inevitable, so she wasn't surprised.

Firemen were everywhere, directing jets of water onto flames; ambulances lurched around debris in the middle of what was left of once familiar roads; bits of brick and splintered wood and clothing, torn off people who took the brunt of the blast, flew about in the air, so Auntie Cath had been right to warn her and Flo about flying wreckage. She heard an elderly man telling a rescue worker in a shaky voice that his windows seemed to bulge in before they shattered. Dust whorled like fog in the night sky and worked its way up her nostrils alongside the smell of escaped gas. Wardens and civilians clambered over rubble and Joyce saw two small children peering into the depths of a hole where a few hours earlier a shop and house had stood. A warden was on his hands and knees, reaching deep into the debris while the little ones stood by, holding hands.

There was nothing left of the house Auntie Cath's flat had been a part of. Joyce stood and looked at the bomb site before she trailed over its bumps and mounds for half an hour, hoping again to find something to tell her definitively that her aunt had gone up or down with the blast. But of course she had. Joyce had told her to stay put in the cupboard, so she didn't need evidence to prove it.

Without anyone to tell except Flo, who she would telegram first thing in the morning or anywhere else to go, Joyce walked back through the chaos to Report and Control.

Controller Davis wanted to relieve her of her duties, saying she could go to his wife in Shepherd's Bush. 'Here,' he said, getting out a piece of paper and a pen, 'I'll write a note you can give her. Knock loudly on the door of the Anderson and she'll open it.'

But Joyce would not hear of it and pleaded with him to let her stay with her map for as long as she was needed. 'I... I'm not being rude or disrespectful to you or Auntie Cath, Sir,' she explained. 'But I think I need to be occupied.'

The Controller studied her for a few moments, then agreed on the condition she tell him if she felt unwell or faint or as if she was going into shock. Once or twice she felt lightheaded and excused herself to sit on the cot in the cupboard, but it soon passed and she was able to carry on.

Towards dawn she laid back on the pillow, telling herself she would close her eyes for just two minutes, and fell into an agitated sleep. When she woke she was shivering, but bathed in sweat. With trembling hands, she splashed water on her face, rinsed her mouth and straightened her hair and clothes. Mrs Bertrand made her a cup of tea and a piece of toast and told her that she and the Controller had decided that Joyce must stay with one or other of them until she could sort out a hostel or bedsit. It hadn't crossed her mind that she had joined the thousands made homeless and would have to find somewhere to live. But now that it had been pointed out, a jolt of panic hit her. The thought of sleeping on a settee or in a corner of a spare room on a makeshift bed in either of those kind people's houses filled her with horror. It had been hard enough moving from Mum's to Nana's to Auntie Cath's and they had been her family. But she couldn't live with Flo in her barracks or stay in Report and Control for ever so she knew she would have to find somewhere of her own.

'Ta, Mrs Bertrand,' Joyce shouted. 'I can't accept, though, as I wouldn't want to be a nuisance to you or the Controller.'

Mrs Bertrand cupped her ear, appeared to understand and said, 'You'd never be that.'

'I'm very grateful,' Joyce said, determined not to sound rude. 'But as soon as the post office opens I'll send a wire to my cousin and she will be here either later today or tomorrow. We'll want to stay together, so I'll find us a room somewhere.'

When she put on her coat, she realised that the only clothes she had were the ones she was wearing and the black, patent pumps she'd left in a cupboard after a night out with

Derek years ago. She would have to grab a bag of castoffs from the WVS or share what Flo brought with her.

In the post office, Joyce chewed the end of a pencil and thought about how to word the telegram to Flo. Whatever she wrote would alarm her cousin, who would know what had happened without Joyce spelling it out, so kept it simple and to the point:

Urgent you come home Stop Find me at R and C Stop Joy

Then she went to the local WVS, joined a long snaking queue of people who looked as though they could barely stand and wondered if she would see Jean or Gladys or Percy while she waited. When it was her turn, she told a woman named Mrs Lewis her plight and was given a cup of tea, a biscuit and a bag of clothes.

'Ta for the bundle,' Joyce said, propping the bag next to her.

'I've popped in some kiddies' things, too,' Mrs Lewis said, whose eyes reminded Joyce of her mum's.

'I don't have any children.' Joyce was bemused and wondered if she was going mad and had said the wrong thing.

'No, my dear,' Mrs Lewis said. 'But you're so petite, I thought some older children's things might fit.'

Joyce nodded. She couldn't do anything about her height, or lack of it and she hadn't realised how thin she'd become. She looked down at her wrists and they were tiny, the bones straining against her flimsy skin. 'I need somewhere to live, too,' she continued. 'Somewhere for me and my cousin who won't have anywhere else to stay when she's on leave from the WAAFs.'

'One moment, please.' Mrs Lewis walked towards a filing cabinet and Joyce wondered how she could be so business-like when she was face to face with people's misery on a daily basis. Perhaps, she thought, that distant detachment was exactly what enabled her to be so capable. Joyce knew that was how she was behaving, too. She was thinking logically and trying not to let her feelings get in her way and that was how she was going to get through.

Mrs Lewis returned with two pieces of paper in her hand. 'I have one room in a ladies' hostel in Bayswater and another in a boarding house in White City.'

'Nothing where we can be together?' Joyce said, afraid now that the tears would start and not stop.

'It's been a terrible night.' Mrs Lewis glanced at the chevrons on Joyce's serge greatcoat. 'From many points of view. As you must be well aware.'

Flicking through her papers, Mrs Lewis said,' Ah, there's a bedsit here in Notting Hill Gate. Oh no, hold fire. No single women allowed.'

Joyce laughed, but there was not a hint of fun in the sound. 'No single women?' She was astonished. 'There won't be anyone left except single women soon. And then where will we go?'

'I agree with you, my dear. It's absurd.' She thought for a moment. 'Do you have any money or can you get your hands on some?'

'Why?' Joyce was alarmed. 'Do you charge a fee?' She hadn't seen any others exchanging coins or notes.

'No, no, my dear,' Mrs Lewis said. 'But there are two small flats, both in privately-owned houses, that require a deposit from the landlord.'

If Mum or Nana or Granddad or Auntie Cath had any money, it had gone down or up with them so all she had was what was in her bag. 'How much?' she asked. 'I have a bit and

I'm sure my cousin will have some when she arrives.' She counted out a few coins and found herself a shilling and sixpence short.

'We have a dwindling emergency fund,' Mrs Lewis said. 'Let me see if there's any left.'

Joyce watched Mrs Lewis as she rummaged through the drawers of the filing cabinet again and seemed to find what she was looking for. Another woman wearing the same uniform wrap over dress joined her and kept her talking for a few minutes. When Mrs Lewis returned, she put the money in Joyce's hand.

'Ta very much, Joyce said. 'I will repay you as soon my cousin gets here.'

The woman's smile was rather jaded. 'We do ask that you try,' she said. 'But most people forget.'

'I won't,' Joyce said. 'You have my word.'

'Right. I've just been told that Powis Terrace has been spoken for. Shall I take you to Talbot Road? It's a basement flat.'

Six stone steps led down to a window facing the street and a tatty brown door tucked away on the left. 'Careful, the woman said. 'The slabs are loose in a couple of places. Same out the back, apparently.'

'Is there a garden?' Joyce asked, not sure how she would manage to care for it.

'I wouldn't call it that. It's paved, but you could grow veg or flowers in pots if you're that way inclined.'

The door stuck after it was unlocked and Mrs Lewis put her shoulder to it, but it still wouldn't budge. 'Try this,' Joyce said, kicking the bottom where the paint had rubbed off the wood. With a rattle, it gave way into a narrow hallway and the women had to shuffle around each other before they could shut it behind them.

Joyce's heart dropped when she looked around at the dark walls and low ceiling; there was an all-pervading smell of damp, too, which if nothing else was a change from smoke and dust. A bathroom with an enamel tub, a small, stained sink and an indoor toilet was behind them; the sitting room with a large window looking out towards the stone steps was first on the right, followed by a bedroom and then the kitchen that led out to the courtyard. The flat wasn't furnished but a cooker, a meat safe, a sideboard with three and a half legs and a tatty settee had been left behind.

Joyce felt proud that she hadn't cried since she'd learned about Auntie Cath, but standing in the kitchen of that dreary, dank flat she knew she would have to make her next home, she couldn't deny her tears any longer. Mum's house had been cosy and comfortable and even with the blackouts pulled she had managed to create a bright, cheerful feeling – one that Joyce had always been happy to go home to. Nana's house had been a bit of a jumble, with funny old things in every corner, but it had been clean and smelled of baking and washing. And Auntie Cath's flat had gone from crowded to roomy without losing its welcoming feel. What would they think of this place that Joyce was going to call home? They would be appalled and sorry for her, but perhaps they would boast, too, if they could, that she was getting on with it and not wallowing in self-pity.

'It's alright, my dear.' Mrs Lewis touched Joyce's arm. 'Have a good cry. You've been through a lot.'

'No more than thousands of others,' Joyce sniffled. 'And it

doesn't help to feel sorry for yourself.' Turning her face away from the older woman, she wiped her nose on a hanky.

'It will be better when you get a fire going and some bits and pieces of your own around the place.'

Joyce shook her head. She'd given her last sixpence to the landlord and there wouldn't be any more until she was paid next week. And where would she and Flo sleep until then? On the floor, she supposed.

'Shall I get some furniture put on a cart and sent round?' Mrs Lewis said, practical again.

'Is that possible?' Joyce asked.

'It will be very basic,' Mrs Lewis replied. 'And you won't get to choose. But we can probably start you off with a bed, linen, a couple of pans, a kettle, a few bits of cutlery and crockery and a small table and chairs for the kitchen. It's a good job you had your ration books in your bag. You can use some of them to get other things you need.'

'Yes,' Joyce said. 'I've learned from experience.'

They agreed that Joyce would report back for duty and return to the WVS for her key later after the furniture had been delivered. They walked part of the way to their posts together and when it was time for them to part company, a knotted lump pushed its way into Joyce's throat – she didn't want to let the older woman go. But she drew herself up tall, said thank you and goodbye and as she watched Mrs Lewis march away, she felt more empty and alone than she had ever done before.

But there was Report and Control, Mrs Bertrand, Controller Davis and Jean, her map to attend to – and Flo was on her way.

The Controller said he would ask his wife to look out

some bits and bobs from their home to help her out and Mrs Bertrand had a small bag of provisions to see her over the next few days while Flo was on leave. Jean appeared and told them that her house had been partly damaged and she would be staying with her mother until it could be shorn up. Night fell above them, the telephone breached the quiet, the Controller's hand hovered over the siren, then he set it to wail. Joyce stood by her map, pins and compass ready and they waited for the first boom or blast or labouring clang of a hateful rocket.

Then they heard voices, a clamour on the stairs and there was Flo, exhausted and dishevelled, signalling to her from the doorway. 'Sir,' Joyce said. 'My cousin has arrived.'

'Stand down, Senior Warden Cooper,' Controller Davis said. 'Report back for duty in forty-eight hours.' As she grabbed her bags, the Controller shuffled towards her and in a soft voice, told her not to forget where he was if she needed him.

The lump tried to reassert itself in Joyce's throat, but she swallowed it down. 'Ta, Sir,' she said. 'I'm very grateful for all you've done for me.'

There was no possibility of Joyce or Flo causing a scene in Report and Control, especially as so many who continued with their duties in a composed, impenetrable manner had lost family or the roofs over their heads or both. They nodded to each other and climbed the stairs side by side. At the top, next to the flickering paraffin lamp, Joyce turned to Flo and asked if she wanted her to relate what had happened there and then or wait until they were home.

'Home?' Flo echoed. 'I've been home. Or where it used to be. And I saw with my own eyes what had happened.' She threw her arms around Joyce's neck and cried quietly. 'I can't believe it,' she said at last. 'There used to be so many of us, now there's only...'

'Us,' Joyce finished for her.

'And Vernon,' Flo snuffled into Joyce's collar.

Joyce prised her cousin's arms from around her coat. 'You might think you have Vernon,' she said in a cold, precise manner. 'But he's nothing to do with me.' She turned towards the direction of Auntie Cath's house, remembered her dire circumstances and turned the other way.

'But he'll be part of the family soon,' Flo whined, following close to Joyce's heels.

All of a sudden, intense fatigue bore down on Joyce with such force it felt as if it would crush her. She stopped short, took a deep breath to steady herself and said, 'I don't want to talk about Vernon. I want to get to the flat I've rented for us, have a look at the furniture the WVS delivered, sort through some clothes, have a cup of tea and talk about Auntie Cath. And that's all you should be thinking about, too. Have some respect for your mum, please.'

They walked the rest of the way in silence, although Joyce allowed Flo to grab her arm and hold onto it.

Manoeuvring the concrete steps was difficult in the blackout and the door stuck again until Joyce kicked it in the right place. 'What's that smell,' Flo said, wrinkling her nose.

'Damp,' Joyce replied.

As well as delivering the furniture and bedding she'd promised, Mrs Lewis had also hung shabby blackouts at the windows and put a shilling in the meter so they could turn on the lights. Joyce thought Mrs Lewis was a wonder, but she never borrowed money from anyone and the thought of now owing the WVS two shillings and sixpence troubled her.

The bed had been made and Joyce longed to lay down on

it but knew that if she did she would only toss and turn and not fall into the deep sleep she needed so badly. While Flo wandered from room to room, Joyce filled the kettle and spooned tea leaves into a pot. 'Mrs Bertrand has given us some bread, margarine and a slice of cheese,' Joyce called out to Flo. 'And what looks like a small piece of sultana cake, so that will have to do for tonight.'

Flo walked into the kitchen, inspecting corners, looking up at the ceiling and turning over the mismatched knives and spoons and forks. 'That's fine,' she said. 'I'm not very hungry anyway. Shall I set a fire? I think your Mrs Lewis left some wood and a few coals in the grate.'

'Ta,' Joyce said. 'That will help.'

They nibbled on their supper, listened for buzzbombs and rockets that might be headed their way and Joyce told Flo about the sequence of events from the night before.

Flo wept and Joyce cried, too.

When they'd gathered themselves together, Flo said, 'So, this is where you live now. I suppose the basement is quite safe in a raid.'

'Not unless the whole house falls down on top of it,' Joyce said. 'And this is your home, too, Flo. It's ours.'

'Ta, Joy love,' Flo said, barely able to get the words out.

In the morning, they went once more to the bombsite that used to be Auntie Cath's flat, picked through the rubble and when they were satisfied they would find no trace of her, reported her as missing, presumed dead. In a few weeks, when they got the go-ahead, they would put up a marker for her. They still had to have Mum's name added to Dad's headstone and get two others made, one for Auntie Cath and Uncle Terry and another for Nana and Granddad. But Joyce couldn't begin to think how much that would all cost, so they would have to make do with wooden crosses for now.

That made Joyce think of money and after she and Flo walked through Hyde Park and Flo bought them a drink in a pub, Joyce asked her cousin how much she could contribute to the weekly rent. 'There's also two shillings and sixpence I owe the WVS,' she said, explaining the situation.

Flo's vermouth stopped before it reached her mouth. Then she pursed her lips and flared her nostrils. 'I didn't think I'd have to pay anything,' she said in a sullen voice. 'It's not my flat.'

Joyce could not believe what she was hearing. 'It is your flat, Flo,' she cried out in astonishment, then looked around in case anyone heard her causing a scene.

Flo looked down the length of her nose. 'I wouldn't have chosen to live there.'

Joyce felt herself matching her cousin's defensiveness. 'I didn't choose it either,' she said. 'But where would you have stayed these two nights if I hadn't and where will you stay every time you come home on leave?'

'A hostel would be cheaper.'

'Then we can't be together,' Joyce said, pleading in exasperation.

Flo sighed, took a drag of her cigarette and said, 'I know you don't want to hear his name, but I'll be going out to Vernon soon and then you'll have to manage on your own anyway, won't you?'

'Have you heard from Vernon?' Joyce asked.

'Yes, I have. He said things are progressing slowly, but he hopes to have details of my passage soon.'

Joyce snorted and Flo turned a bright puce. She hung her head over her bag to hide her embarrassment, so Joyce thought, and came out with the two and six in her hand. 'Here,' she said, slamming it on the table between them. 'But don't expect any more as I need every penny for Australia.'

Joyce scooped up the coins. 'I,' she spat under her breath, 'don't even have one penny. This is the only money I have in the world, and I will be handing it over to Mrs Lewis right away.'

For a moment Flo's eyes widened as the truth of Joyce's situation hit her. Delving into her bag again, she took out half a crown, pressed it into her cousin's hand and sat back in her chair.

Staring down at the money, Joyce wanted nothing more than to hand it back, but it was either accept it or borrow from Controller Davis. 'I will repay you,' Joyce said. 'Ta very much.'

Flo waved her hand dismissively. 'Let's call it quits for the next time I'm on leave.' She lit another cigarette and downed her drink. 'I can't believe we've argued about money right after losing Mum,' she said. 'Now who's being disrespectful.'

'We haven't argued about money,' Joyce said. 'We argued about Vernon. Yet again.'

* * *

On the morning of Flo's departure, they remembered Hettie's wedding. 'I'll send a telegram,' Joyce said. 'Do you want me to put your name on it?'

'Of course I do,' Flo said.

'Can you remember her address?'

'No, I can't, sorry.'

'I think it was 72, no 73 Albany Road? If it gets sent to the wrong place, I'm sure the neighbours will pass it on,' Joyce said. 'What about her new husband's name? Was it Sean or Seamus?'

'Seamus,' Flo said. 'Maloney.'

'Malloy!' Joyce said, pleased with herself.

They hugged at the top of the stone steps, patting each other's backs with a good inch of space between them. When Flo disappeared from view Joyce felt a sudden longing to chase after her, hold her tight and say whatever it took to make her promise they would stay close and never bicker again. But she didn't. Instead, she rose up from the top of her head, went into her flat and bolted the door behind her.

TWENTY-ONE

Saturday 20 April 1974

During the week, Joyce thought a lot about Mr Taylor and Jacqueline's invitation to their wedding and whilst she hadn't changed her mind about attending, she came to the conclusion that she hadn't quite minded her manners and that gave her much disquiet. First, she decided to send a telegram but gathered from the girls in the office that wasn't the done thing anymore. 'It's all cards now,' said Audrey. 'Even the message is printed inside for you. All you have to do is sign it.'

'Shame though,' said Alison. 'There must have been something romantic about sending and receiving telegrams.'

You wouldn't think that if you'd been on either end of the dreaded messages I had to write and open during the war, Joyce thought.

'Ta,' Joyce said. 'I'll have a look at some on my way home.'

But that didn't seem quite enough, and she thought it would be a nice gesture to buy them a little something. But what? She'd never met Jacqueline, so didn't know what sort of things she liked, although the Liberty scarf gave her a clue that the young woman had refined taste.

Recently in Bourne and Hollingsworth, a wedding registry service had been initiated and it was a huge success. The engaged couple listed what crockery or cutlery or glassware they liked, then guests could spend as much or as little as they chose and the gifts would be delivered in time for the ceremony.

Wondering if Mr Taylor and Jacqueline had registered with the store, Joyce nipped down and enquired during her lunch break. But no, she was told, there were no Taylors on the books. 'Perhaps I could try Selfridges. Or John Lewis,' she said to the young, perfectly groomed assistant.

'It would be on the invitation.' The woman arched her already curved eyebrows. 'So guests know where to buy their presents.'

That made sense and Joyce should have thought that through for herself. She read the girl's badge – Carol Edwards. 'Of course,' she said. 'Ta, Miss Edwards.'

The young woman must have stolen a glance at Joyce's name tag, too, because she called after her. 'Mrs Cooper, can I make a suggestion?'

'Miss Cooper.' Joyce turned back.

'You seem to be stuck for a present,' she said. 'Have you considered a gift voucher?'

They had also been recently introduced to the store and were very popular, although Joyce wondered if they took the personal touch out of buying for someone else. Not that she would know as the only gifts she'd bought since the war were little things for the office Secret Santa.

Miss Edwards got out a selection of vouchers and cards from her till and arranged them on the counter. 'You decide on the amount you want to give then choose an appropriate card. There are two for weddings.' She turned one towards Joyce. 'I think this one is lovely.'

'Yes, it is.' Joyce picked it up and thought the silver horseshoe design matched the smaller versions around the edges of Mr Taylor and Jacqueline's invitation. It would be a nice touch. 'But would it seem as though I hadn't put much thought into it?'

'Not at all,' Miss Edwards sounded confident. 'I presume they're a young couple?'

'Yes, they are,' Joyce said.

'Young people love gift vouchers because they can use them to buy whatever they like or put them towards something they wouldn't otherwise be able to buy. And it saves their embarrassment if they have to ask you for a receipt so they can exchange the third kettle or bread knife they've been given.'

Joyce was convinced, so bought ten pounds' worth with the horseshoe card to put them in. While Miss Edwards was ringing up the transaction she said, 'If you're still worried it might be too impersonal, you can always get half a bottle of champagne to go with it. Someone did that for my sister's wedding last year and she loved it.'

So Joyce had bought a special carrier from the stationery department and filled it with a bottle of fizz from the wine merchant's she visited on her way home. That evening, she wrote congratulations and her name inside the card, sealed the envelope and popped it down next to the bottle in the bag, which was also festooned with horseshoes.

Now once again Joyce stood on her balcony, but this time her hair wasn't wet and she was pressed against the French door leading from the flat with the wrapped gift in her hands. Her plan now was to wait until she heard Mr Norris leave his flat then run down the stairs and hand him the present. She knew he wouldn't try to persuade her to change her mind and go with him as she'd made sure she was dressed in the practical clothes she wore to clean her flat and get her weekly shopping. And he wouldn't detain her because she'd overheard two women talking in the convenience store about a minibus that was collecting them, and he wouldn't want to be late for that.

Straining her ears at every sound, she jumped when she heard the click of his gate. She'd put her key in her pocket earlier in case she forgot it in her rush to get to him, so let the door close behind her and ran, as fast as was dignified, down the central staircase. Mr Norris had moved quickly, but she could see him walking away from her towards the street in a very well-cut dark blue suit, whistling Stanley Holloway's song, 'Get Me to the Church.'

'Mr Norris.' She tried to catch up with him.

When he turned, Joyce was impressed with how smart he looked in his white, pressed shirt, striped tie and pink buttonhole. His hair had been cut and groomed and he'd had a close shave. 'Miss Cooper,' he sounded delighted to see her. 'Have you changed your...' Then he eyed her clothes and knew she hadn't.

'No, Mr Norris, I haven't.' She handed the bag to him. 'But would you be so kind as to give this to the bride and groom for me?'

'Miss Cooper,' he sounded as taken aback as if the present was an unexpected surprise for him. 'This is so thoughtful of you. Paul and Jacqueline will be touched by your kindness, I'm sure. And they'll want to thank you themselves at their house-warming party. I'm sure you'll be invited.'

There were parties to celebrate everything these days, she thought. People no longer took anything in their stride.

'I hope the day goes well,' she said and turned to make her way back upstairs.

But as usual, the blasted Mr Norris couldn't leave well enough alone. 'Do come and have a cup of tea with me tomorrow and I can tell you all about it,' he said.

'Oh, there's really no need,' Joyce tried to take her leave.

'Then one afternoon next week.'

'I work, Mr Norris.'

'Next Saturday?' he ventured.

'My Saturdays are full because I work all week.' A horn sounded from the street. 'That must be for you,' she said. 'They're all waiting.'

He waved his hand in the general direction of the idling minibus and said, 'Friday when you get home, then. There's no work the next day so no excuses. Seven o'clock?' He started to jog backwards. 'Shall I come to you or you to me?'

Joyce felt flustered and off her guard. Really, the blasted man was too insensitive. But perhaps if she agreed, they could put a line under it once and for all. She would make sure they did. 'Please come to me for half an hour,' she said and she could hear that her voice was less then welcoming.

* * *

What do you serve someone for a late tea or early supper on a Friday evening, she wondered as she went from the shops to the market in Portobello Road? Would Mr Norris really be happy with a cup of tea or should she get in a couple of bottles of beer? She didn't want to make the half hour too amiable and comfortable or she'd never get rid of him, but she had to give him something to eat and drink. A few sausage rolls, maybe, and a pork pie. That with a slice of ham, a piece of Cheddar and a small salad would be enough. Then she would offer him a bit of Battenburg cake or a vanilla slice, after which it would be time for him to go and she could lock the door behind him.

Around 2.30 it started to drizzle and Joyce ducked into the library. She sat in an empty chair, flicked through a couple of books she'd picked up and considered them for this week. Then she pictured Mr Taylor and Jacqueline in their bridal attire and hoped it wasn't raining in Edmonton, although she didn't suppose they would let it put a damper on their day. She could see Mr Taylor's chin wobble as he took his vows and Jacqueline's broad smile as she faced him, her hands in his. There would be pungent pink and white flowers all over the church; the music would be traditional but uplifting; their parents would be beaming and Mr Norris, in the middle of his friends from the estate, would have a soft, knowing, avuncular look on his face. When the couple exchanged rings, the guests would breathe out a murmur of approval.

Suddenly, the reverie made Joyce feel ridiculous and she wondered if she'd inadvertently picked up a silly romance. But no, the book in her hand was a spy thriller which she decided would be a good read. She checked out her choices and as she was leaving, she passed a notice for book clubs in the area to register their interests so the library could provide copies of the books they were reading. Now that was one group she might be interested in, if she knew where to find one. Mr Norris would know and before she could stop the thought she wondered if she might ask him, without committing herself, when he came for tea. The idea of meeting up with people on a regular basis made her heart race and a thin film of sweat appear on her upper lip, but if nothing else, she might get some good ideas for books to read in the future. Then she dismissed the idea as the library had sufficed perfectly well as a source of inspiration until now.

As she filled her pull-along trolley, she found herself looking at her watch at regular intervals, each time imagining what was transpiring at the wedding party. There would be the procession out of the church with Jacqueline's veil pulled back so her lovely face was on view. A tiny bridesmaid would be scattering pink rose petals. Photos would be taken; old friends would catch up and new ones would be introduced. On the long trudge home she pictured the wonderful food served at the wedding breakfast; the laughter as people pushed back their chairs for the speeches; raised glasses of champagne; balloons; the cake. She picked out one or two faces from the flats in the crowd she'd conjured up. All of them, she supposed, would have their own stories to tell about the war years, why they'd moved to the new estate, how they'd come to be on their own or why they'd married who they had, if they'd had children or not and how they'd found themselves working in the jobs they'd held down. In that respect, they were all cut from the same cloth as her except, and the thought hit her hard, none of them, or so it seemed, had let those years define them like she had.

She was glad when her flat was in sight; her legs ached from the long walk, her arm felt like it was being pulled out if its socket and she was fed up with thinking about that blasted wedding. She couldn't wait to get in, hang her washing on the clotheshorse, make a cup of tea and drink it whilst reading the paper.

Despite the showers, children were playing with a bat and ball on the grass in front of Malvolio Mansions. One of them fell and skidded along on his bottom which made the others laugh and Joyce smile. A woman came to her back door, called to the children and handed each of them a coloured ice lolly.

Joyce's block, though, was quiet and subdued. She bumped her trolley up the concrete stairs without fear of Mr Norris rushing out and trying to rescue her. Along the landing, she gazed out towards the street and started to imagine the cake being cut and handed round, but abandoned the picture in favour of one of herself eating her custard tart. There must have been a stone caught in the wheel of the trolley, because every few steps a scraping noise followed behind her. Then there was the sound of metal sliding against metal and she knew Mr Frenchay had opened his spyhole to see where the noise was coming from. She sighed. There were times she wished she swore at people who annoyed her and this was one of them.

At least she knew she wouldn't be bothered by noise from next door; Mr Taylor had been right, and her neighbour was as quiet as a church mouse except for the occasional murmur or mumble when she was convinced he was talking to himself. She never saw him leave or return to the flat so didn't know if he worked or not. A few times she'd seen him walking home with a small bag of shopping, but it must have been just for him as he never had visitors. She thought he must be lonely, rattling around in there on his own, then she wondered if that was how he perceived her. But her situation, she reminded herself, was different. She had chosen to live the way she did and that was how she liked her life to be.

Putting her shopping away, she noticed that the rain had stopped and the sun was struggling to make an appearance from behind the clouds. *That's good,* she thought, *at least there are a few rays of sun on Mr Taylor and Jacqueline's day.* Then she told herself they were taking up way too much of her time and she was firm that she had other things to think about. She sat down to drink her tea and eat her custard tart, but she couldn't settle. For some reason or another, she wanted desperately to see Derek's pen and his medals. She dug deep into her bag, unzipped the special, safe compartment, pushed aside the spare key and took out Derek's belongings. Studying them, she noticed that the plastic medal was scratched and dust had gathered around the cap on the pen.

Unwanted tears pressed against the backs of her eyes when she thought about her tall, ungainly boyfriend with the bright, crooked smile and how different her life might have been if he were still here. Or if Mum, Auntie Cath, Uncle Terry, Granddad and Nana hadn't been taken from her. How long ago had all of that happened? Thirty years and more. She felt silly for being so sentimental and was glad no one could see her as she quickly put the things away. There had been times in all those years, she had to admit, when she wished she had someone to talk to about what was passing through her head. Perhaps she should take a leaf out of Mr Frenchay's book and tell herself everything in a low voice, but she didn't want to start with that nonsense.

For the first time in ages she thought about Flo and how lovely it would be to write to her about everything in her life, as boring and mundane as it was, and to receive a letter from her, or from Hettie or one of the children. But she reminded herself it was no use dwelling on any of them, as the door to the friendships they'd had many years ago had been well and truly slammed shut and bolted.

Rain threatened again so she moved her table and chair under cover, locked the French doors and drew the curtains. Then she broke her Saturday routine by watching the television, instead of reading, while she ate her supper of cold cuts, cheese, pickles and the custard tart.

TWENTY-TWO

FLO

April 1945

Three days after the buzzbomb hit that claimed Auntie Cath, another V-1 exploded in Hertfordshire and two days later, Orpington in Kent took a packet from a V-2. Then – nothing. And in between the two hits, the government was so certain it was over they issued orders for the Civil Defence to stand down at the beginning of May, with all part-timers released immediately and full-time workers given two months' notice.

Of course they must have known what they were talking about, but Joyce wished she could share in their confidence and the fervour that had gripped everyone she came into contact with. She wondered if she were the only one in London whose stomach rolled and pitched with worry that Winnie might have got it wrong and another onslaught from the Jerries would assault them at any minute. Or what if, she thought as her nerves jangled and she turned first one way then the other in her hand-me-down bed, a weapon more vicious and deadly than the V-2 was being finalised by

Germany at that very moment and would find them with ease as both the blackout and dim-out had ended.

Women were beside themselves with happiness as they ripped up the blasted black curtains, but not Joyce – she refused to take hers down and drew them every evening before she made her way to Report and Control. It wasn't until the days went by and her map remained unchanged, the same number of pins and labels set out on the table and the compass unused, that Joyce began to let herself believe the government had not been too hasty.

Every night she studied the tiny, savage knives that scarred the places on the map where Bill, Mum, Nana, Granddad, Uncle Terry and Auntie Cath had taken their packets, then she would find the plot where her basement flat stood and stare in disbelief that it – and she – remained standing.

With that in mind, she gave the flat a good few airings and the smell of damp slowly dissipated. She found net curtains and a tablecloth at the WVS and with a bit of mending and a lot washing, they looked fresh and cheerful. True to her word, the Controller's wife gave her a bedside cabinet, a mat for the bathroom, a picture of Big Ben which she put up in the kitchen, a lamp, a small coffee table and a battered, but surprisingly comfortable, leather armchair. In Portobello Market she gathered blankets, a bolt for the front door and a few knick-knacks which the stallholder tried to tell her were antiques, but sold to her for a few pennies when she laughed out loud at his gumption. And her pride and joy was a second-hand wireless she bought on tick from the pawn shop. Thrup-pence a week which she squeezed out of her wages with diffi-culty, but it was worth every penny.

She had everything she needed now and if she continued

to buy only what was necessary she could pay her rent and keep her head above water. Because she wasn't going anywhere. When she unlocked the door, kicked the spot that sent it flying inwards and bolted it behind her, she felt safe and cloistered and protected.

Since the stand down had been announced, Joyce had lost count of the number of times she'd walked into Report and Control and was greeted by Controller Davis saying, 'It's over,' a huge smile on his face.

'We've seen the buggers off,' Mrs Bertrand would agree, with glee in her voice.

That the end was in plain sight continued to elude Joyce until two days before the stand down date, when she was faced with an empty space where her map had hung for six years. Her stomach tumbled and anxiety made her skin prickle as she stood gawping at the wall, the outline of the frame and the holes where the nails had held it up staring back at her. She thought perhaps it had fallen and was propped against a table waiting for her to refix it to the crumbling plaster, but it was nowhere in sight.

Controller Davis was talking on the telephone in a nonplussed manner and this time he wasn't sweating and his finger wasn't hovering over the air raid button that had been dismantled the day before, a web of wires now standing in its place. He waved at her but didn't seem to think she might be shaken to find her piece of art, as he'd often called it, nowhere in sight. She took off her outdoor things, stored her bag under the table and stood to attention. When the Controller wrapped up his conversation with a hearty laugh, he limped across to her and said, 'The Centre is beginning to look like one of those puzzles in a kiddie's comic. You know, spot what's missing,' he said, sounding very happy.

'I know that quite a few bits and pieces have gone already,' Joyce said. 'But I didn't know my map was going today.' An unexpected swelling filled her throat, but she reminded herself she was on duty and it wouldn't do to allow herself to become soppy.

'Nor did I,' Controller Davis said. 'But some of the lads came in this morning and said they were collecting all the maps in West London and taking them back to their offices.'

'Which lads?' Joyce asked.

'The lads who distributed them in the first place. Architects and Surveyors.' He chuckled again. 'I expect they'll be pleased to get back to their desk jobs after leading the Rescue Services these past years.'

That's when she knew, too, that the end had truly arrived. A kaleidoscope of butterflies took flight in her stomach and lifted her up tall. She'd lost so many houses and so many people and now her faithful, nightly companion – her map – had been taken from her, too. But she quickly reminded herself that she still had Flo, after a fashion and Flo had her and they both had the flat in Talbot Road.

'So,' Controller Davis said, rubbing his hands together. 'We'll be out of here by the second of May and I have a date with my allotment on the third.'

Jean joined them and said she and her husband had liked Norfolk so much when their twins were evacuated there that they hoped to make it their permanent home. 'The house hasn't been the same since the hit,' she explained. 'And it's so difficult to find anything in London. You were fortunate to get your little place, Joyce,' she said.

'Yes,' Joyce said. 'I was.' And she knew that was the truth, but she didn't feel lucky when she thought about what had happened to lead her there.

'What about you, Senior Warden Cooper?' the Controller asked. 'Have you given any thought to what you'll do after we stand down?'

Over the last week Joyce had started to think about that dilemma, but now it seemed the time to decide was looming. She'd been told she would be paid for two months and then given assistance to find work, but that plan sounded too precarious.

'I've read that the government wants to train young people to teach,' the Controller said. 'You'd make a wonderful teacher, Miss Cooper. Have you ever thought about that as a possibility?'

She shook her head.

'What did you do before the war?' Jean asked. 'Oh, I remember. You worked at Bourne and Hollingsworth, didn't you?'

'That's right,' Joyce said. 'In the Accounts Department.'

'I'll bet it was a lovely place to work.'

'I was happy there,' Joyce said.

'Well, you needn't rush to make up your mind,' said Controller Davis. 'You can make the most of the grace period to have a good think about it.'

But Joyce didn't want to take any chances and find herself stranded, so the following morning she didn't nap or have breakfast or dust the flat. She put her hair up in a neat knot, applied a tiny bit of mascara, rouge and red lipstick, looked through her bag of clothes for a decent, matching outfit but decided to wear her uniform instead. Then she eased her feet into the black pumps and made her way to Oxford Street.

She tried to remember the last time she'd been in that direction and decided it was when she'd met Derek for a drink one afternoon before they'd gone their separate ways to work.

The V-1s and V-2s had wreaked havoc and she was diverted this way and that, traipsing down streets that were completely unrecognisable. The mess and the rubble and the buildings with enormous chunks bitten out of them must surely be causing people like the architects and surveyors huge amounts of worry, but that didn't come across on the faces of the people moving around her. She couldn't describe their expressions as elated, the word that sprang to mind was relieved, as though soothing honey had been poured over everyone. That mixed with a sense of obdurate determination was what she gleaned from the crews clearing up. She could appreciate how gratifying it must feel to mend a wall or a roof, fill in a crater or shore up a terrace of houses, tentatively believing that the whole lot wouldn't be blown apart the next night. If only people could be rebuilt in the same way, she thought.

Workmen were crawling all over Oxford Street, too and there were plenty of servicemen walking smartly, some with girls on their arms. When she approached Bourne and Hollingsworth, she stopped for a minute and took in the façade. She remembered the night it had been hit in the Blitz and how the staff had turned up for work the following day ready to help in any way they could to clear the debris and re-open.

She had loved her time there; she'd been made to feel she was an important and valued part of the running of the store, although now she realised what a small player she'd been. Life had been different then; she'd been hopeful and optimistic and although she'd always been conscientious, she'd had fun, too. And that had been easy, knowing Mum and Nana, Auntie Cath and Flo had been waiting for her at home.

Despite not recognising the doorman and having to negotiate her way around a changed labyrinth of counters, Joyce

414

felt an immediate sense of warmth and familiarity swamp her – just as it did when she walked off the street and into her basement flat. She drew herself up and told herself she would not be leaving Bourne and Hollingsworth without securing her old job.

The Accounts Department might have been relocated to a different part of the building, but she made her way past the hats and toiletries and gentlemen's ties to the stairs she used to climb to her office. 'Can I be of assistance, Madam?' A middle-aged man in a rather worn, shiny, dark grey suit and tie appeared at her side. 'Mr Carter,' he said. 'Floor Manager.'

'Miss Cooper,' Joyce said. 'I worked in the Accounts Department before the war started and Mr Harris, the manager, told me that when I finished my war work I could reclaim my old post. I suppose you've had a number of girls asking for the same.'

'Not too many,' the man said. Joyce noticed he had a scar that ran down from his ear and disappeared into his stiff, white collar. 'I think most of them have moved on. And Mr Harris is no longer with us.'

That caused Joyce a stab of worry. There might not be anyone left who could vouch for her.

'He retired in 1943 and would you believe it, a week later he took a heart attack and that was that. Terrible shock,' he said.

'Dreadful,' Joyce agreed. 'He was such a kind man.'

'Now we have the young Mr St John, nephew of one of the owners. Nice chap. He was a Colonel in the army but was decommissioned on medical grounds so took up his post here rather earlier than expected. Shall I take you up to meet him?'

'Ta,' Joyce said. 'I would be most grateful.'

'You look smart in your uniform,' Mr Carter said. 'Making the most of it before you're stood down. Soon, isn't it?'

'Tomorrow,' Joyce said, shaken for a moment to think that after six years that day was imminent. It had seemed never ending, now she could have sworn that just yesterday she'd bounded up the same stairs to tell Mr Harris she had been seconded to Senior Warden, in charge of the sector map.

Mr St John was, as Mr Carter described him, a nice chap. He smiled at Joyce when Mr Carter introduced them and pointed towards a chair for her sit down. He also wore a grey suit, but his was in an impeccable tweed that looked new and tailored. A pair of regimental cufflinks shone at the ends of his sleeves and his hair was slicked back off his forehead.

Again, Joyce told her story, then waited for Mr St John to tell her she could start in two days' time or perhaps the following Monday. But he sat back, crossed his legs, twiddled his thumbs and shook his head. 'I'm afraid there are no vacancies in Accounts,' he said. 'I'm not saying there won't be, but at the moment everyone in that department is staying put.'

'I understand,' Joyce said. 'But Mr Harris assured me I could have my job back when the war finished.' She felt emboldened by desperation. 'In fact, he gave me his word.'

Mr St John looked up when she said that, a flicker of guilt crossing his face.

Joyce waited patiently and gave him time to think.

'Let me see if we still have your file,' he said, disappearing into another office and coming back with a buff folder that looked as if it had been in the wars. 'You're in luck,' he said. 'We've been going through these and throwing away those that no longer seem relevant.'

Joyce could see her name on the tab and hoped Mr Harris

had written more on her record than her starting and finishing dates.

While she watched, Mr St John leafed through several pages, followed a few lines with his finger and flipped through the papers again. 'Well,' he said at last. 'You were quite the promising bright spark.'

'Ta, Mr St John. I loved working here,' Joyce said in a rush. 'And I'm sure I can take up where I left off.'

'The problems I'm faced with, Miss Cooper,' Mr St John said, 'are twofold. There are no places in Accounts and even if there were, you didn't finish your accountancy training.'

'As I said,' Joyce drew herself up to her full height, 'I can continue to train.'

Mr St John leaned back and looked down from his window to the pavement in front of the store, just as Mr Harris had done on the day she told him she was leaving to be a Senior Warden. Then, her old manager had been studying the bomb damage on the frontage, which Mr St John probably couldn't remember although he must have been witness to some shocking sights he'd much rather forget. When he turned back to look at her, he said, 'The King and Queen are most impressed and thankful for what you Civil Defence ladies and gentlemen have done for us. They said we wouldn't have made it through without you.'

'Ta, Mr St John,' Joyce said, the recognition inflating her with pride.

'So on that basis, we must honour Mr Harris's promise and show our thanks by having you back.'

For a moment, Joyce thought she might disgrace herself and faint with relief. 'Ta,' she said. 'I won't let you down.'

'However,' he continued, 'would you accept a post in Payroll? Then if and when a vacancy comes up in Accounts you will get first refusal to transfer and continue your training. How does that sound?'

Joyce thought it sounded like the answer to keeping her flat. Mr St John gave her a wad of forms to fill in and said she should bring them in on the following Monday, her start day. They shook hands, she thanked him and then went through the ritual again with Mr Carter on the way out.

She thought she might punch the air with excitement or click her heels; instead, she felt lightheaded, remembered she'd had nothing all morning except a cup of tea so found a café and treated herself to a hot drink and a rock bun. While she was fishing the coins out of her bag, her fingers closed tightly around the key to her flat and she brought it to her lips and kissed it.

That evening, she was pleased to let everyone at Report and Control know that she had secured a place back at Bourne and Hollingsworth. Controller Davis wasn't surprised, 'That's our Senior Warden Cooper,' he said. 'Organised and ahead of the game.'

The basement room was bare, with only a few essentials left that would be collected during the following weeks. For a few hours, they tidied and cleaned in relative quiet, unable to comprehend that the following day would be their last.

Controller Davis called everyone together and said in a thick voice, 'It has been my privilege to have called you my dedicated crew during the last six, long years. Every one of you has worked in an exemplary manner and each of you has been indispensable.' He stopped and looked them straight in the eye, one after the other. When it was Joyce's turn, she held his gaze and nodded her thanks. 'The King spoke for the whole country when he said that we could not have been victorious without you.'

'Or you,' Joyce called out before she could stop herself.

'Hear, hear,' Percy joined in.

'I'm sure I speak for all of us when I say we could not have hoped to work under the command of a finer or more courageous man,' Joyce said.

'Three cheers for the Controller,' Mrs Bertrand shouted.

For one awful minute, Joyce thought she'd gone too far and Controller Davis might become tearful, something that would have caused him disgrace, but he held his own while everyone whooped and threw their hats in the air.

Then he banged on the table with the flat of his hand until the cheers stopped and he said he had one more order for them. There was a groan, followed by laughter and Controller Davis carried on, 'Tomorrow evening at twenty hundred hours I command all you to report to The Volunteer for a drink on me. After that, I will see you on the tenth of June in Hyde Park for the farewell parade, where you will receive medals based on your years of service and rank. And I have been asked to put forward the names of two wardens who I consider should have special thanks for splendid and successful service.'

Joyce was glad she wouldn't have to make that decision.

'I could have given each of your names as I know you all merit specific appreciation, but I was forced to choose and those two will receive a letter and might be chosen from the hundreds of other commended to shake hands with the Queen on the day.'

That pronouncement was greeted with another cheer, Mrs Bertrand brought round cups of tea and biscuits and the Controller let them go home well before dawn.

The last day at Report and Control could have been emotional, but Joyce knew that would be silly in light of why they were being stood down. The thought of a drink at the pub helped, too. The Volunteer was packed, but the landlord dragged a table and chairs out from somewhere and they stood around it, downing pints and shandies and Gin and Its. They talked about funny incidents that had happened over the years, like Gladys shouting, 'For God's sake, put that bloody light out!' to a rather grim-faced vicar who opened the door of the vicarage to apologise. Or the times Percy had been so overcome with fatigue, he'd slipped into a deep sleep leaning against a wall with a cup of tea in his hand.

By unspoken agreement, no one mentioned whose son or daughter wasn't coming home or whose child had lost their sight or their toes; whose pets had gone and who had been made homeless. There was a lot of talk about what next, with back slapping and intermittent laughter. Joyce joined in and talked about how stunned she'd been to see a blank wall instead of her map but how, since that day, she'd realised she was glad to see the back of the blasted thing. She said she was looking forward to Bourne and Hollingsworth the following Monday and to Flo coming home sometime soon. But more than anything she felt as if the people she'd worked with for so long were now in the wrong time and the wrong place. She had been used to carrying out serious and sober duties with them and here they were, letting their hair down and having a party in the pub. Suddenly she wanted to be in her flat by herself and feel the stable, durable walls and ceilings around her. Without finishing her drink, she placed her glass on a table and edged out the door before anyone could call her back.

* * *

Somehow, she cobbled together three outfits she could wear for work from her clothing rations or the WVS or the market. She would have loved a new pair of shoes, but they would have to wait as she'd yet again had to spend her rations on underclothes and stockings. Some of the girls from Report and Control had talked about getting permanent waves, but she definitely didn't need that and only had to pin her hair up or twist it in a bun to look neat, which was just as well as she couldn't afford to visit the hairdresser. The few items of make-up she had would suffice and although she didn't have a bottle of scent, her faithful coal tar soap would ensure she was clean and fresh.

Without enough money to catch the bus she was up early, gulping down a hasty breakfast of toast, margarine and tea and walking to Oxford Street again. It had been strange during the few days since stand down to try and get used to staying awake and keeping occupied during the day and then sleeping at night, but a regular pattern of work should help with that. She wondered what duties she would have in the Payroll Department, but imagined that whatever they entailed she would have to be methodical, meticulous and diligent which she was well-suited for. When she said good morning to the doorman, she was struck by the fact that she had come full circle – not a smooth circle, like the ones she'd drawn onto her map with the compass, but a jagged, misaligned, serrated circle that had threatened many times to break, but had somehow remained intact.

Joyce's manager this time around was a woman, as were the four other employees in the Payroll Department, which would have been unheard of before the war. As she was shown to her desk, she smiled to herself when she recalled Auntie Cath telling Uncle Terry, in no uncertain words, that the men would have to fight for jobs the women had so ably stepped into. While that might be true in a Payroll Department, she also knew that women involved in other things like manual labour and the day to day running of the railways were being told they had to stand aside for a man. She sat, stored her bag in a drawer and claimed her place. This was all she had. There was no one else she could rely on so she wasn't going to be moved from her desk or her flat for man or woman. The manageress came towards her with a stack of papers and Joyce prepared herself to learn what was expected of her with a notepad and pencil at the ready.

There had barely been enough time to get into the swing of her new routine before they were all given the day off to celebrate the official end of the war, in Europe at least. The news that the peace treaty was going to be signed the next day had brought people who couldn't wait to celebrate out in their droves, if the sounds of the feet running up and down outside Joyce's flat were anything to go by. She felt as if she'd been holding her breath for the last twenty-four hours as she waited to hear that the Jerries had signed on the dotted line. When the announcement was broadcast on the wireless, she thought she would always remember the exact position of her hands where they had frozen on their way to pinning her hair and how her eyes, round and startled, had stared back at her from the mottled bathroom mirror. Then she gripped the basin and heaved, her heart racing with relief and incredulity.

She wondered if Flo would arrange to come home when she heard the news, but there was no sign of her so Joyce thought she would go out, wander around and perhaps make her way to the West End, where the girls from work said everyone would be heading.

The smell of smoke was the first thing to hit her and for a

moment she was back in the thick of it during the Blitz. But she'd heard on the wireless that bonfires were being lit all over the country and Notting Hill didn't want to be left out. In the distance, she could see the lick of flames from gardens and allotments and wondered if Controller Davis was busy burning sticks, twigs and dried grass somewhere in Shepherd's Bush. There was the distant sound of raucous singing and children laughing; red, white and blue bunting swayed on houses and bombsites. A young couple, holding each other up, meandered past with bottles of beer in their hands.

She thought about calling on Jean, but thought again when she imagined her celebrating with her mother or her sister or some of the old school friends she'd stayed in touch with. It passed through her mind that Madame Beaupre might be running a dance lesson as today would be the perfect day to twirl and pivot around the floor, but no queue of giggling girls was waiting in line and the double doors to the church hall were locked. Towards Bayswater Road the crowds thickened and were more boisterous and when she turned the corner, she was caught up in it right away. An American serviceman grabbed her from behind, spun her around and didn't hold back when he kissed her on the mouth. Surfacing, the surprise of it made her laugh out loud. A woman tapped him on the shoulder and said, 'Oi, what about me?' So he bent her in half and let her have it on the lips.

Hyde Park was packed with people sitting on blankets and tucking into sandwiches and cakes that looked as though they would have taken a month's worth of rations to buy. Everyone had beer or pop or flasks of tea. Little ones wearing paper crowns chased after each other, bits of ragged flags trailing in the breeze behind them, their parents letting them go without a warning to come back immediately they heard the siren. She bought herself a shandy from a kiosk, sat on a bench that she and Derek used to snuggle up on and watched the festivities. It was a new beginning and she was as overjoyed as everyone, but she couldn't help thinking about how much still needed to be mended, and that included people as well as streets and buildings. Churchill had said as much himself when he broadcast on the wireless that they should have their brief period of rejoicing, but not forget the toil and efforts that lie ahead.

Then she told herself that she deserved a day to be jubilant as much as the next person, so she joined the throng again and let herself be carried along to Whitehall where Winnie was expected to speak from one of the balconies. The wide street was jam packed, young men climbing lamp-posts and monuments or hoisting girls up on their shoulders so they could see; civil servants, their ties loose around their necks; a chorus of 'Bless 'Em All' from one side, and 'I'll Be Your Sweetheart' from another. Then a hush descended. Winnie appeared, cigar in mouth, brandishing his fingers towards the crowd in the V for Victory sign which was returned to him in thousands. And then a roar to compete with a swarm of V-2 rockets rose up towards Churchill and echoed around them.

The Prime Minister waited for quiet again and then he started to speak. He reminded them that during the first year of the war they had stood alone. That simple, factual statement brought tears to Joyce's eyes as at the beginning she hadn't been on her own, but now at the end, here she was – a lone, solitary individual. 'Were we downhearted?' Churchill asked and every voice shouted, 'No!' And in a nod towards the speech he'd made in Parliament just before D-Day, he said that in all the years to come, all over the world, when people had their freedom threatened they would look back to this period of time and the stubborn determination and stoic endurance of the British people would be an example to them and they'd say that like them, they would rather die than be conquered.

What a wonderful sentiment, Joyce thought, and she cheered until she was hoarse along with everyone. To think, that this day could go down in history and children all over the world might be taught about her – Senior Warden Cooper – and everyone else who had lived and died during this blasted war. Carried away, she followed a group of young people into a pub and one of them must have thought she was a friend of one of the others because he ordered her a port and lemon and they stood in a circle counting, 'One, two, three, bottoms up!' and drank deeply all at the same time.

She drifted away from that crowd and stood outside Buckingham Palace while the King, Queen and the two princesses waved from the balcony. Churchill joined them there, too. He didn't speak again, but puffed on his cigar, waved and looked as proud as a father basking in the outstanding achievements of his children.

There was a conga line she could have joined, a crazy hokey-cokey she stood and watched for a little while, laughing at two older women who were pulled to the ground exposing the tops of their knotted stockings as they fell, all the blokes around them shouting to see more. Everywhere she went, she looked out for someone she knew – one of the girls from work, Controller Davis, Mrs Bertrand, one of the stallholders from Portobello Market, Gladys or Jean or Percy. But she didn't see anyone, so turned towards home, waving at each and every beeping jeep or lorry covered in Union Jacks that went past.

In her tiny sitting room, Joyce put up her feet and turned on the wireless in time to hear a repeat of the King's speech from earlier, praising his subjects and calling for lasting peace.

He paid special tribute to the men and women in all the services who couldn't join in the celebrations and asked that those who could not rejoice at the end of the country's tribulations be remembered.

Well said, Joyce thought. And she was grateful to the King for reminding her that she should have been thinking about those very people who she knew couldn't join in the fun, instead of going out chasing kisses and speeches, silly dances and drinks in pubs. So she stayed in for the rest of the evening and watched a multitude of feet going backwards and forwards above her until she fell asleep in the old, crinkled leather chair.

* * *

It was back to work the next day and Joyce realised, within half an hour of starting, that she was one of the only members of staff who didn't have a thumping headache and a hangover of euphoria. The girls in the office exchanged news of what they'd done the day before, from serving trifle and brawn sandwiches at a tea party to dangling their feet in the Thames, a drink in one hand, a cigarette in the other. She told them, when asked, what she'd seen and heard, but didn't say she'd spent the evening on her own in her flat.

Flo wrote that she'd had a fantastic couple of days with her crew and was then confined to bed with a throbbing head for the following twenty-four hours. *I reported to sick bay with what I insisted was a nasty bug, but I don't think I fooled anyone. Even the sister who showed me to a bed looked green around the gills. What did you get up to, Joy? I'll bet London was heaving.*

Joyce replied in almost the exact words she'd used when

she'd described her day to the women in her office. Then she told Flo, in case she hadn't heard, about the Civil Defence Farewell Parade in Hyde Park in June; she couldn't ask her outright to attend as that was too presumptuous given how they'd last parted company, but she hoped the hint would persuade Flo to book a train ticket, arrive in time for the ceremony and perhaps stay for a few extra days.

But another letter arrived from Flo saying she hoped Joyce had a marvellous time at the parade and she was sorry she couldn't be there but there would be no more leave until she was demobbed. Flo didn't have an exact date for her demobilisation, but said it would be very soon and asked if she could then stay with Joyce until she received her sailing date from Vernon.

There would be no such communication from Vernon, Joyce was sure of that, but as she and Auntie Cath had decided four months ago, Flo would have to find that out in her own good time. So of course Flo could stay for as long as she liked and Joyce set about finding another single bed, the covers to go on it, a pillow and a few other things like extra towels and cutlery and a frying pan. She bought a bashed-about companion set for the fireplace and began to store coal and wood in a basket next to it and cleared a space in the kitchen cupboard in case Flo preferred to keep their things separate.

Like it or not, Flo was going to have to do something as Joyce wouldn't be able to feed both of them on her wages, even taking into account the fact that Flo would have her rations. Joyce wondered if she might consider going back into a hairdressing salon, not Mrs Neville's of course, but a fancy place that would appreciate her. She had, after all, enjoyed the work when she left school. Or she could easily get a job in a pub or restaurant, or Joyce could put in a good word for her at Bourne and Hollingsworth where they would be happy to have her gracing one of the counters on the shop floor. She considered writing again and reminding Flo that she would need her to help out, but decided against it as she didn't want any more bad feeling between them before her cousin had a chance to move in.

Her own job was going well and, as she'd thought, she enjoyed the structure it gave her days and weeks. She was up early, had a light breakfast, walked to Oxford Street, performed her duties, took dinner in the staff canteen, caught the bus home and read or listened to the wireless or watched the feet walking by in the evenings. At weekends she washed her hair and her clothes, cleaned the flat, visited the library and the market and if she could afford it, treated herself to a small cake from the bakery.

One morning she was summoned to Mr St John's office. Her heart thumped in her chest and her mind whirled. Had she given someone too much in their pay packet? Or calculated someone's overtime incorrectly and short-changed them?

Mr St John was wearing the same suit with a different tie and when he came from behind his desk and shook Joyce's hand, she could see that his shoes had been buffed to a blinding shine. She sat opposite him in the same chair as before, threaded her damp fingers together and waited. 'How are you settling in, Miss Cooper,' he asked.

'Rather well,' Joyce said. 'From my point of view.'

'And from your manageress's,' he said. 'I've had glowing reports about the standard of your work.'

Joyce felt her shoulders soften and her stomach settle, but she remained baffled as to why he'd asked to see her.

'A longstanding member of the Accounts Department has

decided to retire a few months early so, as promised, I'm offering you the position.'

This had happened much sooner than Joyce had anticipated and she was rather taken aback. Quickly, she weighed up the pros and cons of moving to another office, taking up new duties and meeting different colleagues. She would be able to train in accountancy, she knew, but that no longer seemed important to her.

'Would you like to talk it over with your family?' Mr St John said. 'Or friends?'

Joyce didn't want to tell him there was no one she could turn to for advice, except her cousin whose choices in life so far were dubious. What would be the point as he'd only feel sorry for her and she couldn't bear that.

'No, ta, Mr St John,' Joyce said. 'I do appreciate you thinking of me, but I enjoy the work in the Payroll Department and I get on with the other girls, so I'd like to stay where I am.'

'Well, don't be swayed by the fact that you like your colleagues,' he said. 'I do believe that the end of the war will see people moving in and out of jobs at a much higher rate than they ever did.'

Joyce pictured collecting her things from her drawers and placing them where she might not feel comfortable or having to sit next to someone who asked her endless questions about boyfriends or parents or sisters and brothers and if she'd like to meet them for a drink at the weekend. No, she would prefer to stay where she liked the position of her desk and no one bothered with her very much.

'I'm not one of those people,' Joyce said. 'So thank you again, Mr St John, but I'm quite happy where I am.'

* * *

The weekend before the parade, Joyce got out her uniform and inspected every inch of it for dirt and tears and loose threads. She brushed it and checked that the insignia and chevrons on the sleeve of her jacket were lined up correctly. Looking through her sewing basket for a spool of fine thread to mend her stockings, she was surprised and then immediately excited by the rattle of the letterbox. Perhaps it was a note from Flo, saying she would be demobbed in time for the celebration.

But on the mat was an official-looking buff envelope with her details typed on it. She slit it open, thinking that it couldn't possibly be notice of eviction as she made sure she paid her rent on time every week without fail.

Drawing out a lovely piece of good quality paper with the royal seal emblazoned at the top, she read through the one sheet of typing quickly, then once again more slowly so she could take in the details. The Controller had put her name forward for a special letter of congratulations from the King for her outstanding contribution towards the civil defence of the United Kingdom in its darkest hour. During the parade, the Queen would welcome her onto the platform of the Royal Box, shake her hand and present her with a medal cast to mark the occasion. Joyce could not think of one incident she'd been involved in that could have led to her being singled out for such an honour. There were others who'd been seriously injured rescuing people whose names they would never know; Percy had hurt his back pulling a door off its hinges to use as a stretcher and the top of Gladys's foot had been left with a permanent swelling after she'd fallen down a flight of broken stairs in pursuit of a small child's toy. All she'd done was plot the devastation on a map.

She thought of all the small acts of heroism performed by the others she had worked with for those six terrible years and determined she would accept the medal on their behalf as well as her own and that made her feel more deserving. As she boiled a kettle to clean and reshape her felt hat, she smiled and thought that this really would have given Mum something to boast about.

She kept her promise and when she accepted the commendation from the Queen she thought of her colleagues, some of whom were standing to attention amongst the thousands upon thousands of Civil Defence members being stood down. Mrs Bertrand, who had turned up day after day and did whatever was asked of her to help out when she could have sat at home instead, was also commended and for a moment they stood on the platform together but were then ushered down the steps on the other side of the box to make way for the next lot coming through – the Queen had hundreds of hands to shake that day.

A band played, military and civilian personnel as well as officers on horseback paraded past the Royal Box, saluting smartly, while an audience of family and friends looked on. The King gave a speech in which he acknowledged the bravery of all branches of the Civil Defence, especially in light of them carrying out their duties alongside other work. He called them a great host of men and women who had willingly endured hardship and danger and weariness to bring help, comfort and hope to others. The acclamation was beautifully put, but what else could they have done?

When it was over, Joyce strolled around the park with Controller Davis and his wife, Mrs Bertrand and two of her grandchildren and Jean and her mother. They stood at the Serpentine and watched some of the little ones throwing bread to the ducks and Joyce remembered sitting there with Derek and wondering how many children they would have together. She wished he was with her now. And she was in no doubt that he would have been issued with a commendation of his own, as she couldn't think of anyone more worthy of praise for selflessness than him.

Then they had one drink together in Kensington, said their goodbyes at the Marlborough Gate and Joyce went home to her flat to get ready for work the next day.

* * *

Weeks went by without a letter from Flo and Joyce began to wonder if she'd taken herself off to Australia to hunt for Vernon. Then one Saturday afternoon as she was waiting for her hair to dry, Flo turned up looking lovely in a brown suit and a new perm.

When she opened the door, Flo greeted her with a cheery, 'Hello, Joy love,' as if they'd never argued in their lives.

Eager not to let the moment pass, Joyce hugged her cousin and returned the familial endearment. 'Flo, love,' she said. 'You look terrific. Come in.' Joyce stood aside and they shuffled around until Flo and her cardboard suitcase were in the hall, then she closed and bolted the door. 'Why didn't you let me know you were coming? I've nothing in except tea.'

'They gave me a good breakfast to see me off,' Flo said. 'So tea would be perfect.' She sniffed, her nose in the air. 'How ever did you manage to get rid of that awful smell?'

Joyce laughed aloud as she led the way to the kitchen. 'It

was rather putrid, wasn't it? Plenty of airings and cleaning,' she said. 'Tell me about being demobbed.'

Flo sat and felt the cloth covering the kitchen table. 'This is nice,' she said. 'And look, there's our Big Ben on the wall. It's feeling very homely, Flo.'

'I've tried to make it welcoming. And I managed to get a bed for you and some other things to get you started.'

'Joy, love,' Flo said. 'How kind of you. The settee would have been fine.'

'You'll break your back on that old thing.' Joyce filled the teapot and set out two cups and saucers.

Kicking off her shoes, Flo sighed. 'Demob was a bit of a let-down really,' she said. 'Everyone got their papers at different times, so we all just sort of drifted off. How about your parade?'

'It was lovely,' Joyce said. 'Do you remember me writing to you that I was chosen to shake the Queen's hand?' She held up her fingers and wiggled them. 'I've hardly dared wash since. Here's my letter of commendation.' Joyce went to a drawer in the sideboard where she kept her important papers. She beamed when she handed it to Flo. She'd read it a number of times after it had been delivered and thought about how she would have loved to show it to someone – Mum or Sid or Derek – anyone at all. So it made her happy to be sharing it with her cousin.

'At last,' Flo said. 'Something positive to show from the war.'

Joyce thought Flo might have added that she had Vernon as a good outcome from the war years, but she didn't mention his name, so Joyce hoped she'd come to her senses.

'I was about to get some shopping,' Joyce said. 'Want to tag along or would you rather have a rest?'

'I'm not used to resting,' Flo said. 'I'll change my shoes and come with you.'

A bit of building work was going on, but nothing to comment on. There were plenty of men about in demob suits, some so ill-fitting that they came across as comical rather than serious in their pursuit of daily life as civilians. They walked the long way – down Chepstow Road, Pembridge Road and through Ladbroke Square Gardens – to the market, Joyce gathering provisions along the way, using her rations as Flo didn't offer hers. But Joyce decided to let that go as her cousin had just arrived home.

Flo suggested a drink which annoyed Joyce a bit as she couldn't afford to go to the pub after she'd paid for rent and essentials out of her wages. But, she reasoned, perhaps Flo was in a party mood now that she was demobbed so she accepted the invitation. Then, as she waited for her port and lemon, the truth hit her as surely as if a V-1 had landed on her head. Flo always wanted to go to the pub when she had something difficult she wanted to say that would otherwise cause a ruckus at home.

'Ta, Flo,' Joyce said. She sipped her drink and waited. Then it came.

'It's good of you to have me, Joy love,' Flo said.

'I told you before, the flat is your home, too. And I meant it.'

Flo lit a cigarette and smiled. 'It won't be for long. Five or six weeks at the most.'

'And after that,' Joyce asked. 'Will you be getting a place of your own?'

Flo looked annoyed and when she answered, it was in a tone of voice that she might use for a toddler who didn't understand a thing. 'No,' she said slowly and deliberately. 'I will be going to Vernon.'

After all this time, Joyce thought, part of her not believing it could be true and the other half not wanting to believe the truth of it. 'Has he written with a date?' she asked in a clipped voice.

Flo's eyes narrowed. 'You don't believe me, do you?' she accused. 'You think I'm holding on to something that's never going to come to anything.' She dug in her bag, pulled out an envelope and slapped it down on the table. 'There, read that.' Then she mumbled something about Joyce not being happy for her or giving her a shred of congratulations.

Joyce unfolded the piece of paper and she could tell right away Flo had been right when she'd said Vernon wasn't a good letter writer. The sentences were short, the grammar and punctuation uneducated. But the gist of it was that he had sorted out his affairs and within the next month would be writing again with details of where she could collect her ticket for Australia. Joyce passed the letter to Flo who snatched it and sat back in her chair with a triumphant look plastered all over her face. 'Your round,' she said.

'I don't have enough money,' Joyce said.

'Not that again.'

'I'm afraid,' Joyce said in a controlled, polite voice. 'That in order to keep a roof over our heads and food on our plates, I have to be very careful.'

A hint of guilt crept into Flo's eyes. 'I'll get these then,' she said. 'It might go some way to helping out your only living flesh and blood.'

In bed that night, Joyce lay awake and listened to Flo snoring softly as if she were a baby with a clear conscience. Joyce moved from one side of the lumpy bed to the other, turned on her back then towards the wall, next she folded her thin pillow in half and tucked it under the nape of her neck.

She thought about how unhappy Auntie Cath, Uncle Terry, Nana and Granddad had been with Flo's association with Vernon and she wondered if they would have been happier now that Vernon appeared to have come up trumps. She didn't think they would, given Vernon's age and background and the thousands of miles Flo was going to travel to be with him. She wasn't happy about any of it either and still could not believe that there wouldn't be some hitch that would enable Vernon to back out of his promise. But most of all, she had to admit to herself, she was utterly disbelieving that Flo could leave her completely and utterly alone when they were, as her cousin had said, each other's only family. As a leaden dawn broke, she faced up to the reality of Flo's intention to do just that and she forced herself to get up, rise tall from the top of her head and get on with things as she'd always done.

For a month they went on living in the flat, with Joyce forking out for almost everything they needed. Flo contributed the occasional drink and she did give Joyce some of her food rations which helped, but she kept almost everything she had for herself and her new life with Vernon. They spoke and walked and ate together but a gulf as wide as the one that had existed between the Allies and the Axis gaped between them. There was so much Joyce wanted to say and could have said, but she was loath to open her mouth in case Vernon cried off and Flo wanted to stay longer.

But notification came in the form of a telegram telling Flo that a ticket had been booked for her on the HMS *Maloja* sailing out of Liverpool for Sydney on the 7th of July. Joyce thought Flo would look like the cat who'd stolen the cream, but she was subdued and polite and carried herself with grace and dignity. Joyce tried to do the same as she watched her cousin pack her trunk and cardboard suitcase and organise a seat on the train to Liverpool.

On the morning of her departure, Joyce went about her usual routine for work. Flo hadn't offered an address, so it was left up to Joyce to ask. 'I can give you this Post Office Box number, but it's out in the sticks where Vernon used to live with his ex-wife and I'm not sure how often it's checked. Perhaps not at all from now on.'

'But where's Vernon living now?' Joyce thought she should have asked these questions when there had been more time.

'With a pal in Sydney. He's looking for a flat for us there. As soon as I arrive and find out where we'll be living I'll write with the details.' Then she looked at Joyce with more sincerity in her lovely grey eyes than Joyce had seen for ages. 'I promise, Joy love.' Flo opened her arms for a hug. 'Wish me luck,' she said in a husky voice.

'Best of luck,' Joyce said, then she prised herself away from Flo's embrace, put on her coat and shoes and asked her cousin to post her key through the letterbox when she left.

* * *

Every day Joyce hoped to see an envelope waiting for her when she walked in from work, but weeks went by and there was nothing. In desperation, she wrote to Flo care of the Post Office Box and when that didn't produce a result, she sent a letter addressed to Vernon. Three months later a large, stiff envelope was on the mat when she came back from shopping and she ripped it open in a fever. Inside was a black and white photo of Flo wearing a lacy white wedding dress with three quarter length sleeves and a white feathered hat that swept over her head. Her waved hair had been cut very short and her fingernails were painted a dark colour. Vernon stood behind her, his arms about her waist and together they were holding the handle of a knife they were using to cut into a tiered cake. They were both grinning broadly and Joyce thought they looked very happy.

The only message attached was a note from Flo that read: *We made it! X*. Tearing the envelope apart looking for a return address, Joyce finally came across it on the outside left-hand corner, but it was smudged and all she could make out was Sydn and the numbers 840. She fell into the leather chair and put her face in her hands. To think she had longed to receive any sort of communication from Flo and now it had arrived, her stomach and her spirits plunged.

She eked out her money and bought a strong magnifying glass from the market but couldn't read anything else from under the smear of ink. She traipsed to Australia House with the envelope but they weren't much help, giving her no more information than a general suburb of Sydney the numbers might refer to.

She wrote and then wrote again to any permutation of the address she could conjure up and to the Post Office Box, but there was no reply. Joyce tossed and turned at night, worrying that something terrible might have happened to Flo and she would never know. But of course it was more likely that Flo thought Joyce hadn't written at all because she was still angry with her for what she'd put the family through. With a wrench, it reminded her that she had never heard from Hettie after the invitation to her wedding. So the telegram she'd sent probably hadn't found its way into her sister-in-law's hands, either.

She was desperate to let both of them know she hadn't forsaken them and wanted nothing more than to be in a part of their lives, but without addresses there seemed to be no possibility of that. All she could hope for was that one or other – or both of them – would try again, but the years went by and that never happened.

Eventually, she bought a bulldog clip and clamped the photo and the envelope to her other papers, put them in a drawer, sat in the old leather chair and watched the feet going about their business in the street above her.

TWENTY-THREE

Friday 26 April 1974

Barbara and Elaine had fallen out, which was most unlike them or any of the girls in the office and all morning the atmosphere had been quite unpleasant. During their dinner break, Elaine sat next to Joyce in the staff canteen and by the time Barbara put a plate of lamb hotpot and a bowl of steamed roly poly on her tray five minutes later, there were no empty places except at their table. She joined them and a chill hovered in the air.

Politely, Joyce asked first one then the other what they were doing at the weekend.

'Watching Clifford play football,' Barbara said.

'Planting the garden.' Elaine looked at Joyce but not at Barbara. 'You?'

Joyce studied each of her colleagues, frown lines on their foreheads and their mouths set rigid. She knew they would assume she'd reel off her usual – shopping trip to the market, exchange her books at the library, washing, cleaning, a decision between the custard tart and the vanilla slice. And she could have left it at that, but perhaps she should let them in on what was, for her, a once in a twenty-nine-year occasion. After all, she listened endlessly to the ins and outs of their lives.

So she told them about Mr Norris's impending visit and before she knew it, Barbara and Elaine were talking over her about the pros and cons of salad dressing and if it would be best to have thick or thinly sliced ham. Elaine said she had a lovely recipe for a chocolate cake. But Joyce wasn't about to go that far and let Mr Norris think he could get his feet under the table.

'It's not like that.' She shrugged. 'He's just a neighbour who might...'

'Become a friend?' Barbara asked softly.

Joyce thought about that. 'Perhaps,' she said. 'In time.'

'Or a friendly neighbour,' Elaine offered.

Barbara laughed. 'A neighbourly friend.'

'Yes,' Joyce joined in. 'Something along those lines.'

By the time their dinner break came to an end, they'd helped her decide on exactly what to lay out for the tea and that excluded beer as they thought that would give Mr Norris the wrong idea. 'Anyway, if he wants a drink, he might suggest you both go to the pub which would be nice. Wouldn't it, Joyce?'

Picturing them at a table in The Elgin or the Earl of Lonsdale just for the one drink did seem quite alright. But Mr Norris probably wouldn't suggest that and if he did, she probably wouldn't be able to bring herself to accept.

He'd occupied her thoughts all week. Not him exactly and not only what to give him to eat but what to talk about when he was there and how to get rid of him, without being impolite, if he stayed too long. Of course, she could ask him about the wedding and he might have a few snapshots to show her which, she admitted to herself, would be lovely to see. She could ask him about all the hobbies Mr Taylor had said he was involved in, and she might make a mental note of any book groups in the area. That then led her to think about his MIA Club and there her thoughts stuck fast on Flo and Hettie.

She had taken out Flo's wedding photo and wondered whether to have it framed and put on display, but what was the point as it would only serve to remind her that it was the last contact she'd had with her cousin. Tracing the contours of Flo's lovely face and hands with her finger, she had tried to imagine what she would look like now; if she had any children and whether they were boys or girls and what their names might be. With a tingling shock that shot through her, she wondered if one of them might be named Joyce or Margaret, Catherine or Terence. She wondered whether her cousin's life had been happy, busy and filled with laughter and not lonely as hers, she could finally admit, had been.

Late evening sun cast splashes of light on the low coffee table as she set out the tea things. There were coasters, cake plates and forks, room for the teapot, sugar and milk. Under wraps in the kitchen sat the ham and cheese sandwiches, scones and Battenburg cake Barbara and Elaine had assured her were enough but not too much for a light supper.

Standing in the doorway, Joyce surveyed the scene from what would be Mr Norris's initial perspective and moved a vase filled with lilac from on top of the telly to the sideboard, straightened the rug in front of the balcony doors and triple-checked the favourite haunts of spiders for their elusive, diaphanous webs. It might be warm enough for them to sit on the balcony until it was too dark to see, then they could come inside and eat at the table – if Mr Norris didn't hold her to the half an hour she had initially dictated as being the length of their time together.

Then she turned her attention to herself. In the bedroom, she put on the light over the mirrored wardrobe door so she could inspect her face, but clicked it off again when she didn't like what was reflected back at her. She wasn't a vain woman, but filling in the cracks under cover of shadow seemed kinder somehow. Eye pencil, face powder, one sweep of mascara, pale lipstick and she was ready to brush her hair in the full light. Pulling the bristles through her curls from the roots to the ends, there was something about the tilt of her head or the curve of the collar on her neck, a cloud that passed over the sun in a certain sequence or the faintest trace of lilac from the living room, that made her stop stock still.

For several seconds she was thirty years younger and walking through a dappled garden with Flo, who had let her in on her plans to join the WAAFs. They'd linked arms, put their heads together and laughed at Flo's reluctance to tell her parents. The pictures in her mind were so clear she felt as though she could step into them. But more tangible was the inexplicable feeling of anticipation that had overwhelmed her then – she remembered thinking something was just out of her reach, something unformed and obscure and undefinable. But it was there. And all she had to do was wait for it to show itself so she could grab it and claim it for her own.

The fleeting moment of clarity passed and Joyce felt jaded and cynical again. She sat on the bed and gathered strands of hair from the brush. Of course she understood that the elusive expectancy was a phenomenon experienced by young people and that none of them, at any time, could explain what it was they were waiting for with such confident hope. For many of them it arrived in the shape of a partner, children and a home. For others as a career, travel, possessions. Then there were those, she amongst them, for whom the anticipated intrigue crept further and further out of reach until it was nothing more than a vague memory. She thought that must be true for the countless numbers who had been young during the war years; they'd been so busy looking for lights in the blackout or sticking pins in a map, marching in uniform, nursing, driving ambulances, working in munitions factories, living on rations, grieving, surviving, that when the world settled again, the fleeting time for chasing youthful hope had been lost. They couldn't pick up where they'd left off – it simply was not possible.

Some people, like Cressida, settled for second best. Others, like Flo and Vernon, refused to believe their period of yearning for the evasive had been and gone and chased after it, determined to see it through. Most people, though, accepted their place in time and became more practical and realistic about what life held in store for them. That had been the road she'd followed, and she'd been, if not happy with it, at least safe and protected. Except on those occasions when a scent or a shadow or a smile reminded her that there had been a time when she'd believed there was something more for her to look forward to. It was then she wondered how she could ever have let those longings and feelings escape from her grasp.

Joyce placed her hairbrush on top of the dresser and checked her hair in the mirror – still thick and wavy and not too grey. The clock read 6.50 and her stomach churned. It wasn't too late to write a note telling Mr Norris she had to cancel because of a headache or a toothache or an unforeseen circumstance. If she hurried, she could pop it in his door and lock herself back in her flat before he began to climb the stairs. But then what would she do with the sandwiches and the scones and the cake? She'd never get through all of them before they went off and that would be a waste. *And what,* she thought, *would I do with this growing sense of anticipation that's so like the eagerness I felt years ago?*

The shock of recognition almost floored her. It wasn't merely duty and courtesy that had compelled her to invite Mr Norris to tea. And it wasn't the thought of having him or anyone else in particular in and out of her flat and her life. It was not wanting to be left behind any longer, not wanting to spend the next decade or two watching others live their lives from above or below street level. She wanted to be in the thick of it or to at least give that perspective a go.

A jaunty whistle carried along the hallway followed by a rap at the door. Joyce stood, wiped her hands on her skirt then sat down again. She felt awkward and unprepared. She wanted to make the most of what was, for her, an unparalleled occasion.

The bell rang and Joyce knew she was taking too long to answer the door. Mr Norris would think her rude or disorganised, but there was something she wasn't prepared to leave to the mere hope that it might come up in conversation. Going back to the drawer, she found the spoiled envelope from Flo and the scrap of paper on which she'd written what she remembered as being Hettie's last known address. She propped them, with the photo of Flo and Vernon, against the vase where they couldn't be ignored or hidden from view or dismissed as anything other than what they were – a plea for help from Mr Norris's MIA Club.

Then Joyce surveyed the scene once more. She took a

deep breath, patted down her hair, took one last look behind her, drew herself up from the crown of her head and opened the door.

* * *

Thank you so much for taking the time to read *The Woman with The Map,* we hope you loved it as much as we do!

The best thing that you can do to support an author or a book you love is to write a review. We would really appreciate your help spreading the excitement for *The Woman with The Map*. Whether you review on Netgalley, TikTok, Goodreads, social media or retailer websites, we'd love to hear what you think! If you post online about *The Woman with The Map*, please do tag us @AriaFiction on Twitter.

Happy reading!
The Aria Team

ACKNOWLEDGEMENTS

I am very grateful to my lovely daughter, Kelly, who read each chapter as it was written and gave me her invaluable feedback.

Thank you to all my family and friends who have been so supportive of me and of this book: Nick Abendroth, Lizzie Alexander, Libby Aitchison, Basil and Maya Al Omari, Jo Bishop, Cate Casey, Kathleen Casey, Erin Casey and all my Casey family around the world, Helen Chatten, Penny Clarke, Liam and Arie Collinwood, Jill Davis, Fiona Emblem, Jo Emeney, Ozzie Erdinc, Steve Farmer, Natalie Farrell, Mat Garman, Ally and Sharon Gilchrist, Danny and Sonia Gilchrist, Don Gilchrist, Duncan and Lisa Gilchrist, Tom Gilchrist, Eman Gilligan, John Gilligan, Angie Gilligan, David Gilligan, Jan and Jon Gray, Eli Heinrich, Chris Holmes, Paula and David Horsfall, Jan and Gary Hurst, Sheila and Alan Jefferys, Maureen John, Nick John, Liz Koch-prapha, Katy Marron, Tom Mathew, Stuart McKay, Fran Nygaard, Lena Nygaard, Patrice and Mark Nygaard, Liz Peadon, Liz Prescott, Dave Pountney, Mark Priestley, Martin Shrosbree, Sally Tatham, Sue and Gerald Ward, Pete and Fran Ward, Phil and Helen Ward.

I am thankful to my beautiful grandchildren who keep me amused and happy and proud: Toby Gilchrist, Kaan Erdinc, Ayda Erdinc, Alya Erdinc, Aleksia Collinwood and Cleo Gilchrist.

My thanks go to the first editor of this book, Hannah Todd

and to my current editor, Martina Arzu and everyone at Aria Fiction/Head of Zeus for their commitment to me as an author.

I would also like to thank Larry Rostant for the beautiful cover design.

And a huge thank you to Kiran Kataria at Keane Kataria Literary Agency for her support and advice.

ABOUT THE AUTHOR

JAN CASEY's novels, like her first - *The Women of Waterloo Bridge* - explore the themes of how ordinary people are affected by extraordinary events during any period in history, including the present. Jan is fascinated with the courage, adaptability and resilience that people rise to in times of adversity and for which they do not expect pay, praise or commendation. Jan is also interested in writing about the similarities as opposed to the differences amongst people and the ways in which experiences and emotions bind humans together.

Jan was born in London but spent her childhood in Southern California. She was a teacher of English and Drama for many years. When she is not writing, Jan enjoys yoga, swimming, cooking, walking, reading and spending time with her grandchildren. Before becoming a published author, Jan had short stories and flash fictions published.